People are saying *intriguing* things about these authors!

DEBRA WEBB

"Webb's Colby Agency stories just keep getting better... Colby stories are always filled with action, crossover story lines and fascinating, brave and complex characters."
—*RT Book Reviews* on *His Secret Life*

DELORES FOSSEN

"Delores Fossen creates the perfect Harlequin Intrigue with suspense, heat and situations that—we hope—only occur within the pages of a romance novel!"
—*RT Book Reviews* on *Security Blanket*

ALICE SHARPE

"Alice Sharpe knows how to wrap a mystery within a mystery, and her flawless plotting and complicated clues add a bright spark to *Royal Heir*."
—*RT Book Reviews*

D1473119

ABOUT THE AUTHORS

Debra Webb was born in Scottsboro, Alabama, to parents who taught her that anything is possible if you want it badly enough. With the support of her husband and two beautiful daughters, Debra took up writing, looking to mystery and movies for inspiration. In 1998 her dream of writing for Harlequin Books came true. You can write to Debra with your comments at P.O. Box 64, Huntland, Tennessee 37345, or visit her Web site at www.debrawebb.com to find out exciting news about her next book.

Delores Fossen says to imagine a family tree that includes Texas cowboys, Choctaw and Cherokee Indians, a Louisiana pirate and a Scottish rebel who battled side by side with William Wallace. With ancestors like that, it's easy to understand why the Texas author and former air force captain feels as if she was genetically predisposed to writing romances. Along the way to fulfilling her DNA destiny, Delores married an air force top gun who just happens to be of Viking descent. With all those romantic bases covered she doesn't have to look too far for inspiration.

Alice Sharpe met her husband-to-be on a cold, foggy beach in Northern California. One year later they were married. Alice and her husband now live in a small rural town in Oregon, where she devotes the majority of her time to pursuing her second love, writing. Alice loves to hear from readers. You can write her at P.O. Box 755, Brownsville, OR 97327. SASE for reply is appreciated.

DEBRA WEBB

DELORES FOSSEN

ALICE SHARPE

THE
INTRIGUE
COLLECTION

HARLEQUIN®

TORONTO • NEW YORK • LONDON
AMSTERDAM • PARIS • SYDNEY • HAMBURG
STOCKHOLM • ATHENS • TOKYO • MILAN • MADRID
PRAGUE • WARSAW • BUDAPEST • AUCKLAND

If you purchased this book without a cover you should be aware that this book is stolen property. It was reported as "unsold and destroyed" to the publisher, and neither the author nor the publisher has received any payment for this "stripped book."

Recycling programs
for this product may
not exist in your area.

ISBN-13: 978-0-373-83756-4

THE INTRIGUE COLLECTION
Copyright © 2010 by Harlequin Books S.A.

The publisher acknowledges the copyright holders of the individual works as follows:

COLBY LOCKDOWN
Copyright © 2010 by Debra Webb

SHOTGUN SHERIFF
Copyright © 2010 by Delores Fossen

A BABY BETWEEN THEM
Copyright © 2010 by Alice Sharpe

All rights reserved. Except for use in any review, the reproduction or utilization of this work in whole or in part in any form by any electronic, mechanical or other means, now known or hereafter invented, including xerography, photocopying and recording, or in any information storage or retrieval system, is forbidden without the written permission of the publisher, Harlequin Enterprises Limited, 225 Duncan Mill Road, Don Mills, Ontario, Canada M3B 3K9.

This is a work of fiction. Names, characters, places and incidents are either the product of the author's imagination or are used fictitiously, and any resemblance to actual persons, living or dead, business establishments, events or locales is entirely coincidental.

This edition published by arrangement with Harlequin Books S.A.

For questions and comments about the quality of this book please contact us at Customer_eCare@Harlequin.ca.

® and TM are trademarks of the publisher. Trademarks indicated with ® are registered in the United States Patent and Trademark Office, the Canadian Trade Marks Office and in other countries.

www.eHarlequin.com

Printed in U.S.A.

CONTENTS

COLBY LOCKDOWN
Debra Webb

CAST OF CHARACTERS

Slade Convoy—As a Colby Agency investigator, Slade is on the side of what is just and right. He is the first investigator to be thrust into new territory that will ultimately have him breaking the law.

Mia Dawson—As former D.A. Gordon's personal assistant she knows too much.

Former District Attorney Timothy Gordon—He's retired. He has a seven-figure book deal. He isn't about to pay for the past...but the past has other plans.

Victoria Colby-Camp—The head of the Colby Agency. When the agency is overtaken, she must do all within her power to protect her staff.

Ian Michaels—One of Victoria's seconds-in-command. As one of only two staff members not taken captive, he must do whatever is necessary to keep all those inside—including his own wife—safe.

Jim Colby—Victoria's son. He arrives on the scene and is determined to save his mother. The next twenty-four hours prove an emotional turning point for him.

Lucas Camp—Victoria's husband. He must keep the peace between Ian and Jim. More importantly, he must help find a way to rescue his wife and her staff.

Nicole Reed-Michaels—She works with Victoria to help keep the rest of the hostages calm and cooperative. It's the only way to stay alive.

The man in charge—His identity is unknown but his ruthless tactics keep all involved on the edge of their seats.

The shackled man—His identity is unknown as well. But somehow there is a plan for him. Victoria and Nicole are certain this plan involves his death.

ONE

Colby Agency, Chicago
Monday, January 20, 7:45 a.m.

"VICTORIA."

Victoria Colby-Camp looked up from the Monday-morning briefing agenda she had prepared and smiled for the investigator waiting in her open door. "Good morning, Nicole. Did you have a nice weekend?"

Nicole Reed-Michaels moved across the office and settled into a chair in front of Victoria's desk. "I did, indeed." Nicole's lips slid into a pleasant upward tilt. "Ian and I discussed the possibility of a vacation this year." Her gaze searched Victoria's. "One that doesn't include the children."

"Ah," Victoria said, understanding now, "a second honeymoon." Ian and Nicole had been married for nine years. Two children, both school age, and their work had been the couple's focus for nearly a decade. It was past time the two took some alone time for themselves. Victoria was more than a little pleased to learn this news. "No one deserves it more." She didn't have to say that she knew this from experience. Victoria had long denied her own needs for her work and her family. "That's excellent news. Do you have a particular destination or time frame in mind?"

Nicole relaxed fully into her chair. Before coming to work at the Colby Agency she had served with the Federal Bureau of Investigation. No one should be fooled by her silky blond hair or that tall, runway physique. Nicole Reed-Michaels was not only extremely intelligent, but she was also an expert marksman and she knew how to take down an assailant with her bare hands. She was one of the agency's very best investigators. Not to mention she was married to Ian Michaels, Victoria's longtime second-in-command.

Another of those warm smiles appeared, emphasizing the tiny laugh lines that were the only indicators of age on Nicole's otherwise flawless face. "The Caribbean, I think. We're still discussing when and for how long."

"Two weeks," Victoria suggested, "at least." Before long she and Lucas would need to take a nice, indulgent vacation. They'd celebrated their sixth anniversary recently. It was time.

Last summer Victoria's son, Jim, had taken an exciting vacation to Africa with his wife, Tasha. It seemed everyone was taking vacations…except Victoria.

Yes, it was well past time.

A stifled scream echoed beyond Victoria's open door, hauling her attention there. Both she and Nicole were on their feet immediately.

"What was that?" Nicole whirled toward the sound.

Before Victoria could round her desk, Mildred burst into

the office. "You've forgotten your salon appointment," she urged Victoria. "You must go *now!*" Her eyes were wide with fear.

Nicole and Victoria's gazes met briefly even as they rushed across the room.

Both knew what that seemingly silly phrase meant.

Danger had descended upon the Colby Agency. Victoria had to leave via the stairwell next to her office.

Now.

But what about Nicole? Mildred? And the others?

"Go," Nicole reaffirmed as she paused in the doorway. "I'll take care of things here."

Victoria hesitated.

"Go," Mildred repeated.

Fear expanded in Victoria's throat even as her heart threatened to rupture from her chest. She hurried through the small private lobby where Mildred greeted Victoria's appointments, opened the door to the stairwell in the narrow corridor beyond and flung herself through it.

Dear God. How could she leave everyone else behind? She should go back…assess the threat.

What was happening?

Don't think, Victoria ordered.

Go!

Her staff would need her to get through this. She couldn't help anyone with whatever situation was unfolding if she allowed herself to be overtaken. Whatever was going on…she had to escape.

Victoria hurried downward as fast as she dared. She ticked off a mental list of what she would do as soon as she was clear of the building.

Call Ian. He was off duty today. Having just completed an assignment, he had the mandatory forty-eight hours off.

Of course she would call Lucas. He had arrived home only last night from a four-day-long business trip to D.C. An hour ago she'd left him poring over the newspaper and drinking coffee. He might even be on his way here by now. He usually dropped by the agency every day that he was home.

And Jim. Dear God, she had to call her son.

Then the police.

Victoria couldn't be sure if Mildred had had time to activate the silent alarm system that would notify the authorities.

The agency's security system was state-of-the-art. As was the entire building's for that matter. Why hadn't the security guards alerted her to the threat? Both men had been at their posts in the lobby when she arrived half an hour ago.

"Good morning, ma'am."

Victoria drew up short as she reached the landing on the second floor. Only one more floor to go…but she wouldn't make it.

Dread congealed in her stomach.

The man dressed in black, including a ski-type mask to keep his face hidden, held a weapon aimed directly at her chest.

"We should return to your office, Mrs. Colby-Camp," he said quite cordially. "I'd hate for you to miss the opening act of the show."

Fury whipped through Victoria, taming her fear and stiffening her spine. "What the hell do you want?"

"Let's not get ahead of ourselves now." He gestured with the weapon for her to get moving. "Back up the stairs, ma'am."

Determination instantly replaced the dread, fueling the fury building inside her. "Not until you tell me what you want and who you are."

The evil bastard had the gall to laugh. "You've been in this business a long time, Victoria. I'm certain you've been faced with all kinds of situations and all sorts of people." Those vile lips split into a grin. "I'll bet that on occasion you've even run in to someone you really wish you hadn't messed with…." His gaze bored into hers, relaying just how little he cared whether she lived or died. "Well, that someone is me."

TWO

HE was going to be late this morning.

Slade Convoy didn't actually have to be at work today, but the excitement of closing another case had to be shared. And no one understood that better than his colleagues at the Colby Agency.

His last case had been a tough one. A missing child and dys-functional parents. The agency had been contacted by the child's paternal grandparents. Seven days missing, the child was presumed by many to be dead. Slade himself had had his doubts about finding her alive.

A triumphant smile slid across his lips. But he'd found her, very much alive. Right where her bipolar mother had hidden her.

The child was back with her father under the supervision of loving grandparents. All was right in their world once more.

The story had to be shared. He had to bask in the glory of

victory with the folks who had become his family. The only family he'd ever had, really.

Slade shook off the ugly thoughts and focused on maneuvering the Magnificent Mile. As a kid he'd never imagined that one day he would work in the area. He'd considered himself lucky to have a decent meal before bedtime each night.

Life was good...now.

He appreciated every single moment.

His cell vibrated as he slowed for a traffic signal. He tucked his fingers into his pocket and fished out the phone.

He glanced at the screen and immediately recognized Ian Michaels's number. Ian was his boss. One of them anyway. Ian and Simon Ruhl were at the top of the Colby Agency food chain. Victoria ran the show, but never without the input of those two.

Slade slid the phone open. "What's up?" Strange, Slade thought, that Ian would call at this hour. Ian had bragged that today he intended to do something special with his kids.

"We have a situation."

Ian Michaels wasn't one to mince words and his tone was always calm and reserved. The man never lost his cool. Never raised his voice. And never, ever backed down or sugarcoated anything. He was about as soft as an eight-pound sledgehammer. But Slade could tell from Ian's tone something was wrong.

Slade shifted his foot to the accelerator as the light changed to green. Whatever the situation, it was bad. Very bad.

"A situation?" Slade returned.

"Meet me at Maggie's across the street from the agency. I'll be waiting on the second floor."

"I'm close. Be there in a sec," Slade assured him. The connection ended so he slid the phone closed and tucked it back into the pocket of his jeans as he scouted for a parking slot on a side street. Maggie's Coffee House had once been a ritzy restaurant that had slowly shifted focus over the years to become a street-level café. The second floor of the artsy coffeehouse that had once been a private dining room was now used mainly for storage.

Why the hell would Ian be waiting there?

After parking his four-wheel-drive truck, Slade double-timed it up the sidewalk toward the front entrance of Maggie's. He hesitated when he saw a familiar face heading in the same direction from the street.

"Lucas?"

Lucas Camp stopped, one hand on the door leading into Maggie's. "Convoy," the older man acknowledged, obviously not surprised.

This was getting more bizarre by the moment. Lucas was Victoria's husband, but he wasn't on the staff of the Colby Agency. Slade hustled over to the door. "What's going on?"

Lucas shook his head. "I don't know the details yet. Ian asked that I meet him here ASAP." A glimpse of worry flashed in the man's eyes before he moved forward, leading the way through the door. At the hostess's questioning look, Lucas gestured toward the stairs beyond the serving counter. She nodded as if she understood exactly what was going on.

Slade sure as hell wished he knew what was going on as he climbed the stairs behind Lucas. Well into his sixties, Lucas was damned fit, but he'd lost a leg in a long-ago war and the prosthesis he wore slowed him down a bit. But Lucas Camp didn't need any sympathy from Slade or anyone else. The man could be lethal when the need arose. He'd worked numerous deep-cover operations with the CIA for years. Even since retiring he still returned to D.C. monthly to advise the agency on the best way to conduct upcoming operations.

On the second floor, the big single room was cluttered with boxes of paper goods. Across the room near the windows overlooking the Mag Mile, Ian Michaels waited. He turned to face the new arrivals and there was no mistaking the grim expression he wore.

Whatever was going down, it was bad.

"What's going on, Ian?" Lucas demanded as he and Slade weaved their way through the stacks of boxes.

"Jim is on his way," Ian advised, avoiding a direct answer to the question.

Slade stared at the building across the street as he neared Ian's position. His gaze zeroed in on the windows of the floor where the Colby Agency suite of offices should have been buzzing with activity. It was Monday morning after all. From the outside the situation appeared to be like any other snowy January day. No smoke billowing, no shattered glass, no official emergency vehicles in the vicinity of the building. What could be wrong?

"That's good," Lucas said in response to Ian's statement regarding Jim, "but that doesn't answer my question."

Ian shifted his attention to the windows of the Colby Agency offices Slade still surveyed. "At seven forty-five this morning, a group of armed men dressed as SWAT agents laid siege to the agency and everyone inside."

"That's…crazy…." A chill penetrated deep into Slade's bones. Mondays were early days. The weekly briefing. Not only was Victoria—Lucas's wife and the head of the agency—in there, but so was every single member of the staff except for Slade and Ian…including Ian's wife, Nicole.

"How many men?" Lucas asked the question before Slade could gather his wits and utter the same.

With an uncharacteristic shake of his head, Ian turned once more to face them. "I don't know for certain. Nicole managed to get a call through to my cell but she was cut off before…" He swallowed with difficulty. "Before she could fully assess the situation. She mentioned five, then seven. But there could be more."

The same terror humming beneath Ian's tone had claimed the usually unreadable expression on Lucas's face. "Was Nicole aware of any injuries?"

"She didn't get a chance to relay anything more."

"The security guards on duty have most likely been neutralized," Slade suggested, now visually measuring the front entrance. He hoped no one had been killed but there was always that possibility. Anyone else from the businesses housed on the other floors who might have opted to go into work early that morning had likely been taken prisoner or were dead. "We should call LSS and have them issue a warning to stay clear of the building."

LSS, Lockdown Security Systems, were the folks in charge of the building's physical security.

"That was going to be my next—"

"That was the first call I received this morning," Ian said, cutting off Lucas. "LSS called to inform me that the building was in lockdown mode due to a gas leak and no one was to enter until the all clear was given. Before I could question the directive or pass along that the agency already had people inside, Nicole's call came in."

Lucas surveyed the building in question once more. "I don't see any official vehicles. No city maintenance crews."

"I assume the so-called leak was a ploy to enact lockdown. I've had no further word from LSS so I have to assume someone is running interference there."

Ian was right. Whoever had set this game in motion had done their homework. "Have you called the Chicago P.D.?" Slade asked. Since there were no cruisers in the vicinity he imagined the answer was no, but Ian could certainly have informed one of the agency's many contacts within Chicago P.D. to come in dark. The real SWAT folks could be on standby out of sight.

"That's not a move I want to make until I fully comprehend the terms of this situation."

Understandable. Until the terms were known, their hands were tied to a great degree.

"What's happening, Lucas?"

All three turned as Jim Colby crossed the room. The man hadn't made a sound on the stairs. Slade never ceased to be impressed by Victoria's son. He'd been trained as a mercenary as a boy. Could kill a man in mere seconds with nothing but his bare hands. As tall and muscled as he was, he could still move as stealthily as any predator of the jungle.

Lucas quickly explained what little Ian knew at this point. The fury that started to throb in Jim's temples warned that he would not stand by and wait for terms. Slade wanted to act as well. But, as Ian had shown already, this was the time for patience and levelheadedness. Jim Colby possessed neither.

"I'll assemble my team," Jim announced. "We'll move in within the hour."

Jim ran a private investigations shop. But his staff worked around the law more often than not. They called themselves the Equalizers. In sharp contrast, the Colby Agency maintained a stellar reputation, going to great lengths to cooperate fully with law enforcement. Victoria and Jim didn't see eye to eye on the way business was to be conducted.

"No."

The single syllable echoed in the silence that followed. Only two men on this planet had the guts to stare Victoria's son in the eye and tell him no: Lucas Camp and the one who'd just said the word—Ian Michaels. This was about to get hairy.

"If we're not going in," Jim growled, his gaze narrowing with the rage climbing inside him, "then what are you suggesting we do?"

"We do nothing," Ian said flatly, "until we know what the terms of this takeover are. Any step we take might be the wrong one. We wait for the man in charge to make his demands."

Jim walked two steps away, his hands planted on his hips, apparently to regain some measure of control. Or maybe to mentally pull together an entrance strategy.

Lucas took a breath. "Jim," he said as calmly and quietly as could be expected under the circumstances, "Ian has a valid point. We have to think tactically here. Allowing an emotional reaction could cause more harm than good."

Jim glared at his stepfather, then at Ian. "Reacting is not my specialty. This calls for action. *Now.*" He said the last with a pointed stare at Ian. "Waiting will only allow the intruders to gain a stronger foothold."

Ian's grim expression remained in place as he held the other man's lethal glare. "I am Victoria's second-in-command. I am and will continue to be in charge. We will proceed with caution."

Jim reclaimed the steps he'd taken, putting him toe-to-toe with Ian. "Victoria is my mother. We'll do things my way. No negotiations."

Slade shared a look with Lucas. The circumstances were sensitive to say the least. Both men were strong-willed and each had a legitimate point. But, as a staff member of the Colby Agency, Slade's alliance had to be with Ian. Jim was operating solely on emotion. Bad business at a moment like this.

Lucas stepped between the two men, forcing both to take a much-needed step back. "Everyone in this room has a vested interest in how this turns out." He glanced at Jim, then at Ian. "We will all remain calm and we will lay out a proper strategy. There will be no going in blind or taking unnecessary risks before we have a single detail to go on."

Slade relaxed marginally. If anyone could control this out-of-control moment, Lucas could.

The chirp of a cell phone shattered the tense silence.

Ian reached into the pocket of his suit jacket and pulled out his cell. "Michaels."

A muscle throbbed in Jim's hard-set jaw. Lucas stared hopefully at Ian. Slade waited, also hoping that this would be some kind of news. A first move.

Time was slipping by. Every second that lapsed could be one that may have been pivotal to saving one or more lives. The lives of people Slade knew and cared for deeply. Whatever happened, in all probability the Colby Agency would never be the same.

"Yes," Ian said, "I understand." He drew the phone from his ear and touched the screen. "As requested, you are on speakerphone."

Adrenaline moved through Slade's veins.

"Fourteen staff members as well as Victoria Colby-Camp are now my hostages," the male voice announced. "All communications inside the building, including the Internet, cell phones and landlines, have been disabled. The building is stalled in lockdown mode and under my control. No one gets in or out. If anyone tries, the hostages will die. If the authorities, local or federal, are contacted, the hostages will die."

No one made a sound or even breathed. The distant hum of conversation and coffee mugs sliding across tables and counters from below were the only sounds.

"Are you prepared to issue your demands for the release of the hostages?" Ian inquired with amazing calm and self-assurance.

Jim looked away, the fury now visibly pulsing across his brow.

"There are only two."

Only two. *Great,* Slade mused.

All four men waited for the harsh nightmare to become a stone-cold reality.

"Former District Attorney Timothy Gordon will be brought, by whatever means necessary, to the front entrance of the building. This demand is nonnegotiable."

Now Slade got the picture. This wasn't about the Colby Agency at all. It was about one of Chicago's most prestigious political figures.

"Is it your intent to exchange the hostages for Gordon?" Ian asked, his tone still incredibly calm.

"I have two demands, Mr. Michaels," the man said, his voice equally calm and absolutely firm. "When you have met this first demand, we will discuss the status of the hostages as well as the next step."

"This is Lucas Camp," the oldest of those gathered in the storeroom asserted. "Before we go any further, we will need proof of life. And a detailed listing of the physical condition of all hostages."

The caller made a sound, not really a laugh but something on that order. "We have three injuries, none life-threatening. But, Mr. Camp, if you're asking about the condition of your wife, she is indeed among the injured."

Jim swore loudly. Ian and Lucas shot him a glare. Slade moved to Jim's side, placed a hand on his arm and urged him with his eyes to stay calm. The slightest wrong move or comment could set off a chain reaction no one wanted.

"Under the circumstances," Ian offered, "we must demand that you release the injured hostages before we proceed with negotiations."

The sound that echoed in the air was an outright laugh this time. "Mr. Michaels, this is a one-way negotiation. You will bring Gordon to the front entrance. As I've already explained, we will discuss the release of the hostages at that point and not a moment sooner."

"You," Jim warned, stepping forward, "have made a grave mistake. Release the hostages now and we'll forget this ever happened. Refuse and you have my word that your life will never again be your own."

"You have sixty seconds to agree to this demand."

Shock throbbed in the silence that followed.

"If you do not agree to this demand in the next fifty-five seconds," the voice demanded when no one responded, "one of the hostages will die."

"This is—" Ian began.

"Fifty seconds," the man on the phone interrupted. "Another hostage will die with each minute that passes after that."

More of that choking silence.

"Forty seconds, gentlemen. Perhaps I'll start with one of the females." There was a muffled sound followed by the caller shouting to one of his cohorts, "Bring me the deaf woman. I doubt anyone will really miss her."

Slade held his breath. Dear God...

"We will do everything in our power," Ian said, shattering the tension, "to meet your demand."

"Not good enough, Michaels," the voice warned. "Thirty seconds."

"How long do we have to bring Gordon to you?" Jim roared.

Ian looked from Lucas to Jim as if he wanted to argue, but fear for his wife as well as the others kept him from voicing his concerns.

"Twenty-three hours and nineteen minutes. You will deliver D.A. Gordon to the front entrance of the building by seven forty-five tomorrow morning or everyone dies. And I do mean everyone."

"He'll be there," Jim announced. "You have my word."

"Remember, gentlemen," the voice cautioned, "any contact with the authorities, any attempts to gain entrance to the building, and everyone dies."

"You have my word," Jim repeated without reservation. "Gordon will be there on time as requested. We will cooperate fully with all your terms."

"Excellent. I'm always relieved when no one has to die. But," the man added, his voice pulsating with pure evil, "I will without remorse execute one hostage after the other until they're all dead if the need arises. My men will disappear as quickly and untraceably as they appeared. Just like smoke. Do we understand each other?"

"Perfectly," Jim stated.

The connection was severed. Ian immediately started

entering numbers on the keypad of his cell. Jim stopped him. "What're you doing?"

"Determining if I can track the call back to a traceable number."

Jim snatched the cell out of his hand. Fury glistened in Ian's eyes.

"We will contact no one," Jim told him in no uncertain terms. "We will deliver Gordon just as he requested."

Again Lucas intervened. "Convoy will get to work on rounding up Gordon," he suggested. "Ian and I will attempt to get to the bottom of who's behind this takeover."

"And my people," Jim said, "will determine if there is a way inside without detection."

Three, then five seconds of traumatic silence elapsed.

"Agreed," Ian said, capitulating.

"Agreed," Lucas chimed in.

All three looked to Slade. He held up his hands. "I'm ready to do whatever needs to be done."

"Good." Jim set his formidable attention on Slade. "Find Gordon. Bring him in."

Not exactly the easiest job he'd ever been assigned. "What if he doesn't want to cooperate?" Slade felt the question was a legitimate one.

"Do whatever is necessary," Jim told him. "Just get him here."

Slade hesitated to see if Ian would object. When he didn't, Slade shrugged. "No problem."

THREE

Inside the Colby Agency, 8:50 a.m.

VICTORIA tightened her lips against the moan that welled in her throat. Her head throbbed and nausea roiled in her stomach.

She couldn't show the first sign of weakness. The others were depending upon her.

All fourteen of her staff members had been shoved into the conference room. Two others were injured as well. Thankfully none appeared to be life-threatening.

"Victoria."

She drew in a deep breath and forced a calm into her voice that she by no means felt. "I'm all right," she assured Nicole. "We're all going to be all right. I'm certain Ian, Lucas and Jim are doing all within their power to regain control of the situation."

Merri Walters most likely had a mild concussion, at the very least a contusion. Victoria ached for the woman. Unable to hear the approach of the bastards who had taken control of the

Colby Agency, Merri hadn't reacted rapidly enough. She'd gotten a brutal whack to the back of the head for the delay. But she was coherent and, mercifully, showed no outward signs of serious trouble.

Fury vibrated through Victoria. Whatever these animals wanted, they would be sorry they had chosen the Colby Agency as their target.

She would see to that. *Somehow.*

Nicole glanced at Merri and the others huddled around her. "She seems okay." Her attention shifted to the newest investigator on the Colby staff, Kendra Todd. The swelling and bruises on her face reminded all the others that back talk would not be permitted. "But I'll need to keep an eye on Kendra. She isn't accustomed to being pushed around."

Several of the men, Ted Tallant and Trinity Barrett in particular, had their share of swelling, bruises and scrapes for having attempted to fight off the attack while the rest, Victoria included, ran for exits.

Their captors had been prepared for just such a diversion. Both fire exits had been covered and the elevators had been locked down.

"You monitor Kendra and help Simon with the others," Victoria agreed. "I'm going to see if I can learn the shackled prisoner's identity." He was the one unknown variable in this equation.

Nicole's gaze followed Victoria's to the man on the other side of the room. He'd been dragged into the conference room and shackled to a chair as far away from Victoria's staff as possible within the confines of the same four walls. A cloth sack covered his face and head, and his plain gray sweatshirt and worn jeans gave no indication of who he was or where he'd come from.

The generic sneakers he wore had seen far better days. There was nothing about his appearance or his bearing that gave the slightest impression of who he was. He hadn't attempted to speak or escape, which could mean he was either gagged or drugged. Not that escape was an option considering the way his ankles and wrists were bound together and his waist was manacled to the chair. His head drooped forward as if he were in fact unconscious.

"His guard doesn't look too friendly," Nicole commented under her breath.

That much was true. The guard wore black like all the others, including the concealing ski mask. The weapon in his hand indicated he didn't trust anyone enough to holster it. Though all visible beyond the mask were his dark eyes, that glimpse into his psyche warned that he wasn't taking any chances or any grief.

"The least I can do is try," Victoria insisted as she struggled from her position on the floor to her feet. Her head swam. She braced against the wall to steady herself. She'd made the mistake of struggling with the two men who had escorted her to this room. Being made an example of wasn't a surprise—she'd expected as much. Her attackers had wanted to ensure all present realized that Victoria was no longer in control. Several of her staff members had gotten roughed up when they'd attempted to come to her aid. All the more reason she had to tread carefully. Her staff would be taking their cues from her.

Their safety depended a great deal on her every action.

Even as the thought echoed in her brain, she slowly crossed the room toward the shackled man and his personal guard. She'd already spotted the tracks of dried blood down the front of his sweatshirt. He no doubt needed medical attention the same as she did and many of her staff members.

"Back on the floor," the man with the gun ordered. He shifted the business end of his weapon in her direction to reinforce his order.

Victoria halted. "He's bleeding." She gestured to the mysterious prisoner. "I just want to check to see that he's not seriously injured. He may need medical attention."

The guard scoffed. "He'll be dead soon enough. Any injuries he sustained are inconsequential."

Victoria refused to flinch. "Surely you don't mean to deprive us of proper care for our injuries, and some water." She indicated the door on the other side of the room. "There's bottled water and coffee in the lounge across the hall. And first-aid supplies." If someone made a run for it, it couldn't be her. She would not leave a single member of her staff behind. Perhaps Nicole would be allowed to go across the hall. She could attempt an escape if the opportunity presented itself.

This very minute Lucas, Ian and Jim would be planning how to resolve this takeover. These bastards had no idea how lucky they would be to survive the coming battle.

"Sit down," the guard ordered. "Or—" he shifted his aim toward the others huddled around Merri "—one of them dies."

Victoria backed up a step. "Fine. I'll sit." She couldn't take the risk that he might not be bluffing. "But you, sir, should think about how to keep your hostages from further harm. We're no good to you unless we're alive."

His glare was his only response.

The unidentified prisoner was apparently unconscious. She hadn't heard a moan or any other sort of sound from him. If he'd been awake and aware of himself, he would surely have tried to communicate as Victoria had questioned the guard about him.

As she settled on the floor near the members of her staff, she and Nicole exchanged a look of defeat.

No. Victoria refused to be defeated. Not by these men. Not by anyone. True, she had lost that battle, but she wasn't through by a long shot.

Simon Ruhl, one of her most trusted investigators and one of her seconds-in-command, kept one arm around Merri as she leaned against his shoulder. He flashed a ghost of a smile at Victoria. She understood what the gesture meant. They would be okay. Lucas, Ian and Jim would not fail. They would find a way to neutralize the hostiles. Simon's confidence affirmed her own.

All Victoria and her people had to do was remain patient and cooperate with these infiltrators. This day, this nightmare, would soon be reversed. The most brilliant minds on the planet were working together.

The conference room door abruptly flew inward. All eyes swung to the man loitering in the open doorway.

"You," the man who appeared to be in charge said to Victoria, "come with me." It was impossible to tell him apart from the others except for his voice. His accent said he wasn't an American by birth. Perhaps he was of European ancestry.

Simon and several others braced to defend Victoria, but she signaled with a small shake of her head for them to stand down.

Whatever happened to her, the most important thing was for the others to remain safe. To survive.

As Victoria dragged herself up once more and walked slowly toward the door, she tried to remember if she'd told Lucas she loved him that morning before leaving for the office. They'd shared a light kiss. That part she remembered vividly, as always.

Tears brimmed on her lashes and the ache deepened in her chest. They hadn't had nearly enough time together. She'd made him wait so very, very long.

And Jim? When they'd spoken by phone last night, had she told him how very much she loved him? Or Jamie, her sweet little granddaughter?

Victoria hoped that was the case.

She might never get the opportunity again.

FOUR

Treamont condo complex, 9:20 a.m.

MIA Dawson checked her reflection in the mirror once more. She could do this. No matter that he was most likely on to her.

She could do it.

No one else had the level of access she did. If she failed to get this done…then he would just get away with his crimes.

It was her duty as a citizen of Chicago—as a human being—to see that he was stopped. And she owed it to her cousin to ensure justice prevailed.

Mia took a deep breath, moistened her lips and strengthened her determination.

There was no one else. It had to be her.

Grabbing her purse and keys on the way to the front door, she pushed aside the fear and reached for the door. She could do this.

A fist pounding on the slab of wood shook the doorknob in her hand.

She blinked, resisted the impulse to draw back a step. It wouldn't be him or one of his men. She was on her way to his home now. He would much rather carry out any confrontation on his own turf.

Just check the security peephole and see who it is.

Mia leaned forward and took a look. A tall man with blond hair stood on the other side of her door. A frown furrowed her brow. She'd never seen this man before. She squinted, looked again. No, he was a stranger. Knowing her boss, he could have hired someone new just for this job.

Taking care of the enemy.

She swallowed back the uncertainty, deliberately slowed her breathing. "Who is it?" No point in pretending she wasn't home. If he'd been sent to take care of her, he would know she wasn't at work and that her car remained in the underground parking garage.

"I'm Investigator Slade Convoy. I have a few questions for you related to your work with former district attorney Timothy Gordon."

Holy hell. She searched her brain, tried to reason what his statement meant. Seemed damned coincidental that an investigator would show up at her door at precisely this moment.

"Do you have some ID?" IDs could be faked, but asking felt like the right thing to do. He would surely expect her to ask.

The man shoved a credentials case close to the peephole. The case was open so that the identification card was displayed.

The Colby Agency. Private Investigator Slade Convoy.

The Colby Agency. The name rang a bell. She'd heard it at some point. Maybe on a case her boss had prosecuted. Maybe from a defendant. She stiffened her posture and demanded,

"Why would you want to talk to me? Who sent you?" The latter was the far better question. *If* he told the truth.

"Ma'am, I really don't want to do this in the hallway. The subject matter is sensitive."

Ah, he avoided the important question altogether. Getting inside was his objective. "Who did you say sent you?" she repeated, though he hadn't said at all.

"Victoria Colby-Camp, the head of the Colby Agency."

That name sounded familiar as well. "Is there a way I can verify that?"

Impatience etched across his face. "You can call my supervisor. His name is Ian Michaels." To her surprise, the man rattled off a number.

Mia chewed her bottom lip. What the hell? She fished her cell phone from her purse and entered the number.

After the first ring, a male voice uttered, "Michaels."

She cleared her throat. "This is Mia Dawson. There's a man at my door. His…name is Slade Convoy. He claims he represents your agency."

This made no sense! He could have given her any number. No matter what this Ian Michaels said, he could be lying as well. She wasn't thinking.

"Ms. Dawson, it would mean a great deal to the Colby Agency if you allowed Mr. Convoy to ask you a few questions. I can't divulge the nature of the situation, as you might well imagine. But your assistance is greatly needed and would be genuinely appreciated."

She had to be out of her mind to even consider opening the door. "I'm sorry, Mr. Michaels, but you and Mr. Convoy are asking me to open my door to a complete stranger. I'm certain you can understand how unwise such a move would be."

"I do understand, Ms. Dawson." He paused. "I don't want to frighten you, but this is a matter of life and death. Without your help, fifteen people stand to lose their lives."

Good Lord. How did she say no to that? Would anyone go that far to gain access to her when all he had to do was wait for her in the basement near or inside her vehicle? "All right. I'll…talk to him." Michaels thanked her before she disconnected. She had to admit that he sounded genuinely sincere.

Mia peered out the security hole once more. "Mr. Convoy, remove your jacket, please, so that I can see whether or not you're armed."

The man rolled his eyes but acquiesced to her demand. He removed the lined leather coat he wore and dropped it to the floor. Then he held up both hands, surrender style, and turned all the way around so that she could ensure there was no weapon tucked into his waistband.

When he faced the door again, he dropped his arms to his sides. "Satisfied?"

Another moment of hesitation lapsed before she relented and opened the door. He stood before her, taller than he'd looked through the tiny hole. One more deep breath. "How can I help you?"

He gestured to the room behind her. "Surely you can understand how I wouldn't want to have this discussion in a public corridor like this."

No way was this man getting her alone inside her condo. "Since I don't know the nature of your business, I'll have to disagree. What can I do for you, sir?" She'd made all the compromises so far—time for him to make one.

Tension started to throb in his square jaw. If he was one of her boss's thugs, he was damned good-looking. She gave herself a mental shake. What the hell was wrong with her?

"Fine." The tightening of his lips warned that he wasn't happy. "The Colby Agency is investigating Mr. Gordon. I'm hoping you can clear up a couple of things for us before we make a wrong step. Whatever you tell me will be completely off the record. No one will connect any of it back to you."

Interest stirred. Gordon was being investigated? This was the first she'd heard of that. "What sort of investigation?"

Convoy glanced around. "I'm sorry." He shook his head. "I just can't talk about this in the open like this. You're going to have to trust me."

Anticipation nudged her. This could be the break she'd been hoping for. All she had to do was take the risk. She reached into her purse and removed her pepper spray, rested her forefinger on the trigger. "Come in." Stepping back, she opened the door wider.

Convoy picked up his coat and crossed her threshold. She hadn't noticed until then that he wore cowboy boots. Faded jeans and a striped button-up shirt. Other than the pricy jacket he didn't exactly look like any high-class investigator she'd ever met. And if she recalled correctly, the Colby Agency was no low-rent P.I. shop.

Keeping her finger ready on the trigger, Mia closed the door and turned to her visitor. "What is the nature of your investigation?"

"Our client," he began, "has requested a face-to-face with Mr. Gordon."

Mia shrugged. "Gordon has a secretary. I'm certain a simple phone call is all you'd need to set up an appointment for your client." Mia wasn't the man's secretary. She'd been his personal assistant for two years, had the rest of this month to go and then they were done. A tingle of fear shimmered through her. Less than one month to go to get what she needed. She was so close, but close wouldn't cut it. The evidence had to be in her possession before she made her next move.

And that all depended upon whether or not he was on to her extracurricular activities.

Convoy glanced around the room. "I'm afraid the usual route for this sort of thing won't work. Our client wants this meeting off the record as well."

A new kind of fear reared its ugly head. "What does that mean?" Good grief, she'd been so fired up to get the goods on Gordon, she very well may have walked into a trap. But what kind of trap? What was the Colby Agency after? Who was this client he kept referring to?

His gaze, the shade so intensely green that it made her quiver, zeroed in on hers. "I'm going to cut right to the chase, Ms. Dawson."

"That would be nice." She braced, mentally and physically.

"We have a hostage situation at the Colby Agency. Contacting the authorities is out of the question. If I don't bring Gordon in for this little tête-à-tête, then folks are going to die. I have only a few hours to accomplish that task."

Mia hadn't seen anyone else in the corridor outside her door. This man was alone. No cameras. No audio recorders visible. He was unarmed, for heaven's sake. Yet, this had to be some kind of scam or setup. It was too bizarre to be real. Mia Dawson had never believed in coincidences.

Not to mention what he was talking about was kidnapping. A felony.

"O-kay." She felt her gaze narrow. "What's going on here?

I don't know what you're up to, but you can tell me the truth now or I'm calling the police." Her free hand went instinctively to her cell phone while her forefinger settled more fully on the pepper spray trigger. This game was over.

"Wait." He held up both hands as she produced her cell. "I'm telling the truth," he urged. "I don't know what else to say to convince you, but this is not a scam or a joke. It's real and people are going to die."

Maybe if he hadn't looked dead serious—or if she didn't want to get her boss so badly—she wouldn't have hesitated.

Could she really have gotten so lucky that an avenue to execute her plans had fallen right into her lap?

"You want me to believe you?" She hiked up her chin in defiance of the skepticism simmering beneath the hope. "Take me to the Colby Agency and let me hear this from someone besides a voice on the telephone."

His hands dropped impotently to his sides once more. "That's the one thing I can't do." That unsettling gaze pierced hers once more. "The truth is, ma'am, I could have waited for you in your little hybrid in the garage. I could have taken you by force. But I'm giving you the opportunity to do the right thing on your own."

Her head was moving from side to side in protest before he completed the discourse on how this was the best for her. "If you need my help to do something that's clearly illegal, then you're going to have to show me that the stakes are as you say." She wasn't stupid. This guy had to be out of his mind if he thought she was going to go along with this crazy plan without some sort of tangible proof.

He thought about her demand for a moment, that tension still keeping a furious rhythm in his jaw. "Going to the agency is impossible. That's where the hostages are being held. But I can take you to the temporary command center we've set up."

"Who's holding the hostages? If someone wants a face-to-face with Gordon, it must be an old enemy of his." That was the only plausible explanation. As much as she wanted to see the scumbag go down, she would not be responsible for turning him over to some recently released criminal he'd once prosecuted. She was already only weeks from being without a job, she wasn't going to make tracks to prison as well. The unemployment line was unpalatable enough.

Slade Convoy was the one shaking his head now. "We don't know the answer to that question just yet. Our people, what's left of them, are attempting to determine the source of the threat. Right now we have no choice but to accede to the demand given. Time is not on our side."

This was one of those moments…when a woman had to decide if she was going to take an obvious leap of faith for what she believed in or just allow an opportunity to pass right on by.

This man…Slade Convoy…and the agency he represented didn't have to know about her own agenda. This could actually work to her benefit. "I suppose that's reasonable." She had to be a lot desperate or a little crazy to go along with this. But she knew Gordon better than anyone else. She might even be able to help with determining who was behind this takeover. "I can also give you a list of the cases he has prosecuted the past couple of years. Your threat may be coming from one of those."

The relief that flashed in the investigator's eyes was palpable. "I'll inform my superior that we're on our way."

If Gordon was on to what she was up to, she was likely on more than one hit list already. Why not take a risk? One that might ensure she survived?

Not daring to return the canister of pepper spray to her purse, she held on to it with her left hand while she adjusted the shoulder strap of her purse with her right. "Fine. But keep in mind that I'm going to be late for work as it is. With Gordon," she added sharply.

"In that case," Convoy said, gesturing to the door, "what're we waiting for?"

Mia bit her lips together. For a way out of this, she didn't say. For someone to save her...from herself.

FIVE

Maggie's Coffee House, 10:40 a.m.

SLADE nodded to one of the waitresses as he weaved his way between customers and behind the counter. The stairs to the second floor were behind a door marked Employees Only. He held it open for Mia, and she hesitated long enough to meet his eyes.

She still wasn't sure about this. The fact of the matter was he'd expected to have to bring her here by force. He should be thankful he hadn't been obliged to take extreme measures. This whole situation was way out of control and rushing well beyond previously respected legal boundaries.

As she ascended the narrow stairs, he considered that besides a great-looking backside, the woman had the bluest eyes he'd ever seen. Like the darkest depths of the ocean. She looked younger than he'd expected. Rather than the twenty-nine her dossier revealed, she looked more like twenty-one. But that couldn't be right. She'd graduated at the top of her class at Northwestern and had worked five years in the Cook County District Attorney's office, two for Gordon himself. Slade wondered why she'd never opted to go to law school. From what he'd read she was damned good at taking care of business.

After moving only a few steps across the room, Mia stopped in her tracks.

Slade couldn't exactly blame her. Since he'd left, things had changed big-time. The boxes containing paper products had been moved to one corner. Several tables had been pushed together to make a conference center of sorts. A blueprint of the building across the street had been taped to a nearby wall. Computers hummed with the work of folks Slade didn't recognize.

Noting his frown of confusion, Ian gestured to the two guys stationed at the computers. "Jim brought a couple of his team members to support our efforts."

Jim Colby, Victoria's son, stared out the windows as if by sheer force of will he could free his mother from the siege that had descended upon the Colby Agency only three hours ago.

"This is Mia Dawson." Slade indicated the woman at his side, then his superior. "Ian Michaels, the Colby Agency's second-in-command."

"Ms. Dawson." Ian approached and extended his hand. "We sincerely appreciate your cooperation under the circumstances."

"Is that because what you're doing is against a number of laws?" Mia demanded, obviously deciding to cut to the chase.

Both Jim and Lucas, Victoria's husband, turned from their station at the window to assess the woman who'd issued such a vehement inquiry.

Slade had a feeling Ms. Dawson had heard all she wanted to from him. Ian could take it from here. Slade had done a hell of a lot of research on the Colby Agency before accepting the position a year or so ago. The one thing that had drawn him to the offered position was the stellar reputation of Victoria Colby-Camp and her entire staff. The agency was highly respected by local law enforcement as well as those on the federal level.

The plan they had no choice but to enact was about as far from reputable as could be gotten.

The Colby Agency stood on the verge of moving into new territory. Irreparable damage was not only possible, but it was also unavoidable.

"We have fifteen staff members, including Victoria Colby-Camp, in the building across the street." He indicated the window where Lucas and Jim still stood. "All communications have been severed. The building itself is in lockdown mode. As of this moment, we have no avenues of entrance. No negotiating chips, save one."

"Gordon," she suggested.

Ian acknowledged her suggestion with a nod. "If we contact the authorities in any capacity the hostages will die. Considering the way the infiltrators were able to shut down all communications and lock down the entire building, I'm inclined to believe their threat that they are aware of our every move."

Slade shifted his attention from Mia's full lips as she moistened them. She was nervous and rightly so. And he, apparently, hadn't taken care of his sexual urges recently. Being attracted to her at a time like this was immensely stupid.

"Which also indicates they know you've brought me into the situation," Mia added.

"No doubt."

She swore, then whipped around to glare at Slade. He blinked, trying to ignore the way her silky black hair flew around her shoulders. The woman was damned gorgeous, and equally stubborn. But neither of those traits would salvage this situation.

"This could cost me my position," she snapped.

"You're already on notice," Ian interjected. "Three or four weeks are all that remain on your contract with the D.A.'s office, correct?"

Outrage tightened her face. "That's right, but I've applied for another position with the new D.A. This kind of move could jeopardize my chances of a new contract."

Ian nodded once more. "Not helping us could cost the lives of fifteen people."

"Including his wife," Slade said quietly. "The mother of his children."

Ian stabbed him with a deadly glare.

"My God," Mia mumbled.

Lucas Camp ambled across the room. "Ms. Dawson, I'm Lucas Camp." He shook the hand she offered, however limply. "Victoria is my wife," he confessed, "but this isn't about that. All fifteen of the Colby employees inside that building are someone's wife or husband, son or daughter. Most are mothers or fathers. Above all else, they're innocent victims of the madman behind this. The only connection, the one avenue for helping them, is Mr. Gordon."

Mia's chest rose and fell with a big breath. Slade gave himself a mental kick for observing that move far too closely. Maybe he needed another day of R & R to clear his head.

"What is it you want me to do?" Mia's compassion overwhelmed the anger and mistrust.

"I'm sure Gordon won't come here willingly," Ian explained. "Certainly he wouldn't threaten his own safety without involving the authorities."

A laugh burst from Mia's lips. Every gaze in the room landed on her. "Are you kidding? He wouldn't threaten his safety for his own mother, much less anyone else's."

Ian and Lucas exchanged a look.

"That's why we need you," Slade ventured. "My job is to make my way into his estate and bring him here…whether he wants to come or not."

Big blue eyes widened. "Are you serious? You want to kidnap him?"

"That's one way to put it," Slade acknowledged.

Jim's foreboding presence abruptly muscled between the men gathered around Mia. "We're not asking your permission here, Ms. Dawson. We're going to do this with or without your agreement."

Slade's attention shot to Ian. Jim's heavy-handedness was a major hot button with Ian.

Purse still hanging from her shoulders, Mia planted her hands on her hips. "You're saying I don't have a choice?" she demanded, staring at Jim Colby. "That I either help you or what? You'll kill me or something?"

"No, Ms. Dawson, certainly not," Ian said quickly. "We feel certain that under the circumstances you'll want to cooperate with our efforts. We will ensure that Mr. Gordon's safety is protected at all times. We won't send him in, under any circumstances, unless we have backup in place."

"How the hell can you promise that?" Jim demanded. His hands hung at his sides and were clenched in fury. "We'll do whatever we have to."

"I'll take Ms. Dawson downstairs for coffee," Slade suggested.

He was relatively certain Ian did not want her to witness the debate about to take place.

"No." She backed away from Slade's outstretched hand. "If you expect me to help with this, I'm going to be in on both sides of the argument."

Then she said something that shocked Slade. "Besides, what makes you think I care about Gordon's safety? The only thing I'm worried about is my future career in the D.A.'s office."

Ian's questioning gaze settled on Slade. Slade shrugged, then said to her, "My background research didn't reveal any hostility between you and Gordon."

Mia glared at him. "You ran a background search on me? What the hell for? I don't have a criminal record and my professional record in the D.A.'s office is above reproach."

"Is there a personal relationship between you and Gordon that we're unaware of?" Ian asked with his typical frankness.

"Absolutely not," she said entirely too quickly. "I just don't care for the man, that's all. And he's history. My focus is on the future. I don't want to see anyone die for him, but I don't want to kill my career, either."

Ian was suspicious. As controlled as the man's calm facade was, Slade understood that his assessment of Mia Dawson had moved to a different level. So had Slade's, for that matter.

"Then you don't have any problem helping Mr. Convoy obtain access to Gordon's estate?" Ian proposed.

She blinked once, twice. "If that's what you need me to do to—" she gestured vaguely to the window "—help you recover this situation."

Slade's instincts went on point. There was something more going on here. He and Ian shared another of those knowing looks.

"Let's go have that coffee now," Lucas suggested, stepping forward. "I'd like to hear more about your working relationship with Gordon."

Mia's expression gave away her uncertainty. "I'm supposed to be at his place right now. I'm helping him transfer his working note files to storage."

Lucas took her arm, wrapped it around his. "You have my word, this won't take long."

Mia didn't resist. Few people had the guts to protest anything Lucas Camp suggested. Neither his age nor his obvious limp overshadowed his ability to intimidate with a single look or word.

When the two had disappeared down the stairs, Ian turned a furious glare on Jim. "We will not send Gordon inside unless we have backup in place. I've already agreed to the *no-cops* edict. That's as far as I'm willing to cross the line on this."

"And if we can't get backup in place," Jim countered. "We're just going to sit back and let them die when the time runs out?"

The pain that flashed in Ian's eyes twisted Slade's gut into knots. "We have just over twenty hours to get someone inside," Ian summed up. "I'm certain we will be successful. Surely you don't expect Slade to drag Gordon out of his compound in broad daylight? This will need to be done after he's retired for the evening so as not to draw attention."

Ian made a valid point.

"At seven-thirty tomorrow morning," Jim said, obviously not backing off, "we will turn Gordon over, no matter our tactical situation."

"If we're waiting until later tonight," Slade asked, only just now seeing how this was going to play out for him over the next few hours, "how am I supposed to ensure Ms. Dawson doesn't have a change of heart and call the police between now and then?"

Considering he couldn't prevent her from going to work, otherwise suspicions would be roused, he couldn't be absolutely certain she wouldn't call the authorities once she was out of his line of sight.

"You'll find a way," Jim said before returning to the window.

"We're missing something," Ian said for Slade's ears only. "She's somewhat too eager. A woman who has spent the past five years working on the side of justice wouldn't suddenly be so amiable to such a plan." He glanced back at the work going on. "Watch her, Convoy. There may be an undisclosed revelation coming."

"Will do," Slade assured him.

He hustled down the stairs, visually located Lucas and Mia. He watched a moment as she sipped her coffee. Her smile was nervous but seemingly genuine.

Ian was right. She was definitely hiding something relevant to all this.

She glanced up as Slade approached. "Time to get you to work," he said, pushing aside his suspicions for the moment.

"Thank you, Mr. Camp." Mia rose from her chair. "I'll keep all you said in mind."

Slade nodded to Lucas then headed back to his truck with the single key they possessed to this incredible mess. Mia Dawson, a woman with an agenda. "What wisdom did Lucas have to offer?"

She paused at the passenger-side door of his truck. "That I had nothing to worry about. He would personally ensure the job I'd applied for was mine if I wanted it." Those long, dark lashes swept down over her eyes, quickly covering a glimpse of fear or uncertainty. "However this thing turns out."

Well, well, maybe the lady really wasn't worried about anything but her job.

The idea didn't sit comfortably in Slade's gut. Whenever a person worked so incredibly hard to ensure all were aware of his or her single goal, one thing was absolutely certain.

It wasn't the true goal at all.

SIX

Gordon compound, 1:25 p.m.

TWO hours had passed since Slade had watched Mia pull her small hybrid sedan through the gate of the Gordon property. Just outside of Chicago, the property reminded Slade of a compound provided for a wealthy political figure in exile. Mammoth, but closed off from the world. No amount of luxury could offset the intimidation of the twelve-foot walls and the state-of-the-art electronic security surveillance system.

Evidently the seven-figure book deal Gordon had landed after retiring as Cook County's D.A. allowed him to step way, way up in the world.

All that money and the man couldn't escape his enemies.

Lethal enemies.

Those enemies were using the Colby Agency to lure their prey into a trap.

It was Slade's job to see that Gordon walked straight into that trap.

Five minutes more and he was scheduled to enter the compound to pick up the boxed files for transporting back to the county's file storage facility.

Ian had ensured that Slade had all he needed. A properly marked van, uniform and an authentic ID. The files would be turned over to the appropriate security guard at the facility as soon as the task was accomplished. The Colby Agency had contacts from the top on down to the lowest echelon of society, as well as professional assets. Slade never ceased to be amazed at what Ian and Simon could come up with.

Doing this right was supremely important for many reasons. One, to ensure no one died. Second, for damage control. No way was the Colby Agency coming out of this smelling like a rose.

Kidnapping was a felony.

Slade fully understood the risk he was taking.

So did Mia, it seemed.

He still didn't get the idea that she'd caved so easily to the demand.

If he were damned lucky, her cooperation was real and wouldn't come back to bite him in the backside.

So far, only a few minor laws had been broken. But the moment he drove off the compound with those files, despite the fact that he would immediately turn them over to the appropriate handler, Slade was crossing a line. The files were county property. Case files. Sensitive. Protected.

Then there was the second step in his task. Ensuring Gordon's full cooperation. Kidnapping.

Both Ian and Lucas had insisted they would take full responsibility. Jim Colby wanted to do this personally, but Lucas and

Ian had convinced him that his time would be better spent focused on finding a way into the building beneath the radar of the gunmen inside.

Slade glanced at the digital clock on the dash. Time to do this. He started the engine and pulled away from the curb. Braking at the intersection, he turned right and headed for the Gordon compound.

At the gate Slade depressed the call button.

"Let's see some ID," the face and voice on the four-inch security monitor told him.

Slade tugged the clip-on badge from his shirt pocket and held it in front of the screen's built-in camera.

"When you enter the gate, drive straight back to the garage," the man, obviously a member of Gordon's private security, ordered.

"Will do." Slade clipped the badge back onto his pocket and waited for the gates to swing inward.

He rolled across the European-style pavers until he reached the garage. A long, low whistle hissed past his lips as he got a full view of the mansion Gordon called home. The building looked more like something a big-time celebrity would call home.

Slade shifted into Park and shut off the engine. "Showtime." He grabbed the jacket that matched the uniform and pulled it on as he got out. The cold January air cut through him before he could shrug the jacket into place.

The second of the three garage doors opened as he reached for the clipboard on the dash, then closed the door.

Mia stood waiting as the overhead door moved upward. "The boxes are inside." She hitched a thumb toward the massive garage behind her. "Just follow me."

Acknowledging her statement with a nod, he walked toward her. "Afternoon, ma'am."

"We…have six boxes with matching bar codes." Her voice was a little shaky, nervous. "You'll need to document that you've accepted each one."

The last thing he needed was for her to blow this. Too many lives were depending on how this went down. And this step was only phase one. "I understand, ma'am," he assured her, hoping to allay her too-evident fears.

She visually inspected him from head to toe before turning to lead the way into the house.

He surveyed the garage. Two classic luxury vehicles, each polished to a high sheen, claimed two of the parking spaces. From the yard the only means of access to the garage were the overhead doors. No walk-through door. A single paneled door, which looked to be steel, separated the garage from a mudroom and pantry-style storage area. No windows in the garage, only one in the first entry point into the home.

Slade visually assessed each room they encountered as Mia led the way to Gordon's home office beyond the kitchen and family room. They encountered none of the three security personnel she had told him would be on duty inside. Another patrolled the perimeter outside the home. At midnight, the number inside was reduced to only one. Since Slade wasn't met and patted down by security, he had to assume that Mia remained a trusted employee.

She turned back to him then, clasped her trembling hands in front of her. "Mr. Gordon prefers that hand trucks are not used in the house, so you'll need to carry each box out to the garage."

He placed his clipboard on the first box in the stack, then lifted it into his arms. The typical boxes designed for legal-size files, each was taped securely and marked with an identifying bar code across the tape to ensure that breaking the seal would be readily visible.

Mia followed him back to the garage. Five more trips. He wondered if she planned to trace his every step. Adrenaline pushed through him. Unless she behaved that way whenever anyone came by to pick up or deliver something, her actions could very well inspire suspicion.

Rather than drop the box onto the garage floor, Slade carried it directly to the van and deposited it into the open back bay. He annotated the bar code number onto the clipboard's document, which he would sign and leave a copy with Mia when the task was complete.

She hovered at the garage door, waiting for the next trip.

"Is it necessary for you to follow me back and forth each trip?" he asked softly as he passed her on his way back inside.

"Yes." She moved up beside him. "That's part of my job."

He couldn't argue with that.

This time, instead of leading him through the kitchen, she made a path through the family room and formal dining area. Slade took his time following her, mentally noting the windows and doors as well as the main security panel near the front entrance.

Mia drew up short and squeaked at the office door.

One of the members of Gordon's security was scrutinizing the boxes.

"Can I help you?" she asked when she'd regained her wits.

Caution nudged Slade. This was not a part of routine procedure, otherwise Mia wouldn't have reacted in such a surprised manner. He hoped not, anyway. His internal alert rose to the next level.

"I recall you listing five boxes," the man with the wireless communications device decorating his right ear commented. He straightened from the stack and studied Mia with a measuring gaze.

Uh-oh. Slade glanced at his clipboard. "Is there a problem?" He met the other man's eyes. "I have a schedule to keep."

Mia moved into the office, pausing across the boxes from the man in the dark suit. "There were five boxes, but Mr. Gordon opted to send a number of his personal notes along with the case files. I was unable to fit the additions into the five boxes I'd packed. I'm sure if you call him he'll tell you as much, Mr. Terrell."

Slade worked at looking bored and impatient. If Mia was lying she did a damned good job of sounding frustrated and slighted that her work had come under question.

Terrell looked over the boxes once more. "This one—" he tapped the next box on the stack "—seems to be the latest addition to the inventory." He leveled a look at Mia that could only be described as dangerous. "I'm sure you won't mind opening it so that I may inspect it and then resealing it if all is as it should be."

"This is ludicrous." Mia stamped over to the desk and scrambled through the drawers until she'd located a box cutter. "I will inform Mr. Gordon about this incident." She all but pushed Terrell aside and efficiently slid the blade along the taped seams.

"That won't be necessary, Ms. Dawson," Terrell challenged. "I'll inform him myself."

Mia stepped back and let the man sift through the contents of the box. She rolled her eyes twice before he'd finished flipping through file folders.

He closed the flaps on the box. "Everything looks to be in order."

Without a word in response, she stormed back to the desk, put the box cutter away and returned with shipping tape and a marker. When she'd secured the flaps once more, she wrote the bar code along the newly taped seam. Shifting her attention to Slade, she said, "Carry on, please."

For the rest of the trips to the van, Terrell trailed after Slade, which prevented any new free maneuvering through the downstairs portion of the house.

Gordon and his security personnel were either ultrasuspicious by nature or suspected Mia Dawson of some infraction.

Not good for Slade and the task ahead, either way.

He needed to leave a monitoring device on the main downstairs security panel. Not going to happen now. Unless he could trust her to do it.

When he'd reached the van for the last time, he placed the box inside and closed the rear doors. He annotated the final number on the pickup order, signed it and passed the clipboard to Mia. Additionally, he included the tiny device. "You'll need to look over the list I've made and ensure that all is in order. If so, you can sign my original."

She blinked, her fingers icy where they touched his. For one seemingly eternal second, she simply stared at Slade. Then she accepted the clipboard and the tiny round stick-on patch that was practically invisible.

Nodding as she read over each line, she completed her review and lifted her gaze to Slade's. The fear in those aquamarine eyes shook him hard.

"Where do I need to sign?"

He pointed to the appropriate line. "Right there will be fine."

When she leaned closer to scrawl her name across the line, Slade was careful to keep his face down. He murmured, "Put the patch on the main security panel downstairs. It's vital to the next step."

"There you go." She returned the clipboard and pen. He slipped her copy free and passed it to her. She immediately took a step back. "Thank you for coming on such short notice. I believe that's everything."

Picking up the files hadn't been on today's agenda, but Mia had worked it into the schedule to give Slade an avenue into the house.

"No problem." For a moment Slade hated to turn his back on her. She looked scared. Not good. But any unnecessary talk could create a domino effect of trouble. Her background hadn't indicated she'd ever been involved in any underhanded activity, much less anything illegal. Most likely this was a natural reaction.

One she needed to get in check.

He climbed behind the steering wheel and drove away, pausing only to wait for the gate to open.

After surveying both directions, right then left, he pulled out onto the deserted street.

Despite the cold, sweat beaded on his forehead like dew. He couldn't complete the next phase of the plan without Mia Dawson's assistance. But unless she got her act together, she would be more of a stumbling block than an asset.

He hoped like hell she pulled herself together between now and later tonight.

Otherwise—

Slade's gaze locked onto the rearview mirror. A police cruiser pulled from a side street and moved up behind him.

"Damn it."

If she'd broken and Terrell had already called for police backup…surely Cook County couldn't have reacted so quickly. That didn't seem possible. But this was a high-class neighborhood.

Just drive. Slade held his breath as the traffic light turned green and he accelerated forward. The cruiser did the same.

A glance in the rearview mirror told him the cop behind the wheel was speaking to someone via his radio or cell phone.

Damn it!

Careful to keep his speed beneath the posted limit, Slade continued forward.

His fingers itched to put through a call to Ian… just in case.

If the blue lights came on, that was exactly what he would do.

Blue lights throbbed in the mirror.

"Oh, hell."

Slade prepared to pull to the curb.

The cruiser shifted into the left lane and barreled around Slade's borrowed van, blue lights pulsing and sirens blaring.

The relief that surged through Slade left his hands trembling.

That was too close.

Too damned close.

He glanced at the time. Three more hours until Mia got off work for the day. He hoped she could hold it together that long. As nervous as she'd appeared moments ago, he wasn't convinced she could go through with her part of the plan without falling apart or breaking under the slightest pressure.

Still, the aspect that bothered him the most with this whole scenario was her motivation.

What did she have to gain by cooperating with what could only be labeled a criminal activity? No matter what Lucas had said to her, she, of all people, would be fully aware of the risk involved.

Yet, she'd lurched her way through phase one, it appeared.

Maybe he was being overly suspicious. Lucas, as well as Ian, could be acutely convincing.

It was entirely possible that the woman just wanted to do the right thing.

Slade stifled the urge to laugh out loud at that concept. What the hell was the bottom-line "right thing" in all this?

Kidnapping and coercion were crimes any way one looked at them.

But no one involved had a choice.

The fifteen members of the Colby Agency being held hostage would die one by one if certain steps weren't taken.

Slade hoped like hell that a way to rescue everyone inside would be found before it was too late.

For Gordon.

And the Colby Agency.

SEVEN

Inside the Colby Agency, 2:15 p.m.

VICTORIA'S head lolled forward. She jerked it upright. She didn't know how long she'd been tied up in the walk-in coat closet next to the lounge. Hours, she was reasonably certain.

She'd been left standing with her wrists secured to the metal rod above her shoulders. The coats had been shoved aside but the familiar scents of cologne and perfume were comforting to some degree. For a moment she closed her eyes and inhaled deeply, letting the familiar smells draw her away from this ugly reality.

Was there anything she could have done differently this morning? Could she have been more watchful…better prepared for an attack?

Victoria opened her eyes and owned the answer to those questions. No. She—they—had done all within their power to protect the agency.

Now she had to protect her staff…and herself.

At some point she had kicked off her pumps. She'd shifted her weight from side to side several times. Her legs ached and cramped. She hoped the others didn't think the worst. The last thing she wanted was for her absence to set off additional despair and desperation. She felt certain that their captors wanted just that.

Bastards.

For the first time since the siege had taken place, her mind wandered to the possibility that she might not survive. She hoped Jim would be able to bring himself to assume control of the agency. Victoria understood that he loved his Equalizers shop, but his father had hoped that his son would grow up and take over the agency. As did she. Destiny had tossed a stumbling block into their path when Jim had only been seven years old. He'd been abducted and had suffered horrible and inhumane treatment for the better part of twenty years. It was an absolute miracle that he had been able to shake all those horrific years of physical abuse and mental conditioning to hate and to kill. He'd achieved a place so very close to normal at this point…she didn't want this to set him back.

She'd come so near to giving up hope on finding him…but she had found him. And now her family was whole again. Surely fate would not allow their reunion to be so very short-lived.

Victoria had to survive. Her son and granddaughter needed her. This agency needed her.

A trembling smile slid across her lips. Lucas needed her. She loved him so very much. For years after her first husband's death, she had been convinced she could never love anyone the way she had loved James.

But she had been wrong.

She loved Lucas with every fiber of her being. There was no question, no hesitation, not the slightest uncertainty. He completed her, just as James, Jim's father, had all those years ago.

Nor had she ever felt concerned that James would resent what she and Lucas shared. He, above all others, would have wanted her to share her life with a man he himself trusted like a brother. James would want nothing less for her than pure happiness.

And to live.

Determination solidified inside her. She would survive, by God. Whoever had set this turmoil in motion, she would not allow his vendetta to destroy her or her world.

The closet door opened.

Victoria's gaze locked with familiar gray eyes. The man in charge. She had learned to recognize him by those steel-gray eyes, and the lingering inflection that marked his voice.

"I think you've been in here long enough," he announced. He reached into his pocket and produced a knife. The blade hissed as it slid from the shaft in the handle. Victoria refused to show even the slightest hint of fear.

Glee glittering in his eyes, he cut one binding then the other. Her arms dropped. She staggered, caught herself against the door frame. Sensation rushed back into her limp arms, reminding her that they'd gone numb hours ago.

"You have a command performance, Victoria," he told her as he hustled her out of the closet.

She didn't bother asking what he meant. No need. She would know soon enough.

As hard as she tried, she stumbled a number of times on the way to her office. Inside that familiar territory, one of the man's henchmen held a video camera. So that was the kind of command performance he meant.

He intended to send Lucas and the others a message of some sort. Nothing original about that.

"Have a seat."

Victoria looked from the man who'd ushered her here to the comfortable leather executive chair behind her desk. She considered asking him what he had in mind, but she doubted he would explain himself. Arguing or delaying would only draw retribution. She was already suffering the effects of the rough treatment and mental abuse of the day so far.

Cooperation, she reminded herself as she followed his instruction. They all had to cooperate until another option presented itself.

"You're going to send a message to your husband and the others," her captor explained. "It's very simple. They are to keep in mind how precarious your situation is. You and the others are safe for now. But there can be no mistakes or your little family in there will die first. You'll watch them go one at a time."

Victoria met his vile gaze. "Anything else?"

He shook his head. "Just be sure to make your plea believable. We don't want anyone screwing up."

Victoria squared her shoulders as the man with the video camera focused in on her. She lifted her chin and stared directly into the lens.

"And—" he pressed a button "—ready."

"Lucas, Jim—" her voice quavered even as she fought to keep it steady "—we have a few injuries but everyone is safe for now. There are seven men heavily armed and as long—"

The man in charge lunged across Victoria's desk. Files and the framed photo of her family flew in different directions. He slammed the back of his hand across her cheek. The skull-rattling sting sent her head flying back. She grunted. She clamped her lips together to prevent any other outward reaction. She blinked back the burn of tears. The coppery taste in her mouth warned that he'd split her lip. She would not give him the satisfaction of tears.

He pulled back, cleared his throat for emphasis. "Let's try that again. This time leave out the number of men."

Victoria swiped her mouth with the back of her hand to clear the blood. Steadying herself, she stared into the camera lens and started again. "Lucas, Jim, despite a few injuries, we're holding up as well as can be expected under the circumstances. You must cooperate to the fullest extent if you want to ensure there is no loss of life. I beseech you to do all within your power to meet the demands you've been given." She paused a moment to swallow back the lump in her throat. "I am dictating using reasons entirely self-supplied. These are my wishes and mine alone, though at least half my staff is in heavy agreement."

"Got it." The cameraman looked to his boss for additional instructions.

"Edit it," the other man ordered, "and we'll send it to her loving husband." He glared at Victoria.

She didn't flinch or even blink. Let him send it. She'd gotten her message across. The phrase "dictating using reasons entirely self-supplied" would signal them that she'd been coerced into the statement. Her final plea let them know that there were at least seven men, all heavily armed.

Whatever these bastards hoped to accomplish with their barbaric tactics, she had done her part to inform those struggling to devise a plan to retake the Colby Agency. There was little she could do now except attempt to keep the rest of her staff safe and cooperative.

It was the only way to stay alive until help arrived or until they could hatch a plan of action from right here inside the Colby Agency.

One that didn't include anyone dying.

The muzzle of a weapon abruptly bored into her temple.

Her breath caught. Victoria stalled. Didn't so much as breathe.

"Now, Victoria," the evil man who appeared to be in charge murmured, "let's see how successful you can be at keeping your staff alive. The first one who attempts a takeover dies."

EIGHT

Gordon compound, 5:15 p.m.

MIA picked up her purse and reached for her coat. All she had to do was make it to the door and out the gate.

Then she was home free.

She steadied herself, checked her shaking hands. *Focus. Be calm.* Drawing attention at this point would ruin everything.

She'd gotten the files she needed. The ones Gordon had asked her to shred. He'd claimed they were nothing more than duplicates. But Mia had taken the time to review each one and compare it with the so-called original documents.

The select group of files had been altered to agree with the outcome of certain trials. The true originals—the ones he'd asked her to shred—had reflected various witness reports and suppressed evidence that might have greatly affected the outcome of those trials. And no lack of personal, handwritten notes. Particularly the ones that pertained to her cousin's case. The one Gordon had fixed right under her nose.

But now she had him.

A smile stretched across her lips. Her shoulders reared back in triumph.

For nearly a year before her cousin's appearance at trial, she had suspected that Gordon was dirty. Now she had proof. Maybe not enough to convict him of anything that would get him life behind bars, but certainly enough to raise pointed questions and perhaps get him a nice little stint in one of the better prisons. He wasn't getting away with this. If she had her way, he would lose the big book deal. And that would only be the beginning. His name would be splashed all over the media outlets. His reputation, professionally and personally, would be ruined. And her cousin would get this life back.

Still, having Gordon end up in jail with a few of the folks he'd put there was her ultimate goal.

Then justice would take care of itself.

Ultimately she understood that without a search warrant, anything she took from his office was inadmissible in court. However, because she had included them with the official D.A.'s office files, she was reasonably sure that little loophole was taken care of.

She'd accomplished all the items on Gordon's cleanup and reorganization list.

Any working files were now a part of the official files of the D.A. office. He hadn't kept a single page. But then he'd already made notes on all cases he intended to refer to in his memoir. The high-profile cases. All except three—those three he couldn't refer to because he'd ensured the evidence was presented in a way that indicated police tampering or other technicalities that allowed for a hung jury or a failure to present sufficient evidence for trial. Those were the ones she'd duplicated.

She had him.

All she had to do now was get out of here....

"Ms. Dawson."

Mia stopped halfway across the kitchen as Mr. Terrell's voice echoed around her.

Schooling her victorious expression, she turned around slowly and met his expectant gaze. "Yes?"

"Mr. Gordon would like to see you in his office."

Her heart lunged into her throat. *Stop. Stay calm.* "I don't have much time." She shifted the purse strap on her shoulder. "I have a doctor's appointment." Good excuse. Surely he wouldn't keep her from something as important as that.

Two seconds, then four ticked off.

"I'm certain Mr. Gordon won't take up much of your time."

Terrell stood there waiting, his arms carefully positioned at his sides. But she knew that beneath that silk jacket he wore a very big weapon in a shoulder holster. He would use it if the need arose. She suspected that he wouldn't think twice about ending the life of someone as insignificant as her, in his opinion.

"Sure." She surrendered to the inevitable and followed the head of security back to Gordon's office. *He couldn't know anything.* She silently chanted that mantra over and over.

Gordon waited behind his desk. Mia hadn't realized he'd returned. She'd only just left this office about ninety seconds ago.

"Please." Gordon gestured to the chair directly in front of his desk. "Have a seat, Mia."

She glanced at Terrell, who loitered in the doorway, then took the seat as directed.

"I have an appointment, Mr. Gordon."

Gordon clasped his hands in front of his face as if he intended to pray. But she suddenly knew better.

The only person who needed to pray was her.

"I'm very disappointed in you, Mia."

Don't let him see the truth! Ignore the accusing gaze and the disappointment lining his craggy brow.

"I'm sorry." She looked from him to Terrell and back. "I don't understand."

Gordon signaled to Terrell, who stepped aside. One of the other security thugs, wearing yet another silk suit that cost more than she earned in a month, entered the office carrying one of the six boxes Convoy had driven away more than two hours ago. Fear coiled around her throat.

She was so screwed.

"I'm not certain why you thought it necessary to include the duplicates I asked you to shred, but—" he directed her attention to the box now sitting on the corner of his desk "—you did nonetheless."

Defeat sucked at her bones. She'd been so careful. She'd tucked the files into the second of the six boxes. One Terrell would never have thought to rummage through. She'd made sure nothing important was in the sixth box, the one he'd questioned her about earlier.

"I must have misunderstood," she offered, feigning innocence. "Didn't you want everything packed up?"

Gordon eyed her for a long moment. She resisted the impulse to squirm. He wasn't a large man. Five-eight or -nine perhaps. Thin and lean. His hair was thinning and gray. The thick lens of his eyeglasses made his pale blue eyes appear far too large. Yet he had been one of the most powerful and influential men in Chicago for nearly a decade.

But he was a sleaze.

"Perhaps that's the case," he allowed. "Still, it seems quite strange to me that the documents I asked you to shred would end up misfiled in the boxes being transferred to permanent storage. You've never made a mistake like that before. That one of the cases involved your cousin can't be coincidence."

Panic tried to choke her. She'd been so careful—no one had known Terry Campbell was her cousin. She would have been taken off the case. For the good it had done her to be a part of that circus act.

Take the offensive. "Are you accusing me of something, Mr. Gordon?"

He flattened his palms together and pressed his fingers to his lips. "I'm not certain."

Terrell stepped toward the desk.

Mia held her breath.

He opened the flaps of the box and reached inside for the manila folder in which she'd deposited the three files in question.

"Imagine my surprise," Gordon said as he accepted the file, "when Mr. Terrell opened this box and found *these*."

Go for broke. "I must have mixed that file up with the others." She nodded to the folder. "Notice that the only items it contains are the ones I was supposed to shred. I'm certain I packed it by mistake." She turned the plea up in her eyes. "Honestly, your papers were in quite a mess, Mr. Gordon, and I've been distracted about my future with the new D.A." She shrugged. "I'm really sorry about making such a ridiculous mistake. As far as my so-called cousin is concerned, we've been estranged for years. He doesn't exist as far as I'm concerned."

Please let that excuse satisfy him.

"Just a mistake," Gordon echoed, his tone as well as his expression skeptical.

She adopted a look of confusion. "What else would it be?" She glanced at Mr. Terrell once more. "I don't understand why you're making such a big deal of this."

That too-large gaze narrowed behind the magnifying lens. "If Mr. Terrell hadn't noticed that you didn't use the shredder, we might not have had the foresight to discover this *mistake*."

Damn. She hadn't thought of that. He'd said the last as if he didn't believe it for a second despite her Academy Award–winning performance.

She leaned forward. "I can assure you, Mr. Gordon," she urged, "this was just a careless mistake. After two years as your personal assistant, I would hope you know my work ethic better than that. This sort of thing has never happened before."

Mia held her breath again. Prayed her plea would divert his suspicion.

She had watched her every move. Every call. Every step. She'd spoken to no one and had carefully duplicated only information, written or oral, to use in building her case. Nothing was ever done at her condo. Instead, she drove to the library or to an Internet café to do her work. Everything she suspected, everything she had witnessed or heard, had been documented using an alias and on a Web site that could not in a million years be linked to her.

"We've been watching you for some time, Mia," Gordon went on. "Noticing your frequent early arrival or how you stayed late to finish up a task that was clearly completed. We noted how you observed my comings and goings. How you looked over my personal calendar each day. I can't prove what you were up to in a court of law, so to speak, but I do know when someone's building a case. And you—" he smiled triumphantly "—have been amassing evidence. No matter that you have the unmitigated gall to sit there and swear that it was all just a mistake."

Terrell approached her chair, placed one hand on the back behind her head, the other on the chair arm to her right, then leaned in close. "This will go much easier and far more quickly if you simply tell us what you were up to and with whom you were working."

She pushed back the clawing fear, stared first at the man glaring down at her and then across the desk at Gordon. "I don't know what the hell you're talking about, but I do know when I'm being harassed. I will not stand for this, sir."

Gordon nodded, held a hand up to his man. Terrell immediately backed off. "I had a feeling you'd plead innocence."

How the hell could he know? She'd been so damned careful! "This is unbelievable." She stood. "Mr. Gordon, I don't fully understand what you're accusing me of, but I am both insulted and appalled."

"That was the answer I anticipated," he confessed. "That leaves me one choice."

Mia resisted the near overpowering impulse to run for the door.

"You're fired, Mia," he announced. "Leave your security badge and go. Your work at Cook County District Attorney's office is finished as well. Your severance pay will cover the weeks remaining in January. If I have my way, you will not work in this city again."

"But I—"

"Save it," Gordon warned, his face twisted with fury. "I know you've been up to something. I just can't prove what that something is. But I will not tolerate disloyalty on any level."

She shook her head. "Mr. Gordon—"

"This way, Ms. Dawson." Terrell gestured to the door. "We don't want to have to do this by force. Mr. Gordon suggested calling the police earlier, but I assured him that you would go quietly."

More than a little afraid to turn her vulnerable side to either man, she went for broke, spun around and headed for the door.

She was back at square one. She knew plenty about Gordon's underhanded deeds, but she now had not one single piece of tangible evidence. Those case files would be shredded within minutes of her departure.

And her cousin's chances of getting his life back were vanishing right before her eyes.

Through the family room and kitchen, out the garage door, she didn't slow or speak to Terrell en route. She hated when men like him used their size and lethal training to intimidate. She hated even worse that somehow her behavior had given away her plans.

She reached into her purse to fish out her car keys.

"Your key is already in the ignition."

Mia stared at the man she had despised from the day she'd met him, then she understood. "You searched my car."

"Any vehicle that comes on the property is subject to search."

The key to her condo was on that ring as well. "And my home? Did you search that, too?" The idea that this bastard or some of his henchmen might have touched her things made her want to slap him.

Terrell smiled. "Good day, Ms. Dawson."

Furious at herself as much as at the two men who'd played her, she jerked the car door open and tossed her purse inside. She twisted the key in the ignition—only after the fact did she consider that something could have been tampered with. Her brakes. The car could have exploded.

Okay, calm down. She'd evidently watched too many movies.

No matter that she'd had all the solid evidence she'd obtained over the past year pulled like the proverbial rug beneath her feet. She still had the knowledge stored in her head and she still had Convoy.

Let the Colby Agency kidnap Gordon and turn him over to one of the many jerks he'd screwed.

Then she would have the last laugh.

She backed her hybrid up and pulled toward the gate.

Funny, she felt more relaxed and determined than she had in a very long time. That, she suddenly realized, was the mark of a truly good strategist.

Always have a backup plan.

This one, she had to admit, sort of fell into her lap, but a good plan was a good plan. Didn't matter where it came from.

Gordon would get his tonight.

NINE

IAN, Lucas and Jim viewed the video of Victoria a third time. Each time the knife in Jim's chest twisted viciously, amping up the agony. Jim wanted to kill whomever was responsible for this. But first he wanted them to pay with slow, thorough torture.

In more than six years he hadn't wanted to kill like this. But right now it was a throbbing compulsion in his veins.

He would not continue to stand by and allow his mother and her staff to be abused this way.

He simply couldn't.

They had gotten the message that Victoria had made the video under duress. That the plea was not one of her own volition was also crystal clear, but many other things were far too apparent.

The swelling in Victoria's cheek warned that she had suffered at the hands of these bastards. The stiffness of her posture spoke of the pain she felt, physically as well as mentally.

They couldn't sit back and allow this to continue.

Something had to be done.

Soon.

"We have to make a move." Jim looked from Ian to Lucas. "We can't wait for permission and allow this to continue."

The argument wasn't new. They'd gone back and forth about this all day. Ian and Lucas wanted to wait, to quietly meet the demand and then make a move. Jim couldn't wait any longer. The idea of what Victoria had suffered already was killing him bit by bit.

"No one wants to end this more than I do, Jim. But until we have Gordon or a better entry strategy," Lucas argued patiently, "there is nothing else we can do without taking unnecessary risks."

Jim turned his back on Lucas and on the monitor where the video had played out its agonizing scene. There was no getting through to Lucas. With all his years of experience in just this sort of situation, he should know better than anyone else that waiting would only increase the likelihood that someone would die. They needed to move now.

"Jim," Ian offered wearily, "your people are doing all within their power to narrow down a way inside the building without alerting the hostiles to our presence. Slade is working with Mia to gain access to Gordon when the time is right. Any other measures we opt to take at this point will carry grave risks to the very people we're attempting to protect."

Yeah, yeah. He'd heard all that before from both Ian and Lucas. He turned to face Ian. "I will not stand back and let this play out any longer. We've already established that as her son, I have the final say in the matter. Though I will continue to take your suggestions under advisement, we will proceed under my orders from this moment forward."

That same argument had been played out earlier that morning and again around noon. There was nothing further on the matter to discuss. Whatever it took to get that concept through the heads of all present, Jim was more than prepared to undertake.

"Jim!"

His attention swung to the man who'd shouted his name. Ben Steele pointed to the monitor at his workstation. "I've managed to access the security cameras inside the agency. They've been disabled so I can't retrieve any real-time images, but I can extract a number from earlier this morning before the cameras were shut down along with everything else inside."

Jim, followed by Lucas and Ian, moved to stand behind Steele. "Let's see what you've got." Jim clenched his jaw in preparation for the images.

"Victoria was right," Steele said, "there are approximately seven men inside. There could be more but I have verified visuals on seven."

Jim's mother had indicated in her message that half her staff was in heavy agreement, which, as best they could determine, translated to there being seven or more hostiles on site, all heavily armed. All present understood that whatever Victoria decided was fine by her staff, so the phrasing had to mean something else. It was an easy leap to the assessment they'd made.

The images Steele had extracted included one or two from each camera stationed inside the suite of offices. Jim flinched as the frozen scenes moved in front of his eyes one after the other. First Victoria, then Merri and Nicole…Simon—all were roughed up, then forced to the main conference room. As were numerous others as they were gathered from the exit stairwells and various hiding places in their offices. Faces were bruised and bloody.

But it was the fear in his mother's eyes that really got to Jim.

He turned to the men on either side of him—first Lucas, then Ian. "If we don't do something soon, someone will die. Mark my words." When Ian would have presented some other logic, Jim headed him off. "Those people, your coworkers—your wife—have been and will be plotting an escape scenario. You know this as well as I do. If we don't strike before they get the chance to launch an escape attempt, one or more will die for their efforts. Examples will be set."

Ian didn't argue this time. He understood that Jim was correct. Lucas kept any disagreements to himself as well. Their silence spoke volumes about the desperation level in the room. It had topped out.

Jim then drove home his point just to make sure neither man wavered in the hours to come. "What're you going to tell your children if Nicole is the one who initiates an escape plan? Ultimately sacrificing her life?"

The pallor that settled into place on Ian's face gave his answer. He didn't want to stand back and allow that to happen.

"Victoria is already resisting," Jim said to Lucas. "You know she will do all within her power to set an escape plan or a takeover into motion. She will not continue to sit back and let the hours pass or the injustices to her staff continue uninhibited. This—" he gestured to the monitor "—passive attitude you've witnessed won't last much longer. When Victoria has had enough, she'll strike back. We're running out of time, gentlemen. Are we going to sit back and let this play out or are we going to act?"

"Building security is questioning the continued lockdown," Ian said, defeat in his tone. "I don't know how much longer we can prevent the authorities from being involved."

"What the hell are the two of you thinking?" Lucas demanded, fury searing away the emotion Jim had seen in his eyes only moments ago.

Startled by his vehemence, Jim's control slipped. "Obviously I'm the only one who *is* thinking."

"What you're doing is hastening the deaths of one or more of the people inside," Lucas snapped. "Didn't either of you listen to what Victoria said? We are to do all within our power to meet the demand given. She isn't going to allow some rash maneuver to go down any more than she's going to commit one herself. She will ensure her people don't take any unnecessary risks."

"You can't possibly agree with doing nothing," Jim protested, allowing everyone in the room to respond to the challenge he'd just thrown on the table.

"We aren't doing *nothing*," Lucas argued fiercely. "We're doing all within our power to find a way in without detection and we're working on giving these bastards what they want, if only temporarily. That's our job. Our only job, for now."

"Perhaps you're the one who doesn't know Victoria as well as you think," Jim argued.

Lucas went toe to toe with him. "I was there for your mother all those years when you were gone. When your father was murdered. I—" he pounded a fist into his chest "—was the one who held her hand and promised she would survive the agony. Victoria will survive this and I will see that she does. We will proceed with caution when the time is right. Anything that happens prior to that will be over my dead body."

For a time Jim could not respond. Fury blocked his ability to speak. As it slowly drained away, he had to confess that Lucas had told the truth. If anyone in this room knew Victoria…he did.

More waiting.

Jim acquiesced to Lucas's decision because it was what his mother would want.

For the first time in his life, Jim hated himself for not calling Victoria "Mother" months ago.

He'd allowed that one sore spot to fester for too long. Victoria was his mother and she deserved that title. He deeply regretted that he had not allowed her to know that he loved her on that level.

The past was not her fault. What happened to him as a child was not a result of her lack of skill as a mother. He would not let these bastards prevent him from having the opportunity to tell her just how much he appreciated all she had done before his abduction, since they had been reunited, and everything in between.

No one was going to take that away from him.

His wife, Tasha, had learned just before Christmas that she was pregnant again. He wanted to share that birth as he had his first child's with his mother.

Ian took an audible breath. "There's something Nicole and I haven't shared with anyone just yet."

Jim turned his attention to the man Victoria—his mother—trusted so completely. Ian had been with her longer than anyone else on staff. Lucas trusted him implicitly as well. Jim had overstepped his bounds.

Another first for Jim Colby. He was wrong and he wasn't about to pretend otherwise.

"Over the weekend, Nicole learned that she's expecting our

third child." The hint of a smile that lingered on Ian's lips looked haunting against the agony chiseled into the planes and angles of his face. The misery had taken its toll. "It's a bit of a surprise, but we're both pleased. We had decided to wait a few weeks before we passed on the news to everyone else."

"Congratulations, Ian," Lucas offered, giving Ian a pat on the back. "Victoria will be thrilled to hear this news. When this is over, we'll celebrate."

The image where Nicole had been pushed to the floor was even more disturbing to Jim now. If that were Tasha...

He turned to his people, Ben Steele and Leland Rockford, two of his most skilled Equalizers, and said, "Find a way in. We have to move soon." He looked back to Ian and Lucas. "We will neutralize this situation before anyone else is hurt or worse," he assured the men who were as much a part of his family as his own mother. "Whatever it takes."

Ian nodded, his dark eyes uncharacteristically bright. "Whatever it takes."

Lucas looked from one man to the next and repeated that mantra. "Whatever it takes."

TEN

Outside the Gordon compound, 6:05 p.m.

SOMETHING was very wrong. Mia should have departed the property by now.

Slade reached for his binoculars yet again, but it was pointless. From his position on a side street, he couldn't see anything beyond that twelve-foot wall.

"Damn."

He couldn't call her cell phone. He couldn't do one damned thing except wait for a move from inside the compound.

The small transmitting device he'd asked her to place on the first-floor security panel would jam the control frequency when activated. Until the device was turned on it remained undetectable. When the moment came that entry to the house was needed, a split second of interruption in the frequency would be all that was required. By the time any remaining security personnel recognized that something had gone wrong, it would be too late to prevent the intrusion. Worked like a charm every time.

Slade was prepared to make the necessary extraction but there was a lot he needed to know about Gordon's movements and an extraction right now would render her assistance impotent to a great degree. Mia would brief him on all he needed to know as soon as she was out of the compound safely.

He glanced at his wristwatch once more—6:12 p.m.

His head moved from side to side with worry.

If she'd broken and given away the plan... Gordon would no doubt call the police. Then... hell, unless Jim, Ian and Lucas came up with a better plan...

Slade didn't want to think about that. Too many lives depended upon this going down exactly as planned.

The gate started its slow swing inward. Slade sat up straighter. Adrenaline lit in his veins. The idea that she was late evoked a whole series of hard questions. Had she been questioned or had she suddenly decided she couldn't be a part of this?

Maybe she'd simply had to work some overtime.

When she'd driven past his position, he waited another five seconds, then pulled out onto the street. He followed her to the rendezvous point—a convenience store well beyond the residential area Gordon called home.

He guided his truck into the slot next to Mia's hybrid. She stared forward, not bothering even a brief glance in his direction.

Bad sign.

Slade swung out of his truck and walked around to the passenger side of her compact sedan. The door was unlocked. He opened it and dropped into the passenger seat.

"What happened?" He couldn't resist stealing a look behind

them to see if the police showed up to haul him in for questioning. Conspiracy to commit kidnapping was a crime. Not one taken lightly. Particularly when the target was rich and famous.

"I was fired."

She didn't look at him as she made this startling statement.

He'd expected a lot of things to come out of her pretty mouth but that wasn't one of them. "Fired? On what grounds?"

Her face turned to his and that blue gaze, the color of the deepest sea, bored into his. "He…said I had failed to live up to the expectations of the position since he left office and that the new D.A. had his own personal assistant."

She looked away before the explanation was out of her mouth. Slade's gaze narrowed. Why would she lie to him about something as seemingly inconsequential under the circumstances as this? He was no trained expert at spotting untruths but an expert was hardly needed to see right through the garbage she'd just passed off as the gospel.

"What about the promotion you'd hoped for?" Something about this was all wrong. The coincidence that this "firing" occurred on the same day that she'd been approached by the Colby Agency for assistance wasn't lost on him.

"There won't be any promotion." She dropped her head back against the seat. "I'm out. End of story. It's over."

There was little he could do about that, though he regretted she'd lost her job. Too much of that going around these days. "Were you able to put the jamming device into place on the main access panel on the first floor?" As painful as this was for her, he had a job to do. Each step was crucial.

She nodded. "Exactly as you instructed."

Another thought occurred to him. "They took away your access to the property, didn't they?" Without her badge, getting through the gate wouldn't exactly be a piece of cake. That was a huge step backward even with the device in place. Climbing the wall would only work if they knew exactly where the motion sensors were placed.

Slade hoped the others could come up with a plan to infiltrate the Colby Agency building without the necessity of dragging Gordon into this. The man behind the siege was clearly out for vengeance. The Colby Agency wasn't in the habit of succumbing to terrorists and those thugs could only be called exactly that.

Mia started the car and turned to face Slade. "There's something I need to show you."

He tapped the button on the key to his truck to secure the doors. "All right." His instincts started humming once more. Mia Dawson was about to give him something relevant to the task before him. A part of him hoped like hell this would prove some sort of turning point, leverage that would work to the advantage of the agency's reputation. Bending the law was one thing, but breaking it was entirely another.

She pulled out of the parking lot and drove to the nearest discount home improvement store. When she'd maneuvered into one of the parking slots, she grabbed her purse and got out of the car.

Slade followed her across the big lot. He didn't ask questions. She didn't offer any explanations. Inside, she snagged a shopping cart and headed down the main aisle as if she had a specific destination in mind.

As the main aisle intersected the extra wide middle aisle, she paused to meet his gaze. "I want you to go into the men's room and wait for me there."

"The men's room?" Had he heard her right?

She selected a light fixture from an end cap. "Yes. I'll be there in three minutes."

"Whatever you say." Slade strolled across the massive warehouse, pausing occasionally to survey the sale items on an end cap just to fit in. When he reached the restrooms, he entered the men's room and scoped out the place. Five stalls, all empty. Now this scenario…was just this side of weird. He leaned against the corner of the first stall and waited for her arrival.

At the end of three minutes, just as she'd scheduled, the door opened and she waltzed inside.

Her expectant look had him assuring her, "All clear. What's this about?"

She chewed on her bottom lip a moment. "I haven't been completely honest with you."

He'd picked up on that. "In what way?"

Reaching up, she ran her fingers through that long, silky black hair. "There's no way I would have even heard you out this morning. What you were suggesting would have seemed ludicrous…except…"

The silence lagged. "Except?" he prompted when she failed to continue. He needed to know what the hell was going on here.

"For the last year I've been watching Gordon a little closer than I used to. I recognized some inconsistencies in a few of his cases and I felt compelled to look into the situation for—" she shrugged "—you know, little discrepancies. The kind that can tilt a case the other way."

He didn't want to spook her by suggesting that they have a conference call with Ian and the others. Taking her to the command center was too risky, particularly since she'd been fired. Gordon could have someone on his security team watching her. The situation at the Colby Agency was precarious enough without adding any additional layers of trouble.

Another snag Slade would have to deal with in the coming hours.

"Did you find anything to back up your suspicions?" Seemed a safe enough question to ask at this point in the conversation.

She licked the lush lip she'd been abusing with her teeth. "Yes. I…I found evidence that Gordon had sold out in three cases in the past fifteen months. There were a couple of others, but some proved more difficult to connect the dots, so I focused on the ones I could decipher more readily."

"Is this why you were fired today?"

Her head moved up and down, affirming his suggestion. "That's also why I was willing to go along with your plan. Gordon has been selling out victims when the price or the outcome was to his advantage. He isn't the pillar of the community everyone believes him to be. I had hoped that I'd be able to pull together enough evidence to blow his cover or at least to topple his self-righteous empire. But his chief of security, Terrell, noticed my indiscretion on the number of boxed files to be moved to permanent storage."

Slade had taken those boxes to the storage facility himself. "The boxes I picked up and delivered to the county facility?"

She nodded. "Terrell apparently went through them before they were shipped out. Both he and Gordon suspected what I'd done."

"Made copies of certain documents?" Seemed like the most logical step. Documentation of wrongdoing would be the easiest evidence to prosecute. After some serious time in a D.A.'s office, she would certainly know this was a good way to at least cover her own back.

"Yes. Handwritten notes on certain aspects of cases. Altered official documents. Notes," she went on, "that were never introduced into the prosecution's game plan. Twice defendants were never bound over to grand jury because of a lack of tangible evidence. Both times the outcome should have been vastly different. In one case, the lack of those very notes ensured that the case was lost by a jury vote. I know because I was a part of that investigation."

"What made you think the evidence you compiled would be admissible in court? You took it without a search warrant." That was something else she had to know without any coaching from him. A technicality could ruin the best case.

She made a little sound. Under other circumstances it might have been a laugh. "I knew what I was doing." She tapped her right temple. "I have lots to tell stored right here. I just wanted a little hard evidence, you know. I figured if I shipped it to the storage facility and then went to the D.A. with what I know, this would lead to where I'd sent the files—"

"He could issue a search warrant for Gordon's files." Slade got the whole picture now. "Could've worked. Definitely."

"No kidding." She dropped her head back and blew out a disgusted breath. "Now…" She lifted her head and stared into Slade's eyes for a bit before continuing. "Now I don't know."

The door opened. Slade's attention swung to the man who'd entered.

"Sorry," Mia said quickly. She backed toward the door, moving wide around the newcomer. "I'm—" she gestured vaguely to the wall that separated the two bathrooms "—supposed to be next door."

Slade started after her. At the other man's confused look, he mumbled, "We're arguing…she wasn't paying attention."

Mia was already shoving the cart down that center aisle once more. Desperation and defeat were fueling her confusion. Slade hustled to catch up with her.

"What do we do now?" she asked without looking at him.

He fell into step with her purposeful stride. "That's the big question. According to the last call I received from Ian, there's still no workable plan for getting into the building. Which leaves us with—"

"Me." Her gaze met his. "Just so you know, Mr. Convoy," she said as she pushed the shopping cart back into the long line of carts near the front entrance, "I'm ready to do whatever it takes to see Gordon go down. Legal or not."

"We'll pick up my truck and go to my place so we can talk." They walked side by side out one of the exits and to her car. "I'll put through a call to Ian and get an update on the situation there."

She moved around to the driver's side while he waited at the front passenger door. After reaching for her door, she hesitated, stared at him across the roof of the vehicle. "I don't know you very well, Mr. Convoy. Why can't we go to my place?"

He took the remark with an acknowledging nod. "Is it safe to talk openly at your place?"

She blinked, considered his question a moment. "Maybe not. We'll go to your place."

Slade hesitated then, his hand on the door handle. She was disgusted, angry, hungry for revenge. If he let her do this…she could go down with the rest of them.

He pushed away the second thoughts. Their options were limited.

She was their one ace in the hole.

Slade Convoy's home, Joliet, 7:49 p.m.

MIA STEPPED INTO the little bungalow Slade called home. He even had a yard with a little fence, though it was too dark to get the full effect. She wondered if that meant he had a dog.

She hadn't had a dog since she was a kid back home on the farm in Iowa. A long, long time ago.

"It's not much," he offered humbly. "A work in progress mainly."

She gingerly stepped around what looked like a huge carpet shampooer. The floors were hardwood, as far as she could see. Maybe he had rugs.

"Floor sander," he explained as he pushed the shampooer look-alike out of the way. "I'm going to refinish these floors one of these days. I actually had plans to start today."

She turned all the way around in the small living room. Pale yellow walls, probably the previous owner's selection. Convoy didn't look like a yellow kind of guy. But she liked it. Felt warm. God knew it was as cold as hell outside tonight.

"If you're hungry, I could order something to be delivered."

Code for: I don't keep food in the house.

"I'm okay for now." She dragged off her coat and tossed it onto the cluttered leather sofa. The furniture looked fairly new and of incredibly good quality. "Can I see the rest?"

"Make yourself at home." He peeled off his coat and dropped it next to hers.

Two bedrooms, one bath and a neat but compact kitchen. She parted the blinds and peered out the back door. A dim light barely cut through the damp gloom. There was no moonlight and no stars in the sky. The perfect creepy atmosphere for her present predicament.

She wandered back into the living room, where Convoy was deep into a call on his cell. After trying but failing in her efforts not to listen, she realized he was ordering pizza. The old reliable. A guy couldn't go wrong with ordering pepperoni and cheese.

"Fifteen minutes," he told her when he ended the call. "I think I have beer and...water."

"Either'll be fine." She shoved aside a newspaper and collapsed on the sofa. God, she was exhausted.

He hurried to declutter the sofa and matching chair.

"Nice furniture." If he'd picked out the furnishings, he had excellent taste.

"My sister showed up one afternoon and had this stuff delivered." He laughed. "All I had to do was pay for it."

"Then your sister has good taste."

He lowered into the chair across the coffee table from her. "I spoke to Ian en route."

He'd mentioned that he intended to make that call. "What's the plan?" Gordon wasn't getting away with what he'd done to her cousin or to her. Fear of legal retribution wasn't going to stop her. Not now. He'd royally screwed over too many people. She could blame her actions on temporary insanity.

"I'm assuming Gordon has cameras inside the house just as he does outside."

She nodded. The man was a security freak. Not that she blamed him, considering what she'd discovered he had been up to.

"Ian suggested that you play the part of uncooperative informant. That way—" Convoy leaned fully back in the chair "—you won't get charged when this is done. If Gordon and the police believe you were coerced into leading me inside, it'll be far better for you."

She couldn't argue with that, but she wasn't so sure she wanted to be eliminated. Plea bargains were given all the time. She could trade her inside knowledge on Gordon for a lighter sentence. Besides, she was proud of the fact that she was doing the right thing.

"Maybe I don't want to appear unwilling." She might as well put that card on the table. It would give her great pleasure for Gordon to know she'd gotten him in the end.

The private investigator rested his forearms on his wide-spread knees and clasped his hands between them. "I'm not sure you're looking at this with a rational view. You're angry right now, that's no place to make a decision from."

"I know what I'm saying and doing, Mr. Convoy." She wasn't a kid. She was a grown, educated woman. If helping him round up Gordon and turn him over to one of his enemies would save more than a dozen lives, she was all for it. He'd had it coming for a very long time.

"And if he ends up dead? Or someone else does, our people or one or more of the thugs inside? Are you prepared to stand charged for those actions?"

Murder One would be hard to beat. There was no denying the premeditation. A plan was not only useful, it was absolutely necessary.

"But you said you had a strategy to help ensure his safety." She recalled that Ian Michaels or Lucas Camp, maybe both, said Gordon wouldn't be sent in without a backup team in place.

"Definitely, but when weapons are involved there is no sure plan. You need to bear in mind what's best for your future."

She pushed to her feet. "I need to use your powder room."

"If you need anything, let me know," he called behind her.

Inside the cramped bathroom, she closed and locked the door.

She turned to the mirror over the sink. She stared long and hard at her reflection. Dark circles traced the area beneath her eyes.

"What're you doing?"

She looked tired and way older than her twenty-nine years. Convoy had explained that two of the women being held hostage were pregnant. Several were mothers. Most of the men were fathers.

Mia couldn't let those people die.

Considering what Gordon had done, he deserved what was coming to him. She's spent half a decade estranged from her cousin—the whole family had. The man had gone from one scam to another for most of his adult life. Then he'd grown a backbone and a conscience and decided to do the right thing by testifying against his superior at the savings and loan. Terry had sat in that courtroom and exposed the lending institution's underhanded deeds—including taking government bail-outs when it was undeserved. Gordon had seen to it that his professional reputation was ruined, ultimately ensuring that his career in pretty much anything was over. And Terry's superior had been acquitted.

Mia couldn't let Gordon get away with this. Lawyers and cops bent the law every day. This was no different.

Except someone could die.

Shaking off the disturbing thought, she attended to her needs. As she was washing her hands, she couldn't help but notice the masculine scent of his soap. Smelled nice. Sexy.

Like him.

Mia promptly dismissed the crazy thoughts. She'd let down her cousin and lost her job today. Gotten caught trying to take down a criminal, who just happened to be her boss. Latching on to the basics, like sexual attraction, was a normal reaction.

But that was one situation she intended to stay far away from.

She'd never been too good at the whole relationship thing. Her work always got in the way.

Moments later, the smell of pizza filtered through the house. Her stomach rumbled.

About time her appetite showed up once more.

Convoy had spread the open box and a couple of beers on the coffee table.

"Smells great." She didn't wait for an invitation. She grabbed a slice and sank her teeth into the thick pie, then moaned her satisfaction.

He did the same, only without the sound effects. By the time they'd reached for their second slices, they'd relaxed.

"Shortly after midnight," she announced before tearing off another juicy bite with her teeth.

"For moving in on Gordon?"

"He's always in bed by midnight and his sole security guard is pretty much covered up with keeping the house and property secure."

"I'll confirm this with Ian and then we'll get some sleep. It's going to be a long night."

She would bet the next slice of pizza that he was the kind of guy who never slept when there was a job to be done.

"I'll keep you safe," he promised. "You have my word on that. Whatever happens."

Funny, she wasn't worried about that in the slightest.

Convoy made his call to his superior then polished off another slice of pizza.

Mia thought about calling her parents. She was the only child. If anything happened to her they would be devastated. But if she called, one or both would instantly recognize that something was wrong.

It was best not to leak the information to anyone. The fewer who knew, the better.

If she died…she wondered what Gordon, assuming he didn't end up dead as well, would release to the media about her.

She'd known soon enough how this would play out.

Assuming any of them survived.

11:35 p.m.

SLADE MOVED SILENTLY to the door of his bedroom. He hated to disturb Mia but it was almost time. He'd urged her to get an hour or so of shut-eye before midnight. She hadn't wanted to, but he'd eventually talked her into taking his bed and at least trying to sleep.

When he'd confirmed that she'd drifted off into dreamland, he'd made a call to Ian. Slade's instincts were nagging at him. Mia Dawson's professional résumé didn't match her story. She was a strict professional. Loyal and dedicated to a fault. The idea that Gordon was a lowlife wasn't nearly enough motive to send her over the legal line she was about to catapult across. Every instinct he possessed screamed that this was *personal*.

Very personal.

But how? She'd sworn she and Gordon weren't intimately involved. Not a single hint that she'd lied existed. That kind of thing was almost impossible to keep under wraps when a high-profile political figure was involved. That meant it had to be something else…something related to a family member or a friend. Something big and ugly.

Ian had found it. One Terry Campbell, first cousin to Mia Dawson. Campbell had decided to rat out his superior at the independently owned and operated Windy City Savings &

Loan. Only it had backfired. The defense had come up with enough dirt to completely discredit him as a reliable witness. Since Campbell's word was all the D.A.'s office had when key pieces of evidence were thrown out on technicalities, the case had gone south. Campbell had lost his job. His gold-digger wife had walked out since he no longer had anything to offer. The man was already estranged from his family, including Mia. He'd attempted suicide twice in the past four months.

Now there was a strong motivation.

Slade crossed the room in sock feet, his movements silent. He leaned down and touched her shoulder. "Mia?"

She bolted upright, her arms coming up in front of her in a defensive manner. The strangled scream sent regret searing through his bones. She had no real comprehension of just how badly this could end.

"Hey, it's me," he urged as he sat down on the edge of the bed. "Time to get ready to go." The light that filtered in from the hall allowed him to see how her eyes had rounded. She was scared to death.

She sucked in a breath, held it, probably to slow her too-rapid respiration. "Sorry." She scrubbed her hands over her face and pushed all that long, dark hair back. "I was having a bad dream."

"About your cousin?" No need to beat around the bush. This mission was far too important to play games.

"I…" She blinked. "I don't know what you mean."

So she was gong to play it that way, was she? "I know what happened to Terry Campbell. I understand why you want to have your revenge, but this isn't about your cousin or revenge. This is about keeping people alive. People I care about." He leaned over and switched on the bedside lamp. She squinted. "If staying focused is going to be a problem—"

"No." She shook her head adamantly. "I can do this. It's the right thing to do."

He searched those gorgeous blue eyes. "You sure about that? Blood is thicker than water. I don't want you going commando on me and trying to mete out justice yourself."

"That's what my cousin said," she offered, her expression determined.

"That you shouldn't settle a score with Gordon?" Slade was confused now. Ian's research had indicated the cousin was estranged from the rest of the family.

"That it was the right thing to do." She drew in another of those deep breaths, the movement luring his gaze to her chest. "He contacted me only days before he turned himself over to the feds. The whole case was supposed to be played out in federal court. But Gordon somehow managed to get the case shifted to his jurisdiction. If Terry's boss had been proven guilty, the feds would have taken the next step. But Gordon made sure that didn't happen. I had my suspicions but I didn't have anything concrete so I kept my mouth shut." She pulled her knees to her chest and hugged them. "Terry lost everything. And I let it happen. No one in the family will believe anything he says. He's lied so much." She searched Slade's eyes then. "If I don't fix this, he'll just keep trying to end everything and…"

She fell silent. A fat tear rolled down her cheek. Slade couldn't help himself, he had to reach up and swipe it away with the pad of his thumb. Her skin felt so soft. Her lips quivered and he wanted desperately to make that fear go away.

"The Colby Agency will help you set the record straight." He traced the line of her jaw, cupped that softness in his hand. It felt good to touch her. "I'll help you." He stretched his lips into a reassuring smile. "You have my word."

"I wanted to fix this...to be the one who made it right since I allowed it to happen. But today I realized I couldn't do it alone." She leaned her cheek into his palm. "It's all so surreal. I don't know what to trust anymore."

"You can trust me." He leaned forward, placed a chaste kiss on her other cheek. "We should—"

She reached her arms around his neck, pulled his mouth to hers. He knew he should resist. They didn't have time...he didn't have the right...but he couldn't draw away. She tasted of fear and desperation and sweet, soft woman. Her fingers threaded into his hair and a sound of approval swelled in his throat.

At last she dragged her lips from his, rested her forehead against his chin. "Sorry," she muttered. "I just needed to know how you kissed." She looked up at him then. "I've never met a man like you. You're..." A shrug of uncertainty lifted her shoulders. "You're different from the guys I usually run in to."

He fingered a length of her silky hair. "Later," he promised, "when this is over, we'll see where *this* goes."

Right now, they had to go kidnap a former district attorney.

ELEVEN

Gordon compound,
Tuesday, January 21, 12:15 a.m.

SHE could smell his scent on her skin.

Mia felt completely idiotic noticing, but after half an hour sitting in his truck—in the dark—alone with him, there was little else to notice. The kiss…she had to have been out of her mind. But she'd needed to feel something real.

Focus, Mia! This is not the time for selfish needs.

He said they were in wait mode. Ian had to call and confirm the orders to move in.

Admittedly, she would be happy when this part was over.

Never in her life had she done anything illegal. Well, maybe she'd stolen a pen or two from work. Come to think of it, the stapler in her home office had come from work. But not any criminal activity for real.

She turned to Slade Convoy. And to commit the act with

a total stranger was a little off the charts for anyone, especially her. Her parents wouldn't understand. Neither would her few work friends. Personal friends were too few to mention. Who had time? She worked long hours…and, secretly, she'd opted to go back to law school last term. One class at a time would be slow. But she would get it done.

Sounded like a good hobby in prison. Lots of prisoners got their educations while behind bars. She could certainly do the same. The idea sent a shudder through her. Or maybe it was the man next to her. She'd never been kissed like that. *Focus!*

They had parked at the corner of the neighboring property just across the street. Though they hadn't waited in this spot for long, she was surprised the police hadn't cruised by and checked them out. The street remained totally empty. The quiet somehow surrounded them like a protective blanket.

Convoy—Slade, he'd insisted she call him Slade, or maybe she'd said it first—reached into his jacket pocket and pulled out his cell phone. The call he'd been expecting, she supposed. Now maybe they would do something besides sit in the dark and wait.

Adrenaline rushed through her body, sending goose bumps spilling across her skin. She gazed out over Gordon's property. If it was time, she was ready. Ready to see his face when he was in the same vulnerable position his victims had experienced. To see him lose everything the way Terry had.

Jerk.

"Understood," Slade said before closing his phone. He turned to her. "We've been cleared to proceed with entering the house and obtaining Gordon's cooperation."

Who was he kidding? Gordon wasn't going to cooperate with anything that didn't benefit him somehow.

At that instant the anticipation bottomed out and fear howled through her veins.

She was really going to do this.

Slade opened his door and got out. She told herself to move, but nothing happened. *Just get out.* Her hand jerked, that same fear coursing along her limbs as she reached for the door handle.

Then she was out of the truck, both feet on the ground. The night air was cold. She shivered. It was January after all. The silence felt deafening. The ambient lighting pooling along the property wall looked too bright.

How could she and Slade possibly hope to get inside? She no longer had her security badge. The codes had surely been changed.

"This way," Slade murmured as he shrugged a backpack into place.

She followed him in the shadows of the tree-lined street until they reached the corner where two properties met. Then they crossed the street. Her heart thumped harder and harder. If anyone looked out their window, drove by or was for some reason out for a late-night stroll, there would be no place for them to hide.

The neighbor's shrubbery lined the exterior of Gordon's stark wall on the west side. Slade moved between the shrubbery and the wall.

When she was close enough, he said, "You said the motion detectors monitoring the other side of the wall were located approximately twenty feet apart."

She nodded. "I remember distinctly Gordon bringing the blueprints for the fancy system into the office. He was extraordinarily pleased with himself about the property and the new security system he'd contracted to be installed. That's what happens when you get a seven-figure book deal."

Slade motioned to the wall. "If I clear the other side without triggering the alarm, you follow the same route."

She nodded her understanding. *She had to be out of her mind.* The phrase kept echoing in her head. This was the first of many laws she would be breaking. She might as well get used to it.

He pulled a square object from his backpack. She couldn't tell exactly what it was. About the size of a small cosmetic case. He aimed the sort of square package and something shot from it. Hit the wall. He checked to see that the line extending to the top of the wall was steady and secure. He reached out and took her hand. She trembled. He placed her hand against the line. "Feel that?"

"Yes," she whispered.

"If you grab hold and squeeze it'll take you up with no sweat."

Her head made that acknowledging up-and-down motion. This wasn't possible. Couldn't be real. She had to be dreaming. Okay, Mia, pull it together.

Then something incredible happened. He held on to the line and it lifted him to the top of the wall. He reached up with one hand, threw one leg up onto the ledge and pulled himself up. When he was safely astride the ledge, the line from the boxlike mechanism slid effortlessly back down to where she waited.

He'd told her to follow the same route if no alarms sounded. Truly crazy. She licked her lips. Grabbed on to the line with both hands. Squeezed. Her breath evacuated her lungs as her body was propelled upward. Just as abruptly the line jerked to a stop.

Slade didn't speak but he reached down to give her a hand up onto the ledge. Her head swam as she settled her bottom onto the broad limestone ledge. The grounds of the property looked eerie in the darkness…or maybe from this position. Had she ever been afraid of heights? Maybe, but she'd never been in a position to find out.

He tinkered with the line and box, settling it so that it would drop down the other side—the inside of the wall. He gestured for her to pay attention. She moistened her lips and watched his every move. When he grabbed securely on to the line, it dropped to the ground, taking him with it. He landed firmly on his feet but not enough so to throw off his balance. Immediately, he flattened against the wall and waited.

For her. Mia took a breath and followed the steps she'd watched him take. She swallowed back a scream as the line reeled her downward. Somehow going down felt faster than going up. Her feet hit the ground, forcing her knees to bend a little.

He pressed his face to her hair. "You said the guard on duty makes a round of the exterior perimeter at half past the hour, correct?"

She nodded, resisting the urge to tremble at the feel of his mouth against her ear.

"As soon as we see him move beyond our position, we're heading for the house."

She understood, let him see her comprehension.

They left the line in place and carefully moved across the yard, using the islands of shrubbery and architecture as cover. Thank God for her vigilant observation of her surroundings. She'd been helping Gordon at the house for several months. Each day when she'd taken her afternoon walk on the grounds, she'd made a mental note of where everything was, including the security sensors.

Not once during that time had she ever considered that she would need to know those things in order to break in to Gordon's house.

Second thoughts twisted in her stomach.

The security guard suddenly appeared around the front corner of the house, flashlight bobbing with each step. Mia held her breath and watched him pass. When he'd done so, Slade went down on one knee next to a group of shrubs only a few feet from the patio. He dropped his backpack to the ground and rummaged through it for the next gadget he would need, she assumed.

One thing was certain, she'd never met anyone like him. Her life was full of lawyer types and court clerks. Not a single one of them would know where to even begin to accomplish a goal like this one.

They didn't teach stuff like this in law school.

He got back to his feet and made a noiseless path to the French doors beyond the patio that led into the family room. She'd already assured him there were no motion sensors around the exterior doors. The remaining motion sensors were inside. Each window and door was outfitted with a magnetic strip to set off the alarm if one was opened while the system was in active mode.

Holding his hands out palms up, she mimicked the move. He placed a small cloth bag in one hand, then rolled it open like a travel cosmetic carrier. Holding a miniature flashlight with his teeth, he knelt down in front of the door and picked the lock with instruments that looked very much like what a dentist would use.

Mia's job was to watch for the return of the guard. She craned her neck to survey both ends of the house. *Just let them get inside without being spotted.*

When he'd returned the instruments to the bag, rerolled it and placed it back in his backpack, he withdrew something resembling a remote control. One click in the direction of the living room and he waited, watching the series of lights on the handheld device.

When all went to green, he grabbed the handle and opened the French door. She followed him inside. Her body was thankful for the warmth but her mind was reeling with denial and fear.

More of that thick silence waited inside.

After closing the door, he said, "We don't have much time. Go over the locations of the interior motion sensors with me."

"At the bottom of the stairs near the front of the house, as well as the second staircase in the kitchen. I can't remember seeing any others."

"Let's go, then. We need to get up the stairs before the system's connection resumes or the guard comes back inside."

She rushed up the stairs behind him, the thick tread runner cushioning the noise their shoes might have made otherwise. If she was ever rich she wouldn't have a runner on her stairs. When an intruder struck, she wanted to hear him coming.

They had cleared the staircase. Relief made her legs quiver. From here, she led the way.

The distinct chime told them the guard had come back inside and deactivated the motion sensors. He would check the interior of the house next, move from room to room and ensure all was as it should be.

Slade had a plan for that, too.

They moved to the guest room nearest Gordon's suite and took up their positions.

The guard typically needed ten minutes to make his rounds downstairs, then moved to the upstairs.

Stretched out like a cat on the guest bed, Mia tried to listen for his approach over the blood roaring in her ears.

The beam of his flashlight moved over the room before she heard him at the door.

She closed her eyes, giving the appearance of sleep. The glow of the flashlight lit on her face. A softly muttered curse echoed in the room. The guard started toward the bed.

Slade stepped out from behind the door and grabbed him from behind, closing one hand over his mouth as he disabled him. Mia hugged herself as she pushed up into a sitting position. She was extremely pleased that Slade didn't really hurt the guy. But his movements had looked…well… brutal.

Nothing at all like his kiss.

"The duct tape," Slade muttered.

She scooted off the bed and dug the duct tape from the pack still hanging on his back.

When he'd carefully secured the man, including his mouth, Slade removed his cell phone, security badge and keys. Grabbing his flashlight from the floor, the two of them relocated the still unconscious guard to the walk-in closet. This was one she hadn't met. Nothing about him looked familiar.

Time to go for Gordon.

Mia stayed close behind Slade's tall frame as they moved down the dimly lit corridor to the double doors that led into Gordon's suite.

She had started to relax. So far, it wasn't so bad. A little scary when one considered the risk. Breaking and entering. Assault with duct tape and some kind of kung-fu-style training. But Gordon was living on borrowed time, whether he realized it or not.

Slade reached for the doors. Mia held her breath. No light shone from beneath the doors. He was most likely asleep by now.

Still, if he was watching the television with the sound muted, or reading the newspaper using nothing but a subtle side-table light.

She wrung her hands together.

Just stop.

They were very close to attaining their goal.

Soon this part of the operation would be over.

Slade opened the doors wide and stumbled back two steps.

Mia blinked, told herself she had to be seeing things.

"Who're you?"

A scantily clad woman stood directly in front of them, just inside the doors leading to Gordon's suite.

"I'm calling security!" she shouted.

TWELVE

Maggie's, Command Center, 1:03 a.m.

IAN Michaels hesitated in his pacing. Convoy should have contacted him by this time.

"Nothing yet?"

Ian met Lucas's worried gaze and shook his head.

"Something's wrong." Jim stepped away from the workstations where his men were getting closer to an entry strategy with every passing moment.

Unfortunately, Ian agreed with Jim's assessment. Convoy should have called in by now. If he had failed to attain his goal of infiltrating the Gordon compound, they needed to know sooner than later.

Even more disturbing, if the police had been involved, the whole operation would be blown.

"We have no choice but to wait for some indication from Convoy or that location." Ian didn't have to clarify what the latter meant. If the police were summoned, they would know very soon.

"I don't understand why that bastard doesn't answer the phone." Jim stalked back over to the front window and peered through the darkness at the building across the street.

The man in charge of the takeover inside the Colby Agency had refused additional contact. He'd given his demand and he had no intention of discussing matters until he had what he wanted.

Gordon.

Until Gordon was in their possession, they had no leverage.

This was the first time in all his years at the Colby Agency that Ian had given the order to break the law. No matter what Lucas or Jim said, this was his responsibility. He would be the one to face charges if worse came to worst. That was as it should be.

As long as Nicole and the others were safe, he did not care what happened to him. Ensuring the safe return of his wife and the others was all that mattered.

Lucas kept checking his cell phone. Ian was certain he hoped Victoria would have an opportunity to get a call through. Or that his former superior would call with the news that one or more members of his old unit, the Specialists, were back in the country and could help with this nightmare.

Ian closed his eyes. He was very tired. He'd called hours ago and spoken to his kids. A neighbor was taking care of the children for him.

Jim had touched based with his wife, Tasha, several times. She wanted to be here, to help. But their daughter, Jamie, needed her at home.

"They're at it again."

At Jim's remark, Ian moved to the window. He watched the

lobby a moment before seeing the flashlight beams scan the area. The group was vigilant about security. He had to give them that. But that reality only made the concept of getting inside without drawing their attention even more impossible.

Ben Steele and the other man from Jim's shop had deconstructed the building via electronic technology. Each new entry point revealed led to a dead end. The building's designers had worked diligently to ensure there was no way to infiltrate the structure.

One of the architects was deceased. The other had been diagnosed with advanced Alzheimer's last year. That left the trial-and-error method Steele and his associate had been conducting for hours nonstop.

Ian's cell vibrated. His heart all but stopped. He looked at the screen, didn't recognize the number.

Jim and Lucas moved in closer. No one wanted this to be the authorities.

"Michaels." Ian told himself to breathe.

"Daddy, I can't sleep."

Relief flooded Ian. "Natalie, what are you doing up at this hour?"

Jim and Lucas backed off, their expressions bearing out the combination of relief and anxiety they both felt.

"Miss Mary said I could call you since I couldn't sleep."

"Nat," Ian coaxed cautiously, "whose phone are you using?" He didn't recognize the number.

"Miss Mary needs a new phone," his daughter explained. "She's using her mother's cell phone."

Thank God. Thank God.

"Where's your brother," Ian had the presence of mind to ask. "Is he sleeping?"

"Yep. He always sleeps."

"I'm sure if you go back to bed, close your eyes and try really hard," Ian suggested, "you'll be able to get to sleep."

"Daddy?"

"Yes, darling?" Ian's chest squeezed.

"When is Mommy coming home?"

Ian collapsed in the nearest chair. He didn't have the heart to respond to his daughter's question.

He didn't know the answer.

THIRTEEN

Gordon compound, 1:59 a.m.

MIA pressed a length of duct tape on the woman's mouth, but that didn't stop her from squeaking and groaning. Mia shook her head. "I'll go see where Gordon is hiding."

"Be careful," Slade called after her before turning his full attention to their unexpected guest.

Who the hell was this woman? Mia hadn't mentioned that Gordon entertained women friends.

Slade lifted the woman into his arms. Her ankles and wrists were bound and still she struggled against him like a frantic fish. He carried her into the guest room and stashed her in the walk-in closet with the still unconscious guard. Since she'd been dressed for bed, her cell phone hadn't been on her person. Leaving any sort of communication device in the closet with them would be plain dumb.

On second thought along those lines, he secured the

woman's wrists to her ankles to prevent her from trying any escape maneuvers. The fear in her eyes tugged at his insides. Like the guard, she was an innocent victim in this disaster. Slade hated like hell to do this to her but he couldn't take any chances. Telling her to go home and forget all she'd seen wouldn't cut it.

"Don't worry," he assured her, "you'll be fine."

Unable to bear the overflowing tears at this point, he backed away, exited the closet and closed the door. After a quick survey of the room, he scooted a chest of drawers in front of the door. He didn't want either of them coming up with any harebrained ideas about escaping and causing trouble anytime soon.

Now for Gordon.

Slade took a deep breath and headed back into the corridor. As soon as his brain had assimilated what his eyes saw, he stopped dead in his tracks.

Mia waited in the middle of the broad upstairs hall, her hands held high above her head.

Gordon, clad only in silk pajama pants, stood in the open doorway to his room. The revolver in his hand was aimed at Mia. A combination of fear and adrenaline exploded in Slade's muscles. Something else Mia apparently hadn't known about.

The gun.

Two realizations penetrated the shock strangling his mind at the same time.

Gordon wasn't wearing his glasses.

And he didn't look at ease with the weapon in his hand.

Both of those factors could work in Slade's favor.

"Put your hands up," he shouted at Slade.

Slade took his time raising his hands. "Take it easy, Gordon. You don't want to shoot anyone."

"Ha!" he barked. "You're both intruders." He waved the barrel at Mia. "Especially you." The accusation came out a snarl. "I'm calling the police."

Slade braced for a move. The man didn't have a house phone or a cell phone in his hand. He'd have to get to a phone to use one.

"You're a criminal," Mia shouted right back at him. "I'm going to prove it. I want to see you pay for what you've done rather than living in the lap of luxury."

Slade took advantage of the distraction to move a few steps closer to Gordon's position. If Mia could keep him focused on his former cases, maybe…

"What're you doing?" The weapon's business end swung in Slade's direction. "Stop right there."

"You're not going to get away with what you've done," Mia warned, determined not to let her fury go. "Whatever I have to do, I'm going to prove it."

Gordon glared at her with utter derision. "No one's going to believe a word you say. I fired you for incompetence. Anything you say now will be considered sour grapes or plain old revenge. You're a fool if you believe you can trump up some sort of ridiculous charges and have a snowball's chance in hell of making them stick. You're a fool, period."

"No." The word was out of Slade's mouth before his brain had had time to clamp his jaw shut.

Gordon glared at him once more. "What the hell do you know? You're just brawn for hire."

"Actually," Slade told him as he took yet another step in the man's direction, "I'm from the Colby Agency and everything she says is true. You have committed atrocities against your office and the citizens you represent. For those you will pay."

"Stop right there!" The gun in Gordon's hand shook. "I will shoot."

Maybe he would. Slade had come unarmed due to the nature of the job. If the police arrived, no member of the Colby Agency was going to be found armed on the premises after breaking and entering. Too risky.

Besides, he'd had no reason to suspect Gordon kept a gun in the house.

Disabling the security guard had been simple. Slade hadn't expected Gordon to brandish a weapon. Mia had never known him to be anything but anti-gun. He sure as hell didn't have a registered license for a weapon. The agency had checked. Slade had to neutralize this situation quickly.

No one was supposed to die.

"No one will get hurt, Mr. Gordon," Slade argued, "if you just put down the weapon."

Gordon shook his head. "Nothing doing. That bitch isn't ruining all I've worked for."

"You did the ruining yourself," Mia countered. "Someone has to stop you."

Mia needed to back off just a little. She was pushing Gordon too hard. Slade's cell vibrated a second time. Ian was concerned… Slade was supposed to have checked in by now.

"First," Slade said to the man, drawing his attention back to him, "she's not a bitch. She's a very smart lady who saw through a lowlife like you."

Gordon's mouth twisted with outrage. "If she's so smart, what's she doing sneaking in here like this?" He aimed another harsh glare at Mia. "Any lawyer or even law student worth her salt would know what is and isn't admissible in court. And this, my dear, is not admissible in any fashion. Whatever you came here to get, you've wasted your efforts."

"This isn't about your arrest, Mr. Gordon," Slade said, more to shock him than anything. He needed the man vulnerable. He needed to gain control of that weapon before someone got hurt. He also needed to call in and confirm that Gordon was in custody.

The minutes were ticking by.

"What are you up to?" Gordon demanded.

"Justice," Mia announced.

Gordon whipped his attention back to her. "Don't you see, Ms. Dawson, there is no real justice. Only the facsimile created by those with enough money or enough influence to determine how the story should end."

"In a few hours we'll see if your definition of justice remains the same."

"Too bad getting fired sent you over the edge, Dawson." He shook his head. "You might have made something of yourself. I don't know what you came here expecting to find or get, but, as I said, you've wasted your time."

Mia shook her head. "Not at all. We came here to get you."

Gordon charged forward.

Mia stumbled back a step.

Slade rushed between them.

The explosion of the revolver discharging shattered the silence.

GORDON HIT THE CARPETED floor with an *oomph*, Slade on top of him. The weapon bounced out of reach.

"Get the weapon!" Slade shouted.

Mia didn't go for the gun. Slade didn't have time to glance her way. He had to get Gordon subdued.

Screaming profanities, the older man squirmed and attempted to kick Slade. Slade twisted to miss the blows but didn't release his grip on the bastard.

"Duct tape," Slade called out. "Get me the duct tape!"

The duct tape suddenly appeared in front of his face. The hand holding it shook but that wasn't what seized Slade's attention. Blood trailed from beneath the coat sleeve's cuff and down Mia's pale hand.

Fear seized his chest. His gaze sought hers. She was as white as a ghost. "You okay?" he demanded, instantly taking note of the rip in the upper portion of the right sleeve of the coat she wore.

Mia nodded once, her expression frozen in one of shock.

Focus, man! "Secure his ankles while I hold him down," he ordered.

Another single nod.

Slade forced the man's hands above his head and settled his weight down the length of him in an effort to keep him as still as possible.

Don't think about the blood. She's upright and breathing. Most likely a flesh wound.

"Don't touch me!" Gordon wailed. "Don't touch me, you crazy bitch!"

"Don't move," Slade growled, ready to head-butt the fool if he didn't shut up and hold still.

"I'll get you both," Gordon threatened. "You'll see!"

Slade's jaw tightened as he crushed downward with his full weight. "Be still," he growled.

"Got it," Mia muttered. She moved to stand near Slade's left shoulder.

He resisted the impulse to stop what he was doing and check

out her arm. He pushed up onto all fours, then rolled Gordon onto his stomach. "Don't fight me," Slade warned. "You're only hurting yourself."

Whatever Gordon said was muffled by the plush carpet.

When Slade had the man's wrists pushed together, Mia dropped to her knees and wrapped the tape around once, twice, three times.

"I'll take it from here." Slade nodded toward her arm. "Take off the coat and see what kind of damage you've got."

He finished securing Gordon. If she was injured badly… He shouldn't have allowed her to leave the room to check on Gordon. This was his fault.

Damn it.

Using more force than necessary, he rolled Gordon onto his back once more and slapped a length of tape across his mouth. His struggles lessened marginally, probably from exhaustion. But Slade wasn't taking any risks. He wanted this sleazebag properly secured.

Slade got to his feet, stepped away from his prisoner and moved closer to Mia. The bullet had torn through the fabric of her coat and the blouse she wore. Red had pooled around the damaged section of the fabric now plastered to her arm.

"Take off the blouse."

Those blue eyes glimmered with fear as she reached up to do as he'd asked, her movements wooden.

"Here—" he reached out "—let me."

She didn't say a word as he loosened the blouse then peeled it away from her torso and arms. His heart rate accelerated as much from seeing the lush rise of her breasts above the satin cups of her bra as from the raw, jagged flesh where the bullet had left its piercing path. His gut tied into knots.

"Thankfully it looks as if it's nothing more than a flesh wound."

She nodded, then leaned her head to the left. "He's trying to get up!"

Slade wheeled around and with one booted foot shoved Gordon back to the floor. He snatched up the duct tape and knelt down next to Gordon. Slade rolled him onto his side and tethered his ankles to his wrists. "Try it now, old man," he challenged.

Getting back to his feet, Slade returned his attention to Mia. "Let's get that cleaned up." He reached down and grabbed Gordon by the arm. With little effort he dragged the bound man into the middle of the master bedroom.

Mia had already turned on the light in the en suite bath. Slade made his way to where she stood before one of the sinks staring at her reflection in the well-lit, ornate mirror. She still hadn't said much and her movements and reactions were stilted at best. Not surprising. He doubted she'd ever been shot.

Slade searched until he found the items he needed. Clean washcloths, peroxide, an antibiotic ointment, gauze and tape. The gauze and tape appeared to have been around awhile, but it was still in the original packaging.

"This may hurt a little," he offered gently as he began the cleanup. "But it won't hurt for long."

A faint laugh whispered across her lips. "I seem to recall hearing that when I was seventeen and on the verge of losing my virginity." That weary blue gaze collided with his. "Next you'll tell me that it'll be more fun next time."

"Seventeen, huh?" he teased as he cleaned the wound and rinsed with peroxide. A couple of stitches wouldn't hurt, but that wasn't happening right now. He'd been right in his assessment that it was a flesh wound. A few minutes of pressure to staunch the bleeding would help.

She winced, but remained steady. "Yep. High school sweethearts. I figured since everybody else was doing it, I might as well see what all the fuss was about."

"I'll bet you asked questions during the whole experience." He thought of all the questions she'd asked when he'd appeared at her door.

Another of those fatigued laughs. "Well, let's just say I wasn't the only one who didn't particularly enjoy it."

"That," he said, applying the ointment, "is because you were with a boy. A real man knows how to make sure his woman enjoys every moment."

She actually smiled. "I'll remember that."

Slade placed the gauze over the wound in layers in case there was more seepage, then secured it with the tape. "I could help refresh your memory whenever you like."

The silence stretched between them as he rinsed the washcloth and cleaned the rest of her arm. He held her hand under the flow of water and washed it clean as well.

When he was all done, she looked down at herself and her cheeks flushed. "What do I do about this?"

"Gordon's lady friend was wearing a negligee. Surely she has something around here."

While Slade gathered the ruined blouse and weapon, Mia slid on the lady's sweater. She flinched a couple of times, but managed the feat alone before grabbing her coat. The torn sleeve wouldn't prevent the garment from keeping her warm. The woman secured in the closet probably had a coat around here someplace, but hunting it down wasn't on the agenda at the moment. The sooner they got out of here, the better.

"You all set?" he asked.

"Yeah." She glanced at Gordon. "Let's get this done."

Slade hesitated. "You're sure this is the way you want to play this?" Gordon understood that she was a willing participant but it wasn't too late to salvage the situation as far as any other witnesses were concerned.

"Yes." She took a breath. "I'm not ashamed of what I'm doing. It has to be done."

Slade couldn't help himself. He leaned down and left another of those soft, quick kisses on her cheek. But her eyes told him that would never be enough.

"You could," she whispered, her face so very near to his, "refresh my memory of that kiss we shared earlier."

"No problem." His lips brushed hers as he spoke. A quake of pure desire vibrated through him. He let his lips cover hers completely…let himself feel the need and desire quivering in her slight body. She leaned into him, allowed him to experience her heart beating against his chest.

All they had to do was survive the next few hours and then he would show her so many pleasures…if she still wanted to explore this thing escalating between them once the adrenaline rush was over.

FOURTEEN

Maggie's, Command Center, 2:50 a.m.

JIM watched Ian's preparations. He would drive to the Gordon compound to check on Convoy and Dawson. There had been no contact and time was swiftly running out. It was imperative that they understand what was going on.

Nothing had been reported on the police band. Whatever was happening over there, so far the police weren't involved.

Steele pushed back his chair and turned to face Jim and the others. "I may have it."

Relief sent a twinge through Jim's chest. "How difficult will it be?"

Steele turned and tapped the screen of his computer monitor. "It won't be easy, but there's a path I believe will work for a man with the proper skills."

"That would be you," Jim remarked.

Lucas moved up behind Steele to get a look at the point of

entry and path for reaching the Colby Agency's suite of offices that had been discovered.

Ian stiffened. He reached into his jacket pocket and removed his cell phone. "Michaels."

The whole room froze, all eyes glued to Ian.

"Open the back door. They're here," he said to Jim.

"What about Gordon?" Lucas asked.

Ian nodded. "They have Gordon in custody."

Jim took the stairs two and three at a time. He rushed through the kitchen to the rear entrance that opened into the alley between the buildings. After shoving the dead bolts back, Jim wrenched the door open, his heart hammering.

Gordon, mouth taped shut, hands secured, was the first face he saw. Dawson and Convoy were right behind him. Jim ushered the former district attorney inside. "Good work," he said to Convoy. "We were beginning to get worried about you."

That was when Jim noticed the blood on the woman's coat. "What happened?"

"It's nothing," she insisted. "The bullet barely scraped the skin."

Jim's gaze locked with Convoy's. "Gordon had a weapon stashed in his nightstand."

Damn. "We'll have someone take a look at that," Jim said to Dawson.

Mia Dawson glared at him, then brushed past him and stomped up the stairs to the command center. Evidently, she wanted no special attention.

SLADE FELT CONFIDENT that having a bullet miss a vital organ by mere inches wasn't exactly how Mia had expected the confrontation with Gordon to go.

Or maybe he'd pushed too far with his suggestions…or the kiss. But she'd seemed willing enough.

Slade settled Gordon into a chair amid the buzz of the command center on the second floor.

"Rocky," Jim said to his teammate Leland Rockford, "take a look at Ms. Dawson's arm. Apparently Gordon got off a shot that grazed her."

Lucas and Ian shared a look with Slade. "Gordon had an un-licensed weapon in the table next to his bed."

Ian shook his head. Lucas let go a weary breath.

Slade's attention rested on their special guest. They were close now…but at what price?

4:00 a.m.

"What the hell are you doing?" Gordon demanded.

Mia ignored Gordon's blustering. She glanced at the new bandage around her upper arm. She'd tried to tell the man called Rocky that she was fine—that Slade had already taken care of her—but the big guy wouldn't listen. If it hadn't been for Slade's quick reaction and that big coat she'd been wearing…it could have been so much worse.

Gordon would have killed her.

Any possible sympathy she may have cultivated for the man had died a sudden death when the hot metal grazed her flesh.

Gordon had been outfitted with bulletproof clothing. Mia had no idea such protective wear existed. He'd refused to cooperate, prompting Ian and Slade to tug and pull and drag the protective wear as well as his slacks and shirt into place. Mia had gotten the clothes from his closet while Slade ushered the man into the garage. Then, despite the fact that her arm had been hurting like hell—still did—she'd driven Gordon's fancy sedan across town with Gordon and Slade safely ensconced in the backseat. Slade would pick up his truck later.

"How are you coming along with that route?" Jim Colby asked one of the men seated at a computer.

"Printing it out now."

They had a little more than three and a half hours before Gordon had to be turned over to the bad guys. If this route into the building panned out, Steele, one of Jim Colby's men, the way Mia understood it, would go in and take care of the threat. Ian Michaels had briefed her and Slade on the plan. Ian had put through a call to another Colby Agency investigator. Well, not exactly a staff member, but a potential one. Penny Alexander's clearance wasn't in place yet, but she possessed certain skills that would be beneficial to this operation. Ian had decided to call her in if she could be located.

"We have a problem."

The collective attention of everyone in the room swung to the man Rocky standing at the window. Mia couldn't react for a moment. They didn't need any more bad news.

Grabbing back her courage, she joined the others at the window. Blue lights flickered and flashed. Four—no five—Chicago P.D. squad cars had descended upon the small visitor parking area in front of the building across the street.

The Colby Agency building.

"Did you hear from the security company?" Jim asked Ian.

"An hour ago," Ian assured him. "They had agreed to stand by until ten this morning."

"Somebody apparently didn't get the message," Jim said, his tone grave.

The tension that spread through the already stressful situation seemed to squeeze the oxygen out of the room.

Gordon laughed like a fool. They should have left the tape on his big mouth. "My guard must've escaped your incompetent attempt at securing him."

Slade nodded. "That's possible. I secured the guard and the woman in a guest room closet."

More of that idiotic laughter from Gordon. "Now we'll see who's the criminal," he said to Mia.

"How would he know where to send the police?" Mia argued.

Gordon's face twisted with stifled mirth. "We have your apartment wired. We heard what your friend proposed to you. We knew what you were up to, we just didn't know the when. That's why I had a gun in my nightstand." Gordon glanced around at the grim faces. "Whoever your client is, he can go to hell."

Ian moved to the stairs. "I'll see what I can do." He jerked his head toward Gordon. "You might want to put him somewhere out of the way, like in the freezer downstairs."

Jim patted the shoulder of the man at the computer. "Keep working on it. We'll take care of this situation."

Slade and Jim escorted the still manacled Gordon down the stairs and to the kitchen. He shouted most of the way, insisting that he could not be put into the freezer.

Mia wished she had the duct tape so she could shut him up again.

Since there was no walk-in freezer, the walk-in cooler had to do. Mia and Slade joined Gordon inside, to stay out of sight as much as to keep him quiet. Slade had grabbed a hand towel en route. He pried Gordon's mouth open and shoved enough of the hand towel inside to shut him up.

It was barely lit inside the cooler and only because Slade had thought to flip the exterior switch before they were locked inside. With Gordon moaning in the corner it was damned depressing as well. Already he'd thrown a stumbling block in the works. How could she possibly hope to bring him down? The only person going down was likely her…and Slade.

"You okay?"

She met Slade's green eyes. She liked his eyes. But she was so tired. Her cousin's future hung in the balance. She had no job. Gordon would see to it that she faced legal charges. "No, I'm not okay."

Careful of her injured arm, Slade put his arm around her shoulders and pulled her to him. "We'll get this all worked out." He tipped her chin up to him then. "Trust me, will you?"

She tried to smile but her lips were too cold and too tired. "I'm trying." Truth was, she did. Was that crazy or what? She barely knew him.

He caressed her cheek with the pad of his thumb. A shimmer of warmth went through her. "I owe you dinner at least. You really hung in there."

"So did you." She liked having his arm around her. She liked him. She liked his kisses even more.

He placed a soft kiss on her forehead. It wasn't the most romantic place she'd ever been kissed, but it was by far the most romantic kiss she'd ever had the pleasure of experiencing.

"I promise we'll finish *this* later."

"Definitely." Taking yet another risk, she stood on tiptoe and brushed her lips to his. The heat that simmered through her veins made her forget all about being in a massive refrigerator. She'd made the first move once already. But he was worth the risk.

The door abruptly opened.

"The police are gone," Ian reported.

Slade and Ian ushered Gordon back to the second floor. Mia kind of floated along behind them. She didn't know how this day was going to end but she did know one thing for certain—she had something to look forward to.

Slade Convoy.

When Gordon was settled and secured to a chair once more, Ian removed the towel from his mouth and slapped a strip of tape there before he could start ranting again.

Jim suddenly let out a whoop. All gazes landed on him.

"We've got it," he explained. "Rocky has gone to bring the necessary gear and Steele is ready to go in."

"Ms. Alexander is on her way," Ian mentioned.

The two men didn't argue, but there was a shared look of mere tolerance.

Ian reached into his pocket and pulled out his cell phone. "Michaels."

Lucas, Slade, Jim and even Mia fixed their attention on him. Had something else gone wrong? Just because the police had left didn't mean they actually believed Ian's story about the ongoing gas/electrical problem in the building. He'd convinced them that Gordon's security guard was no doubt delusional.

Ian started to argue with his caller twice, then a third time. Each time he appeared to be cut off. Finally he said, "I understand."

He closed the phone and dropped it back into his pocket. "We have thirty minutes to turn over Mr. Gordon or a hostage dies."

"What?" Jim demanded.

"He moved up the timeline?" Lucas shook his head. "This is not what we agreed to."

"I can't get in there that fast," Steele said to Jim, who was looking at him hopefully. "That's an impossible deadline."

"That's the point," Ian said. "He says the arrival of the police prompted him to move up the timeline, but I'm convinced it's because we had Gordon on site and he didn't want us to have any extra time to plot a counterattack."

Mia looked from Ian to Slade. "What do we do?"

Slade held her gaze for a long moment. "We give them what they want."

FIFTEEN

Inside the Colby Agency, 4:30 a.m.

VICTORIA stirred. It was dark in the conference room. And so quiet. Her head hurt, but more than that her chest hurt. She, Nicole and Simon had managed to keep everyone calm and cooperative. But she wasn't sure how much longer that strategy would work. Her entire staff was growing more nervous by the hour.

"Victoria."

She turned her face toward Nicole's voice. The other woman moved closer as soundlessly as possible so as not to alert the guard at the door.

"Simon and I believe we have enough manpower to overtake these guys."

The whispered words struck sheer terror in Victoria's heart. "No." She shook her head to emphasize the word. "Not yet. There's still time—"

"Simon overheard them talking," Nicole interrupted. "The timeline has been moved up. Something is supposed to happen very soon. We can't just keep playing dead...or we'll all end up that way."

More of that fear trembled through Victoria. "I'll try a strategy I've been mulling over first." When Nicole would have argued, she cut her off. "That is a direct order, Nicole. I'm trusting you and Simon to keep the others safe. They are your responsibility. Is that clear?"

Nicole heaved a frustrated breath, then nodded.

The door opened and the overhead lights beamed to life. Victoria squinted, blinked to adjust to the brightness.

The man she recognized as the bastard in charge pointed at her. "Victoria, step up here with me."

The man shackled to the chair across the room started to struggle against his bindings. He moaned pitifully. Victoria wished she could see his face. Could help him.

"We still need water," she told the leader of this unholy troop as she scrambled to her feet. Her numb legs tried to buckle under her. The guard rushed to steady her and escort her to his superior.

"That man—" Victoria indicated the man whose identity they didn't know "—needs water."

The leader grabbed her by the face and squeezed. Victoria's staff stirred. She prayed they would be very, very still. Thankfully she heard Nicole's soft voice urging the others to remain still and quiet.

"You have a special job this morning," the man in charge said to Victoria.

She blinked back the sting of tears as his fingers continued to crush her face.

"You," he went on, "have the distinct pleasure of helping me select who will die first."

"I'll go first."

Victoria's breath caught at the sound of Simon's voice.

"Well, well," the bastard gripping her said, "we have ourselves a hero."

Victoria strained to see her wonderful staff—family, really—huddled together on the floor. A moan rose in her throat as Simon Ruhl pushed to his feet.

"That's right," Simon agreed, "that's all you need, right? One hero?"

The man released Victoria's face. "Maybe. Maybe not. Depends upon how long your friends take to respond to my schedule change." He grinned at Simon. "I'm not so sure they have your best interest at heart."

Simon cautiously moved closer to the man in charge. "Let's step outside and give them some motivation."

"No." The single word wrenched from Victoria's throat. When the leader turned back to her, she said, "I am the head of the Colby Agency. I will go first."

Another of those nasty grins stretched across his face. "How sweet. We have two heroes."

"You're wrong."

Victoria's lungs seized as Nicole struggled to her feet. Victoria's head was moving from side to side, but Nicole wasn't looking at her.

"You have three heroes," Nicole announced.

This time the bastard didn't laugh.

As tears poured unimpeded from Victoria's eyes, each and every member of her staff stood, one by one, and offered to die first.

The man cut a look at Victoria, that steel-gray gaze churning with hatred.

He opened his mouth but, before he could say whatever vile remark that was poised on the tip of his tongue, his cell phone rang loudly.

Without taking his eyes off her, he snatched the phone from his waist. "It's about time," he snapped. A long pause indicated whoever had called was speaking at length. "Excellent. Don't be even a second late or—" his gaze shot to Victoria's "—your beloved Victoria will be the first to die."

SIXTEEN

Maggie's Command Center, 4:40 a.m.

"JIM," Lucas implored, "I will escort Gordon. There's no need for you to take that risk. Victoria would not be happy about that."

Jim stood his ground. "This discussion is over. I'm going in." Before Lucas or Ian could argue further, he asked Ben Steele, "How long before you're prepared to move in?"

Rocky had arrived just moments ago with the gear Steele would need. "I'm ready now."

"You'll need assistance," Ian argued. "Penny Alexander will be here in the next five minutes. I'd like her to go in with you. She's fully prepared to meet the necessary physical rigors."

"I don't want him to wait," Jim protested. To Steele he said, "Go."

"Jim, you're moving too hastily."

Jim sent Ian a hostile glare. "I'm not waiting any longer." He glanced at the clock on the wall. "We have less than ten minutes. One second late and Victoria dies. I won't take that risk."

Slade stepped forward. "All of you need to be here to get the backup team ready and in place. I should be the one to take Gordon in."

Gordon groaned against the tape keeping his mouth closed.

"I should do it."

Everyone turned to stare at Mia.

She took a deep breath. "I know more about what he's done than anyone else. I've also been involved with most of the cases he has worked the past two years. I might recognize someone." She shrugged. "Learn something, maybe."

More of that annoying noise from Gordon.

"No way," Slade said. "You're staying right here."

This time Mia was the one standing her ground. "Have you bothered to look at his prosecution history to try and determine who the hell is behind this? This kind of takeover requires some serious motivation."

Lucas held up a hand. "We have. We've confirmed the whereabouts of all the players in every case he prosecuted for close to three years back…except two. We couldn't locate anyone from the Dennison case or the Thorp case. We're still working on that."

"The only family member of the victim in the Dennison case," Mia explained, "died last year. Cancer. So that's likely a dead end."

"That leaves only one," Ian said, pointing out the obvious.

"The Thorp trial," Mia said with a threatening glare at Gordon, "is one of the cases I believe Gordon screwed up. The killer went free."

"That's the one where his daughter was murdered," Ian commented, apparently remembering some headline or news report.

Mia nodded. "Mr. Thorp tried for months to raise aware-ness in the media and at the D.A.'s office, but he was stopped."

"Where is he now?" Slade asked, a bad, bad feeling leeching beneath his skin.

"He was jailed about three months ago on harassment charges." She glared at Gordon again. "Something else you're responsible for."

"Wait." Lucas looked around the room. "How do I know that name? Am I the only one who's heard it before?"

"The victim was actually his stepdaughter. Patricia Henshaw," Mia clarified.

"Oh, good Lord." Lucas's face paled. "That was the murder trial last summer…the one on which Victoria served as a juror."

Understanding dawned on Ian's face. "We can't take Gordon in there. It would surely be a death sentence for him."

"We can," Jim said as he walked over to the man whose hands and mouth were secured and jerked him to his feet, "and we will. There's no time to do anything else. If we don't, it's a death sentence for a lot of innocent people."

"Jim, wait." Slade stepped in front of the big guy. "This will not end well. I'm afraid I agree with Ian. It's time to call the police."

"No way. Step aside, Convoy."

Slade knew enough about Jim's past not to doubt that he would clear his path by whatever means necessary. But he couldn't let this happen. The Colby Agency's reputation was already fractured. This would push it way past merely broken.

"If you go in like this, emotionally charged, you could end up just another hostage," Slade said, throwing out one last argument. "Let me go."

Jim shot Ian a look. "Tell your man to step aside."

The minutes were ticking by too damned fast.

Ian rested his too-somber gaze on Slade. "Step aside, Convoy. We don't have any more time."

Jim Colby marched down the stairs with *their* hostage in tow.

Slade's gut twisted into knots. This could be the end…

"I don't know about the rest of you," Lucas said as he walked stiffly toward the stairs, "but I'm going out front. If anything goes wrong, I want to be as close as possible if there's any chance I can help."

Tears had started to stream down Mia's cheeks. Slade reached out and squeezed her good arm.

"Where's justice when it's needed?" she asked with a hic-cupping sob.

He gave his head a little shake. "I can't say. But the Colby Agency is the one place that it still exists. Maybe, if this is Thorp, this is the only way and place he felt confident he could find it."

They walked down the stairs together.

On the sidewalk, in front of Maggie's Coffee House, Slade, Mia, Ian and Lucas stood together and watched Jim Colby walk away, walk toward the Colby Agency, where the first hostage was scheduled to die in a mere four minutes.

Victoria was to be first.

Maybe Jim was right. Maybe he was the only choice to finish this.

SEVENTEEN

Inside the Colby Agency, 4:58 a.m.

VICTORIA stood before the receptionist's desk in the greeting lobby of her agency. Thankfully the rest of her staff remained in the conference room. She didn't want them to be subjected to this atrocity…particularly if things went wrong.

Her heart pounded so hard she could scarcely catch a breath. The muzzle of the handgun bored painfully into her temple. She refused to show this bastard that he continued to cause her pain. So she stood stoically, without flinching. She would give him no satisfaction on that level. Focused, she watched and waited for the elevator doors to open.

Someone was escorting former D.A. Timothy Gordon to exchange for the release of the hostages. She wanted so desperately for all her people to be safe. She had prayed and prayed that this moment would arrive.

But not at this price.

Victoria had already made up her mind. She wasn't leaving her agency or the man, Gordon. Or the other unidentified hostage. Whatever the reasons for bringing those two men here…she would not leave either to be murdered in her stead. But she would wait until the rest of her staff was released before taking that stance. She wanted all of them out of harm's way. If they learned of her plan, they would refuse to leave.

But this was her ship and she would go down with whoever remained, good, bad or indifferent. It was her duty.

"Sixty seconds," her captor growled. He bored the muzzle more deeply into the thin flesh of her temple. "Maybe they've decided to let you all die. You are getting up there, after all."

Victoria resisted the urge to smile. Obviously this man did not know Lucas or Jim or Ian. Not one of the three would allow this to happen.

She had long taken the stance that the Colby Agency did not negotiate with terrorists. But now she'd seen that there were times when there was no other choice but to negotiate. She thanked God that this was the only time she'd been forced to be a part of a horrific decision like this.

This was a sad day for the Colby Agency.

In far too many ways to count.

The light above the elevator flashed, signaling that a car had arrived. Then the distinct ding announced that the doors would momentarily open.

Victoria held her breath. Prayed for the strength to stand firm with her decision to remain after the others were released.

"About damned time," the man with the gun snarled hatefully.

The doors slid open slowly. The first man she saw she recognized as D.A. Gordon. His mouth was taped closed and his hands were bound in front of him. Her gaze moved beyond him to identify his escort and her pulse seemed to grind to a halt.

Jim…her son…had escorted Gordon into the building. Why would he take such a risk?

Jim pushed Gordon off the car when he clearly did not want to exit. There had to be a way for Victoria to help him survive whatever was to come.

"You have what you asked for," Jim said, his voice gruff, feral. "Now release the hostages." He kept his gaze steady on the man with the gun pressed to Victoria's head. Not even for a split second did his attention deviate to her.

"Well, well," the bastard said, "the venerable Colby Agency came through after all."

"I'm waiting," Jim warned. "Let them go. All of them. Now."

The bastard gripping Victoria's arm like a vise shouted to his men. Two came running to his aid. "Take Gordon," he ordered.

"No way." Jim drew the man back against him. "You let the hostages go first and then you can have him. But not an instant before."

"How brave of you, sir," the leader mused. "I know my men searched you in the main lobby on the ground floor. You have no weapon. No cell phone. Nothing. And yet you would dare to defy my direct order."

One corner of Jim's mouth twitched with the shadow of a smile. "And I will kill you for touching my mother."

Tears welled in Victoria's eyes. He'd called her his mother. She'd waited so long for him to feel that connection strongly enough to use the endearment. Before she could restrain them, the tears billowed over and flowed down her cheeks.

Still, Jim did not look at her. He kept that fierce glare

locked on his target. Victoria wondered if the man had any idea how savage a killer her son had been in the past. Would those statistics scare him in the least? Jim had been a monster, but he'd overcome those lethal impulses. No matter, she loved him for who he was now and for who he'd always been.

The man made a sound that he likely considered a chuckle. But it was far too vile to contain any humor. "Release the hostages in the conference room," he said to his men. "Lead them down the stairs. Have one of those waiting across the street call and verify that all are accounted for."

Relief left Victoria weak. She prayed her son would look at her so she could tell him with her eyes how very much she loved him and how very much what he'd just said meant to her.

Gordon started to squirm. Jim tightened his grip on the smaller man. That was when Victoria saw the tears sliding down Gordon's cheeks as well. Dear God, how could she allow this?

Yet, she had no choice. Too many lives were at stake.

Two minutes, three, then four passed before the bastard's cell phone sounded a warning that a call was incoming. He released Victoria's arm to take the call. The weapon, however, stayed burrowed into her flesh, which held her still.

When he had confirmed that it was Ian calling, he tossed the phone to Jim. "There's your verification, tough guy."

Jim listened while Ian passed on the required information. "Very good." He closed the phone and tossed it back to its owner. "Now, release the final hostage and we're finished here."

"Now," the bastard said, echoing Jim, "this is where things get dicey. You see, I can't release Victoria. She's part of the second phase of this operation. Remember—"

"In that case, the deal is off," Jim roared, cutting him off.

He reached behind him and pounded the call button with his fist. "You don't release Victoria, you don't get Gordon."

"Ah, not so hasty, Mr. Colby," the man in charge began. "If you remember the demand was twofold. One, bring Gordon. Leaving Victoria behind is part two. I opted to keep that to myself until it became necessary to tell you."

"No way." Jim glared at the man, his eyes warning that he was at the very end of his ability to maintain restraint. He would not be able to hold back his baser urges much longer.

"This is nonnegotiable." The flat statement rang in the air.

Victoria wished she could do something, anything to stop this travesty.

"We haven't called the authorities," Jim reminded him. "If that's what you're worried about, we won't until you and your men have cleared out."

"If only that were true," the leader countered. "Whether it is or not is actually inconsequential. Your mother is needed for phase two."

"It's all right, Jim," Victoria urged. "I need to stay. I can't walk—"

"No talking," the man with the gun snapped, grabbing her hair and digging the muzzle deeper into her skull.

Jim postured to make a dive around Gordon.

Victoria pleaded, "Please, Jim, just go."

Jim's gaze locked with hers. For the briefest moment she saw the misery…the unspoken feelings. He didn't want to lose her…he loved her.

Victoria smiled faintly. She told him with her eyes how very much she loved him.

"You have sixty seconds," the man in charge announced. "Release Gordon to my men and leave or she dies."

Jim's attention swung back to the man with the gun. "Release her and keep me instead."

"Won't work, fifty seconds."

Dear God, Victoria prayed, *just let my son walk away.*

Jim's gaze searched hers once more. For three endless beats she was afraid he would attempt to overtake the man with the gun...no matter that two more of his henchmen had joined him.

"Thirty-five seconds," the man roared. "You'd better make up your mind whether your mother's brains are going to be spread all over this lobby or not. I'm running out of patience."

Three, four, five seconds elapsed. Victoria held on to hope that her son would leave safely.

Jim pushed Gordon forward, turned his back and entered the waiting elevator car. Then he faced her one last time.

Victoria would remember those moments before the door closed for whatever remained of her life. Her son loved her deeply. He'd shown her with his eyes.

"Take him to the conference room," the brute said to his men. Then he dragged Victoria over to the window and crushed her face against it. "I want you to watch your son walk away. It's the last time you'll ever see him."

Victoria's heart filled with pride as Jim came into view, exiting the building. His stride was long and strong as he crossed the parking area and then the street. Lucas and the others waited for him on the other side. Her staff, her family, hugged, held each other close. She didn't have to see the tears to know they wept. For each other. For her.

For the day the Colby Agency ceased to be what it once was.

EIGHTEEN

5:50 a.m.

LUCAS'S heart dropped to the sidewalk.

Jim was crossing the street *alone*.

Lucas walked out to meet him, his leg giving him hell. "Where's Victoria?"

Jim's chin jutted upward. "They wouldn't release her. I tried to exchange myself for her but they refused. She refused as well."

A lone tear trekked down the savage man's face. His pain was as real as anyone's here, including Lucas's.

Lucas nodded. "You did all you could. Victoria is a strong woman. She'll figure a way out of this. We have to believe she will triumph."

Ian moved over to join them, Nicole held close at his side. He repeated Lucas's question. Before anyone could answer, his cell chirped. He pulled it quickly from his pocket. "Michaels."

Silence fell over all those gathered.

Ian drew the phone from his ear and set it to speakerphone. "You're on speaker," he said tightly.

The man still holding Victoria, no doubt.

"Enjoy your freedom!" the bastard exclaimed. "But bear in mind that Victoria remains our hostage for the next twenty-four hours."

Pained glances were exchanged by those gathered around.

"The man all of you saw here with the bag over his head is Reginald Clark, the notorious drug and prostitution prince and otherwise thorn in the side of Chicago. During the next twenty-four hours he will stand trial for his crimes. District Attorney Gordon is being given a second chance to do the job right this time. As is Juror Number Eight, Victoria Colby-Camp. The prince will be tried and sentenced and then that sentence will be carried out without delay. If any of you interfere in any way, including contacting the authorities, Victoria and Gordon will suffer the same sentence. Make no mistake," he reiterated, "we are watching and listening. One wrong move and Victoria dies first."

SLADE AND MIA helped Simon attend to the injuries, most of them minor, of the folks who had been held hostage. Ben Steele had returned with bad news—he, indeed, could not reach his target alone. He needed help. Ian had introduced him to Penny Alexander, a potential hire for the Colby Agency, who had just arrived. She wasn't scheduled to come on board for another week, but her special skills were needed now. If she was willing, so was the Colby Agency.

Before this day was over, Steele and Alexander had to attain their goal and stop this mockery of justice before anyone died.

Slade hoped like hell they could manage the feat. The internal workings of this state-of-the-art building were designed to prevent an intrusion. Now, the very design that had protected the agency and all others inside stood in the way of a rescue. By the time the two could reach the Colby offices, it might be too late.

Mia tapped Slade on the shoulder. He turned to face her. "We need to talk."

Slade glanced around the first floor of the coffee shop that would be closed this morning. The owner had graciously allowed the Colby Agency full use of the facility. The members of the Colby Agency were a bit damaged but they weren't beaten. There wasn't one of them who didn't want to do their part to end this nightmare.

Sadly, there was nothing anyone could do at this point except send in Alexander and Steele and hope that teamwork would succeed.

"I feel like I need to go to the new D.A." She bit her bottom lip. "Maybe he can devise a way to resolve this that doesn't alert those insane jerks. You know, bring aspects of the police in without the usual detectable communications."

Slade wasn't sure it would work but it couldn't hurt. He took Mia by the arm and located Ian and Simon, as well as Lucas. Jim's wife had arrived and was tending to his aggrieved soul.

Slade nodded for Mia to go ahead.

"The new D.A., Ashton Flannery," she began, "is a good man who believes in justice for all. I think maybe we can go to him. He would be the last person to just send the police in arbitrarily. He might be able to come up with a doable plan beneath the radar of those men."

The three men Slade knew had to agree considered her suggestion for a moment.

Ian spoke first. "You understand that your participation in this will be revealed in such a way that could expose you to prosecution if you go to Flannery."

Mia nodded. "I understand. It's the right thing to do. I don't care what I'm exposed to."

Slade felt a weak smile tug at his lips. He liked that she was so true and loyal to truth and justice. They might have gotten off on the wrong foot, but he knew her now.

"I can take her," Slade offered, "see that the agency's interests are fully protected."

Jim shouldered his way into the huddle. "What's going on?"

Simon quickly explained what Mia had suggested. "This, of course, has nothing to do with Penny and Ben pursuing that avenue of infiltration. It's merely a backup plan," Simon clarified.

Jim considered the suggestion then turned to Mia. "If you believe you can trust this man, I'm on board. Anything we can do is better than standing here doing nothing."

That was a major step. Slade nearly swayed with the overwhelming relief.

"Jim and I," Ian offered, "will remain here to monitor the infiltration efforts." He looked to Lucas and Simon. "The two of you should get some rest."

"You know better than to suggest that I leave," Lucas retorted. "I'm not going anywhere until my wife is at my side."

"Jolie is on her way here," Simon interjected. "She had to get a sitter for the kids. I'll spend a few minutes with her and then I'm with the rest of you. I'm not leaving until Victoria is safely out of there."

"Go," Ian urged Slade and Mia. "The clock is running."

He didn't have to say the rest.... Time for Victoria was running out.

NINETEEN

Flannery home, 7:50 a.m.

SLADE parked the SUV he'd borrowed from Ian at the curb on the opposite side of the street from D.A. Flannery's house. "If he's up yet there are no signs of life."

Mia peered at the house across the street. Though it was almost daylight, it was still gloomy enough to have lights on inside. Flannery would be expected at work in another hour or so. He should be up. Maybe he was in the shower.

"He's widowed," she explained. "Lives alone. He could be taking a shower."

Slade nodded. "So we should just knock on the door."

They had agreed not to call since they couldn't be sure if their phone lines were being monitored. Slade had picked up on an uneasiness regarding the subject when he'd mentioned it to Mia. But she wasn't used to all the subterfuge.

"We'll knock on the door." Mia reached for her door and

slid out of the SUV. Like Slade's truck, it was a lot higher off the ground than her little hybrid.

Slade came around the vehicle to stand beside her. "Quiet neighborhood."

"The school buses have run already. No kids at home to be noisy."

He nodded. "No outside dogs, either."

"One less worry," she muttered.

As they crossed the street, she couldn't help feeling a sense of doom settling onto her shoulders. Something wasn't right. Then again, maybe she just felt bad because she hadn't been completely honest with Slade about Flannery.

"You know," Slade said, leaning his head close to hers, "this feels wrong somehow."

"We must be on the same wavelength. I was just thinking the same thing." She kept the other part of her worries to herself.

As they approached the door, the intense oppression only heightened. Weird. Mia rapped on the door. Five seconds later, Slade reached around her and pressed the doorbell.

They waited.

Nothing.

Slade knocked this time. He pounded hard enough to wake the dead. She shivered. She'd had all the near-death experiences in the past twenty-four hours that she ever cared to have.

Another minute or two lapsed with no reaction.

"Let's go around back," Slade suggested.

Mia glanced at the house on the right and then the one on the left. No one appeared to be looking. So she followed him around to the gate at the side of the house. It wasn't locked, just a simple latch that let them through into the backyard.

The yard was lavishly landscaped. Even in the dead of winter it was breathtaking. More greenery than she would have expected. Lots of fancy rocks and pavers.

No lights in any of the windows at the back of the house, either, though. That was troubling.

"This is just weird." Mia liked this less and less.

"Time to put some of my less marketable skills to use." Slade winked at her.

She blushed then followed him to the back door, which appeared to lead into a laundry room or mudroom. Putting her hands on either side of her face, she peered through the glass. Washer and dryer. Yep, laundry room.

He pulled out his wallet, removed a credit card and did the niftiest trick she'd ever seen. He slid it between the door and the frame and did some expert wiggling. The next thing she knew he opened the door as if he'd used a key.

"Wow. I'd say *less marketable*," she noted with a soft laugh. What else would she learn about this man?

Other than the very obvious facts that he was tall and gorgeous and kind and loyal and made her heart skip about every other beat. And that he was an amazing kisser.

Mia rolled her eyes. This was certainly not the time or place for such thoughts. Her reasons for breaking yet another law were serious…deadly.

They needed a break. Something had to give. Everything, including justice for her cousin, was riding on how this turned out.

"Mr. Flannery," she called out as they entered the kitchen.

This went on for several minutes. She alternately called his name and frowned when it became obvious that he had certainly been in the process of preparing for work. The shower was running in the master bath. Had been running for a few minutes. The mirrors over the two sinks were fogged. A suit was laid out on the bed.

Back downstairs his briefcase sat by the front door, next to the table where his keys and cell phone lay waiting for his exit.

"We've searched the entire house." Slade shook his head. "We have to be missing something."

Her gaze met his. "Basement?"

They moved back to the broad, sweeping stairs and opened the closet door built beneath. The closet was large, large enough to step into. On the far side was a door that led into the basement.

The moment they descended the first step, the smell of death assaulted Mia's nostrils. Her pulse sped up as did her feet.

Ashton Flannery lay sprawled on the basement floor. He wore white boxers and a white T-shirt. A single bullet hole in his forehead had leaked a significant amount of blood on the concrete floor.

Mia couldn't move. She stood there and stared. Trying to figure out if he'd killed himself...or...

No, no...that couldn't be.

Then she saw the note in his hand. Slade checked the man's carotid artery, shook his head, then tugged the note from his cold fingers. He stood, opened the neatly folded pages and stared at the typed note.

Mia and Slade,
I didn't want to make a mess upstairs. This is a warning. Don't get any more bright ideas or the next body you discover will be Victoria's.
Yours Truly: The MAN in charge.

Dear God! "How could they have known?" Mia couldn't comprehend this. It was crazy!

Slade turned to her, his expression grave. "Did you talk to anyone else before talking to me?"

Emotion lodged in her throat. "I…I used the coffeehouse phone and called…" She indicated the dead man on the floor. "I didn't give him any details. I just told him I needed to talk to him right away. He—" she licked her lips "—said I should come directly here."

Slade closed his eyes. "Great."

Mia hung her head. "I'm sorry. I thought it was okay since I didn't tell him anything." She touched Slade's arm. "I didn't mean to lie to you. I just had to be sure he would welcome our visit. I swear I didn't tell him anything."

"But," Slade countered, "you told *them* everything. Where you were going and who you were going to talk to."

Mia fell into his arms. Exhaustion was clawing at her. She was running on empty. She'd made a mistake. One that had cost a man his life. This was her fault.

Slade held her close, guided her up the stairs and out of the house. When he'd buckled her into the passenger seat of the SUV, he swiped at the tears on her cheeks. "We're going to get through this…together."

She nodded. "That's the only way."

There was no promise of tomorrow…only today…this moment.

It was time to stop planning for another day and start appreciating this one.

Slade closed her door and moved around the vehicle to slide behind the steering wheel. He started the engine and drove away.

Now they had another dilemma. Did they call the police

and report the murder? As far as Mia was concerned, she was leaving that decision up to Ian, Lucas and Slade. She'd screwed up far too much already.

Slade braked for a traffic light. He glanced at her. "Ian and Lucas will know what to do."

The broken laws and accessory charges just kept piling up. But she could survive that… How could she live with being responsible for another human's murder?

How would they ever survive this mess?

She had just wanted justice for her cousin and all the others.

"Hey." He touched her cheek with the tips of his fingers and turned her face to his. "Don't give up on me yet."

She laughed, though she felt no humor. "It's not you I'm giving up on. It's me." How could she have been so foolhardy? So utterly stupid?

"Does it matter that I'm not giving up on you?"

A smile prodded at her lips. "Yes. Yes, it does."

"Good."

He kissed her, softly, sweetly. She cherished this moment, this kiss. And the man.

No matter that everything else about her life was uncertain. He was the certainty she'd been looking for her whole life.

TWENTY

Inside the Colby Agency, 8:05 a.m.

VICTORIA sat on one side of the long mahogany table in her conference room. Across the room Leonard Thorp stood next to his hired guns. Reginald Clark, the prince, remained bound in his chair, but the chair had been relocated to one end of the conference table. Gordon sat at the opposite end, sweat beaded on his forehead, his designer framed eyeglasses askew.

All seated at the table were scheduled to die before this day ended. Thorp and his men would never allow Victoria or Gordon to leave this building alive. Certainly Reginald Clark would not survive if this mock trial was allowed to play out.

Victoria thought of her husband, her son, and the many other family members and friends she loved. She also reflected on the many people her agency had helped, could still help.

A smile lifted the corners of her mouth. Her gaze settled on

Thorp and his evil henchmen. She wasn't beaten. Nor was she finished…not by a long shot.

All she had to do was buy some precious time. The best of the best were waiting just across the street to do what had to be done.

And Victoria, well, she fully intended to do her part. This was not the end.

★ ★ ★ ★ ★

The Harlequin Intrigue® series brings you six new
passionate and suspenseful books a month
available wherever books are sold, including most bookstores,
supermarkets, drugstores and discount stores.

SHOTGUN SHERIFF
Delores Fossen

CAST OF CHARACTERS

Sheriff Reed Hardin—As sheriff of Comanche Creek, he's reluctant to cast his lot with the Texas Rangers because he wants to conduct his own investigation into the town's recent string of murders.

Sgt. Olivia "Livvy" Hutton—The Rangers' CSI who's as suspicious of Reed as he is of her.

Marcie James—A records clerk that someone obviously wanted to silence. Now, Livvy and Reed must work together to find her killer.

Jonah Becker—A powerful rancher who's not afraid to use his money to get what he wants. Is he a cold-blooded killer or just an unscrupulous businessman?

Woodrow "Woody" Sadler—The popular mayor who might have greased the way for Jonah to profit from a shady land deal.

Deputy Shane Tolbert—Marcie's ex who's arrested for her murder. They had a checkered relationship. Despite being a small-town lawman, he's well trained in forensics.

Billy Whitley—The city official who might have done something illegal to orchestrate the land deal that's under investigation.

Charla Whitley—Billy's wife. Did she kill Marcie to hide her own wrongdoing?

Jerry Collier—Head of the land office and Marcie's former boss. He's also connected to the illegal sale of Native American artifacts that were recovered after Jonah got the land.

Ben Tolbert—Shane's father. He wants his son cleared of all charges, but how far is he willing to go to make sure that neither Shane nor he spends any time in jail?

ONE

Comanche Creek, Texas

SOMETHING was wrong.

Sheriff Reed Hardin eased his Smith and Wesson from his leather shoulder holster and stepped out of his mud-scabbed pickup truck. The heels of his rawhide boots sank in the rain-softened dirt. He lifted his head. Listened.

It was what he *didn't* hear that bothered him.

Yeah, something was definitely wrong.

There should have been squawks from the blue jays or the cardinals. Maybe even a hawk in search of its breakfast. Instead there was only the unnerving quiet of the Texas Hill Country woods sardined with thick mesquites, hackberries and thorny underbrush that bulged thick and green with spring growth. Whatever had scared off the birds could be lurking in there. Reed was hoping for a coyote or some other four-legged predator because the alternative put a knot in his gut.

After all, just hours earlier a woman had been murdered a few yards from here.

With his gun ready and aimed, Reed made his way up the steep back path toward the cabin. He'd chosen the route so he could look around for any evidence he might have missed when he'd combed the grounds not long after the body had been discovered. He needed to see if anything was out of place, anything that would help him make sense of this murder. So far, nothing.

Except for his certainty that something was wrong.

And he soon spotted proof of it.

There were footprints leading down and then back up the narrow trail. Too many of them. There should have been only his and his deputy's, Kirby Spears, since Reed had given firm orders that all others use the county road just a stone's throw from the front of the cabin. He hadn't wanted this scene contaminated and there were signs posted ordering No Trespassers.

He stooped down and had a better look at the prints. "What the hell?" Reed grumbled.

The prints were small and narrow and with a distinctive narrow cut at the back that had knifed right into the gray-clay-and-limestone dirt mix.

Who the heck would be out here in high heels?

He thought of the dead woman, Marcie James, who'd been found shot to death in the cabin about fourteen hours earlier. Marcie hadn't been wearing heels. Neither had her alleged killer. And Reed should know because the alleged killer was none other than his own deputy, Shane Tolbert.

Cursing the fact that Shane was now locked up in a jail he used to police with Reed and Kirby, Reed elbowed aside a pungent dew-coated cedar branch and hurried up the hill. It didn't take him long to see more evidence of his something-was-wrong theory. There were no signs of his deputy or the patrol car.

However, there was a blonde lurking behind a sprawling oak tree.

Correction. An *armed* blonde. A stranger, at that.

She was tall, at least five-ten, and dressed in a long-sleeved white shirt that she'd tucked into the waist of belted dark jeans. Her hair was gathered into a sleek ponytail, not a strand out of place. And yep, there were feminine heels on her fashionable black boots. But her attire wasn't what Reed focused on. It was that lethal-looking Sig-Sauer Blackwater pistol gripped in her latex-gloved right hand. She had it aimed at the cabin.

Reed aimed his Smith and Wesson at her.

Maybe she heard him or sensed he was there because her gaze whipped in his direction. She shifted her position a fraction, no doubt preparing to turn her weapon on him, but she stopped when her attention landed on the badge Reed had clipped to his belt. Then, she did something that surprised the heck out of him.

She put her left index finger to her mouth in a *shhh* gesture.

Reed glanced around, trying to make sense of why she was there and why in Sam Hill she'd just shushed him as if she'd had a right to do it. He didn't see anyone other than the blonde, but she kept her weapon trained on the cabin.

He walked closer to her, keeping his steps light, just in case there was indeed some threat other than this woman. If so, then someone had breached a crime scene because the cabin was literally roped off with yellow crime-scene tape. And with the town's gossip mill in full swing, there probably wasn't anyone within fifty miles of Comanche Creek who hadn't heard about the latest murder.

Emphasis on the word *latest*.

Everyone knew to keep away or they'd have to deal with him. He wasn't a badass—most days, anyway—but people usually did as he said when he spelled things out for them. And he always spelled things out.

"I'm Sheriff Reed Hardin," he grumbled when he got closer.

"Livvy Hutton."

Like her face, her name wasn't familiar to him. Who the devil was she?

She tipped her head towards the cabin. "I think someone's inside."

Well, there sure as hell shouldn't be. "Where's my deputy?"

"Running an errand for me."

That didn't improve Reed's mood. He was about to question why his deputy would be running an errand for an armed woman in fancy boots, but she shifted her position again. Even though she kept her attention nailed to the cabin, he could now see the front of her white shirt.

The sun's rays danced off the distinctive star badge pinned to it.

"You're a Texas Ranger?" he asked.

He hadn't intended for that to sound like a challenge, but it did. Reed couldn't help it. He already had one Ranger to deal with, Lieutenant Wyatt Colter, who'd been in Comanche Creek for days, since the start of all this mess that'd turned his town upside-down. Now, he apparently had another one of Texas's finest. That was two too many for a crime scene he planned to finish processing himself. He had a plan for this investigation, and that plan didn't include Rangers.

"Yes. Sergeant Olivia Hutton," she clarified. "CSI for the Ranger task force."

She spared him a glance from ice-blue eyes. Not a friendly glance either. That brief look conveyed a lot of displeasure.

And skepticism.

Reed had seen that look before. He was a small-town Texas sheriff, and to some people that automatically made him small-minded, stupid and incapable of handling a capital murder investigation. That attitude was one of the reasons for the so-called task force that included not only Texas Rangers but a forensic anthropologist and apparently this blonde crime-scene analyst.

As he'd done with Lieutenant Colter, the other Ranger, Reed would set a few ground rules with Sergeant Hutton. Later, that was. For now, he needed to figure out if anyone was inside the cabin. That was at the top of his mental list.

Reed didn't see anyone near either of the two back curtainless windows. Nor had the crime-scene tape been tampered with. It was still in place. Of course, someone could have ducked beneath it and gotten inside—after they'd figured out a way to get past the locked windows and doors. Other than the owner and probably some members of the owner's family, Reed and his deputy were the only ones with keys.

"Did you actually see anyone in the cabin?" he asked in a whisper.

She turned her head, probably so she could whisper as well, but the move put them even closer. Practically mouth to cheek. Not good. Because with all that closeness, he caught her scent. Her perfume was high-end, but that was definitely chocolate on her breath.

"I heard something," she explained. "Your deputy and I were taking castings of some footprints we found over there." She tipped her head to a cluster of trees on the east side of the cabin. "I wanted to get them done right away because it's supposed to rain again this afternoon."

Yeah, it was, and if they'd been lucky enough to find footprints after the morning and late-night drizzle, then they wouldn't be there long.

"After Deputy Spears left to send the castings to your office," she continued, "I turned to go back inside. That's when I thought I heard someone moving around in there."

Reed took in every word of her account. *Every word*. But he also heard the accent. Definitely not a Texas drawl. He was thinking East Coast and would find out more about that later. For now, he might have an intruder on his hands. An intruder who was possibly inside with a cabin full of potential evidence that could clear Shane's name. Or maybe it was the cabin's owner, Jonah Becker, though Reed had warned the rancher to stay far away from the place.

With his gun still aimed, Reed stepped out a few inches from the cover of the tree. "This is Sheriff Hardin," he called out. "If anyone's in there, get the hell out here now."

Beside him, Livvy huffed. "You think that's wise, to stand out in the open like that?"

He took the time to toss her a scowl. "Maybe it'd be a dumb idea in Boston, but here in Comanche Creek, if there's an intruder, it's likely to be someone who knows to do as I say."

He hoped.

"Not Boston," she snarled. "New York."

He gave her a flat look to let her know that didn't make

things better. A Texas Ranger should damn well be born and raised in Texas. And she shouldn't wear high-heeled boots.

Or perfume that reminded him she was a woman.

Reed knew that was petty, but with four murders on his hands, he wasn't exactly in a generous mood. He extended that non-generous mood to anyone who might be inside that cabin.

"Get out here!" he shouted. And by God, it better happen now.

Nothing. Well, nothing except Livvy's spurting breath and angry mumbles.

"Just because the person doesn't answer you, it doesn't mean the place is empty," she pointed out.

Yeah. And that meant he might have a huge problem. He didn't want the crime scene compromised, and he didn't want to shoot anyone. *Yet.*

"How long were Deputy Spears and you out there casting footprints?" he asked.

"A half hour. And before that we were looking around in the woods."

That explained how her footprints had gotten on the trail. The castings and the woods search also would have given someone plenty of time to get inside. "I'm guessing Deputy Spears unlocked the cabin for you?"

The sergeant shook her head. "It wasn't necessary. Someone had broken the lock on a side window, apparently crawled in and then opened the front door from the inside."

Reed cursed. "And you didn't see that person when you went in?"

Another head shake that sent her ponytail swishing. "The place was empty when I first arrived. I checked every inch," she added, cutting off his next question: *Was she sure about that?*

So, he had possibly two intruders. Great. Dealing with intruders wasn't on his to-do list today.

Now, he cursed himself. He should have camped out here, but he hadn't exactly had the manpower to do that with just him and two deputies, including the one behind bars. He'd had to process Shane's arrest and interrogate him. He had been careful. He'd done everything by the book so no one could accuse him of tampering with anything that would ultimately clear Shane's name. Kirby Spears had guarded the place until around midnight, but then Reed and he had had to respond to an armed robbery at the convenience store near the interstate.

Lately, life in Comanche Creek had been far from peaceful and friendly—even though that was what it said on the welcome sign at the edge of the city limits. Before the spring, it'd been nearly a decade since there'd been a murder. Now, there'd been four.

Four!

And because some of those bodies had been dumped on Native American burial ground, the whole town felt as if it were sitting on a powder keg. With the previous murder investigations and the latest one, Reed was operating on a one-hour nap, too much coffee and a shorter fuse than usual.

He glanced around. "How'd you get up here?" he asked the sergeant. "Because I didn't see a vehicle."

"I parked at the bottom of the hill just off the county road. I wanted to get a good look at the exterior of the crime scene before I went inside." She glanced around as well. "How'd you get up here?" she asked him.

"I parked on the back side of the hill." And for the same reason. Of course, that didn't mean they were going to see eye-to-eye on anything else. Reed was betting this would get ugly fast.

"Reed?" someone called out, the sound coming from the cabin.

Reed cursed some more because he recognized that voice. He lowered his gun, huffed and strolled toward the front door. It swung open just as Reed stepped onto the porch, and he came face-to-face with his boss, Mayor Woody Sadler. His friend. His mentor. As close to a father as Reed had ever had since his own dad had died when Reed was seven years old.

But Woody shouldn't have been within a mile of the place.

Surrogate fatherhood would earn Woody a little more respect than Reed would give others, but even Woody wasn't going to escape a good chewing-out. And maybe even more.

"What are you doing here?" Livvy demanded, taking the words right out of Reed's mouth. Unlike Reed, she didn't lower her gun. She pointed the Blackwater right at Woody.

Woody eased off his white Stetson, and the rattler tail attached to the band gave a familiar hollow jangle. He nodded a friendly greeting.

He didn't get anything friendly in return.

"This is Woody Sadler. The mayor of Comanche Creek," Reed said, making introductions. "And this is Sergeant Livvy Hutton. A Texas Ranger from New York."

Woody's tired gray eyes widened. Then narrowed, making the corners of his eyes wrinkle even more than they already were. Obviously he wasn't able to hold back a petty reaction either. "New York?"

"Spare me the jokes. I was born in a small town near Dallas. Raised in upstate New York." As if she'd declared war on it, Livvy shoved her gun back into her shoulder holster and barreled up the steps. "And regardless of where I'm from, this is my crime scene, and you were trespassing," she declared to

Woody and then fired a glance at Reed to declare it to him as well.

"I didn't touch anything," Woody insisted.

Livvy obviously didn't take his word for it. She bolted past Woody, grabbed her equipment bag from the porch and went inside.

"I swear," Woody added to Reed. "I didn't touch a thing."

Reed studied Woody's body language. The stiff shoulders. The sweat popping out above his top lip. Both surefire signs that the man was uncomfortable about something. "You're certain about that?"

"I'm damn certain." The body language changed. No more nerves, just a defensive stare that made Reed feel like a kid again. Still, that didn't stop Reed from doing his job.

"Then why didn't you answer when I called out?" Reed asked. "And why'd you break the lock on the window and go in there?"

"I didn't hear you calling out, that's why, and I didn't break any lock. The door was wide open when I got here about fifteen minutes ago." There was another shift in body language. Woody shook his head and wearily ran his hand through his thinning salt-and-pepper hair. "I just had to see for myself. I figured there'd be something obvious. Something that'd prove that Shane didn't do this."

Reed blew out a long breath. "I know. I want to prove Shane's innocence, too, but this isn't the way to go about doing it. If there's proof and the New York Ranger finds it, she could say you planted it there."

Woody went still. Then, he cursed. "I wouldn't do that."

"I believe you. But Sergeant Olivia Hutton doesn't know you from Adam."

Woody's gaze met his. "She's gunning for Shane?"

Probably. For Shane and anyone who thought he was innocent. But Reed kept that to himself. "Best to let me handle this," he insisted. "I'll talk to you when I'm back in town. Oh, and see about hiring me a temporary deputy or two."

Woody bobbed his head, slid back on his Stetson and ambled off the porch and down the hill, where he'd likely parked. Reed waited until he was sure the mayor was on his way before he took another deep breath and went inside.

He only made it two steps.

Livvy threw open the door. "Where's the mayor?" she demanded.

"Gone." Reed hitched his thumb toward the downside of the hill. "Why?"

Her hands went on her hips, and those ice-blue eyes turned fiery hot. "Because he stole some evidence, that's why, and I intend to arrest him."

TWO

LIVVY was in full stride across the yard when the sheriff caught up with her, latched on to her arm, whirled her around and brought her to an abrupt halt.

"I'm arresting him," she repeated and tried to throw off his grip.

She would probably have had better luck wrestling a longhorn to the ground. Despite Sheriff Reed Hardin's lanky build, the man was strong. And angry. That anger was stamped on his tanned face and in his crisp green eyes.

"I don't care if Woody Sadler is your friend." She tried again to get away from the sheriff's clamped hand. "He can't waltz in here and steal evidence that might be pertinent to a murder investigation."

"Just hold on." He pulled out his cell phone from his well-worn Wranglers, scrolled through some numbers and hit the call button. "Woody," he said when the mayor apparently answered, "you need to get back up here to the cabin right now. We might have a problem."

"Might?" Livvy snarled when Sheriff Hardin ended the call. "Oh, we *definitely* have a problem. Tampering with a crime scene is a third-degree felony."

The sheriff dismissed that with a headshake. "Woody's the mayor, along with being a law-abiding citizen. He didn't tamper with anything. You said yourself that someone had broken the lock, and Woody didn't do that."

"Well, he obviously isn't so law-abiding because he walked past crime-scene tape and entered without permission or reason."

"He had reason," Reed mumbled. "He's worried about Shane. And sometimes worried people do dumb things." He looked down at the chokehold he had on her arm, mumbled something indistinguishable, and his grip melted away. "What exactly is missing?"

"A cell phone." Livvy tried to go after the trespassing mayor again, but Reed stepped in front of her. Worse, her forward momentum sent her slamming right against his chest. Specifically, her breasts against his chest. The man was certainly solid. There were lots of corded muscles in his chest and abs.

Both of them cursed this time.

And Livvy shook her head. She shouldn't be noticing anything that intimate about a man whom she would likely end up at odds with. She shouldn't be noticing his looks, either. Those eyes. The desperado stubble on his strong square jaw and the tousled coffee-brown hair that made him look as if he'd just crawled out of bed.

Or off a poster for a Texas cowboy-sheriff.

It was crystal-clear that he didn't want her anywhere near the crime scene or his town. Tough. Livvy had been given a job to do, and she *never* walked away from the job.

Sherriff Hardin would soon learn that about her.

By God, she hadn't fought her way into the Ranger organization to be stonewalled by some local yokels who believed one of their own could do no wrong.

"What cell phone?" Reed asked.

Because the adrenaline and anger had caused her breath and mind to race, it took her a moment to answer. First, she glanced at the road and saw the mayor inching his way back up toward them. "One I found in the fireplace when I was going through the front room. You no doubt missed it in the initial search because the ashes were covering it completely. The only reason I found it is because I ran a metal detector over the place to search for any spent shell casings. Then, I photographed it, bagged it and put it on the table. It's missing."

His jaw muscles stirred. "It's Marcie's phone?"

"I don't know. I showed it to Deputy Spears, and he said he didn't think it was Shane's. That means it could be Marcie's."

"Or the killer's."

She was certain her jaw muscles stirred, too. "Need I remind you that you found Deputy Shane Tolbert standing over Marcie's body, and he had a gun in his hand? Marcie was his estranged lover. I hate to state the obvious, but all the initial evidence indicates that Shane *is* the killer."

Livvy instantly regretted spouting that verdict. It wasn't her job to get a conviction or jump to conclusions. She was there to gather evidence and find the truth, and she didn't want anything, including her anger, to get in the way.

"Shane said he didn't kill her," Reed explained. His voice was calm enough, but not his eyes. Everything else about him was unruffled except for those intense green eyes. They were warrior eyes. "He said Marcie called him and asked him to meet her at the cabin. The moment he stepped inside, someone hit him over the head, and he fell on the floor. When he came to, Marcie was dead and someone had put a gun in his hand."

Yes, she'd already heard the summary of Shane's statement from Deputy Kirby Spears. Livvy intended to study the inter-rogation carefully, especially since Reed had been the one to question the suspect.

Talk about a conflict of interest.

Still, in a small town like Comanche Creek, Reed probably hadn't had an alternative, especially since the on-scene Ranger, Lieutenant Colter, had been called back to the office. If Reed hadn't questioned Shane, then it would have been left to his junior deputy, Kirby, who was greener than the Hill Country's spring foliage.

The mayor finally made his way toward them and stopped a few feet away. "What's wrong?"

"Where's the cell phone that I'd bagged and tagged?" Livvy asked, not waiting for Reed to respond.

Woody Sadler first looked at Reed. Then, her. "I have no idea. I didn't take it."

"Then you won't mind proving that to me. Show me your pockets."

Woody hesitated, until Reed gave him a nod. It wasn't exactly a cooperative nod, either, and the accompanying grumble had a get-this-over-with tone to it.

The mayor pulled out a wallet from the back pocket of his jeans and a handkerchief and keys from the front ones. No cell phone, but that didn't mean he hadn't taken it. The man had had at least ten minutes to discard it along the way up or down the hill to his vehicle.

"Taking the cell won't help your friend's cause," she pointed out. "I already phoned in the number, and it'll be traced."

Woody lifted his shoulder. "Good. Because maybe what you learn about that phone will get Shane out of jail. He didn't kill Marcie."

Reed stared at her. "Can the mayor go now, or do you intend to strip-search him?"

Livvy ignored that swipe and glanced down at Woody's snakeskin boots. "You wear about a size eleven." She turned her attention to Reed. "And so do you. That looks to be about the size of the footprints that I took casts of over in the brush."

"So?" Woody challenged.

"So, the location of those prints means that someone could have waited there for Marcie to arrive. They could be the footprints of the killer. Or the killer's accomplice if he had one. Sheriff Hardin would have had reason to be out here, but what about you? Before this morning, were you here at the cabin in the past forty-eight hours?"

"No." The mayor's answer was quick and confident.

Livvy didn't intend to take his word for it.

"You can go now," Reed told the mayor.

Woody slid his hat back on, tossed her a glare and delivered his parting shot from over his shoulder as he walked away. "You might do to remember that Reed is the law in Comanche Creek."

Livvy could have reminded him that she was there on orders from the governor, but instead she took out her binoculars from her field bag and watched Woody's exit. If he stopped to pick up a discarded cell phone, she would arrest him on the spot.

"He didn't take that phone," Reed insisted.

"Then who did?"

"The real killer. He could have done it while Kirby and you were casting the footprints."

"The real killer," she repeated. "And exactly who would that be?"

"Someone that Marcie got involved with in the past two years when she was missing and presumed dead."

Livvy couldn't discount that. After all, Marcie had faked her own death so she wouldn't have to testify against a powerful local rancher who'd been accused of bribing officials in order to purchase land that the Comanche community considered their own. The rancher, Jonah Becker, who also owned this cabin, could have silenced Marcie when she returned from the grave.

Or maybe the killer was someone who'd been furious that Marcie hadn't gone through with her testimony two years ago. There were several people who could have wanted the woman dead, but Shane was the one who'd been found standing over her body.

"See? He didn't take the cell phone," Reed grumbled when the mayor didn't stop along the path to retrieve anything he might have discarded. The mayor got into a shiny fire-engine-red gas-guzzler of a truck and sped away, the massive tires kicking up a spray of mud and gravel.

"He could be planning to come back for it later," Livvy commented. But probably not. He would have known that she would search the area.

"Instead of focusing on Woody Sadler," Reed continued, "how about taking a look at the evidence inside the cabin? Because naming Shane as the primary suspect just doesn't add up."

Ah, she'd wondered how long it would take to get to this subject. "How do you figure that?"

"For one thing, I swabbed Shane's hands, and there was no

gunshot residue. Plus, this case might be bigger than just Shane and Marcie. You might not have heard, but a few days ago there were some other bodies that turned up at the Comanche burial grounds."

"I heard," she said. "I also heard their eyes were sealed with red paint and ochre clay. In other words, a Native American ritual. There's nothing Native American or ritualistic about this murder."

Still, that didn't mean the deaths weren't connected. It just meant she didn't see an immediate link. The only thing that was glaring right now was Deputy Shane Tolbert's involvement in this and his sheriff's need to defend him.

Livvy started the walk down the hill to look for that missing phone. Thankfully, it was silver and should stand out among the foliage. And then she remembered the note in her pocket with the cell number on it. She took out her own phone and punched in the numbers to call the cell so it would ring.

She heard nothing.

Just in case it was buried beneath debris or something, she continued down the hill, listening for it.

Reed followed her, of course.

Livvy would have preferred to do this search alone because the sheriff was turning out to be more than a nuisance. He was a distraction. Livvy blamed that on his too-good looks and her stupid fantasies about cowboys. She'd obviously watched too many Westerns growing up, and she reminded herself that in almost all cases the fantasy was much hotter than the reality.

She glanced at Reed again and mentally added *maybe not in this case.*

In those great-fitting jeans and equally great-fitting blue shirt, he certainly looked as if he could compete with a fantasy or two.

When she felt her cheeks flush, Livvy quickly got her mind on something else—the job. It was obvious that the missing cell wasn't ringing so she ended the call and put her own cell back in her pocket. Instead of listening for the phone, she'd just have to hope that the mayor had turned it off but still tossed it in a place where she could spot it.

"The mayor's not guilty," Reed tried again. "And neither is Shane."

She made a sound of disagreement. "Maybe there was no GSR on his hands because Shane wore gloves when he shot her," she pointed out. Though Livvy was certain Reed had already considered that.

"There were no gloves found at the scene."

She had an answer for that as well. "He could have discarded them and then hit himself over the head to make it look as if he'd been set up."

"Then he would have had to change his clothes, too, because there was no GSR on his shirt, jeans, belt, watch, badge, holster or boots."

"You tested all those items for gunshot residue?"

"Yeah, I did," he snapped. "This might be a small town, Sergeant Hutton, but we're not idiots. Shane and I have both taken workshops on crime-scene processing, and we keep GSR test kits in the office."

It sounded as if Sheriff Hardin had been thorough, but she would reserve judgment on whether he'd learned enough in those workshops.

"But Shane was holding the murder weapon, right?" Livvy clarified.

"Appears to have been, but it wasn't his gun. He says he has no idea who it belongs to. The bullet taken from Marcie's body is on the way to the lab for comparison, and we're still searching the databases to try to figure out the owner of the gun."

Good. She'd call soon and press for those results and the plaster castings of the footprints. Because the sooner she finished this crime scene, the sooner she could get out of here and head back to Austin. She didn't mind small towns, had even grown up in one, but this small town—and its sheriff—could soon get to her.

Livvy continued to visually comb the right side of the path, and when they got to the bottom, they started back up while she examined the opposite side. There was no sign of a silver phone.

Mercy.

She didn't want to explain to her boss how she'd let possible crucial evidence disappear from a crime scene that she was working. She had to find that phone or else pray the cell records could be accessed.

"What about the blood spatter in the cabin?" Reed asked, grabbing her attention again.

"I'm not finished processing the scene yet." In fact, she'd barely started though she had already spent nearly an hour inside. She had hours more, maybe days, of work ahead of her. Those footprint castings had taken priority because they could have been erased with just a light rain. "But in my cursory check, I didn't see any spatter, only the blood pool on the floor. Since Marcie was shot at point-blank range, that doesn't surprise me. Why? Did you find blood spatter?"

"No. But if Shane's account is true about someone clubbing him over the back of the head, then there might be some. He already had a head injury, and it had been aggravated with what looked like a second blow. But the wood's dark-colored, and I didn't want to spray the place with Luminol since I read it can sometimes alter small droplets. Judging from the wound on Shane's head, we'd be looking for a very small amount because the gash was only about an inch across."

She glanced at him and hoped she didn't look too surprised. Most non-CSI-trained authorities would have hosed down the place with Luminol, the chemical to detect the presence of biological fluids, and would have indeed compromised the pattern by causing the blood to run. That in turn, could compromise critical evidence.

"What?" he asked.

Livvy walked ahead of him, up the steps and onto the porch and went inside the cabin. "Nothing."

"Something," Reed corrected, following her. He shut the door and turned on the overhead lights. "You'd dismissed me as just a small-town sheriff."

"No." She shrugged. "Okay, maybe. Sorry."

"Don't be. I dismissed you, too."

Since her back was to him, she smiled. For a moment. "Still do?"

"Not because of your skill. You seem to know what you're doing. But I'm concerned you won't do everything possible to clear Shane's name."

"And I'm concerned you'll do anything to clear it."

He made a sound of agreement that rumbled deep in his throat. "I can live with a stalemate if I know you'll be objective."

The man certainly did know how to make her feel guilty. And defensive. "The evidence is objective, and my interpretation of it will be, too. Don't worry. I'll check for that blood spatter in just a minute."

Riled now about the nerve he'd hit, she grabbed a folder from her equipment bag. "First though, I'd like to know if it wasn't Woody Sadler, then who might have compromised the crime scene and stolen the phone." She slapped the folder on the dining table and opened it. Inside were short bios of persons of any possible interest in this case.

Reed's bio was there on top, and Livvy had already studied it.

He was thirty-two, had never been married and had been the sheriff of Comanche Creek for eight years. Before that, he'd been a deputy. His father, also sheriff, had been killed in the line of duty when Reed was seven. Reed's mother had fallen apart after her husband's murder and had spent the rest of her short life in and out of mental institutions before committing suicide. And the man who'd raised Reed after that was none other than the mayor, Woody Sadler.

She could be objective about the evidence, but she seriously doubted that Reed could ever be impartial about the man who'd raised him.

Livvy moved Reed's bio aside. The mayor's. And Shane's. "Who would be bold or stupid enough to walk into this cabin and take a phone with me and your deputy only yards away?"

Reed thumbed through the pages, extracted one and handed it to her. "Jonah Becker. He's the rancher Marcie was supposed to testify against. He probably wouldn't have done this himself, but he could have hired someone if he thought that phone would link him in any way to Marcie."

Yes. Jonah Becker was a possibility. Reed added the bio for Jonah's son. And Jerry Collier, the man who ran the Comanche

Creek Land Office. Then Billy Whitley, a city official. The final bio that Reed included was for Shane's father, Ben Tolbert. He was another strong possibility since he might want to protect his son.

"I'll question all of them," Reed promised.

"And I'll be there when you do," Livvy added. She heard the irritation in his under-the-breath grumble, but she ignored him, took the handheld UV lamp from her bag and put on a pair of monochromatic glasses.

"Shane said he was here when he was hit." Reed pointed to the area in front of the fireplace. It was only about three feet from where Marcie's body had been discovered.

Livvy walked closer, her heels echoing on the hardwood floor. The sound caused Reed to eye her boots, and again she saw some questions about her choice of footwear.

"They're more comfortable than they look," she mumbled.

"They'd have to be," he mumbled back.

Though comfort wasn't exactly the reason she was wearing them. She'd just returned from a trip to visit her father, and one of her suitcases—the one that contained her favorite work boots—had been lost. There'd been no time to replace them because she had been home less than an hour when she'd gotten the call to get to Comanche Creek ASAP.

"I do own real boots," Livvy commented and wondered why she felt the need to defend herself.

With Reed's attention nailed to her, she lifted the lamp and immediately spotted the spatter on the dark wood. Without the light, it wasn't even detectable. There wasn't much, less than a dozen tiny drops, but it was consistent with a high-velocity impact.

"Shane's about my height," Reed continued. And he stood

in the position that would have been the most likely spot to have produced that pattern.

It lined up.

Well, the droplets did anyway. She still had some doubts about Shane's story.

Livvy took her camera, slipped on a monochromatic lens and photographed the spatter. "Your deputy could have hit himself in the head. Not hard enough for him to lose consciousness. Just enough to give us the cast-off pattern we see here. Then, he could have hidden whatever he used to club himself."

Reed stared at her. "Or he could be telling the truth. If he is, that means we have a killer walking around scot-free."

Yes, and Livvy wasn't immune to the impact of that. It scratched away at old wounds, and even though she'd only been a Ranger for eighteen months, that was more than enough time for her to have learned that her baggage and old wounds couldn't be part of her job. She couldn't go back twenty years and right an old wrong.

Though she kept trying.

Livvy met Reed's gaze. It wasn't hard to do since he was still staring holes in her. "You really believe your deputy is incapable of killing his ex-lover?"

She expected an immediate answer. A *damn right* or some other manly affirmation. But Reed paused. Or rather he hesitated. His hands went to his hips, and he tipped his eyes to the ceiling.

"What?" Livvy insisted.

Reed shook his head, and for a moment she didn't think he would answer. "Shane and Marcie had a stormy relationship. I won't deny that. And since you'll find this out anyway, I had to suspend him once for excessive force when he was making an arrest during a domestic dispute. Still…I can't believe he'd commit a premeditated murder and set himself up."

Yes, that was a big question mark in her mind. If Shane had enough forensic training to set up someone, then why hadn't he chosen anyone but himself? That meant she was either dealing with an innocent man or someone who was very clever, and therefore very dangerous.

Because she was in such deep thought, Livvy jumped when a sound shot through the room. But it wasn't a threat. It was Reed's cell phone.

"Kirby," he said when he answered it.

That got her attention. Kirby Spears was the young deputy who'd assisted her on the scene and had carried the footprint castings back to the sheriff's office so a Ranger courier could pick them up and take them to the crime lab in Austin.

While she took a sample of one of the spatter droplets, Livvy listened to the conversation. Or rather that was what she tried to do. Hard to figure out what was going on with Reed's monosyllablic responses. However, his jaw muscles stirred again, and she thought she detected some frustration in those already intense eyes.

She bagged the blood-spatter sample, labeled it and put it in her equipment bag.

"Anything wrong?" Livvy asked the moment Reed ended the call.

"Maybe. While he was in town and running the investigating, Lieutenant Wyatt Colter made notes about the shoe sizes of the folks who live around here. He left the info at the station."

That didn't surprise Livvy. Lieutnenant Colter was a thorough man. "And?"

"Kirby compared the size of the castings, and it looks as if three people could be a match. Of course, the prints could also have also been made by someone Marcie met during her two years on the run. The person might not even be from Comanche Creek."

Livvy couldn't help it. She huffed. "Other than you, who are two possible matches?"

"Jerry Collier, the head of the land office. He was also Marcie's former boss."

She had his bio, and it was one of the ones that Reed had picked from the file as a person who might be prone to breaking into the cabin. Later, she'd look into his possible motive for stealing a phone. "And the other potential match?"

Reed's jaw muscles did more than stir. They went iron-hard. "The mayor, Woody Sadler."

"Of course."

She groaned because she shouldn't have allowed Reed to stop her from arresting him. Or at least thoroughly searching him. Mayor Woody Sadler could have hidden that phone somewhere on his body and literally walked away with crucial evidence. Lost evidence that would get her butt in very hot water with her boss.

"I'll talk to him," Reed said.

"No. *I'll* talk to him." And this time she didn't intend to treat him like a mayor but a murder suspect.

In Reed's eyes, she saw the argument they were about to have. Livvy was ready to launch into the inevitable disagreement when she heard another sound. Not a cell phone this time.

Something crashed hard and loud against the cabin door.

THREE

REED drew his Smith and Wesson. Beside him, Livvy tossed the
UV lamp and her glasses onto the sofa so she could do the same.
Reed had already had his fill of unexpected guests today, and this
sure as hell better not be somebody else trying to "help" Shane.

"Anyone out there?" Reed called out.

Nothing.

Since it was possible their visitor was Marcie's killer who'd
returned to the scene of the crime, Reed approached the door
with caution, and he kept away from the windows so he
wouldn't be ambushed. He tried to put himself between Livvy
and the door. It was an automatic response, one he would have
done for anyone. However, she apparently didn't appreciate it
because she maneuvered herself to his side again.

Reed reached for the doorknob, but stopped.

"Smoke?" he said under his breath. A moment later, he confirmed that was exactly what it was. If there was a fire out there,
he didn't want to open the door and have the flames burst at them.

There was another crashing sound. This time it came from the rear of the cabin. Livvy turned and aimed her gun in that direction. Reed kept his attention on the front of the place.

Hell.

What was happening? Was someone trying to break in?

Or worse. Was someone trying to kill them?

In case it was the *or worse,* Reed knew he couldn't wait any longer. He peered out from the side of the window.

And saw something he didn't want to see.

"Fire!" he relayed to Livvy.

She raced to the back door of the cabin. "There's a fire here, too."

A dozen scenarios went through his mind, none of them good. He grabbed his phone and pressed the emergency number for the fire department.

"See anyone out there?" Reed asked, just as soon as he requested assistance.

"No. Do you?"

"No one," Reed confirmed. "Just smoke." And lots of it. In fact, there was already so much black billowy smoke that Reed couldn't be sure there was indeed a fire to go along with it. Still, he couldn't risk staying put. "We have to get out of here now."

Livvy took that as gospel because she hurried to the table, grabbed the files and the other evidence she'd gathered and shoved all of it and her other supplies into her equipment bag. She hoisted the bag over her shoulder, freeing her hand so she could use her gun. Unfortunately, it was necessary because Reed might need her as backup.

"Watch the doors," he insisted.

Not that anyone was likely to come through them with the

smoke and possible fires, but he couldn't take that chance. They were literally under siege right now and anything was possible. The smoke was already pouring through the windows and doors, and it wouldn't be long before the cabin was completely engulfed.

The cabin wasn't big by anyone's standards. There was a basic living, eating and cooking area in the main room. One bedroom and one tiny bath were on the other side of the cabin. There was no window in the bathroom so he went to the lone one in the bedroom. He looked out, trying to stay out of any potential kill zone for a gunman, and he saw there was no sign of fire here. Thank God. Plus, it was only a few yards from a cluster of trees Livvy and he could use for cover.

"We can get out this way," Reed shouted. The smoke was thicker now. Too thick. And it cut his breath. It must have done the same for Livvy because he heard her cough.

He unlocked the window, shoved it up and pushed out the screen. The fresh air helped him catch his breath, but he knew the outside of the cabin could be just as dangerous as the inside.

"Anyone out there?" Livvy asked.

"I don't see anyone, but be ready just in case."

The person who'd thrown the accelerant or whatever might have used it as a ruse to draw them out. It was entirely possible that someone would try to kill them the moment they climbed out. Still, there was no choice here. Even though he'd already called the fire department, it would take them twenty minutes or more to respond to this remote area.

If they stayed put, Livvy and he could be dead by then.

"I'll go first," he instructed. He took her equipment bag and hooked it over his shoulder. That would free her up to run faster. "Cover me while I get to those trees."

She nodded. Coughed. She was pale, Reed noticed, but she wasn't panicking. Good. Because they both needed a clear head for this.

Reed didn't waste any more time. With his gun as aimed and ready as it could be, he hoisted himself over the sill and climbed out. He started running the second his feet touched the ground.

"Now," he told Livvy. He dropped the equipment bag and took cover behind the trees. Aimed. And tried to spot a potential gunman who might be on the verge of ambushing them.

Livvy snaked her body through the window and raced toward him. Despite the short distance, she was breathing hard by the time she reached him. She turned, putting her back to his. Good move, because this way they could cover most of the potential angles for an attack.

But Reed still didn't see anyone.

He blamed that on the smoke. It was a thick cloud around the cabin now. There were fires, both on the front porch and the back, and scattered around the fires were chunks of what appeared to be broken glass. The flames weren't high yet, but it wouldn't take them long to eat their way through the all-wood structure. And any potential evidence inside would be destroyed right along with it. If this arsonist was out to help Shane, then he was sadly mistaken.

Of course, the other possibility was that the real killer had done this.

It would be the perfect way to erase any traces of himself. Well, almost any traces. There was some potential evidence in Livvy's equipment bag. Maybe the person responsible wouldn't try to come after it.

But he rethought that.

A showdown would bring this fire-setting bozo out into the open, and Reed would be able to deal with him.

"Will the fire department make it in time to save the cabin?" Livvy asked between short bursts of air.

"No." And as proof of that, the flames shots up, engulfing the front door and swooshing their way to the cedar-shake roof. The place would soon be nothing but cinders and ash.

Reed was about to tell her that they'd have to stay put and watch the place burn since there was no outside hose to even attempt to put a dent in the flames. But he felt Livvy tense. It wasn't hard to feel because her back was right against his.

"What's wrong?" Reed whispered.

"I think I see someone."

Reed shifted and followed her gaze. She was looking in the direction of the county road, which was just down the hill from the cabin. Specifically, she was focused on the path that Woody had taken earlier. He didn't see anyone on the path or road, so he tried to pick through the woods and the underbrush to see what had alerted Livvy.

Still nothing.

"Look by my SUV," she instructed.

The vehicle was white and barely visible from his angle so Reed repositioned himself and looked down the slope. At first, nothing.

Then, something.

There was a flash of movement at the rear of her vehicle, but with just a glimpse he couldn't tell if it was animal or human.

"There's evidence in the SUV," she said. Her breathing was more level now, but that statement was loaded with fear and tension. "I'd photographed the cabin and exterior with a highly sensitive digital camera. Both it and the photo memory card are inside in a climate controlled case, along with some possible hair and fibers that I gathered from the sofa with a tape swatch."

Oh, hell. All those items could be critical to this investigation.

"The SUV's locked," she added.

For all the good that'd do. After all, the person out there had been gutsy enough to throw Molotov cocktails at the cabin with both Reed and a Texas Ranger inside, and he could have broken the lock on the SUV or bashed in a window.

Livvy grabbed her equipment bag from the ground and repositioned her gun. Reed knew what she had in mind, and he couldn't stop her from going to her vehicle to check on the evidence. But what he could do was assist.

"Stay close to the treeline," he instructed.

He stepped to her side so that she would be semi-sheltered from the open path. Another automatic response. But this time, Livvy didn't object. However, what she did do was move a lot faster than he'd anticipated.

Reed kept up with her while he tried to keep an eye on their surroundings and her SUV. None of the doors or windows appeared to be open, but he wouldn't be surprised if it'd been burglarized. Obviously, someone didn't want them to process that evidence.

He saw more movement near the SUV. A shadow, maybe. Or maybe someone lurking just on the other side near the rear bumper. Behind them, the fire continued to crackle and burn, and there was a crash when the roof of the cabin gave way and plummeted to the ground. Sparks and ashes scattered everywhere, some of them making their way to Livvy and him.

Livvy didn't stop. She didn't look back. But when Reed saw more movement, he latched on to her arm and pulled her behind an oak. This was definitely a situation where it would do no good to try to sneak up on the perp because the perp obviously was better positioned. Despite the cover of the trees, Livvy and he were in a vulnerable situation.

"This is Sheriff Hardin," he called out. "Get your hands in the air so I can see them."

He hadn't expected the person to blindly obey. And he didn't. Reed caught a glimpse of someone wearing a dark blue baseball cap.

Reed shifted his gun. Took aim—just as there was a crashing sound, followed by a flash of light. Someone had broken the SUV window and thrown another Molotov cocktail into the vehicle.

"He set the SUV on fire," Livvy said, bolting out from cover.

Reed pulled her right back. "He might have a gun." Except there was no *might* in this. The guy was probably armed and dangerous, and he couldn't have Livvy running right into an ambush.

"But the evidence…" she protested.

Yeah. That was a huge loss. Like Livvy, his instincts were to race down there and try to save what he could, but to do that might be suicide.

"He could want you dead," Reed warned.

That stopped Livvy from struggling. "Because of the evidence I gathered from the cabin?"

Reed nodded and waited for the rest of that to sink in. It didn't take long.

"Shane couldn't have done this," she concluded.

"No." Reed kept watch on the vehicle and the area in case the attacker doubled back toward them or tried to escape.

"But someone who wanted to exonerate him could have," Livvy added.

Reed nodded again. "That means the fire starter must have thought you saw or found something in the cabin that would be crucial evidence."

That also meant Livvy was in danger.

Reed cursed. This was turning into a tangled mess, and he already had too much to do without adding protecting Livvy to the list.

In the distance Reed heard the siren from the fire department. Soon, they'd be there. He glanced at the cabin. Then at Livvy's SUV. There wouldn't be much to save, but if he could catch the person responsible he might get enough answers to make up for the evidence they'd lost.

More movement. Reed spotted the baseball cap again. The guy was crouched down, and the cap created a shadow that hid his face. He couldn't even tell if it was a man or a woman. But whoever it was, the person was getting away.

"Stay put," Reed told Livvy.

Now it was her turn to catch onto his arm. "Remember that part about him having a gun."

Reed remembered, but he had to try to find out who was behind this.

"Back me up," he told her. That was to get her to stay put, but the other reason was he didn't want this cap-wearing guy to sneak up on him. Reed wouldn't be able to hear footsteps or much else with the roar of the fire and the approaching siren.

Keeping low as well, Reed stepped out from the meager cover of the oak. He kept his gun ready and aimed, and he started to run.

So did the other guy.

Using the smoke as cover, the culprit darted through the woods on the other side of the SUV and raced through the maze of trees. If Reed didn't catch up with him soon, it'd be too late. He ran down the hill, cursing the uneven clay-mix dirt that was slick in spots. Somehow, he made it to the bottom without falling and breaking his neck.

Reed didn't waste any time trying to save the SUV. The inside was already engulfed in flames. Instead, he sprinted past it, but Reed only made it a few steps before there was another sound.

Behind him, the SUV exploded.

He dodged the fiery debris falling all around him and sprinted after the person who'd just come close to killing them.

FOUR

LIVVY dove to the ground and used the tree to shelter herself from the burning SUV parts that spewed through the air. She waited, listening, but it was impossible to hear anything, especially Reed. Beyond the black smoke cloud on the far side of what was left of her vehicle, she saw him sprint into the woods.

Since Reed might need backup, she got up, grabbed the equipment bag and went after him. Livvy kept to the trees that lined the path and then gave the flaming SUV a wide berth in case there was a secondary explosion. She'd barely cleared the debris when the fire engine screamed to a stop on the two-lane road.

"Sergeant Hutton," she said, identifying herself to the men who barreled from the engine. "Sheriff Hardin and I are in pursuit of a suspect."

Livvy hurried after Reed but was barely a minute into her trek when she saw Reed making his way back toward her. Not walking. Running.

"What's wrong?" she asked.

Reed drew in a hard breath. "I couldn't find him, and I was afraid he would double back and come after you."

Because the adrenaline was pumping through her and her heart was pounding in her ears, it took Livvy a moment to realize what he'd said. "I'm a Texas Ranger," she reminded him. "If he'd doubled back, I could have taken care of myself."

Reed tossed her a glance and started toward the fire department crew. "I didn't want him to shoot you and then steal the evidence bag," he clarified.

Oh. So, maybe it wasn't a me-Tarzan response after all. And once again, Livvy felt as if she'd been trumped when she was the one in charge.

By God, this was her case and her crime scene.

She followed Reed back to the chaos. The fire department already had their hose going, but there was nothing left to save. Worse, with everyone racing around the SUV and the cabin, it would be impossible to try to determine which footprints had been left by the perpetrator.

Reed stopped in front of a fifty-something Hispanic man, and they had a brief conversation that Livvy couldn't hear. A minute later, Reed rejoined her.

"Come on," he said. "We'll use my truck to take that evidence to my office."

Livvy looked around and realized there was nothing she could do here, so she followed Reed past the cabin to a back trail. It wasn't exactly a relaxing stroll because both Reed and she hurried and kept their weapons ready. With good reason, too. Someone had just destroyed crucial evidence, and that same someone might come after them. The woods were thick and ripe territory for an ambush.

Reed unlocked his black F-150 and they climbed in and sped

away. He immediately got on the phone to his deputy, and while Reed filled in Deputy Spears, Livvy knew she had to contact her boss, Lieutenant Wyatt Colter.

She grabbed her cell, took a deep breath and made the call. Since there was no way to soften it, she just spilled it and told him all about the burned cabin, her SUV and the destroyed evidence.

On the other end of the line, Lieutnenant Colter cursed. "You didn't have the evidence secured?"

"I did, in the locked SUV, but the perp set it on fire." She was thankful that she'd already stashed her personal items at the Bluebonnet Inn where she'd be staying so at least she would have a change of clothes and her toiletries. Of course, she would have gladly exchanged those items, along with every penny in her bank account, if she could get back that evidence.

More cursing from the lieutenant, and she heard him relay the information to someone else who was obviously in the room with him. Great. Now, everyone at the regional office would know about this debacle.

"Things are crazy here," Lieutenant Colter explained. "I'm tracking down those illegally sold Native American artifacts, and I'm at a critical point in negotiations. But I'll be out there by early afternoon."

"No!" Livvy couldn't get that out fast enough. "There's no need, and there's nothing you can do. I have everything under control."

The lieutenant's long hesitation let her know he wasn't buying that. "I'll talk with the captain and get back to you."

"I don't need reinforcements," she added, but Livvy was talking to herself because Lieutenant Colter had already hung up on her.

"Problem?" Reed asked the moment she ended the call.

"No," she lied.

He made a sound to indicate he knew it was a lie.

Since it was a whopper, Livvy tried to hurry past the subject. "After I get this evidence logged in and started, I'd like to question Shane about the murder."

Reed didn't answer right away. He had her wait several moments, making Livvy wish she'd made it sound more like an order and not a request.

"Shane will cooperate," Reed finally said. He paused again. "And while you're talking to him, I'll call your lieutenant and let him know this wasn't your fault."

"Don't." She stared at him as he drove onto the highway that led to town. "I don't need your help." Though she probably did. Still, Livvy wouldn't allow Reed to defend her when she was capable of doing it herself. "I'll call him in an hour or two and explain there's no need for him to be here."

And somehow, she would have to make him understand.

"This case seems personal to you," Reed commented. "Why? Did you know Marcie?"

"No." But he was right. This was personal. Murders always were. "My mother was murdered when I was six, and she was about the same age as Marcie. This brings back…memories."

And she had no idea why she'd just admitted that. Sheez. The chaos had caused her to go all chatty.

"Was the killer caught?" Reed asked.

Livvy groaned softly. She hadn't meant for this to turn into a conversation. "No. He escaped to Mexico and has never been found."

"That explains why you're wrapped so tight."

She blinked. Frowned. "Excuse me?"

"You think if you solve Marcie's murder, then in a small way, you'll get justice for your mom."

She was sure her mouth dropped open when she scowled at him. "What—did you take Psych 101 classes along with those forensic workshops?"

He shook his head. "Personal experience. My dad was shot and killed when I was a kid. Every case turns out to be about him." Reed lifted his shoulder. "Can't help it. It's just an old wound that can't be healed."

Yes.

Livvy totally understood that.

"That's why I jumped to defend Woody back there," Reed continued. "He raised me. He became the dad who was taken away from me." But then he paused. "That doesn't mean I can't be objective. I can be."

She wanted to grumble a *hmmmp* to let him know she had her doubts about that objectivity, but her doubts weren't as strong as they had been an hour earlier. Livvy blamed that on their escape from death together. That created a special camaraderie. So did their tragic pasts. For that matter so did this bizarre attraction she felt for him. All in all, it led to a union that she didn't want or need.

"Oh, man," Reed groaned.

Livvy looked ahead at the two-story white limestone building with a triple-arch front and reinforced glass doors. It was the sheriff's office, among other things. Livvy had learned from Deputy Spears that it also housed the jail and several municipal offices.

Right next to the sheriff's building was an identical structure for the mayor's office and courthouse. However, it wasn't the weathered facades of the buildings that had likely caused Reed's groan. As he brought the truck to a stop, he had his attention fastened to the two men and a Native American woman standing on the steps. Another attractive woman with long red hair was sitting in a car nearby.

"Trouble?" Livvy asked.

"Maybe. Not from the redhead. She's Jessie Becker, but her father's the one on the right. He's probably here to stir up some trouble."

Jonah was the owner of the cabin. And, as far as Livvy was concerned, he was a prime murder suspect. Even if he hadn't been the one to actually kill Marcie, he might have information about it.

Though she'd scoured Jonah's bio, this was Livvy's first look at the man, and he certainly lived up to his reputation of being intimating and hard-nosed. Jonah might have been wearing a traditional good-guy white cowboy hat, but the stare he gave her was all steel and ice.

"You let somebody burn down my cabin," Jonah accused the moment Reed and she stepped from the truck. "The fire chief just called. Said it was a total loss."

"We didn't exactly *let* it happen," Reed snarled. He stopped. Met Jonah eye-to-eye. "There was a phone stolen from the cabin before the place was set on fire. Know anything about that?"

Jonah's mouth tightened. "Now, you're accusing me of thievery from a place I own?"

"I'm asking, not accusing," Reed clarified, though from his tone, it could have been either. "But I want an answer."

The demand caused a standoff with the two men staring at each other. "I didn't take anything from the cabin," Jonah finally said, "because I haven't been out there. Last I heard, you'd roped off the place and said for everybody to stay away. So, I stayed away," he added with a touch of smugness.

If Reed believed him, he didn't acknowledge it.

"I'm Billy Whitley," the other man greeted Livvy, extending his hand to her. He tipped his head to the Native American woman beside him. "And this is my wife, Charla."

Livvy shifted her equipment bag and shook hands with both of them. "Sergeant Hutton."

Unlike Jonah, Billy wasn't wearing a cowboy hat, and the khaki-wearing man sported a smile that seemed surprisingly genuine. "Welcome to Comanche Creek, Sergeant Hutton."

"Yes, welcome," Charla repeated, though it wasn't as warm a greeting as her husband's had been. And she didn't just look at Livvy—the woman's intense coffee-brown eyes stared.

Livvy didn't offer her first name, as Billy had done to her. Yes, it was silly, but she wanted to hang on to every thread of authority she had left. After what'd just happened, that wasn't much, but somehow she had to establish that she was the one in charge here. That wasn't easy to do with Reed storming past Jonah and Billy.

And her.

That left her trailing along after him.

"I'm the county clerk here," Billy continued. "Charla is an administrative assistant for the mayor." All three followed into the building, too. "I handle the records and such, and if I can help you in any way, just let me know."

That *such* might become important to Livvy since Billy would be in charge of deeds, and the land that Jonah had bought might play into what was happening now. Of course, Livvy had a dozen other things to do before digging into what might have been an illegal land deal.

Jonah caught up with them and fell in step to her left. Since the entry hall was massive, at least fifteen feet wide, it wasn't hard for the four to walk side by side, especially with Reed ahead of them. "I'm not even gonna get an apology for my cabin?" Jonah complained.

"I'm sorry," Livvy mumbled, and she was sincere. Losing the cabin and the evidence inside was a hard blow to the case.

Reed turned into a room about midway down the hall, and he walked past a perky-looking auburn-haired receptionist who stood and then almost immediately sat back down to take an incoming call.

They walked by a room where Deputy Spears was on the phone as well, but he called out to her, "The castings are on the way to the lab. The courier just picked them up."

"Thanks," Livvy managed but didn't stop.

She continued to follow the fast-walking Reed into his office. Like the man, it was a bit of a surprise. His desk was neat, organized, and the slim computer monitor and equipment made it look more modern than Livvy had thought it would be. There was a huge calendar on the wall, and it was filled with appointments at precise times, measured not in hours but in quarter hours.

"You can put the equipment bag there," Reed instructed, pointing to a table pushed against one of the walls. There was also an evidence locker nearby. Good. She wanted to secure the few items she had left.

Reed snatched up the phone. "I need to call some of the other sheriffs in the area and have them send over deputies to scour the woods for anything the arsonist might have left behind. After that, I'll take you up to the jail so you can talk to Shane."

Reed proceeded to make that call, but he also shot a what-are-you-still-doing-here? glare at Billy, Charla and Jonah, who were hovering in the narrow doorway and watching Livvy's every move. Livvy didn't think it was her imagination that all three were extremely interested in what she had in the equipment bag. Still, Billy tipped two fingers to his forehead in a mock salute and Charla and he left.

Jonah didn't.

"So, did you come to town to arrest me for Marcie's murder?" Jonah asked her.

Livvy spared him a glance and plopped her bag onto the table. "Why, are you confessing to it?"

"Careful," Jonah warned, and his tone was so chilling that it prompted Livvy to look at him.

"I'm always careful. And thorough," she threatened back. She tried not to let her suspicions of this man grow. After all, they had a suspect in jail, but she wondered if Shane had acted alone.

Or if he'd acted at all.

It wouldn't be a pleasant task to challenge Shane's guilt or innocence because if she proved Shane hadn't murdered Marcie, then she would have to prove that someone else had. That was certain to rile a lot of people.

She remembered the uncomfortable stare that Charla Whitley had given her. And the way the mayor had reminded her of Reed's authority. She wasn't winning any Miss Congeniality contests—and probably wouldn't.

"Good day, Mr. Becker," Livvy said, dismissing Jonah, and she took out the bag with the sample from the blood spatter. If this was indeed Shane's blood, and if future analysis of the pattern indicated that it was real castoff from blunt force, then that would put some doubt in her mind.

Since Reed was still on the phone, Livvy secured her bag in the evidence locker, and with the blood sample clutched in her hand, she walked to the doorway. Jonah was still there, but she merely stepped around him and went to Deputy Spears's office. She shut the door so they'd have some privacy.

"I need this analyzed ASAP," she instructed. "It's possible that it's Shane's blood."

Kirby Spears nodded. "I can run it over to the coroner. He does a lot of this type of work for us, and we have Shane's DNA on file in the computer so we can compare the sample." He took the bag and put his initials on the chain of custody form.

Again, Livvy was surprised with the efficiency. "What about the murder weapon and the bullet?"

"The bullet's still being analyzed at the Ranger crime lab, and there's no match to the gun. We have the serial number, but so far, there's no info in the database about it."

Livvy made a mental note to call the crime lab, but first she wanted to visit Shane. Without Reed. Even though Reed had said he would be the one to take her, she didn't need or want his help during this particular interrogation. She knew how to question a suspect.

"Where's the jail?" she asked the deputy.

"Up the stairs, to the right."

Livvy thanked him and walked back into the hall. She halfway expected Jonah to be waiting there, but saw thankfully he had left. Since Reed was still on the phone, she made her way up the stairs to where she found a guard sitting at a desk. He wore a uniform from a civilian security agency, and he obviously knew who she was because he stood.

"Shane's this way," he commented and led her down the short hall flanked on each side with cells. All were empty except for the last one. There, she found the deputy lying on the military-style cot.

Livvy's first thought was that he didn't look like a killer. With his dark hair and piercing blue eyes, he looked more like a grad student. A troubled one, though.

"Sergeant Hutton," he said, slowly getting to his feet.

"Word travels fast," she mumbled.

The corner of his mouth lifted into a half smile that didn't quite make it to his eyes. "There aren't many secrets in Comanche Creek. Well, except for the secret of who murdered Marcie. I loved her." He shook his head. "I wouldn't have killed her."

"The evidence says differently."

He walked closer and curved his fingers around the thick metal bars. "But since I didn't do it, there must be evidence to prove that. Promise me that you'll dig for the truth. Don't let anyone, including Jonah, bully you."

She shrugged. "Why would Jonah want to bully me?"

"Because you're a woman. An outsider, at that. He won't respect your authority. For that matter, most won't, and that includes the mayor."

Well, Livvy would have to change their minds.

"What do you know about a cell phone that I found in the ashes of the fireplace?" she asked.

There was a flash of surprise in his eyes. Then, another headshake. "I don't know. Is it Marcie's?"

"Maybe. Any reason the mayor would steal the phone to try to help you out?"

"Woody? Not a chance. He might not care for outsiders like you, but he wouldn't break the law. Why? You think he had something to do with the fire at the cabin?"

Livvy jumped right on that. "How'd you know about it?"

"The guard. His best friend runs the fire department."

"Cozy," Livvy mumbled. But she didn't add more because she heard the footsteps. She glanced up the hall and saw Reed making his way toward them.

"You could have waited," Reed mumbled.

Livvy squared her shoulders. "There was no reason. I'm trying to organize my case, and questioning Deputy Tolbert is a critical part of that."

Reed gave her a disapproving glance—she was getting used to those—before he looked at Shane. "We found blood spatter on the mantel in the cabin." It definitely wasn't the voice of a lawman, but it wasn't exactly friendly, either.

Shane blew out his breath as if relieved. "I've been going over and over what happened, and I'm pretty sure the person who clubbed me was a man. Probably close to my height because I didn't get a sense of anyone looming behind me before I was hit. I think you're also looking for someone who might be left-handed because the blow came from my left."

"Did you notice any particular smell or sound?" Livvy asked at the same moment Reed asked, "Did you remember what he used to hit you?"

Reed and she looked at each other.

Frowned.

"No smell or sound," Shane answered. "And I saw the object out of the corner of my eye. I think it might have been a baseball bat."

Livvy was about to ask if the bat had possibly been in or around the cabin, but her phone rang. One glance at the caller ID, and she knew it was a call she had to take—her boss, Lieutnenant Colter. She stepped away from the cell and walked back toward the desk area. Behind her, she heard Reed continue to talk to Shane.

"Livvy," Lieutenant Colter greeted her. "I wanted to let you know that I won't be able to get to Comanche Creek after all. There's too much going on here. And with a suspect already arrested—"

"Don't worry. I can handle things."

His pause was long and unnerving. "I talked with the captain, and we've agreed to give you three days to process the scene and the evidence. By then, we can send in another Ranger. One with more experience."

Oh, that last bit stung.

"Three days," Livvy said under her breath. Not much time, but enough. She would use those three days to prove herself and determine if the evidence did indeed conclude that the deputy had murdered his former girlfriend. "Thank you for this opportunity."

"Don't thank me yet. Livvy, there's one condition about you staying there."

Everything inside her went still. "What?"

"You're not in charge of this case. Sheriff Reed Hardin is. And while you're there in Comanche Creek, you'll be taking your orders from him."

FIVE

REED made his way across the back parking lot of the sheriff's building. With the sun close to setting, the sky was a dark iron-gray, and the drizzle was picking up speed. He hadn't even bothered to grab an umbrella from the basket next to his desk, but then he hadn't thought Livvy would creep along at a snail's pace either.

"This isn't necessary," Livvy complained again. She was a good ten feet behind him, and she had her equipment bag slung over her shoulder. "I can walk to the Bluebonnet Inn on my own."

Reed ignored her complaint and opened his truck door so she could climb inside. "The inn's a mile away, and in case you hadn't noticed, it's raining." And because her expression indicated she was still opposed to a lift, he added, "The sooner you get settled into your room, the sooner you can go over the recording of my initial interview with Shane."

Since Livvy had the envelope with the disk tucked under her arm, Reed knew she was anxious to get to it. But then, she was also anxious to be away from him, and a ride, even a short one, would only remind her that she'd essentially been demoted as lead on this case.

And he was in charge.

Reed didn't know who was more ticked off about that—Livvy or him. Even though he'd wanted to handle this investigation himself, he certainly hadn't asked to play boss to a Texas Ranger who already thought he was lower than hoof grit.

When Livvy stopped and stared at him, Reed huffed, blinked away the raindrops spattering on his eyelashes and got into his truck, leaving the passenger's-side door open. The rain had caused wisps of her hair to cling to her face and neck. No more sleek ponytail. The rain had also done something to her white shirt.

Something that Reed wished he hadn't noticed.

The fabric had become somewhat transparent and now clung to her bra and breasts. And the rest of her.

You're her temporary boss, he reminded himself.

But the reminder did zero good. Nada. Zip. His male brain and body were very attentive to Livvy's ample curves and that barely-there white lace bra she was wearing.

As if she'd realized where his attention was, her gaze dropped down to her chest. "Oh!" leaped from her mouth. And she slapped the large manila envelope over the now-transparent shirt. She also got in the truck. Fast. And slammed the door.

"You could have said something," she mumbled, strapping on her seat belt as if it were the enemy.

"I could have," he admitted, "but let's just say I was dumbfounded and leave it at that."

He drove away with her still staring at him, and her mouth was slightly open, too.

Reed didn't want to defend himself, especially since gawking at her had been a dumb thing to do, but her continuing stare prompted him to say something. "Hey, just because I wear this badge doesn't mean I'm not a red-blooded male."

"Great." And that was all she said for several moments. "This won't be a problem."

"This?" Yeah, it was stupid to ask, but Reed couldn't stop himself.

"My breasts. Your male red blood."

Well, that put him in his place and meant the attraction was one-sided. His side, specifically. Good. That would make these next three days easier.

Parts of his body disagreed.

Reed stopped in front of the Bluebonnet Inn, a two-story Victorian guesthouse that sported a crisp white facade with double wraparound porches and a ton of windows. Livvy got out ahead of him and seemed surprised when he got out as well and followed her up the steps.

"I just want to check on a few things," he explained.

"Such as?"

"Security."

That stopped her hand in mid-reach for the cut-glass doorknob. She studied his eyes, and then her forehead bunched up. "You think the person who burned the cabin might come after me?"

"It's a possibility." Reed glanced at her equipment bag. "He might be after that."

"There's no evidence in it. The blood's being analyzed, and I left the photos of the spatter pattern at your office in the secure locker." Then she quickly added, "But the arsonist doesn't know that."

Reed nodded and opened the door. He didn't want to feel uneasy about Livvy's ability to protect herself. After all, as she'd already informed him, she was a Texas Ranger, trained with a firearm. And he was reasonably sure his feelings had nothing to do with her being a woman and more to do with the fact there was someone obviously hell-bent on destroying any and everything that might have been left at the crime scene.

Someone he likely called a friend or a neighbor. Not exactly a comforting feeling.

"Reed," the landlady greeted him when he stepped inside. Like most of the townsfolk, he'd known Betty Alice Sadler all his life. She was Woody's sister and the owner of the Bluebonnet Inn and she had a smile that could compete with the sun.

"Betty Alice," Reed greeted her back. He tipped his head to Livvy. "You've met Sergeant Hutton?"

The woman aimed one of her winning smiles at Livvy. "For a second or two when she dropped her things off this morning. In and out, she was, before we hardly had time to say a word." The smile faded, however, when she glanced at the bulky-looking suitcase and garment bag in the corner. "One of those McAllister boys was supposed to help me out around here today, but he didn't show up."

Reed knew what Betty Alice didn't explain. The woman had a bad back, and all the guestrooms were upstairs. No elevator, either. Taking up the bags herself would have been next to impossible.

"I'll carry them up," Reed volunteered. "Has anyone dropped by today? Maybe someone who could have slipped into the rooms?"

Betty Alice pressed her left palm against her chest. "Lord have mercy, I don't think so. But you know I'm not always at this desk. When I'm in the kitchen or watching my soaps, it's hard to hear if somebody comes in."

Yes, he did know, and that meant he needed to do some further checking. "I'm sure everything's fine. It's just we had some more problems out by Jonah Becker's cabin, and I want to take some precautions."

Betty Alice's hand slipped from her chest, and her chin came up a fraction. "Nobody around here would try to set fire to my place. Now, Jonah's cabin—well, that's a different story. Most folks know he's got money and things to burn so that cabin was no real loss to him. Still, I'm real sorry about the sergeant's car."

"How did you know about my car?" Livvy asked.

"My second cousin's a fireman, and he was at home when he got the call to respond. His wife heard what was going on and phoned me. I hope your car was insured."

"It was," Livvy assured her. And she walked toward her bags.

Reed walked toward them, too. "Let me guess—you put Sergeant Hutton in the pink room?" Reed asked Betty Alice.

The woman's smile returned. "I did. You know it's where I put all my single female guests. That room's my pride and joy. I hope you like it, Sergeant."

"I'm sure I will," Livvy answered, and in the same breath added, "I can carry the things myself."

He would have bet his paycheck that was what she was going to say, but Reed took the suitcase and garment bag anyway, and since Livvy had the equipment and the envelope, she couldn't exactly snatch the items away from him.

"You'll set the security alarm tonight?" Reed said to Betty Alice. "And lock all the windows and doors?"

"Of course. I'll keep my gun next to my bed, too. Since all that mess with Marcie, I'm being careful, just like you told me."

"Good. But I want you to be extra careful tonight, understand?"

Betty Alice bobbed her head and nibbled on her bottom lip that'd been dabbed liberally with dark red lipstick. Reed hated to worry the woman, but he wanted Livvy and her to be safe.

"I really can carry my own bags," Livvy repeated as they made their way up the stairs.

Reed stopped at the top of the stairs in front of the pink room and set down the bags. Yes, it was dangerous, but he turned and met Livvy eye-to-eye. Since she was only about four inches shorter than he was, that made things easier because he wanted lots of eye contact while he cleared the air.

"Three days is a long time for us to be at odds. Yeah, I know you can carry bags. I know you can protect yourself, but I'm an old-fashioned kind of guy. A cowboy. And it's not in my genes to stand back when I can do something to help. Now, if that insults you, I'm sorry. And I'm sorry in advance because I'm about to go in your room and make sure it's safe. Just consider that part of my supervisory duties, okay?"

The staring match started. Continued. Reed had been right about the eye contact. And the other close contact. After all, Livvy was still wearing that transparent blouse, and she smelled like the smoky bacon cheeseburger and chocolate malt the café had delivered not long before Reed and she had called it a night and left the office. Normally, Reed wouldn't have considered a burger and malt to be tempting scents, but they were working tonight.

"Okay," she said, her voice all silk and breath.

Or maybe the silk part was his imagination.

Nope. When she cleared her throat and repeated it, Reed realized this close contact was having an effect on her as well.

Both of them stepped back at the same time.

"I want to go back out to the cabin in the morning." She cleared her throat again. "Will you be able to arrange a vehicle for me?"

Reed mentally cleared his own throat and mind. "I can take you. Two of the nearby sheriffs sent deputies out to scour the woods. Don't worry, they all have forensic training. They won't contaminate the scene, and they might be able to find and secure any evidence before the rain washes it all away."

That was a Texas-size *might* though since it'd been drizzling most of the afternoon.

She turned toward the door. Stopped. Turned back. "I'm sorry."

Puzzled, Reed shook his head. "For what?"

"For being so…unfriendly. I'm just disappointed, that's all."

He didn't know which one of them looked more uncomfortable with that admission. "I understand. I didn't ask Lieutenant Colter to be in charge."

"I know. He doesn't trust me."

Reed shrugged. "Or maybe he just wanted you to have some help on a very tough investigation."

She made a sound to indicate she didn't agree with that and opened the door. He supposed the room had some charm with its lacy bedspread and delicate—aka prissy—Victorian furniture, but it was hard to see the charm when the entire room looked as if it'd been doused in Pepto-Bismol.

"It *really* is pink, isn't it?" Livvy mumbled.

"Yeah. You could ask for a different room, but trust me, you don't want to do that because then you'd have to listen to Betty Alice explain every décor decision that went into the final result."

"This'll be fine. After all, it's where she puts all her single female guests."

And that was one of the primary reasons Reed had wanted to accompany her to the room. Everyone in town would know Livvy was staying there. It wouldn't help to put her in a different room either because secrets had a very short shelf life in Comanche Creek.

Reed set down the bags and went to the adjoining bathroom to make sure it was empty. It was. No one was lurking behind the frilly shower curtain ready to start another fire. No threatening messages had been scrawled on the oval beveled mirror.

Maybe, just maybe, the threat had ended with the destruction of the SUV and cabin.

Reed was in such deep thought with this suite examination that it took him a moment to realize Livvy was standing in the bathroom door, and she was staring at him. "You're really concerned that I can't take care of myself. But I can. My specialty might be CSI, but my marksmanship skills are very good."

He didn't doubt her. Didn't doubt her shooting ability, either. But after the past few days, he wasn't sure any skill was good enough to stop what was happening.

"I have a spare bedroom at my place just on the edge of town," he offered. "And it's not pink," he added because he thought they both could use a little levity.

The corner of her mouth lifted. Not quite a smile, though. And her eyes came to his. "Thanks but no thanks. I'll have a hard enough time getting people to respect me without them thinking that I'm sleeping with the boss."

He nodded. Paused. Reed walked past her and back into the bedroom. "They're likely to think that anyway."

Reed waited for her to look shocked. Or to protest it. But she didn't. "I take it you don't have a fiancée or long-time girl–friend?" she asked.

"No." And he left it at that.

Of course, Livvy would soon hear all about the breakup with Elena Carson four years ago when his high-school flame had decided to move to London to take a PR job. Heck, she'd even hear about the attorney from San Antonio that Reed had dated for a couple of months. The one who'd pressed him to marry her because her biological clock was ticking. And yeah, Livvy would even hear about the cocktail waitress who'd worn an eye-popping dress to the city hall Christmas party. No one would say he was a player, but he wouldn't be labeled a saint.

"What about Charla Whitley?" Livvy asked. "Did you date her?"

Reed was sure he was the one who looked a little shocked now. "No. What made you think that?"

"She was giving me the evil eye, and I thought it was maybe because of you. Probably had more to do with the fact that her husband could be a suspect, and she doesn't want me here investigating things."

Probably. But then, just about everyone in town was a suspect. Livvy could expect a lot of evil eyes in the next few days.

"What about you?" Reed asked, knowing it was a question that should be left unasked. "No fiancé or long-time boyfriend?"

She shook her head. "I don't have a lot of time for serious relationships."

"Ever?" And, of course, he should just hit himself so he'd stop prying, but for some stupid reason, a reason that had gen-

erated below his belt, he wanted to know more about Livvy
Hutton.

"I dated someone in college, and it got serious. Well, on
his part. You probably know it's hard to keep up with a
personal life when the badge is there. And my badge is always
there," she added, tapping the silver star on her chest while
eyeing the one clipped to his belt.

He couldn't stop himself. "Must make for interesting sex if
you never take off your badge."

There was another flash of surprise in her eyes. Then, she
laughed. It was smoky and thick, the laugh of a woman who
knew how to enjoy herself when the time was right. But she
clamped off the laugh as quickly as she had the smile.

"You should go," she murmured. There it was again. The
sound of her voice trickled through him. Warm and silky.

Reed looked at her face. At her mouth. And knew Livvy
was right. He should go. Betty Alice was probably already on
the phone to her garden club, telling them that the sheriff had
been in the lady Ranger's room for a whole ten minutes.

A lot could happen in ten minutes.

His imagination was a little too good at filling in the possibilities. Sex against the door. On the floor. Location wasn't
important. It was the sex that he wanted.

But he wouldn't get it.

Reed forced himself to repeat that several times until it
finally sank in.

"I'll pick you up at 7:00 a.m.," he told her. "And after a bite
or two of breakfast at the café, we can drive out to the cabin."

"Can we get the breakfast to go?" she asked. "I'm anxious
to return to the crime scene, and we can eat on the way."

Reed nodded. "Takeout, it is. I'll even see if the cook can

figure out a way to add some chocolate to whatever's on the breakfast menu."

Livvy blinked. "How did you know I like chocolate?"

"Your breath, this morning. I smelled it. Milky Way?"

"Snickers," she confessed.

He didn't know why, but that confession seemed just as intimate as the sex thoughts he'd been having about her. He obviously needed to remember that he was a badass Texas sheriff. A surly one at that. Certainly not a man who cared to make a mental note to buy Livvy a Snickers bar or two.

"I'll see you in the morning." Reed headed out the door. However, he did wait in the hall until Livvy had closed it and he heard her engage the lock. She also moved something—a chair, from the sound of it—in front of the door.

Good.

Livvy was at least a little scared, and though that likely meant she wouldn't get much sleep, her vigilance might keep her safe. Now, Reed had to make sure that that safety extended to other things.

As soon as the borrowed deputies got to his office, he would send one of them out to patrol Main Street. Specifically, the Bluebonnet Inn. And he'd make copies of anything Livvy had left in the storage locker. That way, if the arsonist struck again, they wouldn't lose what little evidence they had left.

While Reed was making his mental list, he also added that he needed to call about the bullet, the missing cell phone, the gun and the DNA sample that Livvy had sent to the coroner.

It'd be another night short on sleep.

Reed went down the stairs, said goodnight to Betty Alice and watched as the woman double-locked the door and set the security alarm. Since the inn was also Betty Alice's home, it meant she, too, would be staying there, and Reed hoped everything would stay safe and secure. No more fires.

Because the drizzle had turned to a hard rain, he hurried down the steps toward his truck. But something had him stopping. He glanced around and spotted the black car parked just up the street in front of the newspaper office. That office had been closed for several hours, and there should have been no one parked there.

Reed tried to pick through the rain and the darkness and see if anyone was inside.

There was.

But because the windows were heavily tinted, he couldn't see the person. Nor the license plate. However, Reed could see the sticker that indicated it was a rental car. Definitely not a common sight in Comanche Creek.

He eased his hand over the butt of his Smith and Wesson and started toward the car. Maybe this had nothing to do with anything. Or maybe the fact it was a rental meant this was someone not local. Maybe someone Marcie had met while she was in hiding.

Either way, Reed braced himself for the worst.

The farther he made it down the sidewalk, the less he could see. That was because the only streetlights in this area were the two that flanked the front of the Bluebonnet Inn. The person had chosen the darkest spot to park.

And wait.

Reed was about fifteen feet away from the vehicle when he saw the movement inside. Someone gripped onto the wheel. A moment later, the engine roared to life. Reed kept moving toward it, but the sudden lurching motion of the car had him stopping in his tracks.

It happened in a split second. There was more movement from the driver, and the car barreled forward.

Right at Reed.

Drawing his gun, he dove to the side. And not a moment too soon. He landed on the wet grass of the vacant lot, his shoulder ramming into a chunk of limestone.

The car careened right into the spot where seconds earlier he'd been standing.

Reed cursed and came up on one knee. Ready to fire. Or to dive out of the way if the car came at him again.

But it didn't.

The driver gunned the engine, and before he sped away, Reed caught just a glimpse of the person inside.

Hell.

SIX

"WHERE the heck is he?" Livvy heard Reed demand.

He'd been making such demands from everyone he'd called, and this wasn't his first call. Reed had been on the phone the entire time since he'd picked her up at the Blue-bonnet Inn ten minutes earlier. And while Livvy ate her scrambled-egg breakfast taco that Reed had brought her from the diner, she tried to make sense of what was going on.

"Leave him another message," Reed added, his voice as tense as the muscles of his face. "Tell him to call me the minute he gets back." And with that, Reed slapped his phone shut and shoved it into his pocket.

Livvy waited for an explanation of what had gotten him into such a foul mood, but he didn't say a word. She wondered if it was personal, and if so, she wanted to stay far away from it. There was already too much personal stuff going on between Reed and her, including that little chat they'd had about chocolate, badges and relationships.

She'd dreamed about him.

Not a tame dream either, but one that involved kissing and sex.

Hot, sweaty sex.

She would have preferred to dream about catching a killer or processing evidence, but instead she'd gotten too-vivid images of what it would be like to be taken by a man who almost certainly knew how to take.

Livvy felt herself blush. And decided she needed a change of thoughts. "Is there a problem?" she asked Reed.

Still no immediate answer, which confirmed there was indeed something wrong. "When I was leaving the Bluebonnet last night, I saw a rental car parked just up the street. When I went to check it out, the driver gunned the engine and nearly plowed right into me."

Oh, mercy. "Any reason you didn't tell me this sooner?"

More hesitation. "I wanted to check into a few things first."

Which, of course, explained nothing. Well, nothing other than why during the night there'd been a deputy positioned in a cruiser on the street directly in front of the inn. When Livvy had noticed him, she'd gotten upset with Reed because she'd assumed once again that he thought she couldn't take care of herself. But the rental-car incident was what had prompted him to add some extra security to the inn.

Reed had wanted someone in place in case the guy returned.

With her appetite gone now, Livvy wrapped up the rest of the breakfast taco and shoved it back into the bag. "Were you hurt?" she asked, starting with the most obvious question.

"No." That answer was certainly fast enough, though she did notice the scrape on the back of his right hand. It was red and raw.

Livvy moved on to the next questions. "Any idea who the driver was, and why he'd want to do something like this?"

The possible theories started to fire through her head, but the one at the forefront was that the person who'd done this had also destroyed the cabin and her SUV. And this person wanted all the evidence destroyed and the investigation halted so the real killer wouldn't be caught. Or maybe the person thought the real killer was already behind bars and wanted him free.

Shane's father, maybe.

Or the other suspects.

Jerry Collier, Billy Whitley, Charla, Jonah Becker or Woody.

Reed stopped his truck just off the road that led to the burned-out cabin. Just yards away there was a police cruiser from another county. The vehicle no doubt belonged to the backups that Reed had called in. But it wasn't the activity that had her staring at him. Suddenly, the calls and his surly mood made sense.

"You saw the driver," she accused.

He scrubbed his hand over his face. "I saw his hat. A white Stetson with a rattler's tail on the band." Reed got out and slammed the door.

It didn't take her long to remember where she'd seen one matching that description. "Woody Sadler's hat," she clarified, getting out as well. Since Reed had already started to storm up the hill, she had to grab her equipment bag and hurry to keep up with him.

"A hat like his," Reed corrected.

"Or his," Livvy corrected back. She thought of the calls Reed had made in the truck. "And you haven't been able to speak to Woody to ask where he was last night."

The glance he gave her was hard and cold, but he didn't deny it. "Woody's secretary said he'd decided to take a last-minute fishing trip. His cell phone doesn't have service at the lake." He stopped so abruptly that Livvy nearly lost her balance trying to do the same. He aimed his index finger at her. "But let's get one thing straight. Woody wouldn't have tried to run me down."

Livvy wanted to argue with that, but it was true. It wouldn't make sense. Now, if Woody had come after her, that would have been more believable.

"Okay." Livvy nodded. "Then that means someone wanted you to think it was Woody. Who would have access to a hat like that?"

"Anyone in Texas," he grumbled.

Of course. It was dumb of her to ask. "But you're sure it was a man behind the wheel of the car?"

"Pretty sure. The person had the hat angled so that I couldn't see his face. And I got just a glimpse."

She glanced at the scrape on his hand again. Reed had gotten lucky, because even if this had been a stunt to scare them, it could have gone terribly wrong and he could have been killed. The thought made her a little sick to her stomach.

Okay, not sick sick.

Troubled sick.

She didn't like to think of anything bad happening to him, even though they were, for all practical purposes, still on opposite sides of a very tall fence.

"What?" he asked, glancing down at his hand and then at her.

"Nothing." And so that it would stay that way, she started up the hill again.

Reed snagged her by the arm and stopped her in her tracks. *"Something,"* he corrected.

She thought of her dream, felt the blush return. Livvy tried to shrug, and she quickly tried to get her mind off those raunchy images. "I know you're the boss, but from now on, please don't keep anything from me that might relate to the case."

And to make sure this didn't continue, she pulled away from his grip and started toward the uniformed deputy standing near the burned-out swatch of her SUV. Someone had already gathered up the debris. Nearby, just several feet inside the start of the thick brush and trees, she spotted a uniformed officer.

Livvy also spotted the soggy, muddy ground that was caking onto her boots. That mud wasn't good for her footwear or the crime scene. It had certainly washed away any tracks, and it'd sent a stream of ashes down the hill from the cabin. The black soot slivered through the crushed limestone, creating an eerie effect.

Reed said something to the uniformed officer and then looked at her. He motioned for Livvy to follow. Despite the mud weights now on her soles, she did. Not easily though. Reed began to plow through the woods like a man on a mission.

"They found something," he relayed to her without even looking back to make sure she was there.

That got Livvy moving faster, and she followed him through the maze of wet branches, underbrush and wildflowers. "What?"

But Reed didn't answer. He made his way to some yellow crime-scene tape that had been tied to a scrawny mesquite oak. "They didn't collect it," he explained. "They figured you'd want to do that."

Livvy walked around the tree and examined what had caused Reed to react the way he had. It didn't take her long to see the swatch of fabric clinging to a low-hanging branch. It was fairly large, at least two inches long and an inch wide. She immediately set down her equipment bag and took out the supplies she needed to photograph and tag it. Thank goodness she had a backup camera because her primary one was destroyed in the fire.

"It looks as if it came from the cuff of a shirt," Reed pointed out.

Possibly. It was thick, maybe double-layered, and there was enough cloth for her to see that it was multicolored with thin stripes of dark gold and burgundy on a navy blue background. It wouldn't have been her first choice of clothing to wear to commit a crime because the pattern really stood out.

Livvy snapped pictures of the swatch from different angles. "Did you see the perp's clothing when he was by my SUV and then running into the woods?"

"Just the baseball cap. But it's possible he had on a jacket, and that's why I didn't see the shirt."

Yes, or maybe this didn't belong to the suspect. Still, Livvy continued to hope because something like this could literally solve the case.

"You think it has DNA on it?" Reed asked.

"It might. If not on the fabric itself, then maybe the tree branch snagged some skin." It looked as if the fabric had been ripped off while someone was running past the branch.

Reed got closer, practically arm to arm with her, and took his own photograph using his cell phone. "I'm sending this to Kirby at the office." He pressed some buttons on his phone to do that. "I'll have him ask around and see if anyone recognizes the fabric."

Good idea. She wished she'd thought of it first, and then

Livvy scolded herself for even going there. Reed and she were on the same side, and maybe if she repeated it enough, she would soon believe it. She certainly wasn't having trouble remembering everything else about him.

Livvy finished the photographing, bagged the fabric and then snipped the tip of the branch so she could bag it as well. While she did that, Reed walked deeper into the woods.

"See anything else?" she asked.

"No." He stopped, propped his hands on his hips and looked around. "But if I were going to commit a crime and then make a fast escape, this is the route I'd go. If he'd gone east, that would have put him on the road. There's a creek to the west, and this time of year it's swollen because of the spring rains. With the fire and us behind him, this was the only way out."

Picking up the equipment bag, she went closer. "So, you're thinking the person was local?"

He nodded. And remained in deep thought for several long moments. "Jonah doesn't exactly encourage people to go traipsing onto his land, so there aren't paths through here." Reed pointed to the even thicker brush and trees ahead. "And once the arsonist made it to that point, I wouldn't have been able to see him. If that fabric belongs to him and if he ran in a fairly straight line, he would have ended up there."

Reed pointed to a trio of oaks standing so close together they were practically touching. Around them were thick clumps of cedars.

"The deputies searched that area?" Livvy asked.

Reed glanced around at the tracks on the muddy ground. "Yeah. But I'd like to have another look."

So would she, so Livvy followed him. She checked for breakage on the branches and shrubs, but when she didn't see any, she went farther to her right because the perp could have wavered from a straight-line run, especially once he was aware that Reed was in pursuit.

Since any point could be the escape route, she took some pictures, the flash of the camera slicing through the morning light. She was aware of the sound of Reed's footsteps, but Livvy continued to photograph the scene while moving right.

"Stop!" Reed shouted. But he didn't just shout.

He grabbed on to her shoulder and jerked her back so that she landed hard against his chest. Suddenly she was touching him everywhere and was in his arms.

"What are you doing?" she managed to ask. She looked up at him, but Reed's attention wasn't on her. It was on the ground.

"Trap." He pointed to a clump of soggy decaying leaves.

Livvy didn't understand at first, but she followed Reed's pointing finger and spotted the bit of black metal poking out from the clump.

Reed reached down, picked up a rock and tossed it at the device. It snapped shut, the claw-like sides closing in as they were meant to capture whatever—or whoever—was unfortunate enough to step on it. If she'd walked just another few inches, that trap would have clamped on to her foot.

"The perp probably wouldn't have had time to set that," Livvy managed to say. Not easily. Her heart was pounding and her breath had gone so thin that she could barely speak.

"Not unless he put it here before he started the fires."

Yes, and if he'd done that, then this crime had been premeditated. Worse, if there was one trap, there might be others.

"I need an evidence bag," Reed told her, moving toward the trap. "The trap might have fingerprints on it."

Livvy handed him a large collection bag and watched as he carefully retrieved the trap. "I'll have the deputies go through the area with a metal detector. After we're sure it's safe, we'll come back and keep looking."

She wasn't about to argue with that. First the fires. Then, Reed's encounter with the rental car. Now, this. It didn't take any CSI training to know that someone didn't want them to investigate this case.

Reed's cell phone rang, and he handed her the bagged trap so that he could take the call. Livvy labeled the item and eased it into her evidence bag so that she wouldn't smear any prints or DNA that might be on it.

"Billy said what?" Reed asked. And judging from his suddenly sharp tone, he wasn't pleased about something.

Since she couldn't actually hear what the caller was saying, she watched Reed's expression and it went from bad to worse.

"What's wrong?" she asked the moment he ended the call.

Reed turned and started back toward his truck. "Kirby faxed the picture of the fabric to all the town agencies, and Billy Whitley said he'd seen that pattern before, and that it'd come from a shirt."

Billy Whitley. The county clerk she'd met in front of the sheriff's office the day before. The one who might also have ties to Marcie and her murder. "And did Billy happen to know who owns that shirt?"

"Yeah, he did." That was all Reed said until they made it back into the clearing. "Come on. We need to question a suspect."

SEVEN

REED pulled to a stop at the end of the tree-lined private road that led to Jonah Becker's sprawling ranch house. He couldn't drive any farther because someone had closed and locked the wrought-iron cattle gates. Since he'd called about fifteen minutes earlier to let Jonah know he was on the way to have a *chat,* Reed figured the surly rancher had shut the gates on purpose.

It wouldn't keep Reed out.

Livvy and he could simply use the narrow footpath to the side of the gates. But it would mean a quarter-mile walk to question Jonah about how the devil a piece of his shirt had gotten torn on a tree branch mere yards from a double crime scene.

Though he figured it was futile, Reed called the ranch again and this time got the housekeeper. When he asked her to open the gate, she mumbled something about her boss saying it was to stay shut for the day. She further mumbled there was trouble with some of the calves getting out.

Right.

Jonah just wanted to make this as hard as possible.

Even though Reed hadn't specifically mentioned the shirt fabric they'd found, Jonah no doubt suspected something was up, and that *something* wasn't going to work in his favor. Of course, the real question was—had Jonah really committed a felony by burning Livvy's SUV and destroying evidence at a crime scene? And if the answer to that was yes, then Reed also had to consider him a candidate for Marcie's murder.

Livvy and he got out of the truck and started the trek along the deeply curved road. Thankfully, the road was paved so once they made it through the turnstile pedestrian gate, they didn't have to continue to use the muddy ground or pastures that fanned out for miles on each side of the ranch.

"It's a big place," Livvy commented, while shifting her equipment bag that had to weigh at least twenty-five pounds, especially now that it had the trap inside.

Reed figured it would result in a glare, but he reached out and took the bag from her. He waited for the argument about her being able to do it herself, but she simply mumbled "Thanks."

"Thanks?" he repeated.

Her mouth quivered a little. A smile threatened. "This doesn't mean anything. Well, other than you're stronger than I am."

But the smile that finally bent her mouth told him it might be more than that. The slight change of heart was reasonable. They were spending nearly every waking moment together, and they were both focused on the case. That created camaraderie. A friendship, almost. It definitely created a bond because they were on the same side.

Reed frowned. And wondered why he felt the need to justify his attraction to a good-looking woman. True, he hadn't planned on an attraction that might result in a relationship, but he was coming to terms with the notion that not having something in his plans didn't mean it wasn't going to happen anyway.

"Hold up a minute," Livvy said. She picked up a stick and used it to scrape some of the mud from those city heels on her boots.

"Those boots aren't very practical out here," Reed commented.

"No. My good pair was lost with some luggage when I was visiting my dad. I ordered another pair last night off the Internet, and I'm hoping they'll get here today."

So, this wasn't normal for her. What was, exactly? And what did she wear when she wasn't in her usual Ranger "uniform" of jeans and a white shirt? While Reed was thinking about that, he realized she'd stopped scraping mud and was staring at him.

"We, uh, both started off with some misconceptions about each other," she admitted.

"You're still from New York," he teased. But Reed immediately regretted his attempt at humor. He saw the darkness creep into her eyes and realized he'd hit a nerve. "Sorry."

"No. It's okay." She looked down and started to scrape at the mud again.

Since she wobbled and seemed on the verge of losing her balance, Reed caught on to her arm. He immediately felt her muscles tense. And her eyes met his again. Not a stare this time. Just a brief glance. But a lot of things passed between them with that glance.

Both of them cursed.

It'd been stupid to touch her, and Reed upped the ante on that stupidity by moving in closer still, lowering his head and putting his mouth on hers. Reed expected profanity. Maybe even a slap. He certainly deserved it, and a slap might just knock some sense into him.

But Livvy didn't curse or slap him.

She made a sound of pleasure, deep within her chest. It was brief and soft, barely there, but she might as well have shouted that the kiss was good for her, too. It was certainly *good* for Reed. Her mouth was like silk and, in that kiss, he took in her breath and taste.

That taste went straight through him.

And for just a moment he had a too-vivid image of what it would be like to kiss her harder and deeper. To push her against the nearby oak and do things he'd wanted to do since the first time he'd laid eyes on her.

Now, Livvy cursed and jerked away from him. "I know what you're thinking," she grumbled.

Hell. He hoped not. "What?"

"You're thinking that was unprofessional."

"Uh, no. Actually, I was thinking you taste even better than I thought you would, and my expectations were pretty damn high."

The smile threatened again, but it was quickly followed by a full-fledged scowl that she seemed to be aiming at herself. Livvy grabbed the equipment bag from him and started marching toward the ranch house.

"I have to do a good job here," she said when Reed fell in step alongside her. "I have to prove I can handle a complex crime scene on my own."

Reed understood the pressure, though he had never experienced it firsthand. "It's been the opposite for me," he admitted. "My father was the sheriff so folks around here just accepted that I was the best man for the job."

"Lucky you." But she didn't say it as a snippy insult. More like envy.

"Well, maybe that luck will rub off on you." Which sounded sexual. His body was still begging for him to kiss her again. That would be a bad idea, especially since they were now close to the ranch house.

Livvy must have realized that as well because she looked ahead at the massive estate that peeked through the trees. "Jonah will probably try to convince us that the fabric's been there for a long time."

"Probably. But it hadn't been there long because it showed no signs of wear or of being exposed to the elements."

Jonah would try to refute that as well, but the man was still going to have a hard time explaining how he tore his shirt in that part of the woods, just yards from a murder scene.

As they got closer, Reed saw Jonah. He was waiting for them on the front porch.

And he wasn't alone.

Jonah's daughter, Jessie, had just served her father and his guest some iced tea. She tipped her head toward them in greeting.

"Don't work yourself up into a state," Jessie told her father, and she gently touched his arm. Her gaze came back to Reed, and she seemed to issue him a be-nice warning before she disappeared into the house.

Seated in a white wicker chair next to Jonah was a sandy-haired man Reed knew all too well: Jerry Collier.

"He's the head of the Comanche Creek Land Office," Livvy pointed out.

Reed nodded. "Jerry was also Marcie's former boss. And on various occasions, he acts as Jonah's attorney."

"Jonah lawyered up," she grumbled.

Apparently. And that was probably wise on Jonah's part. The man's temper often got in the way of his reason, and he must have guessed something incriminating had turned up.

"Reed," Jerry snapped, getting to his feet. Everything about him was nervous and defensive. That doubled when he turned his narrowed dust-gray eyes on Livvy. "Sergeant Hutton. I'm guessing you're responsible for this visit because Reed knows Jonah didn't have anything to do with what went on in his cabin."

"Is that true?" Livvy asked the rancher.

Jonah stayed seated and didn't seem nearly as ruffled as Jerry. "I understand you found a piece of cloth."

Reed groaned and didn't even bother to ask who'd told the man, but he'd ask Kirby about it later. His deputy apparently hadn't kept quiet as Reed had ordered.

Livvy set the equipment bag on the porch steps and took out the bagged swatch of fabric. She held it up for the men to see. "Does this belong to you?"

"Don't answer that," Jerry insisted. He wagged his finger at Reed. "First you accuse Woody of wrongdoing, and now Jonah? Am I next?"

"That's entirely possible," Reed calmly answered. "The investigation's not over. Who knows what I'll be able to dig up about you."

"And everybody else in town?" Jerry tossed back.

"No. Just the folks with motive to kill Marcie. Like you, for instance. I can't imagine you were happy when she showed up, ready to testify against you. And you couldn't have been pleased about it, either," Reed added, tipping his head toward Jonah.

Jerry aimed his comments at Livvy. "Marcie could testify

all she wanted, but that doesn't mean Jonah and I did anything wrong."

"You're talking to the wrong person," Jonah told his lawyer. A faint smile bent the corner of Jonah's mouth. "Reed's in charge of this investigation, aren't you? The Rangers don't have a lot of faith in Sergeant Hutton."

Reed didn't have to look at Livvy to know that brought on a glare.

"Oh, they trust her," Reed corrected before Livvy could get into a battle of words with Jonah and Jerry. "The only reason I'm in charge is because the Rangers believe I know folks around here well enough that I can help Livvy get to the truth. And one way or another, we will get to the truth," Reed warned.

Jerry motioned toward the road. "You're looking for truth in the wrong place. Neither one of us had anything to do with Marcie's death."

Reed stepped closer, making sure he got way too close to Jerry. He knew Jerry wouldn't like that. For lack of a better word, the man was anal. Everything in its place. Everything *normal*. It wouldn't be normal for Reed to get in his face.

"Jerry, if I thought for one minute you were innocent in all of this, I wouldn't be talking to you. I believe you're just one step above being a snake-oil salesman. *One step,*" Reed emphasized, showing him a very narrow space between his thumb and index finger. "And I think you'd kill Marcie in a New York minute and then come here and pretend that you need to defend your old friend Jonah."

That caused the veins to bulge on Jerry's forehead, and he opened his mouth, no doubt to return verbal fire.

"Jerry, why don't you head back to your office?" Jonah ordered. "Just use the code I gave you to open the gate."

"I'd rather stay here," Jerry insisted, glaring at Reed.

Jonah angled his eyes in Jerry's direction. "And I'd rather you didn't. Go ahead. Head on out."

But Jerry didn't. Not right away. It took Jerry turning to Jonah, probably to plead his case as to why he should stay, but Jonah's eyes held no promise of compromise.

"Leave now," Jonah growled.

That sent Jerry cursing and storming off the porch and toward his silver-gray Mercedes. He gave Reed and Livvy one last glare before he got in, slammed the door and sped off.

Jonah calmly picked up his glass of iced tea and had a sip. He looked at Reed over the top of his glass that was beaded with moisture. "That fabric you found—it came from a shirt I used to own."

"Used to own?" Livvy questioned.

Jonah lazily set the glass aside as if he had all the time in the world. "I did some spring cleaning about two weeks ago and sent a bunch of old clothes to the charity rummage sale the church put on. That shirt was just one of the things I donated."

Well, there *had* been a rummage sale two weeks ago, but Reed had never known Jonah to be a charitable man.

"You donated it," Livvy repeated. "That's convenient."

"It's the truth." Jonah didn't smile, but there was a smug look on his face. He took a folded piece of paper from his pocket and handed it to Reed. "That's a copy of the things I donated."

Reed glanced over the dozen or so items, all clothing, and there were indeed three shirts listed on the tax receipt form.

Livvy leaned over and looked at it as well. "I don't suppose the church group would know who bought the shirt."

"No need," Jonah said before Reed could answer. "I already

know because I saw him wearing it in town just a couple of days ago. I guess some people don't have any trouble with hand-me-downs."

Reed waited. And waited. But it was obvious Jonah was going to make him ask. "Who bought the shirt?"

"Shane's father, Ben Tolbert."

If Jonah had said any other name, Reed would have questioned it, but Ben probably did buy his clothing at rummage sales. Better yet, Ben had a powerful motive for burning down that cabin and Livvy's SUV.

Shane.

Ben wasn't a model citizen, but no one in Comanche Creek could doubt that he loved his son. Add to that, Ben did have a record and had been arrested several times. Nothing as serious as this, though.

"I already called Ben," Jonah continued, "and he didn't answer his phone. When you get a chance to talk to him, tell him I'm none too happy with him burning down my place and that I'm filing charges. I want his butt in a jail cell next to his murdering son."

Reed figured it was a good thing that Jonah's own son, Trace, wasn't around to hear his dad call Shane a killer. Trace and Shane had been friends since childhood, and Reed knew for a fact that Trace believed Shane to be innocent and had even tried to pay for a big-time lawyer to be brought in if the case went to trial.

"If I find out you're lying about Ben having the shirt, then you'll be the one in a jail cell next to Shane," Reed warned.

"And I'll be the one right there to make sure you're fired," Jonah warned back. "I won't be railroaded into taking the blame for something your own deputy and his loony father have done."

Since Reed knew there was no benefit to continuing this discussion, he turned and motioned for Livvy to follow him. "I need to talk to Ben before I go any further with this," Reed told her when they were a few yards away from the porch. He could practically feel Jonah staring holes in his back.

"If Ben doesn't corroborate Jonah's story about the shirt, will you be able to get a search warrant?" Livvy asked.

"Yeah. But it wouldn't do any good. If Jonah set those fires, then trust me, that shirt is long gone."

"True. He doesn't seem like the kind of man to keep incriminating evidence lying around." Livvy shrugged. "Which makes me wonder why he would have worn such a recognizable shirt to commit a crime."

Reed could think of a reason—to throw suspicion off himself by drawing attention to himself. A sort of reverse psychology. Still, that didn't mean Jonah hadn't hired someone to wear that shirt and destroy the evidence.

"I'll talk to Shane," Reed assured her. "He might know something about all of this."

"And he'd be willing to incriminate his father?"

"He has in the past. Three years ago when Ben got drunk and trashed some cars in the parking lot of the Longhorn Bar, Shane arrested him."

"Yes, but this is different. This is a felony. His father could go to jail for years."

Reed couldn't argue with that. But if Shane couldn't or wouldn't verify the shirt issue, then there were other ways to get at the truth, even if it meant questioning everyone in town.

"Look," Livvy said. She pointed to a storage barn in the pasture to their right.

Reed immediately saw what had captured her attention. There were several traps hanging on hooks. Traps that looked identical to the one someone had set near the cabin.

"You think they'll have serial numbers or something on them to link them to the other one?" she asked.

"Possibly. But even if they do and if they match the one we found, Jonah could say he set the trap because he owned the property and was having trouble with coyotes or something."

She shook her head. "But I have the feeling the trap was set for us. For me," Livvy softly added. "Someone in Comanche Creek doesn't want us to learn the truth about what happened to Marcie."

Reed had a bad feeling that she was right.

He thought about her alone at night in the inn and considered repeating his offer for her to stay at his place. She'd refuse, of course. Probably because she knew that would lead to a different kind of trouble. But even at the risk of Livvy landing in his bed, he wanted to do more to make sure she stayed safe while working on this case.

Reed mentally stopped.

Cursed.

"What's wrong?" Livvy asked, firing glances all around as if she expected them to be ambushed.

Reed wasn't sure this would sound any better aloud than it did in his head. "I'm thinking about staying at the inn. Just until this case is wrapped up."

She stopped, turned and stared at him. "And the profanity wasn't because of the element of danger. You know that being under the same roof with me isn't a good idea."

He tried to shrug. "Depends on what you consider a good idea."

Her stare turned flat. "Having a one-night stand with you wouldn't be a good idea. Or even a two-night stand, for that matter. Besides, you wouldn't even make the offer to stay at the inn if I were a man."

"True," he readily admitted. "But if you were a man, I wouldn't be torn between wanting you and protecting you."

She huffed and started to walk again. She was trying to dismiss all of this. But Reed figured the time for dismissing was long gone.

"My advice?" she said, her voice all breathy and hot. "We forget that kiss ever happened."

"Right." And he hoped his dry tone conveyed his skepticism. He'd have an easier time forgetting that he was neck-deep in a murder investigation. "We'll head back to the jail and talk to Shane about his father."

And once they'd done that, he'd think about his possible upcoming stay at the inn.

The cattle gates were wide open when they approached them. Jerry had no doubt left in a huff, especially since Jonah had essentially told him to get lost. That was something else Reed needed to give some thought. If Jonah hadn't wanted Jerry there in the first place, then what had the man been doing at Jonah's ranch? Reed trusted Jerry even less than he did Jonah, and he hoped Jerry hadn't made the visit because he had something to plot with Jonah.

Or something to hide.

They passed through the gate just as his phone rang. From the caller ID, he could see that it was Kirby.

"Don't tell me something else has gone wrong," Reed answered.

"No. Well, not that I know of anyway. I still haven't been

able to reach Ben Tolbert like you asked. But I did just get a call from the crime lab about the gun Shane was holding when he was found standing over Marcie's body."

Reed took a deep breath and put the call on speaker so Livvy could hear this as well.

"That gun was the murder weapon," Kirby confirmed.

Hell. Reed glanced at Livvy. No I-told-you-so look on her face. Instead, her forehead was creased as if she were deep in thought.

"They also IDed the gun owner. A dealer in San Antonio who said he sold the piece over a week ago to a man named Adam Smith."

Reed shook his head. "Let me guess—Adam Smith doesn't exist."

"You're right. The documents he provided for proof of identity are all fake."

So, either Shane had faked them, or this was looking more and more like a complex, premeditated murder of a person who could have been a potential witness against both Jonah and Jerry for their involvement in that shady land deal.

Yeah. Reed really needed to do some more digging on both men.

"Kirby, could you please have the lab courier the murder weapon back to Reed's office?" Livvy asked. "I want to take a look at that gun."

"It's already on the way. Your boss figured you'd want to examine it so he sent it with the courier about an hour ago. Should be here any minute."

"Thank you."

Reed hung up and opened the door so that he could toss in Livvy's equipment bag. He heard the sound.

The too-familiar rattle.

And he reacted just as much from fear as he did instinct. He pushed Livvy to the side.

It wasn't a second too soon.

Because the diamondback rattler that was coiled on the seat sprang right at them.

EIGHT

EVERYTHING was a blur. One minute Livvy was getting ready to step inside the truck, and the next, she was on the ground.

She heard the rattling sound, and it turned her blood to ice. Livvy rolled to her side and scrambled to get away.

The rattler shot out of the truck again, aiming for a second attempt to strike them, and she shouted for Reed to move. He did. And in the same motion, he drew his gun.

And fired.

The shot blasted through the countryside, and he followed it up with a second one. That didn't stop the snake. Livvy watched in horror as the rattler made a third strike. Its fangs stabbed right into Reed's leather shoulder holster. He threw it off, fired a fourth shot, and this time the bullet hit its intended target.

Still, the snake didn't stop moving. It continued to coil and rattle before it slithered away.

"Did it bite you?" Livvy managed to ask. Her heart felt as if it were literally in her throat.

Reed shook his head and looked at her. "Are you okay?"

She took a moment to assess her situation. "I'm fine, but what about you?" Livvy got to her feet and checked out his arm and shoulder.

"I wasn't hurt." He checked her out as well, and when his gaze landed on her now-muddy jeans and shirt, he cursed. "This wasn't an accident. That snake didn't open my truck door and crawl in."

No. And that meant someone had put it there. "Who would do this?"

"The same person who's been trying to make our lives hell for the past two days." He paused to curse again. "The snake probably wouldn't have killed us even with multiple bites, and the town doc keeps a supply of antivenom. But it would have made us very sick and put us out of commission for God knows how long."

"And it scared us. Scared *me*," she corrected. Livvy flicked the loose bits of mud off her clothes. "But it won't scare me enough to stop this investigation."

"No, it won't," Reed readily agreed. He checked his watch, eyed the truck and then eyed her. "You think you can get inside?"

She could. Livvy had no doubts about that, but she couldn't quite control her body's response to nearly being the victim of a snake attack.

"You believe Ben Tolbert is capable of this?" Livvy took a deep breath and got inside.

Reed did the same, and he started the engine. "He's capable all right. Rattlesnakes aren't exactly hard to find around here, and some people trap and sell them. There's a trapper about twenty miles from here who runs a rattlesnake roundup. I'll call him and see if anyone's recently purchased a diamondback from him."

It would be a necessary call, just to cover all bases, but Livvy doubted the culprit would go that route where he could be easily identified. "What about Jerry Collier? He left the ranch house in plenty of time to plant the snake."

Reed nodded. "And he was riled enough to do it."

Yes, he was. "But that would indicate premeditation."

"Maybe. Or maybe he spotted the snake as he was driving out and did it on the spur of the moment."

She tried to imagine the suit-wearing, nervous head of the Comanche Creek Land Office doing something like picking up a live rattler on a muddy road, but it didn't seem logical. Well, not logical in her downtown office in Austin, but out here, anything seemed plausible.

"Don't worry—I'll question Jerry," Reed continued, his voice as tight as the grip he now had on the steering wheel. "Ben, too. And I'll have the outside of the truck dusted for prints. We might get lucky."

"I'm sorry," he added a moment later.

Since his tone had just as much anger as apology, she looked at him. Yes, he was riled. Maybe it was simply because of the leftover adrenaline from the attack, but Livvy got the impression that he was angry because of her, because she'd been placed in danger.

And because there was now *something* between them. Something more than the job.

She was about to remind him that the kiss and attraction really couldn't play into this, but he grabbed his phone from his pocket, scrolled down through the recent calls he'd made and pressed the call button.

"I want to speak to Jerry," Reed demanded of whoever answered. There was at least a five-second pause. "Then take a message. He needs to call me immediately, or else I'll arrest his sorry ass."

Reed ended that call and made another. This time, he put it on speaker, and she heard the call go straight to Ben Tolbert's voice mail. Reed issued another threatening order very similar to the one he'd left for Jerry. But he didn't stop there. Reed continued to call around: to the mayor, then someone on the city board, and he asked both men to help him locate Jerry Collier and Ben Tolbert. He was still making calls when he pulled to a stop in the parking lot of his office.

Livvy knew it wasn't a good time to be close to Reed, not with so much emotion still zinging around and between them, so she grabbed her equipment bag, got out of the truck and, with Reed right behind her, she hurried inside.

Eileen, the receptionist, gave her a warm smile and a hello. Livvy tried to return the greeting but wasn't pleased to hear the tremble in her voice. Her hands were shaking, too, and since she didn't want to risk a meltdown in front of anyone, she mumbled something that she hoped would sound composed and raced into Reed's office.

Livvy hurried to the desk that he'd set up for her to work, and she took out the trap and fabric swatch so she could start the paperwork to send them to the lab in Austin.

It also gave her hands and her mind something to do.

She wasn't a coward and knew full well that danger was part of the job, but she wasn't immune to the effects of coming so close to Reed and her being hurt.

She heard the door shut and glanced over her shoulder at

Reed. He stood there as if trying to collect himself, a response she totally understood.

"Here are the trap and the fabric," she said. Her voice was still shaky, and Livvy cleared her throat hoping it would help. "When the courier gets here with the murder weapon, I'll have him go ahead and take the items to the crime lab for testing."

Livvy picked up a note. A message left for her by Kirby. She read it out loud: "'The lab checked on the number I gave them for the missing phone. It was one of those prepaid cells, and the person who bought it must have paid cash because there's no record of purchase. That means we can't trace the buyer, and we won't be able to find out about any calls he might have made.'"

Reed didn't respond to that latest dose of disappointing news. Instead, he reached behind him, locked the door and pushed himself away. But he did more than just walk toward her. When he reached her, he latched on to her arm and hauled her against him. Reed pulled her into a tight embrace.

"I'll try very hard not to let something like that happen again," he said.

Confused, Livvy looked up at him. "You mean the snake or the kiss?"

He smiled, but it was short-lived and there was no humor in it. "The snake."

Yes, but both were dangerous in their own way, and Reed and she knew that. Still, Livvy didn't move away, even when he slid his arm around her waist and pulled her closer. Not even when her breasts pressed against his chest. Not even when she felt his warm breath push through the wisps of her hair.

Livvy could have sworn the air changed between them. The nerves and adrenaline were still there, but she felt another emotion creep into the already volatile mix.

Attraction.

Yes, it was there, too, and all the talk and head-shaking in the world wouldn't make it go away. She opened her mouth to say, well, she had no idea what to say. But despite the hot attraction, she knew she had to say or do something to stop the escalation of all these crazy emotions.

But she didn't stop it.

Instead, she did the opposite. She came up on her tiptoes…

And she kissed him.

Not a peck, either, like the other one at the ranch, though it started that way. Reed took things from there. He made sure this one was hard, French.

And memorable.

Livvy didn't do anything to stop this either, despite the intense argument going on between her head and the rest of her body. No. She made things better—and worse—by slinging her arm around his neck and moving even closer.

That taste.

It was amazing. And the man moved over her mouth as if he owned her. She did her own share of kiss-deepening as well, and they didn't break the intimate contact until they both realized they needed to catch their breaths.

Reed looked stunned and confused when he drew back. Livvy knew how he felt. They were both in a lot of trouble, and she didn't think they'd be getting out of this trouble any time soon.

"The evidence," she said as a reminder to both herself and Reed.

"Yeah." Still, he didn't pull away. He pressed his forehead against hers and groaned. "I would promise not to do that again, but you and I both know it's a promise I can't keep."

"We can't just land in bed, either." Though that suddenly seemed like a great idea. Sheez. Her body really wasn't being very professional.

Now, he smiled and looked down at her. "The bed is optional. Sex with you? Not so optional." He pressed harder against her. So hard that she could feel the proof of their attraction. "I want you bad, Livvy, and all the logic and the danger in the world won't wish that away."

That seemed to be a challenge, as if he expected her to dispute what he was saying. She couldn't.

The sound of his ringing cell phone shot through the room, and that sent them flying apart. Good. They weren't totally stupid.

Just yet, anyway.

"Kirby?" he answered after glancing at the caller ID screen.

Livvy welcomed the reprieve. Well, part of her did anyway. But she knew it was just that: a reprieve. Somehow, she would have to force herself away from Reed. Maybe she could move her side of the investigation to the inn, just so they wouldn't be elbow to elbow. That might minimize the temptation of the mouth-to-mouth contact.

But then she looked at him.

All six feet plus of him. With that rumpled dark hair and bedroom eyes, he wasn't the sort of man that a woman could *minimize*.

"As soon as he steps foot in his office, let me know. Thanks, Kirby." He closed his phone and shoved it into his pocket. He tipped his head to the fabric and trap. "I'll have Eileen arrange to have that taken to the crime lab, but it might not happen before we get to question Jerry. He's on his way back to his office."

"Good. We can ask him about the rattlesnake." Livvy put the evidence into the locker so it would be safe until the courier arrived.

"We can ask him more than that. Kirby just learned the results from the footprint castings that you took. And they're a perfect match to Jerry Collier."

Livvy sank down into the chair just a few inches from her worktable. "Is there any valid reason why his footprints would be there?"

"None that I know of. Plus, he has one of the strongest motives for wanting Marcie dead. If she had managed to stay alive long enough to testify against him, Jerry would have ended up in jail. Without her testimony, the state doesn't have a strong enough case."

That was a huge motive indeed, and Livvy was about to use her laptop to request a full background check on Jerry, but there was a knock at the door. Reed crossed the room, unlocked the door, and when he opened it, Kirby was standing there. The young deputy looked puzzled and maybe even suspicious as to why the door had been locked.

Great.

If Kirby sensed the attraction between Reed and her, God knew how little time it would take to get around town. She was betting everyone would know by lunchtime.

Livvy took the bagged and tagged gun from Kirby and initialed the chain of custody form. He also handed her the report file from the lab. While Kirby and Reed discussed whether or not they should issue an APB for Ben Tolbert, Livvy put on her gloves and got to work examining the gun.

It was a Ruger .22 Rimfire pistol. Common and inexpensive. A person could buy it for under three hundred dollars at any gun store in the state. Just about anyone who wanted a gun badly enough could afford it.

Including all of their suspects.

The Ruger had already been processed, and even though it was indeed the murder weapon, according to the report, it contained no DNA. Just fingerprints that had been dusted and photographed. The photographs had then been fed into AFIS, the Automated Fingerprint Identification System. The result?

They were Shane's prints.

The fact there was no DNA was odd, especially since the lab had run a touch test, which should have been able to detect even a minute amount of biological material.

Yet, nothing.

Since Shane had supposedly shot Marcie at close range, there should have been some blood spatter or maybe even sweat from Shane's hand. First-time killers normally weren't so calm and cool that they didn't leave a piece of themselves behind at the crime scene.

She set the gun aside, and went through the report file. There were several photos of the fingerprints on the weapon, and the tech who'd taken them had been thorough. Livvy could see the placement of every print, including the one on the trigger, which had a much lighter point of pressure than the others.

Also odd.

It should have been about the same, or maybe even heavier. Killers didn't usually have such a light touch when it came to pulling a trigger.

She picked up the gun again and took a magnifying glass from her case so she could look at the actual pattern. Even though some of the fingerprint powder and the prints themselves had been smeared during transport and processing, she could still see where the shooter had gripped the gun. That created a vivid image in her mind.

Shane pointing the gun at Marcie.

Then firing.

Livvy replayed the scene again. And again. Each time, she made tiny mental changes to see if she could recreate the end result: Marcie's murder with Shane pulling the trigger.

"Something about this doesn't look right," she mumbled. She glanced over her shoulder to see if Reed had heard her, but his attention wasn't on her. It was on the phone call that he'd just answered.

"Good, because we want to talk to you, too," Reed snarled. But his expression morphed into concern. "We'll be right there."

"What happened?" Livvy asked when he slapped the phone shut.

"That was Jerry Collier, and he's back in his office. He says someone is out to kill you, and he knows who that person is."

NINE

"IF you'd rather stay at the office and finish examining the gun, I can do this alone," Reed offered, though he knew what Livvy's answer would be.

"No, thanks." Her response was crisp and fast, like the speed at which she exited the building. "I'd like to learn the identity of the person who wants me dead."

So would Reed, but he wasn't certain they would be getting that information from Jerry. Still, he wasn't about to pass up the opportunity to question the man about the dangerous attempts that had been orchestrated to prevent Livvy and him from doing their jobs.

They went into the parking lot, and he spotted one of the loaner deputies who was examining his truck for prints and other evidence. Reed didn't want to interrupt that or destroy any potential evidence by using the vehicle. The other deputies were apparently still at the crime scene or else on patrol because his official vehicle was nowhere in sight. That left the one cruiser, which Reed hated to tie up in case Kirby had to respond to an emergency.

The Comanche Creek Land Office was just up the street about a quarter of a mile away, but it wouldn't be a comfortable stroll. It was already turning into a scorcher day with the heat and humidity. Plus, there was the potential danger, which mostly seemed to be aimed at Livvy. Maybe it wasn't wise to have her out in the open.

"It'd be safer if I have someone drive us," Reed suggested.

She looked at him as if he'd sprouted a third eye. "I won't let this scare me. We're both peace officers, and if we can't walk down the street in broad daylight without being afraid, then that sends a message to the perp that I don't want to send."

And with that, she started walking again. "Besides, I need a few minutes to clear my head," Livvy added. "I don't want to go storming into Jerry's office like this."

Reed was on the same page with her. First, the footprints that were a match to Jerry, and then his bombshell comment about knowing who wanted to kill Livvy. Up to this point, Reed had hoped and believed that the incidents were meant to scare her off. Not kill her. But by God, if that was someone's intention, then there'd be hell to pay.

He didn't curse himself or groan at that thought. Somewhere along the way, he'd crossed the line with Livvy, and cursing and groaning weren't going to make him backtrack even if that was the sensible thing to do.

"You said there was no gunshot residue anywhere on Shane?" she asked, pulling him out of a fit of temper that was building because of Jerry.

"None. Why?"

She lifted her shoulder. "I've just been trying to get the picture straight in my mind."

Yeah. He'd done that as well, and this was one picture that hadn't fit right from the start. Well, unless Shane truly was a cold-blooded killer who'd set all of this up.

"You make a fine-looking couple," someone called out.

Reed glanced across the street and spotted Billy Whitley, the county clerk, and his wife, Charla, who were just going into the diner, probably for an early lunch.

"Careful," Billy teased. "People will say you're in love."

Reed stopped to set him straight, but Charla got in on the conversation.

Charla nudged her elbow into Billy's ribs. "I know you got better sense than that, Reed," Charla countered. "That woman's trying to tear this town apart."

"Actually, I'm just trying to do my job," Livvy fired back.

That earned Livvy a *hmmmp* from Charla, and the woman threw open the door of the diner and stormed inside. Billy gave an apologetic wave and followed her.

Reed didn't know which was worse—Billy's innuendo or Charla's obvious dislike of Livvy. "Sorry," he mumbled to Livvy once they started walking again.

"No need to apologize. Will this cause trouble for you?" she asked but didn't wait for his answer. "Would it be better if we did separate investigations?"

Reed didn't even have to think about this. "It wouldn't help. You're a woman and I'm a man. We're both single. If people don't see us together, they'll just say we're staying apart so we don't raise suspicions about a secret relationship."

And that was really all he wanted to say about that, especially since the gossip was really going to heat up because

Reed planned to spend a lot more time with her at work and at the inn.

Reed would break that news to Livvy later.

"We were discussing the gun," he prompted.

"Yes." She wiped the perspiration from her forehead and repeated it. "I think there's a problem with the pressure points. The print isn't that strong on the trigger."

Despite the heat, Reed slowed a bit so he could give that some thought. Now, he got that picture in his mind. "The person who hit Shane over the head could have used gloves when he shot Marcie. Then, he could have pressed Shane's prints onto the weapon."

Hell. Why hadn't he thought of that sooner? Probably because this case had come at him nonstop. It was almost as if someone wanted to make sure that his focus was disrupted. Maybe that was the real reason for all the diversions, like that snake.

"I need to do some further testing," Livvy added. Her forehead creased. "It could mean that Shane just has a light touch when it comes to his trigger finger. I'd like to compare this weapon to his service pistol, just to see how the grip pattern lines up."

That would give her information if Shane hadn't recently cleaned his gun. For the first time in Reed's law-enforcement career, he was hoping his deputy had been lax about that particular standard procedure. "You can do that as soon as we finish with Jerry because I have his gun locked up in the safe in my office."

Ahead of them on the steps to the county offices were three men and a woman, all Native Americans, and all carrying signs of protest.

"Sheriff Hardin," the woman called out, and her tone wasn't

friendly, either. Not that Reed expected it to be, since she was carrying a big poster that demanded justice for her people.

"Ellie," Reed greeted her. He caught onto Livvy's arm and tried to maneuver her around the protesters, but the trim Comanche woman, Ellie Penateka, stepped in front of them.

Reed had known Ellie all his life, and though she was passionate about her beliefs, she could also toe the line of the law.

"When will you do your job and arrest Jonah Becker and his cronies?" Ellie demanded.

"When I have some evidence that warrants an arrest." Reed wasn't unsympathetic to her demand. After all, Jonah probably had participated in a dirty deal to get land that belonged to the Native American community. Jerry might have helped him, too, but he couldn't arrest anyone without probable cause.

Since it was obvious that Ellie didn't intend to move, Reed met her eye-to-eye. "If and when I get proof, any proof, that Jonah's done something wrong, I'll arrest him. You have my word on that."

Ellie stared at him and then turned her dark eyes on Livvy. "Help us," she said, her voice still laced with anger. "This land deal has to be undone."

Livvy opened her mouth, looking as if she were about to say she was there to solve a murder, not get involved with community issues, but she must have rethought that because she nodded. "If I find anything, the sheriff will be the first to know."

That seemed to soothe Ellie enough to get her to move to the side, and Livvy and Reed continued up the steps to the county offices.

"How long has the protest been going on?" Livvy asked under her breath.

"On and off since the land deal over two years ago." And what Reed had said to Ellie hadn't been lip service. He would arrest Jonah if he could, and that arrest might go a long way to soothing the split that was happening in Comanche Creek.

He opened the door to the office building, and the cool air-conditioning spilled over him. Inside, there were some curious folks who eyed Livvy and him and then did some behind-the-hand whispers. Reed doled out some warning scowls and made his way down the hall. Jerry's office door was wide open, and he was seated at his desk, apparently waiting for them.

They stepped inside, and Reed shut the door. Not that they would have much privacy since the glass insert in the door allowed anyone and everyone to see in.

Livvy and he took the seats across from Jerry's desk. "Start talking," Reed insisted.

But Jerry didn't. Instead, he pulled out a manila file and slid it toward them. Reed opened it and saw that it was case notes from a murder that had happened over twenty years ago. The name on the file was Sandra Hutton.

Livvy's mother.

He aimed a raised eyebrow at Jerry and passed the file to Livvy. "What does this have to do with anything?" Reed asked.

"Sandra Hutton's killer has been hiding out in Mexico," Jerry explained with a tinge of smugness. "Maybe he's decided to return to Texas and create some havoc with Sandra's daughter. He could be the person who set fire to that cabin."

Livvy's reaction was slight. Just a small change in her breathing pattern. She moistened her lips, closed the file and tossed it back on Jerry's desk. "How did you get this information?" she asked.

"I requested it from the county sheriff's office. I told them it could be relevant to the investigation into the land deal that's got the Comanches so riled up."

In other words, Jerry had pulled strings so he could pry into Livvy's past.

"My mother's killer has no part in this," Livvy insisted.

"You're sure?" Jerry challenged.

"Positive."

Reed only hoped she was, but he'd do some checking when he got back to his office. For now though, he wanted answers and not a possible smokescreen.

"Were you at the cabin around the time Marcie was killed?" he asked Jerry.

There was no quick denial. Jerry studied Reed's expression and then nodded. "Why?"

"Because we found your tracks there." Reed studied Jerry as well, and the man certainly didn't seem particularly rattled by all of this. Of course, maybe that's because Jerry always seemed on edge about something. Like a pressure cooker ready to start spewing steam.

"I was at the cabin the morning of the murder." But then, Jerry hesitated. He had a pen in his hand, and he began rolling it between his fingers. "I got a call, telling me Marcie would be there, and I wanted to talk to her, to ask if she intended to go through with her testimony against Jonah Becker."

"And you," Livvy supplied. "Because if she'd testified against Jonah, you also would have been implicated."

Jerry bobbed his head, and rolled the pen faster. "At the time I put it together, I didn't know the land deal could be construed as illegal. I'm still not convinced it is. But I understand why the Native American community is upset. That's why they're protesting outside. I also understand they want someone to blame, but I wanted to make sure Marcie was going to get me a fair shake when she was on the witness stand."

"And did Marcie agree?" Reed asked.

"I didn't see her. She wasn't at the cabin when I got there so I left. That following morning, I heard about her murder. I swear, I had nothing to do with her death."

Reed wasn't sure he believed that. "So who called you to tell you about Marcie being at the cabin?"

This hesitation was a lot longer than the first, and the pen just started to fly over his fingers.

"Billy Whitley," Jerry finally said.

"Billy," Reed repeated, not that surprised but riled that he hadn't been given this information sooner. "How did he know Marcie was going to the cabin?"

Jerry picked up his phone. "I don't know, but you can ask him yourself." He pressed some numbers. "Billy, could you come over here a minute? Reed and the lady Ranger want to know why I was at the cabin that morning." He hung up. "He'll be here in a couple of minutes."

Reed wasn't going to wait for Billy to continue this interrogation. "When Billy called to tell you about Marcie being at the cabin, you didn't ask him how he'd come by that information? Because Marcie hadn't exactly announced her whereabouts."

Jerry shook his head, tossed the pen on his desk and grabbed a Texas Longhorns mug near where the pen had landed. He gulped down enough coffee to choke himself. "I didn't ask. I was just thankful to finally have a chance to talk to her."

"And you're positive she wasn't there when you arrived?" Livvy asked.

"No sign of her. I didn't go in, but I looked in the windows. No one was in that cabin."

Livvy made a sound of disagreement. "She could have been hiding. I can't imagine that Marcie would have been happy to see her former boss, especially when she was scared to death of you."

Jerry couldn't and didn't deny that. It was common knowledge around town that Marcie had been afraid of him, so maybe she had indeed been wary enough to hide when she saw him skulking around the place.

"Did you happen to notice Shane while you were there?" Reed wanted to know.

"No." His answer was fast and prompted him to drink yet more coffee. "I told you, there was no one at that cabin."

Still, it was possible that both Shane and Marcie had come later. Jerry could be telling the truth.

Or not.

Reed wasn't ready to buy the man's story when Jerry had so much to lose from this situation.

There was a knock at the door, one sharp rap on the glass insert, before it opened and Billy strolled in. "You wanted to see me," he said, aiming the not-too-friendly comment at Jerry. Charla was there, too, but she stood back in the doorway and didn't come in. "Charla and I were in the middle of eating lunch."

"I told them you were the one who called me about Marcie being at the cabin," Jerry volunteered.

"And we want to know how you came by that information," Reed added.

"I see." Billy pulled in a long weary breath and sat on the

edge of Jerry's desk. "If you don't mind, I'd rather not divulge that information."

Reed stopped his mouth from dropping open, but that comment was a shocker. "I do mind." He got to his feet. "And if you don't tell me, I'll arrest you on the spot for obstruction of justice."

The usually friendly Billy suddenly didn't seem so friendly, and he tossed a glare at Jerry, probably because he wasn't pleased that the man had given Reed what Billy would have thought was private information.

Charla obviously ignored Billy's glare. "Ben Tolbert told Billy that Marcie was going to be at the cabin," the woman confessed.

Livvy and Reed exchanged glances, and he was certain neither was able to keep the surprise out of their eyes. "How did Ben know?"

Billy wearily shook his head and sighed. "He said he found out from Jeff Marquez."

Reed was very familiar with the name. Jeff Marquez was the EMT who'd helped Marcie fake her own death. "He's in county jail on obstruction of justice charges, and he won't be getting out anytime soon."

Billy nodded. "But he told Ben before he was arrested. Why, I don't know. Maybe Ben bribed him."

Ben didn't have the money for that, but Jonah sure did. Which brought them back full circle without eliminating any of the suspects. Jerry, Billy, Ben and Jonah all had the means, motives and opportunities to kill Marcie, but Reed was having a hard time believing that Ben would have allowed his son to take the blame for something he'd done.

That meant, he could focus more on the two men in the

room, and the one rancher friend they had in common: Jonah. He wouldn't take Ben off his suspect list, but he did mentally move him to the bottom.

"I've done nothing illegal," Billy reiterated. "Neither has Jerry. And you're barking up the wrong tree, Reed. You already have the killer in custody."

"Maybe," Livvy mumbled. She got to her feet and stood next to Reed. Reed followed.

"Maybe?" Jerry challenged, and Reed didn't think it was his imagination that the man suddenly seemed very uncomfortable. Also, that wasn't a benign glance he aimed at Billy. And then Charla.

"Maybe," Livvy repeated, keeping a poker face. She walked out past Charla and into the hall.

Since there were lots of people milling around, too many, Reed didn't want to say anything that would be overheard and reported to Charla and the men. He waited until they were outside and away from the protestors.

"Smart move," he said under his breath, "to let them think you might have some evidence to prove Shane's innocence. And maybe their guilt."

"Well, I wanted to say something to shake them up a bit."

Mission accomplished. Now, they would have to wait to see who would react, and how, to the possibility that the charges against Shane weren't a done deal.

"I'm sorry Jerry brought up your mother," Reed told her.

"Not your fault. And this has nothing to do with her. That was an attempt to muddy the waters on his part. Makes you wonder just how deep he is into this. After all, other than Jonah, Jerry has the strongest motive because Marcie could have sent him to jail for years."

"Yeah, and he doesn't have Jonah's big bankroll to fight a long legal battle."

Livvy stayed quiet a moment. "So, of all our suspects who would be most likely to kill a woman and set up her former lover to take the blame?"

"Jerry," Reed said without hesitation. Still, that didn't mean Jonah or someone else hadn't put him up to it or even assisted. "While you're reexamining the gun, I want to talk to Shane again. Maybe he remembers something that'll help us unravel all of this."

He heard Livvy respond, but he didn't actually grasp what she said. That was because Reed saw something that got his complete attention.

The black rental car parked just up the street less than a block from his office.

"That's the vehicle that nearly ran me down," he told Livvy.

She put her hand over the butt of her service pistol. Reed did the same and tried to walk ahead of her so he could place himself between the car and her. Of course, Livvy wouldn't have any part of that. She fell in step beside him, and they made their way to the car.

"Can you see if anyone's inside?" she asked.

"No. The windows are too dark." And with the sunlight spewing in that direction, there was also a glare.

With each step they took, Reed's heart rate kicked up. It certainly couldn't be Billy, Charla or Jerry in that car since he'd just left them in Jerry's office, but it could be someone who'd been hired to intimidate Livvy and him.

Reed and Livvy were only a few yards away when the engine roared to life.

Livvy stopped and drew her weapon. Reed was about to push her out of harm's way, but it was already too late. The driver slammed on the accelerator, the tires squealing against the hot asphalt.

Reed cursed as the car sped past them. He cursed again when he got a glimpse of the driver.

This time it was Shane's father, Ben Tolbert.

TEN

LIVVY stepped from the claw-footed tub and wrapped the thick terry-cloth towel around her. The hot bath had helped soothe some of her tight back and shoulder muscles, but it hadn't soothed her mind.

She dried off, slipped on her cotton nightgown and smeared her hand over the steam-coated mirror. A troubled face stared back at her, and she tried to assure herself that neither her career nor her personal life were in deep trouble.

But they were.

The Ranger captain had hit the roof when he learned about the destroyed crime scene, and it didn't help matters that she hadn't been able to confirm the arrest of their main suspect.

In fact, she'd done the opposite.

She'd created doubt with her questions about the murder weapon, and those doubts were fueling animosity between the Native American community and the rest of the town. According to the inn's owner, Betty Alice, there were whispers that

Livvy was trying to clear Shane because of her personal involvement with Reed.

Maybe the new lab tests she'd ordered on the gun would help. Well, they might help clear Shane anyway, so they could concentrate on other suspects. But that wouldn't clear the rumors about Reed and her.

Worse, those rumors were partly true.

Other than that kiss, Reed and she hadn't acted on this crazy attraction, but that was no guarantee it wouldn't happen in the future.

And that was a sobering thought.

Despite all the problems a relationship with Reed would cause, she still wanted him. Bad. She wanted more than kisses. Livvy wanted sex.

No.

Sex wouldn't have been as unnerving as the fact that Livvy wanted Reed to make love to her. Something long, slow and very, very hot. And not a one-time shot, either. She was thinking of starting an affair with a lawman who could put some serious dents not just in her heart but in her professional reputation.

Cursing herself, Livvy brushed her teeth and reached for the door.

She heard it then.

A soft bump.

The sound had come from the bedroom.

Livvy turned to reach for her gun, only to realize she'd left it holstered on the nightstand. She hadn't wanted the gun in the steamy bathroom with all the moisture and humidity. Thankfully, she remembered she did have her cell phone with her, though, because she had been concerned that she might not be able to hear it ring while the bathwater was running.

Of course, she'd locked the door to the room, and it was entirely possible that Betty Alice had come up to bring her some towels or something. Still, with everything that'd happened, Livvy wished she had her gun.

She walked closer to the bathroom door, listening. And it didn't take long before she heard a second thump. Then, footsteps.

Someone was definitely in her room.

"Betty Alice?" she called out.

Nothing. The heavy footsteps stopped just outside the bathroom door.

Livvy grabbed her phone from the vanity, flipped it open but then hesitated. Calling Reed wasn't at the top of her list of things she wanted to do, but she might not have a choice.

"Who's out there?" she tried again.

No answer.

So, she waited, debating what she should do. She wasn't defenseless since she'd had some martial arts and hand-to-hand combat training, but she didn't want to go hand-to-hand with someone who was armed.

Like Marcie's killer.

The doorknob moved, and her heart dropped to her knees. This wasn't Betty Alice or even someone with friendly intentions, or the person would already have answered her.

There was another rattle of the doorknob, and then someone bashed against the door. That caused her heart to bash against her ribs. Oh, God. The door held, but Livvy knew she had no choice. She called Reed.

"This is Livvy. There's an intruder outside my door."

She didn't stay on the line. Livvy tossed the phone back onto the vanity so she could free her hands for a fight.

The person rammed against the door again, and she heard some mumbled profanity. She was almost positive it was a man's voice.

Another bash, and this time the wood cracked. It wouldn't hold up much longer, and she had to do something to improve her chances of survival if this turned into a full-fledged assault.

Livvy grabbed the scissors from her makeup bag and slapped off the lights. Since the lights were still on in her room, she hoped the intruder's eyes wouldn't have time to adjust to the darkness if he managed to get through that door.

Or rather *when* he got through.

The next bash sent the door flying open right at her, and Livvy jumped to the edge of the tub so she wouldn't get hit. Her heart was pounding. Her breathing was way too fast. And she had no hopes of being concealed in the dark room since her white nightgown would no doubt act as a beacon.

The man came at her.

Because the room was dark, Livvy couldn't see his face, but she caught his scent, a mixture of sweat and whiskey. He reached for her, but she swung the scissors at him and connected with his arm. She heard the sound of tearing fabric, and prayed she'd cut skin as well. He cursed in a raspy growling voice.

A voice she didn't recognize.

In the back of her mind, she was trying to identify this intruder. No. He was an assailant now, not merely an intruder, and with the profanity still hissing from his throat, he latched on to her hair and dragged her away from the tub. His grip was strong, and was obviously being fed with booze and adrenaline. Still, Livvy didn't just stand there and let him assault her.

Using the scissors again, she slashed at his midsection and

followed it with a kick aimed at his shin. She missed. But he released the grip he had on her.

"Livvy?" someone shouted.

Reed.

She'd never been more thankful to hear someone call out her name. Better yet, he was nearby, and she could hear him barreling up the stairs. Her attacker must have heard Reed as well because he turned and raced out of the bathroom.

Livvy went after him.

Only the lamp was on, but she had no trouble seeing the man's back as he dove through the open window that led to the second-floor balcony.

"Livvy!" Reed shouted again.

He banged on the door, which was obviously still locked because the intruder hadn't entered that way. He'd apparently entered the same way he exited through the window. A window she was certain she'd locked as well because the balcony had steps that led down in the garden. She had known full well it was a weak security point.

Livvy hurried across the room to unlock the door, threw it open and faced a very concerned-looking Reed. "Are you okay?" There were beads of sweat on his face, and his breath was gusting.

Livvy didn't trust her voice. There'd be too much fear and emotion in it. Instead she pointed to the window where the evening breeze was billowing the pink curtains.

She dropped the scissors on the nightstand and grabbed her gun so she could go in pursuit, but Reed beat her to it.

He bolted through the window and started running.

REED RACED across the balcony, following the sounds of footsteps. Unfortunately, whoever had broken into Livvy's room had a good head start, and Reed caught just a glimpse of the shadowy figure when he leaped off the bottom step and raced through the English-style country gardens that were thick with plants and shrubs.

There were too many places to hide.

And worse, too many ways to escape.

Reed barreled down the steps, but he no longer had a visual on the guy. Heck, he couldn't even hear footsteps on the grounds. Since finding him would be a crap shoot, Reed ran straight ahead because where the gardens ended there was a thick cluster of mature oaks. Beyond that was a greenbelt and then another street lined with businesses that would already be closed for the night. If the intruder was local, then he knew all he had to do was duck into one of the many alleys or other recesses.

And that was probably what had happened.

Because once Reed tore his way through the greenbelt and onto the street, he saw no one.

He stopped, listened and tried to hear any sound over the heartbeat that was pulsing in his ears.

Nothing.

Well, nothing except for his racing imagination. Maybe the escape had been a ruse. Maybe the guy was doubling back so he could have another go at Livvy. That put a knot in Reed's gut, and he whirled around and raced toward the inn.

A dozen scenarios went through his head. None were good. But he forced himself to remember that Livvy could take care of herself. Most of the time.

Tonight had obviously been the exception.

It might take a lifetime or two for Reed to forget the look of sheer terror he'd seen on her face when she'd unlocked the door to let him in.

He took out his cell phone and called his office so he could request backup. "Get any and all officers to Wade Street and the area back of the Bluebonnet Inn," he told the dispatcher. "We're looking for an unidentified male. About six feet tall. Dressed in black. Find him!" he ordered.

Reed didn't have to make it all the way back to the inn before he spotted Livvy. Dressed in her gown and bathrobe— and armed—she was making her way down the balcony stairs.

"Did you catch him?" she called out.

"No." And even from the twenty feet or so of distance between them, he saw her expression. The fear had been quickly replaced by anger.

Reed understood that emotion because he was well beyond the anger stage. He wanted to get the guy responsible for putting Livvy through this.

"Are you hurt?" he asked. He closed the distance between them and glanced around to make sure they weren't about to be ambushed.

"I'm fine," Livvy insisted.

But they both knew that was a lie. He caught onto her arm to lead her back up the steps because he didn't want her out in the open.

"Betty Alice called a couple of minutes ago," Livvy explained. Her voice sounded calm enough. It was a cop's tone. Clinical, detached. She would have pulled it off, too, if he hadn't been touching her. Reed could feel her trembling. "She heard the noise and wanted to know what was going on. I told her to stay put and make sure all the windows and doors were locked."

"Good." He didn't want anyone in the path of his guy.

Because it was entirely possible they weren't just dealing with an intruder but a killer.

Marcie's killer.

Reed led her back into her room, and closed the gaping window that had been used as the escape route. Because he didn't want anyone seeing their silhouettes, he turned off the lights as well.

"He broke through the bathroom door," Livvy explained. Her voice was soft now, practically a mumble, and she cleared her throat. "It was dark, and I couldn't see his face."

"But you're sure it was a man?"

"Positive. He smelled of sweat and liquor. And he had a strong grip." She rubbed her wrist. Even though she was a peace officer, that didn't make her bulletproof or spare her the emotion that came with an attack. Soon, very soon, the adrenaline would cause her to crash. "I'd left my gun in here so I couldn't get to it."

The fear in her voice was hard for Reed to hear, but he wouldn't be doing either of them any favors if he gave in to it. He had to have more answers if they hoped to catch this guy.

"Did he have a weapon?" Reed asked.

She hesitated a moment and then shook her head. "If he did, he didn't use it. He just grabbed me."

Now, that was odd. A killer, especially the one who'd shot Marcie, would likely have a gun. Or he could have grabbed Livvy's own weapon before going after her in the bathroom. But he hadn't.

Why?

Maybe this wasn't about harming Livvy but rather about scaring her. *Again*. If so, this SOB was persistent.

"I might have cut him with those scissors," Livvy added,

tipping her head to where they lay on the nightstand. "I need to bag them."

"Later," Reed insisted. The scissors could wait.

She was shaking harder now, and Reed looped his arm around her and eased her down onto the bed so they were sitting on the edge. It wouldn't be long, maybe a few minutes, before he got an update from the deputies. If they got lucky, they might already have the attacker in custody. But just in case, Reed wanted to hear more.

"What about the possibility of transfer of DNA from him to you?" he asked.

"No," she answered immediately. "I wasn't able to scratch him, and other than his hand on my wrist, there was no physical contact."

Reed was thankful for that. Livvy hadn't been hurt. But the DNA proof would have been a good thing to have. Still, if she'd managed to cut him, that would give them the sample they needed.

"The door was locked," she continued, "but I guess he broke in through the window." Her voice cracked. The trembling got even worse.

And Reed gave up his fight to stay detached and impersonal. He pulled her even closer against him, until she was deep into his arms, and he brushed what he hoped was a comforting kiss on her forehead.

It didn't stay at the comfort level.

Livvy looked up at him, and even though the only illumination was coming from the outside security lights filtering through the curtains, he could clearly see her face. Yes, the fatigue and fear were there. But there was also an instant recognition that he was there, too, touching her.

Maybe it was just the adrenaline reaction, but Reed forgot all about that possibility when he lowered his head and kissed her.

There it was. That jolt. It slammed through him. So did her taste. After just one brief touch of their mouths, Reed knew he wanted more.

He slid his hand around the back of her neck so he could angle her head and deepen the kiss.

Yeah, it was stupid.

French-kissing his temporary partner and subordinate was a dumb-as-dirt kind of thing to do, but he also knew he had no plans to stop. He could justify that this was somehow easing Livvy's fear, but that was BS. This wasn't about fear. It was about this white-hot attraction that had flared between them since they first met.

Livvy didn't exactly cool things down, either. She latched on to him, bunching up his shirt in her fist, and she kissed him as if he were the cure to the trauma she'd just experienced.

And maybe he was.

Maybe they both needed this to make it through the next few minutes.

Her gown was thin. Reed quickly realized that when her chest landed against his. No bra. He could feel her breasts warm and soft against him. He felt even more of them when Livvy wound herself around him, leaning closer and closer until it was hard to tell where she started and he began.

Reed made it even closer.

He hauled her into his lap. Again, it was a bad idea. Really bad. But his body was having a hard time remembering why it was so bad because Livvy landed not just on his lap but with her legs straddling his hips.

The kisses continued. It was a fierce battle, and they got even more intense. So did the body contact. Specifically, her sex against his. And that was when Reed knew. This might have started as a kiss of comfort, but this was now down-and-dirty foreplay.

He made it even dirtier.

Reed slid his hand up her thigh, pushing up the flimsy gown along the way. She was all silk and heat, and the heat got hotter when he reached the juncture of her thighs. He paused a moment, to give Livvy a chance to stop things, but she only shoved her hips toward his hand.

And he touched her.

There was a lot more silk and heat here, and even though she was wearing panties, it wasn't much of a barrier. Part of him—okay, all of him—wanted to slide his fingers and another part of him into that slick heat. Only his brain was holding him back, and it just wasn't making a very good argument to convince the rest of him.

"This will have to be quick," she mumbled and took those wild kisses to his neck.

Quick sounded very appealing. Heck, any kind of sex with Livvy did. He wanted her. Worse, he wanted her now.

And that was why he had to stop.

She slid her hand over his erection and reached for the zipper on his jeans. However, Reed snagged her wrists. That didn't stop the other touching and, fighting him, she ground herself against his erection until he was seeing stars.

And having a boatload of doubts about stopping.

"Livvy," he managed to get out.

She finally stopped. Stared at him. Blinked. "You don't want to do this."

"Oh, I want it, and that's the understatement of the century. But you know what I'm going to say."

"The timing sucks." Her weary sigh shoved her breasts against his chest again.

He nodded and used every bit of willpower to ease her off his lap and back onto the bed. It didn't exactly end things. She landed with her legs slightly apart, and he got a glimpse of those barrier panties.

Oh, yeah. Definitely thin and lacy.

Reed had to clench his hands into fists to stop himself from going after her again.

"I'm sorry," she mumbled, shoving down her gown and scrambling away from him.

Hell. Now, she was embarrassed, and that was the last thing he wanted her to feel.

Even though it was a risk, Reed latched on to her shoulders and forced eye contact. "We will have sex," he promised. "It doesn't matter if it'll complicate the devil out of things, we'll land in bed. I'd just prefer if it happened when you weren't minutes off surviving an attack. I want to take my time with you. I want to be inside you not because you're scared but because you really want me inside you."

Her stare held, and for the briefest of moments, the corners of her mouth lifted into a smile. "I'm pretty sure the want was real. *Is* real," she corrected.

But Livvy waved him off, sighed again and scooped her hair away from her face. "I didn't think you'd be the sensible one."

He shrugged. "I don't feel too sensible. Actually, I'm damn uncomfortable right now."

They shared a smile, and because Reed thought they both could use it, he leaned over and kissed her. Not a foreplay kiss. But not a peck, either. He hoped it would serve as a reminder that this really wasn't over.

"Tonight's shot," he told her, pulling back. "We'll have reports to do. Maybe a suspect to interrogate. But tomorrow, why don't you plan on spending the night at my house?"

Her right eyebrow came up. "That'll get the gossips going."

"Yeah." It would. And it wouldn't be pretty. "I figure having you in my bed will be worth the gossip."

Livvy's eyebrow lifted higher. "You're sure about that?"

He was, but gossip was only part of it, and the look in her eyes indicated she understood that.

"I'm a Texas Ranger," she stated. "You're married to that badge, and this town. You don't have time to have an affair with me. Besides, judging from the way women around here look at you, you're the number-one catch. Husband and daddy material."

Reed couldn't disagree with any of it. He didn't consider himself a stud, but being single, male and employed did put him in big demand in a small town like Comanche Creek.

"What?" she questioned. "Did I hit a nerve?"

"No. I want marriage and kids someday," he admitted. Or at least he had at one time. Lately, however, those things seemed like a pipe dream. "What about you?"

But she didn't get a chance to answer. There was a knock at the door. "It's me, Kirby."

The sound of his deputy's voice sent them scurrying off the bed. "Did you find him?" Reed immediately asked.

"Not yet. But there's someone who wants to see you. He says it's important."

Livvy grabbed her clothes from the back of a chair and hurried into the bathroom. "I need to dress, but I won't be long," she assured him. Since the bathroom door was off its hinges, she got into the tub and pulled the shower curtain around her so she'd have some privacy. "And talk loud so I can hear what you're saying."

Reed unlocked the bedroom door, eased it open, and came face-to-face with someone he certainly hadn't expected to see.

Ben Tolbert.

Reed drew his weapon, surprising Kirby almost as much as he did their visitor.

Shane's father stared at the gun, then him. Actually, it was more of a glare with intense blue eyes that were a genetic copy of his son's. The dark brown hair was a match, too, though Ben's was threaded with gray.

"Did you come back to finish the job?" Reed asked.

"I don't know what you mean." He tipped his head to Reed's gun. "And is that necessary?"

"It is." Reed leaned in so he could get right in Ben's face. "Now, you're going to tell me why you've been harassing Sergeant Hutton."

"I haven't been," Ben insisted.

Reed had to hand it to him. It certainly didn't look as if Ben had just committed a B and E and then escaped on foot. However, Reed couldn't rule out that it was exactly what had happened.

"You want me to believe it's a coincidence that you're here tonight, less than thirty minutes after Sergeant Hutton was attacked?" Reed tried to keep the anger from his voice. He failed.

"Call it what you will. I didn't attack anyone, including that Texas Ranger. I'm just here to set the record straight."

Good. But Reed figured there would be a lot of lies mixed in with Ben's attempt to explain anything. First though, Reed looked at Kirby. "I'll handle this situation. Go ahead and help out the others by securing the place. I want the whole area checked for prints or any other evidence."

Kirby issued a "Will do," and headed down the stairs.

Reed heard the shower curtain rattle, and Ben's gaze flew right to Livvy. His snarl deepened. "So, there you are. I understand you're hell-bent on keeping my boy behind bars."

Livvy walked across the room and stood next to Reed. "Actually, I'm hell-bent on examining the evidence. Too bad I keep getting interrupted." She paused just a heartbeat. "Did you try to kill me tonight?"

"I already answered that. No. Got no reason to go after you. *Yet.*"

That did it. Reed was already operating on a short fuse. He grabbed Ben with his left hand and slammed him against the doorjamb. "Threatening a peace officer's a crime, Ben. One I won't take lightly."

It took a moment for Ben to get his teeth unclenched. "I've done nothing wrong."

"What about burning down the cabin?" Reed challenged.

"I didn't do that." No hesitation. None. But Reed wasn't ready to believe him. Ben had one of the best motives for wanting Livvy out of town.

"In the woods near the cabin, we found a piece of a shirt that belongs to you," Livvy challenged.

"Yeah. I heard about that. Jonah said I bought it from a charity sale. Well, you know what? Jonah was lying, probably to save his own rich butt. But I'll be damned if I'll take the blame for something that man's done."

"So you're saying you're innocent?" Livvy clarified.

"Damn right I am."

Ben began a tirade of why he was being railroaded, but Reed was no longer paying attention to him. That was because he had spotted something.

Something that could blow this case wide open.

Reed latched on to Ben and got him moving toward the stairs. "Ben Tolbert, you're under arrest."

ELEVEN

LIVVY gulped down more coffee and hoped the caffeine would help clear the fog in her head. The adrenaline from the attack had long since come and gone, leaving her with a bone-deep fatigue that was worse because she'd gotten only an hour or so of real sleep. That probably had something to do with the lumpy sofa in the sheriff's office break room that she'd used as a bed.

But it had more to do with Ben Tolbert's arrest.

God, was he really the one who'd attacked her? If so, Reed and she would soon know. The tiny rip on the sleeve of Ben's shirt had prompted his arrest.

A rip that she was thankful Reed had noticed.

She'd been too shaken from the attack to notice much of anything. So much for all her training. She'd reacted like a rookie, and it didn't really matter that she was one. She expected more of herself.

Livvy checked her watch again. It was 9:00 a.m. The start of the normal workday for most people, but Reed and she had been working this case most of the night. With luck, they would soon know if the small cut on Ben's shirt had been made with her nail scissors. Well, they'd know if the Ranger lab could match the fibers. Reed had had one of the deputies hand-deliver both Ben's shirt and the scissors, and any minute now, they should know if it was a match.

"I'm not releasing Ben Tolbert until I'm sure he's innocent," she heard Reed bark. He was no doubt still talking to Jerry Collier, the head of the land office and also Ben's newly hired attorney.

"Then schedule an arraignment," Jerry insisted. "I don't want you holding him without making it official."

"I'm doing us all a favor. It'll only create a mountain of paperwork if I officially arrest Ben."

"But you can release him until you get back that evidence." And Jerry continued to argue his client's case.

Livvy, however, shut out the conversation when her phone rang. It was the crime lab, but the number on the caller ID wasn't for trace and fibers, it was from the firearms section.

"Sergeant Hutton," she answered.

"It's me. Sam McElroy." This was someone she knew well. A firearms expert who'd been examining the weapon that had killed Marcie. But Livvy hadn't just sent him that particular gun. She had also couriered Sam the primary firearm that Shane used in the line of duty.

"You found something?" Livvy asked.

"I did. Your instincts were right. Someone tampered with the Rimfire pistol used to kill Marcie James."

Livvy let out the breath she'd been holding. She'd tried to stay objective, but because her feelings for Reed had softened to the point of melting, she'd automatically found herself rooting for his deputy. And, yes, that was a blow to her professionalism, but in the end, it was the truth that mattered anyway.

"The fingerprints were planted on the murder weapon," she said, stating a conclusion she'd already reached.

"Yes," Sam verified. "I compared the two firearms, and the grip pattern on the Rimfire is way off. There weren't enough pressure points to indicate Deputy Tolbert fired the gun, even though it was in his hand."

"Probably placed there by the real killer while the deputy was unconscious."

Shane had been set up, just as he said.

But by whom?

Had his father been the one to kill Marcie? Maybe. But why would he set up his son to take the fall? Still, he certainly wasn't the only suspect. Ben's attorney, Jerry, was on the short list. So was the mayor. Billy Whitley. And Jonah Becker.

"There's more," Sam continued. "I checked the lab, and one of the results was ready. I thought you'd like to know."

She listened as Sam explained the results of the sample she'd submitted after examining the cabin crime scene.

Livvy thanked Sam, ended the call and got up from the desk so she could give Reed the news, but the moment she saw his face, she knew he had news of his own.

"I'm getting my client out of jail," Jerry insisted. *"Now."* And with that, he stormed off.

Reed scrubbed his hand over his jaw, drank some coffee and then looked at her. "I just got a call from the lab. The fibers on your scissors didn't match Ben's shirt."

Her heart dropped to her stomach. "But what about the rip on the fabric?"

Reed lifted his shoulder. "It wasn't caused by the scissors."

Livvy forced herself to take a step back. "Ben could have changed his shirt after he attacked me."

"Yeah. He could have." But there was skepticism in Reed's voice.

Livvy shared that skepticism. Why would Ben have chosen to replace the shirt worn during the attack with one that was torn in such a way that it would only cast more suspicion on him?

"I have to let him go," Reed said. "As soon as Jerry and he sign the papers, he'll be out. But I'll keep an eye on him. And I'll take some measures to make sure you're safe."

She remembered his invitation when they'd kissed in her room. "You want me to stay at your place?"

"Yes." More skepticism. "I know what you're thinking. It'll set tongues wagging, but I'd planned on spending more time with you anyway whether that was at work or the inn. This just makes it easier for me to keep you safe because I'm not going to let Ben or anyone else have a go at you."

Livvy wanted to object. She wanted to remind him that she could take care of herself. But she wasn't stupid. And she didn't want to die.

"I have news, too." It seemed a really good time to change the subject. "The fingerprint pattern on the murder weapon doesn't match the one on Shane's service pistol."

She saw the fatigue drain from Reed's face. "You mean he's innocent."

She nodded. "That's what the evidence indicates."

So why was she so reluctant to declare that Shane wasn't a killer?

All the pieces fit for him to have been set up. It was also obvious that someone else was out there, someone who wanted to stop them from learning the truth. Shane certainly hadn't been responsible for those attacks because he had been behind bars when they occurred. But Livvy couldn't totally dismiss the possibility that perhaps Shane was the mastermind who'd set all of this in motion.

Still, there were others with more powerful motives than love gone wrong.

"The firearms expert who called me about the gun also had the results from one of the lab tests," she continued. "The blood spatter we found in the cabin was consistent with the head injury that Shane described. And it was his blood."

Now there was relief in his eyes. Reed looked as if he were about to shout in victory, but his mood changed again.

Did he have doubts as well?

"Thank you," he said.

He reached out and almost idly ran his fingers through the ends of her ponytail. It was the gesture of a man comfortable with touching her. A gesture that shocked Livvy but not nearly as much as her own reaction did. She moved in to the touch, letting his thumb brush against her cheek.

It was intimate.

And wrong.

As usual, the timing was awful. They were both exhausted. Both had a dozen things to do that were important and related to the job. But it was as if those deeply seeded primal urges just weren't going to leave them alone.

"You know, I'll be leaving as soon as we've wrapped up this case," Livvy said. Not that she needed to remind him or herself of that.

"I know." And he seemed genuinely disappointed. "But Austin's not that far from here. Less than an hour away."

Far enough, she silently added.

If she stopped this now…but then she halted that particular thought because it was useless.

She couldn't stop this now.

It was only a matter of time before they landed in bed, and her hope was that this heat between them would be so intense that it would quickly burn itself out and Reed and she could get back to normal.

Reed drew in a hard breath, pulled back his hand and turned. "I need to do the paperwork for Shane's release." Then, he paused. "You're sure he's innocent?"

"No," she admitted. "But the evidence doesn't point to him being guilty."

Reed nodded and walked away, leaving Livvy to wonder if she'd just given a killer a get-out-of-jail-free card.

The phone on Reed's desk rang, and Livvy glanced out into the reception area to see if Eileen was there to answer it. She wasn't, so Livvy took the call.

"It's me, Ben Tolbert," the caller said.

Livvy tried to keep the strain out of her voice. "Are you already out of jail?"

"Yeah, as of thirty seconds ago."

Her heart suddenly felt very heavy. "Where are you?"

"I'm going nowhere near you. Where's Reed?"

"Busy. I'm surprised you didn't see him because he was headed to the jail." She'd let Shane be the one to tell his father that he'd been cleared of the murder charges.

"I musta missed him. I didn't exactly hang around the place after I told my boy I'd be gettin' him out of that cell soon enough."

Sooner than Ben thought. "I don't expect Reed back for ten or fifteen minutes, but I can take a message."

Silence. Several long seconds of it. "Tell him I've been doing some digging."

Livvy had to get her teeth apart so she could speak. "We don't want you to interfere in this case."

"Well, somebody has to. You got the wrong man in jail, and I intend to do everything I can to prove it. So, consider this a tip. I heard from a reliable source that Billy Whitley faked historical documents that allowed Jonah Becker to buy that land—the land that's causing all the ruckus with the Comanches."

Billy Whitley, another suspect. "Why would Billy have done that?"

"Money, what else? Jonah paid him to do it. Jonah's too smart to make a payment that could be traced back to him, but there will be a trail all right. You're just gonna have to hunt hard and find it."

Maybe. If this was a legit lead. "Who's your reliable source?"

"Can't tell you that."

"Then why should I believe you?" Livvy pressed. "You might be saying all of this to take suspicion off yourself."

"No reason for that. I haven't done anything wrong."

The attack came racing back at her. The man's scent. The rasp of his breathing. How he'd come at her. She'd been lucky not to have been hurt. Or worse.

"I think Billy's the one who set up my boy," Ben continued, and that accusation immediately grabbed her attention.

"Why do you think that?"

"Because if Billy did fake those documents, then he's as much of a suspect as Jonah."

"And your lawyer," Livvy pointed out. "Jerry has motive, too."

"A lot of people have motive," Ben admitted, "but I'm betting Billy or his wife is responsible for this."

Yes, Charla could have been in on it. "Again, do you have proof?"

There was another hesitation, longer than the first. "What's the fax number there?" he asked.

Surprised by his request, Livvy looked at the machine and read the fax number that she located on the top of it. "Why do you need it?"

"Because I'm about to send you something. Consider it a gift."

Livvy didn't really want any gift from a suspected killer, but it didn't take long before the machine began to spit out a faxed copy.

"The first page is a copy of the way the deed was filed decades ago," Ben explained. "Look at line eight. When you get the second page, you'll see how it was changed. It no longer says 'the Comanche people.' It lists ownership as none other than Billy and Charla Whitley."

Livvy didn't say a word until both documents had finished printing, and her attention went to line eight on the pages.

There had indeed been a change.

"How did you get these?" she demanded.

"I can't tell you that."

"You stole them," Livvy accused. Then, she cursed under her breath. "And if you did, that means we can't use them as evidence. We wouldn't be able to prove that you're not the one who did the tampering."

His silence let her know that Ben was considering that. "What if I swear on my son's life that those papers are real?"

"That won't stand up in court." But it did in some small way convince her that Ben might be telling the truth, about this anyway. Livvy decided to put him to the test. "Shane will be out of jail soon. It appears someone planted his prints on the murder weapon."

"Are you sure?" Ben snapped.

"Sure enough for Reed to be processing his release as we speak."

Ben paused. "Is this some kind of trick? It is, isn't it? You're just telling me what I want to hear. You want to hang my boy."

"I want to hang the person responsible for Marcie's murder," Livvy clarified. "And if that had turned out to be Shane, he'd still be in jail. That's true for any future evidence we might find. But for now, the evidence isn't enough for us to hold your son."

Ben mumbled something. "Guess that means you're still gunning for him."

Livvy huffed. "Only if Shane's guilty of something. Is he?"

"I knew it." Ben cursed again. "I knew you'd still go after my boy."

Livvy didn't even bother to repeat that she wasn't on some vendetta to convict Shane of anything. But Ben might have a vendetta of his own.

"Did you tamper with these documents to implicate Billy so you could get your son cleared of murder charges?" Livvy asked.

"No. The documents are real, and Billy changed them so Jonah could buy that land."

His answer was so fast and assured that it surprised Livvy. Ben could have taken the easy way out. Heck, he could have hung up the phone and raced to the jail to see Shane.

But he hadn't.

Instead, Ben had stuck to his story about Billy's involvement.

Livvy looked at the documents again. They certainly seemed real, and that meant she had to call Reed.

They needed a search warrant ASAP.

"My advice?" Ben said. "Be careful, Sergeant Hutton. Because once everyone in town knows what Billy and Jonah did, somebody's gonna get hurt. Bad."

Livvy didn't question the threat because she knew Ben was right. The town was already on the verge of an explosion, and this certainly wouldn't help.

"One more thing," Ben added. "Everything we've said here, somebody's probably overheard. Somebody who's probably running to tell Billy to destroy anything that might put these murders on him. He'll be desperate. Real desperate. If I was you, I'd get over there right now."

Livvy didn't argue or disagree. She dropped the phone back onto its cradle and hurried to find Reed.

TWELVE

REED replayed everything Livvy had told him about her conversation with Ben. In fact, Reed had spent a good deal of the day replaying it and trying to figure out what the devil was going on.

He wasn't any closer to the answer than he had been when the day started.

Thankfully, Woody had come back from his fishing trip. Well, he had after Reed had sent his deputy out to tell the man what had been going on in town. Woody had returned immediately, just in time to give Reed permission to search Billy's office in the city building.

Reed had personally gone through every inch of Billy's office. Nothing was out of order, nor were there any signs of tampered documents. It'd helped that Billy hadn't been there during the search, but he would find out about it. That was a given, even though Reed had sworn Billy's secretary to secrecy.

Besides, there was a bigger secret that Reed had to unravel.

Shane was out of jail now. Cleared because of planted evidence that Livvy had discovered. So, that meant there was a killer out there who had to be caught.

Reed just wasn't sure this was the way to go about doing it.

Beside him on the seat of his truck, Livvy was napping. Thank God. She was the only person in town who in the past twenty-four hours had had less sleep than him. Of course, she hadn't wanted the nap. In fact, she'd fought it like crazy, but in the end, the boring stakeout of Billy's house had been too much for the fatigue, and she was now asleep with her head dropped onto his shoulder.

Reed didn't mind the close contact with her rhythmic breath brushing against his neck. He didn't even mind that her left breast was squished against his arm. The touching was a surefire way of remembering that she was a woman, and that in turn was a surefire way of keeping him awake.

Shifting a little so that his arm wouldn't go numb, Reed checked their surroundings again. It was dark now, still hotter than hell, and no one had come or gone from the Whitley house in the entire three hours that Livvy and he had been keeping watch. The area wasn't exactly brimming with activity since it was located just outside the city limits and a good half mile from any neighbors.

Reed had called Billy earlier, before he'd even gone to the man's office to search. Billy had been home then. Sick with a sudden case of the stomach flu, he'd said, and he had a doctor's appointment in San Antonio and wouldn't be home until later in the evening. Then, he'd hung up and hadn't answered the phone when Reed tried to call him again. That'd sent Livvy and Reed out to Billy's place because they didn't want the man to try to destroy any evidence.

But where were Billy and Charla now? Still at the doctor's office or perhaps pretending to be there?

And had someone already tipped him off about Ben somehow finding the doctored land record? Or the office search? Maybe. But if Billy did know, the last thing Reed expected the man to do was go on the run.

Well, unless Billy really was a killer.

Reed checked his cell phone again. Nope. He hadn't missed a call. Not that he thought he had since the phone was set to a loud ring. That meant Kirby hadn't succeeded in getting the search warrant yet. Reed hadn't needed one for a municipal office because Woody had given him permission to search. But he'd need one for a private residence.

He'd get it, too.

There was no way a judge would turn it down with the evidence of the doctored documents, but Comanche Creek wasn't exactly flooded with judges, and Kirby had gotten stuck driving all the way over to Bandana, a good hour away, just to find Judge Calder, who was visiting relatives.

Reed had considered just going in and looking around Billy and Charla's place. But that wouldn't be smart if Livvy and he managed to find something incriminating. If Billy was the killer, Reed didn't want anything like an unlawful search to stand in the way of the man's arrest and conviction. Of course, Reed had considered that this could be an exigent circumstance, where a peace officer could conduct a search without a warrant if there was a likelihood that evidence might be destroyed, but again, he didn't want that challenged. He wanted to follow the letter of the law on this one.

Livvy stirred, her breath shivering as if she were in the throes of a bad dream. But Reed rethought that theory when her eyes sprang open and her gaze snapped to his.

Even though the only illumination came from the hunter's moon and the yellow security light mounted at the end of the drive, he could clearly see her expression. No nightmare. But no doubt disturbing.

This dream was perhaps of the sexual variety.

Or maybe that was wishful thinking on his part. His thoughts were certainly straying toward that variety when it came to Livvy.

"You shouldn't have let me fall asleep," she mumbled and eased her breast away from his arm.

Maybe it was his surly mood, or even his own fatigue, but Reed put his hand around the back of her neck, hauled her to him and kissed her.

He got proof of the direction of her thoughts when she didn't resist. She kissed him right back.

And more.

Livvy caught onto his shoulders and adjusted their positions so that he got more of that breast contact. Both of them. He'd been hot before, but that kicked up the heat even more.

The kiss continued. Deepened. So did the body contact. They were both damp with sweat, and with the moisture from the kiss, everything suddenly felt right for sex.

It wasn't, of course.

And because they were literally sitting in his truck in front of a suspected killer's house, Reed remembered that this was not a safe time to engage in an oral rodeo with a woman he wanted more than his next breath.

He pulled back. Man, his body protested. But before his body could come up with a convincing argument as to why this could continue, Reed moved Livvy back onto the seat so that they were no longer touching.

"I feel like I'm back in high school," she complained.

Not Reed. In high school his willpower had sucked, and he wouldn't have let something like common sense or danger get in the way of having sex.

And if he wasn't careful, he wouldn't let those things get in the way now.

His phone rang, slicing through the uncomfortable silence that followed Livvy's confession. Reed wasn't pleased with the interruption, but he was damn happy about getting this call.

"Kirby," Reed answered. "Tell me you have a search warrant."

"I got it. The judge didn't put any limits on it, either. You can go through the house, grounds and any outbuildings or vehicles. You still waiting at Billy's house?"

"Yeah. Bring the warrant to us."

"Will do. I'll be there in about forty-five minutes."

Reed hung up, knowing he wouldn't wait that long. The warrant had been issued and that was enough. "Let's go," he instructed.

Livvy immediately grabbed her equipment bag, got out and joined him as they walked toward the front of the house. "You plan to bash down the door?" she asked.

"No need." Reed lifted the fake rock to the left side of the porch and extracted a key.

"That's not very safe," she commented.

No, but until recently most people around Comanche Creek hadn't had cause to be concerned about safety.

Reed unlocked the door and stepped inside. "Anyone home?" he called out just to be sure that Billy or his wife weren't hiding out. But he got no answer.

He was thankful that the house wasn't huge and also that he had been there often enough to know the layout. "Billy's office is this way," he said, leading Livvy down the hall that was off the living room. "His wife, Charla, is somewhat of a neat freak so if he brought the land documents home, they'd be in here."

They went into the office, turned on the lights and immediately got to work. The room wasn't large, but it was jammed with furniture, including a desk that held a stack of papers, folders and an open laptop. Reed went there first, and Livvy headed to a filing cabinet.

"What are some possible file names that would be red flags?" she asked.

"Anything that deals with Native American land. Or something called the Reston Act. That's the name of the old law that gave the Comanches the land."

Livvy took out some latex gloves from her bag, put them on and tossed him a pair. She then pulled open the drawer. "So, if that law is on the books, why wasn't the land deal challenged when it happened two years ago?"

"It was, by the activist Native American group. But then Billy produced this document that supposedly superseded the Reston Act. It seemed legit, and there were other documents on file to back it up. Basically, those documents claimed that the land had only been leased to the Comanches and that ownership reverted to the original owner, who was Jonah's great-great-grandfather."

"Convenient," Livvy mumbled.

"Maybe." Reed put on the gloves and thumbed through the papers and files. "Or maybe someone doctored that, too. The activist group didn't have the funds to fight a long legal battle, so they turned to Marcie. They wanted her to testify that at Jonah's urging, Jerry Collier orchestrated the illegal land deal."

"And we know what happened to Marcie." Livvy paused, and he heard her rifling through the files. "Other than Billy, who else could have faked the documents?"

Reed figured she wouldn't like the answer. He certainly didn't. "Anyone with access to the land office."

Woody, Billy, Jerry and, yes, even Jonah. Basically, anyone with enough motive and determination could have figured out a way to get into those files since security was practically non-existent.

That had changed. Since the murders, Reed had insisted the city council install a better security system, one with surveillance cameras. But this crime—the altered documents—had happened long before the murders.

"I might have something," Livvy said.

But when he looked at her, she no longer had her attention on the files. She was studying something in the bookcase behind the cabinet. "There are two books here, one on Comanche burial rituals and another on local Native American artifacts."

That grabbed his attention, especially the one about rituals. Reed pulled it from the shelf, went straight to the index and saw the references for the red paint and ochre clay used in burials. It was critical because two dead bodies found the previous week had been prepared with red paint and clay.

"Hell," Reed mumbled. He continued to thumb through the book and noticed the pages with the clay references had been dog-eared.

Of course, Billy's wife was Native American. Maybe the books were hers. But Reed suspected if they had been, they wouldn't be in Billy's office. "It's circumstantial, but we can still use it to build a case. If Billy's guilty," he added.

"I think we might have something more than just circumstantial," Livvy corrected.

Reed looked up from the book. Livvy was photographing the trash can. She took several pictures and then carefully pushed aside some wadded-up paper and pulled out a latex glove, one very similar to the pair she was wearing.

"Any reason Billy would need this in his office?" she asked.

"None that I can think of." Especially none that involved anything legal.

Livvy eased the glove right side out and examined it. "We might be able to get DNA from the inside," she explained.

She placed the glove back on top of the paper wads, took the spray bottle of Luminol from her bag. She put just a fine mist on a small area that would cover the back of the hand.

It lit up.

An eerie blue glow.

Indicating there was blood.

Reed cursed again. "Is there enough for a DNA match to Marcie's blood?"

"All it takes is a tiny amount." She leaned in closer. "There's a smudge. It could be gunshot residue. Let's go ahead and bag this, and I'll bring the entire trash can in case the other glove is down in there."

Reed took one of the evidence bags to encase the glove while Livvy clicked off more photographs. The trash can and the glove would be sent to the lab that would have the final word on any biological or trace evidence, but it wasn't looking good for Billy.

Was Billy really a killer?

Reed had to admit it was possible. He'd known Billy all his life and had never seen any indication that the man was violent. Still, he'd also seen desperate people do desperate things, and Billy might have been desperate to cover his tracks and therefore kill Marcie.

"Once Kirby gets here with the warrant, I'll have him lock down the place so we can have time to go through everything else," Reed explained.

It also might be a good idea for them to drive the glove and trash can to the lab themselves. If they could get a quick match to Marcie on the blood, then Reed would arrest Billy.

"Are you okay?" Livvy asked.

Reed realized then that he was staring at the bagged glove with what had to be an expression of gloom and doom on his face. "I was just hoping the killer was someone else. Someone I didn't know."

"I understand." She touched his arm with her fingertips. A gesture no doubt meant to soothe him.

And it might have worked, too, if there hadn't been a sound. A slight rustling from outside the house.

"Probably the wind," Livvy said under her breath.

"Probably." But Reed set the bagged glove aside in case he had to reach for his gun. "It's not Kirby. We would have heard the cruiser drive up." Besides, it was too soon for the deputy to have arrived.

There was another sound. One that Reed couldn't quite distinguish, but it had come from the same direction as the first.

"I'll have a look," he insisted, and drew his weapon.

Livvy put down the trash can and did the same. "You think Billy's out there?" she whispered.

Someone certainly was—Reed was positive of that when he heard the next sound.

Footsteps, just outside the window.

He turned, aiming his gun.

Just as the lights went out and plunged them into total darkness.

Reed saw the shadow outside the window and reached for Livvy to get her out of the way. But he was a split second too late.

The bullet tore through the glass and came right at them.

THIRTEEN

LIVVY heard the shot, but she wasn't able to see who had fired at them. That was because Reed shoved her to the floor. She landed, hard, and the impact with the rustic wood planks nearly knocked the breath out of her.

Thankfully, Reed didn't have any trouble reacting.

He rolled to the side, came up on one knee, and using the desk as cover, he took aim. She couldn't see him clearly, but she heard the result. His shot blasted through what was left of the glass on the far right window.

"Who's out there?" she whispered, getting herself into position so she could fire as well.

"I can't tell."

Well, it was obviously someone who wanted them dead.

That hadn't been a warning shot. It'd come much too close to hitting them. And worse, it wasn't over. Reed and she were literally pinned down in a room with three large windows, any one of which could be an attack point. But it wasn't the only way a gunman could get to them.

There was a door behind them.

Livvy rolled onto her back so she could kick it shut. At least this way the culprit wouldn't be able to sneak up on them. And that led her to the big question.

Who exactly was the culprit?

"Billy Whitley," Livvy mumbled under her breath. Livvy scrambled to the side of the desk as well.

Another shot came through the window. Not from Reed this time. But from their attacker. Reed immediately returned fire, but Livvy held back and tried to peer over the desk and into the night. She hoped to get a glimpse of the shooter's location, but the only thing she saw was the darkness.

The next shot tore through the oak desk and sent a spray of splinters right at them. Reed shoved her back to the floor, and she caught onto his arm to make sure he came down as well.

More shots.

One right behind the other.

Livvy counted six, each one of the bullets slamming into the desk and the wall behind them. A picture fell and smashed on the floor next to her feet. The crash blended with the sounds of the attack. The chaos. And with her own heartbeat that was pounding in her ears.

Then, the shooting stopped.

Livvy waited, listening, hoping the attack was over but knowing it probably wasn't.

"He's reloading," she mumbled.

"Yeah." Reed glanced over at her. "How much ammunition do you have on you?"

"A full magazine in the gun and a backup clip. You?"

"Just what I have here. The rest is in the truck."

The truck parked outside where the shooter was.

Livvy didn't need to do the math. She knew. Reed and she wouldn't be able to go bullet-to-bullet with this guy because he probably had brought lots of backup ammunition with him. However, that was only one of their problems.

There was Kirby to consider.

The deputy would arrive soon, maybe in twenty minutes or less. The shooter might gun him down if Reed and she didn't warn him.

"I have to call Kirby," Livvy let him know.

Reed kept his attention nailed to the windows and passed her his phone. "Request backup, too, but don't have them storming in here. Tell him to keep everyone at a distance until they hear from me. But I do want lights and sirens. I want this SOB to know he's not going to escape."

Livvy agreed and made the call. She'd barely got out the warning when the shots started again. Obviously, the gunman had reloaded, and he began to empty that fresh ammunition into the room. He was literally tearing it apart, and that included the desk. It wouldn't be long before the shots destroyed the very piece of furniture they were using as cover.

"Kirby's calling backup," she relayed to Reed and tossed the phone back to him.

"The shots are getting closer."

Because of the noise, it took a moment for that to sink in. Livvy's gaze whipped in the direction of the windows again, and she listened.

God, Reed was right. The shots were getting closer, and that meant the shooter was closing in on them. If he made it all the way to the windows, he'd have a much better chance of killing them.

"He knows we don't have enough ammunition to hold him back," Reed explained. "We have to get out of this room."

Livvy didn't have any doubts about that. But what she did doubt was they'd be able to escape without being shot. The gunman might already be at the windows.

Of course, Reed and she could fire right back.

And they would. Until they were out of bullets. After that, well, they'd still fight. Livvy had no intentions of letting this goon get away, and Reed no doubt felt the same.

With the shots still knifing all around them, Livvy crawled to the door and reached for the knob.

"Be careful," Reed warned. "He might not be alone out there."

Mercy. She should have already thought of that. If this was Billy firing those shots, then he could be working with his wife. Charla could be in the house. Not that there had been any signs of that, but it was something Livvy had to prepare herself to face.

She aimed her gun and used her left hand to open the door. Just a fraction. She peered out into the hall. Thankfully, her eyes had adjusted to the darkness so even though the lights were off, she didn't see anyone lurking outside the doorway.

"It's clear," she relayed to Reed.

That got him moving. With his back to her and his attention still on the windows, he made his way to her and fired a glance into the hall.

"I'll go first, and you come out right behind me," Reed explained over the thick, loud blasts. "Stay low, as close to the floor as possible. You cover the right side of the hall. I'll cover the left."

Livvy's heart sank lower because the shots were even closer now.

Reed came up a little and fired a bullet in the direction of those shots. He didn't even aim, because it was meant to get the guy to back off. It might buy them a second or two of time, but that was all they needed.

Livvy didn't bother with the equipment bag. It was too big and bulky to take with them. She only hoped that it would still be there at the end of this attack. Just in case it wasn't, she snatched the bagged glove and shoved it into the waist of her jeans.

"Now!" Reed ordered.

Livvy didn't waste any more time. She scrambled to the side so Reed could get by her. He practically dove into the hall but as he'd instructed, he stayed on the floor. Livvy did the same, and she landed out in the darkness with her back to his.

She had the easy end of the hall to cover. Only one room that was directly at the end. Probably a bedroom. And the door was closed. However, that didn't mean the shooter wouldn't go through one of the room's windows to get to them and try to stop their escape.

"I don't see anyone," she reported.

"Neither do I."

Livvy didn't exactly breathe easier because that side contained all the main living areas. There were multiple points of entry, and if the gunman was indeed Billy, he would know the way to get in that would cause the biggest threat to Reed and her.

"This way," Reed instructed.

He remained crouched, with his gun aimed and ready, and he began to inch his way toward the front of the house where they'd entered. Livvy did the same while keeping watch on the bedroom. She didn't want anyone blasting through that door.

Then, again, the shots stopped.

Reed and she froze, and Livvy tried to steady her heartbeat so she could listen. But the only thing she heard was their breathing.

"Let's move," Reed insisted.

Yes, because they were still in the line of sight of the office windows, and Livvy couldn't risk reaching up to close the door. The last thing they wanted was for the shooter to have a visual on them.

Reed began to move again, and Livvy followed. She kept watch on both the office and the bedroom door, but there were no sounds coming from either.

Mercy.

Where was the shooter?

She doubted he'd just give up. No. He was looking for a place to launch another attack.

Reed stopped again when they got to the end of the hall, and she glanced at him as he peered out into the living room. It was just a quick look, and then he whipped his attention to the other side, to the kitchen. He didn't say anything, didn't make a sound, but Livvy figured he didn't see anyone or else he would have taken aim.

She heard it then. The knob on the kitchen door rattled. Reed and she both shifted in that direction, but she continued to watch the bedroom and now the office.

Another rattle. Someone was obviously trying to get in, but the door was apparently locked because the third try wasn't just a rattle. Someone gave it a frantic, violent shake.

Livvy had just enough time to wonder why Billy hadn't just used his key to gain entry when she heard another sound.

A siren.

Kirby or one of the backup deputies had finally arrived. Or would soon. Reed and she wouldn't have to hold out much longer.

But that brought a new concern. A new *fear*.

The gunman might get away.

That couldn't happen. Reed and she couldn't continue to go through this. They had to catch the killer and get him off the streets. If not, this wouldn't stop.

Reed obviously had the same concern because he moved out of the hall so he'd be in a better position if the gunman did indeed come through the kitchen door. The siren might scare him off.

Or not.

The *or not* was confirmed when someone kicked at the door. Hard. And then it sounded as if someone was ramming against it.

Livvy considered shooting at the door. Reed likely did, too, but this might not be the gunman. It could be Charla who was trying to get away from her now deranged husband. Or maybe it was someone from backup responding.

"This is Sheriff Hardin," Reed called out. "Who's out there?"

Nothing. And the attempts to get inside stopped.

Livvy couldn't hear if the person moved away because the sirens drowned out any sound the person might have made.

Reed cursed and scurried to the snack bar area that divided the living room from the kitchen. He kept his aim and focus on the door while Livvy tried to keep watch all around them.

"Call Kirby." Reed tossed her his phone again. "Make sure he's locking down the area."

But it might be too late. The killer could already be on the move and escaping.

"Smoke," she heard Reed say.

She lifted her head, pulled in a long breath, and cursed. Yes, it was smoke, and she figured it was too much to hope that it was coming from some innocent source.

Livvy pressed Redial, and Kirby answered on the first ring. She relayed Reed's message and told the deputy to await further orders. She'd barely managed to say that before there was another shot.

This one, however, hadn't been fired into the house. It'd come from outside but in the direction of the driveway.

Reed and she waited for several long seconds. Breaths held. With her pulse and adrenaline pounding out of control. Livvy didn't take her eyes off the bedroom just up the hall, and she was primed and wired for an attack when the cell phone rang.

The unexpected sound caused her to gasp, and she glanced down at the lit screen. It was Kirby.

"There's a fire on the back porch," Kirby shouted. "You need to get out of there."

Maybe Reed heard the deputy because he motioned for her to move toward the front door.

"Do you see the shooter?" Livvy asked Kirby.

"I think so. He's on the west end of the house."

By the driveway, just as she'd expected. "Is he trying to get in?"

"No. He's just sitting there, leaning against the wall."

Sitting? Or maybe crouching and waiting? "Can you see who it is?"

"No," Kirby quickly answered. "I'm using my hunting binoculars. They have night vision, and I'm getting a pretty close look, but he has a hat covering his face."

So if it was Billy, he could be trying to conceal his identity.

"How bad is the fire?" The smoke was starting to billow into the living room.

"Not bad right now, but I wouldn't stay in there much longer. Uh, Sergeant Hutton?" Kirby continued. "I think the guy's been shot. He's got his hand clutched to his chest, and his gun is on the ground beside him."

Shot? It was possible. Reed and she had fired several times, and any one of the bullets could have hit the gunman.

"The shooter might be wounded," she told Reed. "He's by the driveway."

Reed didn't say anything for several seconds. "Tell Kirby to cover us. We're going out there."

Livvy told Kirby their plan while they were on the move toward the front door. Reed opened it.

Nothing.

Certainly there was no gunman waiting just outside.

Reed went first, and Livvy followed him. As they'd done inside, they moved back to back so they could cover all sides. At the end of the road, she saw Kirby standing next to a cruiser. Covering them. She hoped they wouldn't need it.

The night was sticky and hot, and the smoke was already tainting the air. Livvy heard the high, piercing buzzing of mosquitoes that immediately zoomed in on them.

Reed batted the mosquitoes away and hurried to the back of the house. He paused only a few seconds to check the area where the last shot had been fired.

Then, Reed took aim.

And fired.

Livvy tried to scramble to get into position so she could assist, but Reed latched on to her arm and held her at bay. "I fired a warning shot," he told her. "The guy didn't move an inch."

Which could mean the gunman was perhaps too injured to react. Or this could be a trick to lure them out into the open so he could kill them.

"Cover me," Reed insisted.

He stood, braced his wrist for a better aim and started toward the shooter.

Livvy eased out so she could fire if necessary. She saw the shooter then. Dressed in what appeared to be jeans, a dark shirt and a baseball cap that covered his face. His back was against the exterior of the house. His handgun on the ground beside him.

The guy certainly wasn't moving.

Reed inched closer. So did Livvy. And thanks to the moonlight she saw the man did indeed have his left hand resting on his chest.

She also saw the blood.

Ahead of her, Reed stooped and put his fingers against the man's neck. Livvy waited and didn't lower her guard just in case this was a ploy.

"He's dead," Reed relayed.

"Dead," Livvy repeated under her breath.

She walked closer and stared down at the body. Though she was more than happy that this guy wasn't still taking shots at them, it sickened her a little to realize that she might have been the one to kill him.

Reed reached down with his left hand and eased the cap away from the man's face.

Livvy's stomach roiled.

It was Billy Whitley.

"We have to move the body," she heard Reed say, and he reached for Billy's feet. "The fire's spreading fast."

Livvy took hold of Billy as well and glanced at the flames

that were eating their way through the back of the house. Reed was right—they didn't have much time. The fire had swelled to the wood-shake roof, and there were already tiny embers falling down around them.

They had dragged the body a few yards when she saw something fall out of the pocket of Billy's jeans.

A piece of paper.

Since she was still wearing a latex glove, she reached for it, but reaching was all she managed to do. The cabin seemed to groan, the sound echoing through the smoke-filled night. Livvy looked up to see what had caused the sound.

It was the heavy wood-shake roof.

And a massive chunk gave way.

Falling.

Right toward them.

She let go of the body. Reed did the same. And they both dove to the side as the flaming wood came crashing down.

FOURTEEN

"WHAT was the cause of death?" Reed asked the coroner. He had his office phone sandwiched between his ear and shoulder so he could use his hands to type the incident report on his computer.

"The obvious," Dr. McGrath answered. "Gunshot wound to the chest. The single shot hit him in the heart, and he was probably dead before the bullet even stopped moving."

Yeah. It was obvious, but Reed needed it officially confirmed. All the *i*'s had to be dotted and the *t*'s crossed. Behind him at the corner desk, Livvy was doing a report as well. He glanced at her and saw the same stark emotion in her eyes that was no doubt in his.

The adrenaline rush had long since ended for both of them. They were somewhere between the stages of shock and exhaustion, and the exhaustion was slowly but surely winning out. That was why Reed had tried to convince Livvy to go back to the inn and get some rest. He would have had better luck trying to talk a longhorn into wearing a party dress.

Still, he'd keep trying.

"The gunshot was self-inflicted?" Reed asked the coroner.

"That's my official opinion. The angle is right. So is the stippling pattern. Billy also had gunshot residue on his right hand." Dr. McGrath cursed. "How the hell did it come to this, Reed? I've known Billy for years."

"We all have." Thankfully, the fatigue allowed him to suppress the gut emotion and keep it out of his voice. "If Marcie had testified against him, Billy would have gone to jail for a long time."

That was the motive, and it was a powerful one. Everything fit. All the pieces had come together. Billy had killed Marcie, set up Shane and then tried stop Livvy and him from learning the truth.

"I need your report when it's finished," Reed told Dr. McGrath and ended the call.

Two lights were blinking on his phone, indicating he had other calls. Probably from Woody or someone else in town. Maybe even Billy's widow, Charla. The woman had called five times in the past four hours, but Reed didn't want to go another round with her trying to convince him that her husband had been set up. If Billy was innocent, then it would come through in the evidence.

"What are you reading?" Reed asked, looking over at Livvy again.

"A fax from the county sheriff's office. I asked them why they'd given Jerry the file on my mother."

"And?" Because this was something Reed wanted to know as well.

"Apparently, Jerry asked a clerk, who also happens to be his cousin, to get the file for him. Jerry thought I would jump on this lead and wouldn't focus on Jonah, his client."

Damn. Talk about a slimy move. "I hope the clerk was fired."

"He was."

That was a start, but Reed would have a long talk with Jerry about dredging up old wounds just so he could try to help out his client.

Reed ignored the blinking lights on the phone, stood and went to Livvy. Reed caught onto her arm and lifted her from the chair. She wobbled a little, and he noticed her hand was still trembling.

"It's past midnight," he reminded her. "You need some rest."

She opened her mouth, probably to argue with him, but Reed opened his, too. He started to tell her that he could carry her out of there, caveman style. But he rethought that and simply said, "Please."

Livvy blinked. Closed her mouth. That *please* apparently took away any fight left in her, and she sagged against him as they made their way out the door.

The receptionist had gone home hours earlier, and the front office was staffed with loaner deputies, some of whom he barely knew. But Shane was there, and even though he probably needed some rest, too, Reed preferred to have his own men in the thick of things.

"We'll be back in a couple of hours," Reed told Shane. But Reed hoped he could extend that couple of hours until morning. Maybe he'd need a few more *please*s to get Livvy to shut her eyes and try to recover from yet another attempt to kill her.

"I'm waiting on a call about that glove we found in Billy's trash," Livvy said as they walked out. "And that piece of paper that dropped from Billy's pocket. It was too burned for me to read, but I'm hoping the lab will be able to tell us what it says."

"Don't worry," Reed assured her. "They'll call one of us on our cells when the tests are back." Even though it was a short walk, he helped her into his truck so he could drive her to the inn.

She wearily shook her head. "That glove is critical. My equipment bag was destroyed in the fire."

Reed didn't respond to that except with a heavy sigh that he just couldn't bite back. Fires, rattlesnakes and bullets. All of which had been used to get to Livvy. Billy had certainly been persistent.

And maybe he hadn't acted alone.

That thought had been circling around in Reed's mind since he'd seen Billy's body propped against the house. Of course, there was no proof of an accomplice, but once they'd gotten some rest he'd look into it.

Reed stopped his truck in front of the inn, and Livvy didn't protest when he helped her out and went inside. Her silence bothered him almost as much as the trembling. He grabbed the spare room key from the reception desk and led her up the stairs.

"You okay?" he asked her.

A soft burst of air left her mouth. Almost a laugh. But it wasn't from humor. "I'm fine," she lied. Her eyes met his as he unlocked her door. "You?"

"I'm fine," he lied right back.

She stopped in the doorway and stared at him. "Your friend tried to kill you tonight."

Hearing those words aloud packed a punch. "He tried to kill you, too."

"Yes, but I didn't know him the way you did. He certainly wasn't my friend." She touched his arm. Rubbed gently. "I'm worried about you, Reed."

Now, it was his turn to nearly laugh. "You're worried about me? No need. I'm worried about you."

Livvy broke the stare, turned and went into the room. But she didn't turn on the light. "No need," she repeated. "True, I'd never really had my life on the line until I came to Comanche Creek, but this baptism by fire will give me a lot of experience to deal with future cases."

That sounded, well, like something a peace officer would say. But he knew for a fact that this particular peace officer wasn't made of stone. He reached for her, but she moved away from him and waved him off.

"Not a good idea," she insisted. "If you touch me, we'll end up kissing. And then we'll have aftermath sex. It won't be real. We'll be doing it to make ourselves forget just how close we came to dying tonight."

Now, that sounded too damn logical. And she was right. If he touched her, they would kiss, and they would have sex. But Reed was afraid she was wrong about the "not being real" part. He figured Livvy was afraid of that, too.

"I'll take a nap," she continued. "Then, I'll pack." Thanks to moonlight filtering through the gauzy curtains, he could see her dodge his gaze. "Because once the lab confirms that Marcie's blood was on that glove we found in Billy's trash can, the case will be over. I'll need to head back to my office. And Comanche Creek can start returning to normal."

That did it. All this calm logic was pissing him off. So did her packing remark. Yeah, it was stupid, but Reed figured if he didn't do this, then he would regret it for the rest of his life.

He slid his hand around the back of her neck, hauled her to him and kissed her.

Reed expected her to put up at least some token resistance, but she didn't. Livvy latched on to him and returned the kiss as if this would be the one and only time it would ever happen.

Her taste slammed into him. Not the fatigue and the fear. This was all heat and silk. All woman. And the kiss quickly turned French and desperate.

She hoisted herself up, wrapping her legs around his waist, while they continued to wage war on each other's mouths. Reed stumbled, hoping they'd land on the bed, but instead his back slammed into the wall. He'd have bruises.

He didn't care.

Nothing mattered right now but taking Livvy.

She took those frantic kisses to his neck and caused him to lose his breath for a moment or two. Turnabout was fair play so he delivered some neck kisses to her as well and was rewarded with a long, feminine moan of pleasure. So Reed took his time with that particular part of her body.

Or at least that was what he tried to do.

Livvy obviously had other ideas about how fast this was all moving. Her hands were as frantic as her mouth, and she began to fight with the buttons on his shirt. She didn't even bother with the shoulder holster, and speed became even more of a necessity.

Reed tried to slow things down a bit because he wanted to add at least a little foreplay to this, but foreplay didn't stand a chance when Livvy got his shirt unbuttoned. She unhooked her legs from his waist and slid down so she could drop some tongue kisses on his chest. And his stomach.

All right, that did it.

To hell with foreplay because she was playing dirty in the

best way possible. Every part of his body was on fire, and sex with Livvy was going to happen *now*.

LIVVY COULDN'T THINK. Didn't want to think. But she did want to feel, and Reed was certainly making sure that was happening. For the first time in years, every part of her felt alive.

And needed.

Reed was making sure of that as well.

Livvy had him pressed against the wall, literally, and they were both grappling at each other's shirts. Even though Livvy had his open, she still lost the particular battle when Reed threw open her shirt, shoved down her bra and took her left nipple into his mouth.

Everything went blurry and fiery hot.

She had to stop kissing him. Because she couldn't catch her breath. She could only stand there while Reed took her to the only place she wanted to go.

Well, almost.

The breast kisses sent her body flying, but soon, very soon, they weren't nearly enough. She needed more, and she knew just how to get it.

Livvy went after his belt and somehow managed to get it undone. He didn't stop those mindless kisses, making her task even harder, but she finally got the belt unlooped from his jeans, and she shoved down his zipper. She would have gotten her hand inside his boxers, too, if he hadn't pushed the two of them toward the bed. Not gently either.

But she didn't want gentleness anyway.

This was how she'd known it would be with Reed. Intense. Frantic. Hot. Memorable. So memorable that she knew he was a man she'd never forget.

In the back of her mind she thought of the broken heart that was just down the road for her. Their relationship couldn't be permanent. This would have to be it. But even one time with Reed would be worth a lifetime with anyone else.

A thought that scared her.

And got her even hotter.

Because even in the heat of the moment, Livvy knew this wasn't ordinary.

Another push from Reed, and they landed on the bed, with him on top of her. The kisses took on a new urgency. And a new location. With her shirt still wide open, he used that clever mouth on her stomach and circled her navel with his tongue.

He went lower.

And lower.

Kissing her through her jeans and making her very aware yet again of just how good this was going to be.

She felt him kick off his boots and tried to do the same. It didn't work, and Livvy cursed the difficulty of clothing removal when both of them were dressed in way too much and were way too ready for sex.

Livvy changed their positions, flipping Reed on his back so she could reach down and drag off the boots. Reed helped himself to her zipper and peeled off her jeans.

Her panties, too.

With her thighs and sex now bare, she became all too aware that he was still wearing jeans, a barrier she didn't want between them.

Reed obviously felt the same because he turned them again until he was on top. Both grabbed his jeans, pulling and tearing at the denim. Livvy considered trying to use a little finesse but gave up when the jeans and boxers came off and she had a mostly naked Reed between her legs.

"Condom?" he ground out. "I don't have one with me."

"I'm on the pill," she answered, though she didn't try to explain she was taking them to regulate her periods. For once she praised that particular problem because without it, there would have been no birth control pills. And no sex tonight with Reed.

Livvy wasn't sure either of them would have survived that. This suddenly felt as necessary as the blood rushing through her body.

They both still had on their shoulder holsters and weapons, and the gun metal clanged against the metal when Reed grabbed on to her hair, pulled back her head and kissed her. No ordinary kiss. His tongue met hers at the exact second he entered her.

He tried to be gentle.

Livvy could tell.

But gentleness didn't stand a chance tonight. She dug her heels into the soft mattress and lifted her hips, causing him to slide hard and deep into her. She stilled just a moment. So did Reed.

And in the moon-washed room, their eyes met.

Livvy wanted the fast and furious pace to continue. She didn't want to think about the intimacy of this now. But Reed forced her to do just that. The stare lingered, piercing through her. Until she could take no more. She grabbed on to his hips and drew him into a rhythm that would satiate her body.

Too soon.

She couldn't hang on to the moment. Instead, Livvy gave in to that rhythm as well. She moved, meeting him thrust for thrust, knowing that each one was taking them closer and closer to the brink.

Livvy heard herself say something, though she hadn't

intended to speak. But she did. In that moment when she could take no more of the heat, no more of those rhythmic strokes deep inside her...

She said Reed's name, repeating it with each breath she took. And then she surrendered.

FIFTEEN

REED forced his eyes open. His body was still exhausted, but humming, and already nudging him for a second round with Livvy. It wouldn't happen.

Well, not anytime soon.

She needed to sleep, and what he wanted to do with her involved the opposite of sleeping.

Reed checked the blood-red dial on the clock next to the bed. Four o'clock. Livvy and he had been asleep for nearly three hours, more than just the catnap stage. He should get up and make some calls to find out what was going on at the station.

Livvy's bare left leg was slung over him, and he eased it aside. She reached for him, groping blindly, and Reed brushed a kiss on her hand before moving it aside as well. Even though he kept everything light and soft, Livvy still woke up.

"I fell asleep," she grumbled and started to climb out of bed as well.

"And you need to keep on sleeping."

"So do you, but you're up."

He couldn't argue with that. Heck, he couldn't argue with his body, which was begging him to climb back into bed with her. She was a sight, all right. Naked, except for her rumpled white shirt and bra that was unhooked in the front. That gave him a nice peek-a-boo view of her breasts.

And the rest of her.

Later, after he'd cleared up some things at work, he would see if he could coax her into taking a shower with him. Reed was already fantasizing about having those long athletic legs wrapped around him.

He had to do something to stave off an erection, so he pulled on his boxers and jeans. He, too, still wore his shirt, and it was a wrinkled mess. He also had a bruise on the side of his chest where his gun and holster had gouged him during sex. Livvy and he hadn't gotten around to removing their weapons until they'd finished with each other.

"I need to call the lab," she explained. She peeled off her shirt and bra, leaving herself naked.

There wasn't enough devotion to duty in the world that would make Reed pass up this opportunity. He caught her arm, pulled her to him and kissed her.

She melted against him.

She smelled like sex. Looked like sex. And that was sex melt. A hot body slide against his that let him know it wouldn't take much coaxing to get her back in bed.

Reed pulled away, looked down at her. "Give me just a minute to check in at work. *Just a minute,*" he emphasized.

Smiling, she kissed him again. "Tempting. Very tempting," Livvy added, skimming her fingers along his bare chest. "But we both need to take care of a few things. Then, before I leave, maybe we can spend some time together."

Before I leave.

Yeah. Reed had known that was coming. Still, work could wait at least another half hour, so he leaned in to convince her of that. Their mouths had barely met when the ringing sound had them jumping apart. It was his cell, and when he checked the ID screen, he knew it was a call he had to take.

"Shane," Reed answered.

But before Shane could respond, Livvy's cell phone rang as well.

"We have a problem," Shane explained. "Charla Whitley's out front, and she's got a gun pointed at her head. She says she'll kill herself if we try to come any closer. I've cleared the area, but I haven't had any luck talking her into surrendering."

Hell. Charla was obviously distraught, and with good reason, since only hours earlier she'd lost her husband. "Has she made any specific demands?" Reed wanted to know.

"She's insisted on speaking to you—and to Sergeant Hutton. I wouldn't advise that, by the way. Personally, I think Charla wants to kill both of you because she blames you for Billy's death."

Of course she did. Charla certainly wouldn't want to blame her own husband, even though the guilt might solely be on Billy's shoulders.

"I'll be there in a few minutes," Reed informed him. "I'll drive around back so Charla can't get off an easy shot at me, but if she moves, let me know."

"Will do, Reed. Right now, she's hiding in the shrubs on the west side of the building. Be careful."

Oh, he intended to do that. After he talked Livvy into

staying put so she could get some more rest. However, he quickly realized that would be a losing battle because Livvy was dressing as she talked on the phone. Since he couldn't make heads nor tails of her conversation, he finished putting on his clothes as well.

"Charla's at the station," Reed explained the moment she ended her call. "She's demanding to speak to us."

Livvy blew out a long breath and shook her head. "So, we'll *speak* to her." She collected her boots from the floor. "That was the lab. The blood on the glove was a match to Marcie James. Billy's DNA was on it as well, and in the right place this time. The DNA inside the finger portions of the glove was his."

So, there it was, the proof that connected Billy to Marcie's murder. "What about the charred piece of paper that fell out of his pocket?"

Livvy sat down on the bed and pulled on her boots. "It was a suicide note. Handwritten. Billy confessed to all the murders and the attempts to kill us. The lab tech pulled up Billy's signature from his driver's license, and the handwriting seems to be a match."

Seems. Reed wanted more. After the fiasco with Shane, he wanted layers and layers of proof. "I'll send them more samples of Billy's handwriting so they can do a more thorough analysis. What about fingerprints on the paper? Did they find any?"

"Just Billy's." She hooked her bra, ending his peep show, and grabbed a fresh white shirt from the closet.

That could mean that Billy had indeed written it—voluntarily. But maybe it meant he was coerced and the coercer had worn gloves or perhaps not even touched the paper.

But he didn't want to borrow trouble. Everything pointed to Billy, and for now, Reed would go with that.

Livvy and he strapped on their holsters, and as they hurried down the stairs, she gathered her hair back into a ponytail. They obviously woke Betty Alice because the woman threw open the door to her apartment and peered out at them.

"Is there more trouble?" she asked.

"Could be." Reed tried not to look overly alarmed about the situation with Charla. And he also tried not to look as if he'd just had sex with Livvy. It wouldn't matter, of course. The gossips would soon speculate about both, especially since his truck had been parked in front of the inn for several hours.

Betty Alice clutched the front of her pink terry-cloth robe, hugging it even tighter. "Anything I can do?"

"Just stay put. And you go ahead and lock your door."

Her eyes widened, and she gave an alarmed nod, but she shut the door, and Reed heard her double-lock it.

Livvy and he headed out, locking the front door securely behind them. They hadn't even made it down the steps when his phone rang again. From the caller ID, he could see it was Shane.

"Reed, you said you wanted to know if the situation changed," Shane said, his words rushed and laced with concern. "Well, it changed. Charla disappeared."

Reed's stomach knotted. "What do you mean she disappeared?"

"She'd been hiding in the bushes like I said, and I had one of the deputies on the top floor using night goggles to keep an eye on her. She started running, and the deputy didn't want to shoot her in the back."

Reed could understand that, especially since Charla hadn't actually threatened anyone but herself.

"I'm in pursuit of her," Shane added. "And we're both on foot."

"What direction is Charla running?" Reed asked.

Shane didn't hesitate. "She's headed your way."

When Reed drew his gun, Livvy did the same.

She hadn't heard all of Reed's conversation, but the last part had come through in Reed's suddenly tense expression.

What direction is Charla running?

"She's on her way here?" Livvy clarified.

"Yeah. And according to Shane, she's armed and possibly gunning for us."

Great. Here, Livvy had thought they'd dealt with the last of the attempts to kill them, but she had perhaps been wrong.

"Go after Charla," Reed instructed Shane. "But don't fire unless it's absolutely necessary. We don't know her intentions, and she could mean us no harm." Though Reed didn't sound as if he believed that.

Reed ended the call, and changed the phone's setting so that it would vibrate and not ring. He put away his phone, but he didn't hurry to his truck, probably because it was parked out in the open and not far up the street from the police station. Charla could possibly be on the very sidewalk next to the truck and ready to take aim if either Reed or Livvy stepped toward the vehicle.

"We need to take cover," Reed insisted, tipping his head to the four-foot-high limestone wall that stretched across the entire front and side yards of the inn.

Reed took the left side of the gate, and Livvy took the right. Both crouched low so they wouldn't be easy targets.

And they waited.

Because of the late hour, there were no people out and about. Thank goodness. There was little noise as well. The only sounds came from the soft hum of the streetlights and the muggy night breeze stirring the shrubs and live oak trees. What Livvy didn't hear were any footsteps, but that didn't mean Charla wasn't nearby.

The woman was apparently distraught and ready to do something stupid to avenge her husband's suicide. That meant Reed and she had to be prepared for anything, and that included defending themselves if Charla couldn't be stopped some other way. Livvy didn't want it to come down to that. There had already been enough deaths and shootings in Comanche Creek without adding a recent widow to the list.

Livvy heard a soft creaking noise and lifted her head a fraction so she could try to determine where the sound had originated.

"Behind us," Reed whispered. He turned in the direction of the inn. "Keep watch on the front."

Livvy did, and she tried to keep her breathing quiet enough so it wouldn't give away their positions. It would be safer for everyone if they could get the jump on Charla and disarm her before she had a chance to use her gun.

There was another sound. Maybe the leaves rustling in the wind. But Livvy got the sickening feeling in the pit of her stomach that it was much more than that.

Maybe even footsteps.

The sound was definitely coming from behind them, where there was no fence, only the lush gardens that Betty Alice kept groomed to perfection. Did that mean Charla had changed course so she could ambush them? If so, maybe the woman wasn't quite as distraught as everyone thought she was.

She could possibly even be her husband's accomplice.

That wasn't a crazy theory, since Billy had no doubt profited from the sale of the land that Jonah had ended up buying. Maybe Charla hadn't gotten personally involved and had no idea it would lead to her husband's death.

"My phone," Reed whispered, reaching into his pocket. It'd apparently vibrated to indicate he had a call.

Reed glanced down at the back-lit caller ID screen and put the phone to his mouth. "Shane?" His voice was barely audible, and she was too far away to make out a single word of what Shane was saying.

She continued to wait. The seconds ticked off in Livvy's head, and she held her breath for what seemed to be an eternity. She cursed the fatigue and the fog in her head. She needed to think clearly, but the lack of sleep and the adrenaline were catching up with her.

Reed finally eased the phone shut and slid it back into his pocket. His expression said it all—he was not a happy man. "Charla got into her car and drove off. Kirby and another deputy are in pursuit. Shane's staying at the station in case she heads back there."

"Shane's alone?" she asked.

Reed nodded.

Livvy glanced up both ends of the street. There were no signs of an approaching vehicle. Well, no headlights anyway, but if the car was dark-colored, Charla might have turned off her lights so she could get close to them without being detected.

"You think she'll come this way?" Livvy asked.

"No." But then he lifted his shoulder. "Not unless she doubles back."

Which she could do. *Easily.* After all, Main Street wasn't the only way to get to the inn. She could park on one of the back streets and make her way through the inn's garden.

Of course, that was only one of many places Charla could end up. She might have other people she wanted to confront—including Jonah Becker.

"You should get to the station so Shane will have some backup," Livvy reminded him. "But I'm concerned about leaving Betty Alice here alone. If Charla does double back, she might come here and try to get in."

His gaze met hers, and there was plenty enough light for her to see the argument he was having with himself. Livvy decided to go on the offensive.

"I'm not a civilian, Reed. I'm trained to do exactly this sort of thing."

Reed scowled. "If I leave, then you don't have backup."

"True. But I can go inside. Stand guard. And I can call you if something goes wrong."

He continued to stare and scowl at her. A dozen things passed between them. An argument. Some emotion. Also the reminder that they weren't just partners on a case. Sex had changed things.

But it couldn't stay that way.

Both of them were married to their badges, and they couldn't let sex—even the best sex ever—get in the way of what had to be done.

Livvy tried to give him one last reassuring glance before she checked the street and surrounding area.

No sign of Charla.

"Go to the station," she insisted.

"No." He matched her insistent tone. "We both go, and we'll take Betty Alice with us."

Livvy huffed to show her disapproval at the veto of her plan, but she had to admit it was, well, reasonable. Or at least it would be if they could get Betty Alice safely out. Livvy didn't like the idea of a civilian being brought out into the open when a shooter might be in the area.

"The inn doesn't have a garage," she commented, looking at the house. "Maybe you should pull the truck to the back, and we can get Betty Alice out through the kitchen."

Reed nodded. "Call her and let her know the plan. Then we'll get in the truck together. I don't want to leave you out here waiting."

Livvy took out her phone, and for a moment she thought the sound she heard was from her hand brushing against the pocket of her jeans.

It wasn't.

The sound was footsteps. Frantic ones. And they had definitely come from behind.

Both Reed and she spun in that direction. They had their guns aimed and ready. But neither of them fired.

Livvy tried to pick through the murky shadows in the shrub-dotted yard to see who or what was out there. She didn't see anyone, but that didn't mean they weren't there.

She tightened her grip on her pistol. Waited. And prayed.

The next sound wasn't a footstep. More like a rustling. And she was able to determine that it had come from a cluster of mountain laurels on the west side of the yard.

She aimed her gun in that direction.

Just as the shot blasted through the silence.

Livvy didn't even have time to react. But she certainly felt it.

The bullet slammed right into her.

SIXTEEN

EVERYTHING happened fast, but to Reed, it felt as if he were suddenly moving in slow motion.

He saw the bullet slam into Livvy's left shoulder. He saw the shock on her face.

The blood on her shirt.

Cursing, he scrambled to her and pulled her down onto the ground so she wouldn't be hit again. It wasn't a moment too soon because another shot came flying their way.

"Livvy?" he managed to say, though he couldn't ask how badly she was hurt. That was because his breath and his heart were jammed in his throat.

She had to be okay.

"I'm fine," she ground out.

But it was another lie. The blood was already spreading across her sleeve, and she dropped her gun.

Though the shots continued to come at them, Reed didn't

return fire. He ripped off the sleeve of his shirt and used it to apply pressure to the wound.

The bullet had gone into the fleshy part of her shoulder. Or at least that was what he hoped. Still, that was only a few inches from her heart.

He'd come damn close to losing her.

The rage raced through him, and he took Livvy's hand, placing it against her wound so he could return fire and stop the shooter from moving any closer. He hoped he could blast this SOB for what he'd done.

Or rather what *she* had done.

Charla.

She must have doubled back after all.

Reed sent a couple of shots the shooter's way and took out his phone. He didn't bother with dispatch. He called Shane.

"I need an ambulance. Livvy's been shot. Approach the inn with caution because we're under attack." That was all he had time to say because he didn't want to lose focus on either Livvy or the gunman.

"I'm okay," Livvy insisted. Wincing, she picked up her gun, and holding it precariously, she also tried to keep some pressure on her bleeding shoulder.

"You're not okay," Reed countered. He maneuvered himself in front of her with his back to her so he could keep an eye on the shooter. "But you will be. Shane will be here soon to provide backup, and he's getting an ambulance out here."

She shook her head. "It won't be safe for the medics. We need to take care of this before they get here."

Livvy was right. It was standard procedure to secure the scene before bringing in medical personnel, but Reed wasn't sure he could take the risk of Livvy bleeding to death.

Somehow, he had to get her to the hospital, even if he had to drive her there himself.

He glanced back at the truck.

It was a good twenty feet away, and they'd be right in the line of fire if they stood. That meant Reed had to draw this moron out because he couldn't waste any more time with the attack.

The shots were all coming from the side of the house near some shrubs. It was a dark murky space, most likely why the shooter had chosen it. But it wasn't the only shadowy place. He, too, could use the shrubs and get closer so he could launch his own assault.

Reed looked over his shoulder at Livvy. "Can you shoot if necessary?"

She winced again and forced out a rough breath. But she nodded. "I can shoot."

"Then I'm going out there." He wanted to take a moment to tell her to be safe. To hang in there. Hell, he even wanted to wait until Shane had arrived, but all of that would eat up precious seconds.

Time they didn't have.

Crouched down, Reed inched forward and kept his gun ready in case the shooter came running out of those shrubs and across the lawn. But there was no movement. And the only sound was from the shots that were coming about ten seconds apart.

He went even closer to the shooter, but then stopped when he heard the footsteps. They weren't coming from in front of him, but rather from behind.

"Shane?" Reed said softly.

No answer.

And the shots stopped.

Hell. He turned so he could cover both sides in case the shooter was making his move to get closer. As Livvy leaned against the wall for support, she lifted her gun and aimed it as well.

They waited there, eating up precious moments while Livvy continued to lose blood.

"Shane?" Reed tried again.

"No," someone answered.

Definitely not Shane. It was a woman's voice, and a quick glance at Livvy let him know that she was as stunned as he was.

"It's me, Charla," the woman said.

Since her voice was coming from the area by the gate, an area that was much too close to Livvy, Reed hurried back in that direction.

Just as Charla dove through the gate opening.

Reed caught just a glimpse of her gun, and his gut clenched. No! He couldn't let Charla shoot Livvy again.

This time, the bullet might be fatal.

Charla landed chest-first on the ground, her gun trapped beneath her. Livvy moved, adjusting her position so she could aim her gun at the woman.

Reed did more than that. He launched himself toward Charla and threw his body on hers so she couldn't be able to maneuver her weapon out into the open.

There wasn't time to negotiate Charla's surrender, so Reed grabbed her right wrist and wrenched the gun from her hand. He tossed it toward Livvy and then shoved his forearm against the back of Charla's neck to keep her pinned to the ground.

"Call Shane," Reed instructed Livvy. "Tell him to get that ambulance here now."

With her breath racing and her chest pumping for breath, Livvy took out her phone. Beneath him, Charla didn't struggle, but she did lift her head and look around. Her eyes were wild, and Reed could feel her pulse racing out of control.

"Who was shooting at you?" Charla asked.

The question caused both Livvy and Reed to freeze.

"You," Reed reminded her.

Charla frantically shook her head. "No. It wasn't me. I didn't fire my gun. I heard the shots and took cover on the other side of the fence."

Reed was about to call her a liar, but he didn't manage to get the word out of his mouth. That was because the next sound turned his blood to ice.

Someone fired another bullet at them.

Livvy DROPPED back to the ground.

Her wounded shoulder smashed against the limestone fence, and the pain shot through her. She gasped, causing Reed's gaze to whip in her direction.

"I'm okay," she lied again.

The pain was excruciating, and the front of her shirt was wet with her own blood. She needed a doctor, but a doctor wasn't going to do any of them any good if the shooter managed to continue.

And obviously, the shooter wasn't Charla.

Mercy, what was going on?

Livvy had been so sure those shots had come from the grieving widow, but obviously she'd been wrong. Someone else was out there, and this person wanted them dead.

But who?

There was another shot. Another. Then another. Each of the thick blasts slammed through the air and landed God knew where. Livvy prayed that none of them were landing inside the inn, and while she was at it, she also prayed that Betty Alice would stay put and not come racing out in fear.

Livvy waited. Listening. But the shots didn't continue. That was both good and bad. She certainly didn't want Reed to be wounded, or worse, but the lack of shots could mean the gunman was on the move.

Maybe coming straight toward them.

She heard the sirens from the ambulance and saw the red lights knifing through the darkness. But the lights didn't come closer, and the sirens stopped, probably because Shane had told them to stay back. Livvy hadn't managed to call him as Reed had ordered. And that was a good thing. If she had, if she'd told them that Reed had the shooter subdued, the medics would have driven straight into what could be a death trap.

Reed jerked his phone from his pocket, and since the screen was already lit, it meant he had a call.

"Shane," Reed answered. "Where are you?"

Because Reed had his hands full with the call, keeping watch and with Charla, Livvy hoisted herself back up to a sitting position so she could return fire if necessary. Maybe, just maybe, her body would cooperate. The pain was making it hard to focus, and Livvy was afraid she wouldn't be able to hear anything over her heartbeat pounding in her ears.

"We don't know who the gunman is," Reed told Shane. "But it's not Charla. She's with us." He paused, apparently listening to Shane. "Okay. But Livvy and Charla are staying put. Call Livvy if there's a change in plans."

With that, Reed shut his phone and shoved it back into his pocket. "Shane's going to try to sneak up on the gunman," he whispered. "And I need to help him."

Livvy understood. Reed couldn't help if he had to hang on

to Charla. Though it took several deep breaths and a lot of will-power to force herself to move, Livvy reached out with her left hand and began to pull Charla in her direction. Reed moved to the side, and together they maneuvered the woman in place just to the side of Livvy.

Charla didn't resist.

She went willingly and pressed her body against the fence. She also covered her face with her hands. Livvy didn't think the woman was faking her fear, so that probably meant Charla had no idea who their attacker was.

"I'm going straight ahead," Reed mouthed. But he didn't move. He paused just a moment to meet her gaze, and then he started to crawl forward again.

"Don't get hurt," Livvy mumbled under her breath, but she was sure he didn't hear her.

She instantly regretted that she hadn't said more, something with more emotion and volume. But that would have been a stupid thing to do. Reed didn't need emotion from her now. He needed her to keep Charla subdued and safe, and for that to happen, she had to stay alert and conscious.

The next shot put her right back on high alert. The bullet slammed into the limestone just inches from Charla's head. Charla yelped and dropped on her stomach to the ground, and Livvy sank lower. She couldn't go belly-down as Charla had done, she needed to be able to help Reed, but she did slide slightly lower.

Another bullet.

This one hit just inches from the last one. God, she hoped the shooter hadn't managed to pinpoint them somehow. But there was some good in this because the shots didn't seem to be aimed at Reed.

She heard Reed move forward, making his way across the lawn. Livvy couldn't see him, but she knew he would use the shrubs for cover. Maybe that would be enough, but bullets could easily go through plants and leaves. She choked back the rest of that realization because the physical pain was one thing, but she couldn't bear the thought of Reed being hurt.

Beside her, Charla began to sob. Livvy was about to try to stop her when her phone rang. Unlike Reed, she hadn't put hers on vibrate, so the ringing sound was loud.

There was a shot fired.

Then another.

The third one bashed into the limestone and sent a spray of stone chips flying through the air. Livvy tried to shield her eyes, and she snatched up her phone so it wouldn't ring again.

"It's me, Shane," the caller said.

Livvy released the breath she'd been holding. It wasn't Reed calling to tell her that he'd taken one of those bullets.

"Where's Reed?"

"I'm not sure. Somewhere between the fence and the west side of the inn." She tried to pick through the darkness and shadows, but she couldn't see him either. "Where are you?"

"The back porch of the inn. I'm going to try to sneak up the stairs to the upper porch."

It was a good idea. That way, he might be able to spot the shooter. If the shooter didn't spot Shane first, that was. The outside stairs weren't exactly concealed, and the shooter might have an unobstructed view of both the stairs and the upper porch.

"Be careful," Livvy warned. "But hurry. Whoever's doing this isn't giving up."

She got instant proof of that. The shooter fired again, and this time the bullet didn't go into the fence. It went into the wooden gate just on the other side of Charla. The woman screamed, covered her head with her hands and tried to scramble behind Livvy.

"Were you hit again?" Shane immediately asked.

"No." Livvy pressed the phone between her right shoulder and ear so she could focus on keeping aim. No easy feat. The pain was worse now, and it seemed to be throbbing through every inch of her body.

"Just hang in there," Shane told her. "We'll get the medics in ASAP."

He'd obviously heard the pain come through in her voice. Livvy hoped the shooter didn't sense that as well because she was in no shape to win a gunfight.

"I've got to hang up now," Shane continued. "I'm at the stairs, and— Wait…"

That *wait* got Livvy's complete attention. "What's wrong?"

"I see the shooter. He's wearing dark clothes, and he's behind the oak tree."

Not the mountain laurels as Reed had thought. She quickly tried to remember the landscape, and if her memory was right, Reed could soon be crawling right past the gunman.

Or right at him.

Shane cursed, and the call ended.

Livvy mumbled some profanity as well. She considered phoning Reed but figured it was too late for that.

"Reed?" she shouted. "Watch out!"

But her warning was drowned out by the gunfire that blasted through the air. Not from the direction where the shooter had originally been.

The shots came from directly in front of them.

SEVENTEEN

REED heard Livvy's warning, but it was too late for him to do anything but duck his head and hope the bullets missed him.

And her.

God knew how much pain Livvy was in right now, and she certainly wasn't in any shape to be in the middle of this mess.

"Stay down!" Reed called out to Livvy, Charla and Shane. He hoped they all listened and had the capability to keep out of the line of fire. Shane certainly wasn't in the best of positions. Or at least he hadn't been when Reed had last spotted his deputy at the base of the stairs. Then Shane had disappeared, and Reed hoped like hell that he'd taken cover.

Since there was no safe way for him to go forward and because he was worried about Livvy, Reed turned and began to make his way back to her. It was obvious the gunman was on the move, and Reed didn't want him to manage to sneak up on Livvy.

Moving as fast as he could while trying to keep his ear attuned to the directions of the shots, Reed maneuvered his way through the damp grass and the shrubs. He spotted Livvy. She was crouched over Charla, protecting her, but Reed knew Livvy needed someone to protect her.

God, there was even more blood on her shirt.

He scrambled to her, keeping low because of the barrage of bullets, and he clamped his hand over her wound again. It wasn't gushing blood, but even a trickle could cause her to bleed out.

"We can't wait for the ambulance," he whispered. "I need to get you out of here."

She didn't argue. Well, not verbally anyway. He saw the argument in the depths of her eyes, but he also saw that the blood loss had weakened her.

"I'm going to stay in front of you," he instructed Livvy. "Do you think you can crawl through the gate and onto the sidewalk?"

"Yes." Now, she shook her head. "But I won't leave you here to fend for yourself."

He nearly laughed. *Nearly.* So, there was some fight left in her after all. "I have Shane for backup. I'll cover you while you get to the sidewalk. Get as far away from the inn as you can, and I'll have the medics meet you."

Charla moved when Livvy did, but Reed latched on to the woman. "You're staying here." Though he doubted Charla was truly involved in the shooting, he didn't want Livvy to have to worry about watching her back.

Livvy had barely made it to the gate when Reed heard the sound. Not more gunfire, but movement. It wasn't just foot-steps either. There seemed to be some kind of altercation going on, and whatever it was, it was happening in front of them.

Shane.

Hell, his deputy had likely come face-to-face with the gunman.

Reed motioned for Livvy to keep moving, but she didn't. She stopped and aimed her gun in the direction of those sounds. Someone cursed. It was definitely Shane, and then there was a loud thump. Reed had been around enough fights to know that someone had just connected with a punch.

The silence returned.

But it didn't last.

It was mere seconds before the footsteps started. This wasn't a quiet skulking motion. Someone was running straight toward them.

Reed couldn't call out Shane's name because it would give away Livvy's and his positions. Besides, whoever this was, it wasn't Shane. His deputy was well-trained and would have identified himself to avoid being shot.

The gunman darted out from one of the eight-foot-high mountain laurels.

Reed fired.

And missed.

But he'd gotten a glimpse of the person. Shane was right about the dark clothes, and it was definitely a man.

Reed got a sickening feeling. He hoped it wasn't Woody out there.

The shots started again, and the man rushed out, coming closer. Each shot and each movement was wasting time, and Reed was fed up. He needed to get Livvy out of there.

He motioned for Livvy to stay down. Whether she would or not was anyone's guess. Reed picked up a chunk of the limestone that'd broken off in the attack, and tossed it to the center of the yard. When the stone landed on the ground, the gunman left cover.

Reed fired again.

This time, he didn't miss.

The shooter howled in pain and clamped his hands onto his left thigh.

"Fire a couple of shots into the ground but in that direction and then get to the medics," he told Livvy, pointing to the area on the west side of the inn but still far enough away from where he would be heading. He needed a diversion in case their attacker could still manage to shoot.

Reed hurried, racing toward the gunman who'd done his level best to kill them. And this wasn't over. He had no idea just how badly Livvy, and maybe even Shane, were hurt. There had to be a good reason his deputy wasn't responding.

When he was closer, Reed saw that the shooter was wearing a black baseball cap that was tilted down to cover the upper portion of his face. Reed didn't stop or take the time to figure out who this was; he dove at the guy.

The shooter lifted his gun.

Aimed.

But he didn't get off another shot before Reed plowed right into him.

Both of them went to the ground, hard, and the guy's gun rammed into Reed's rib cage. It nearly knocked the breath right out of him, but Reed fought to pull air into his lungs while he fought to hang on to his gun.

But he wasn't successful.

The man swiped at Reed's arm, and it was just enough to send his weapon flying.

Still, Reed wasn't about to give up. He used every bit of his anger and adrenaline so he could slam his fist into the man's face.

It worked.

The guy's head flopped back. He wasn't unconscious, but

the movement caused his baseball cap to fall off. And Reed got a close look at the gunman's face.

He cursed.

Because it was a face he knew all too well.

The shock stunned Reed for a moment. Just a moment. But that was apparently all the time the man needed to get his weapon back into place.

The gun slammed hard against the side of Reed's head.

LIVVY COULD no longer feel the pain. That was good. Because one way or another she was going to make her way to Reed, and dealing with the pain was one less obstacle that could get in her way.

Charla was still sobbing and cowering against the fence. It was a risk to leave her there alone, but it was an even bigger risk to let Reed take on the gunman without backup. Yes, Shane was out there somewhere, but he didn't seem to be responding. She hoped he hadn't been shot, or killed.

Livvy forced herself to stand, and since there were no more bullets flying, she didn't exactly crouch. Her goal was to make it to Reed as quickly as possible.

Still, that wasn't nearly fast enough.

She felt as if she were walking through sludge, and it didn't help that she had to keep her shooting hand clamped to her shoulder. That meant her gun was out of position if she had to fire, but she would deal with that if and when it came down to it. She couldn't let the blood flow go unchecked, or else this rescue mission would fail, and she would be in just as much serious trouble as Reed and Shane.

She trudged through the grass and shrubs, and she heard the sounds of a struggle.

Reed and the gunman, no doubt.

At least they weren't shooting at each other, and even though she dreaded the idea of Reed having to fist-fight his way out of a situation, he'd apparently cornered the shooter, and maybe that meant this was on its way to being over.

Just ahead of her, Livvy heard a different sound. Much softer and closer than the battle going on at the other side of the yard. This was a moan, and it sounded as if someone was in pain. The person was lying on the ground just ahead of her. She unclamped her arm so she could aim and moved closer.

It was Shane.

He moaned again and touched his head. "Someone knocked me out," he whispered.

Livvy didn't take the time to examine him further. The deputy was alive and could fend for himself for a little while so she could get to Reed.

She silently cursed. The sex had indeed changed everything. Or maybe the sex was just the icing on this particular cake. Livvy had to admit that the reason the sex had happened in the first place was because she'd fallen hard and fast for the hot cowboy cop.

Worse, she was in love with him.

She hadn't realized that until she'd seen him rush away after the gunman. And he'd done that to save her. That's the kind of man he was. A man worth loving. Too bad that wouldn't solve all their problems. Still, that was a matter for a different time and place. Right now, she needed to focus all her energy on helping Reed.

Oh, and she needed to stay conscious.

She didn't think she'd lost too much blood, but the shock

was starting to take over. Soon, very soon, she wouldn't be much help to Reed.

"I'll be back," she whispered to Shane and stepped around him.

Livvy didn't have to walk far before she saw Reed and the other man. They were fighting, and in the darkness she couldn't tell where Reed's body began and the other man's ended. She certainly couldn't risk firing a shot because she might hit Reed.

The man bashed his forearm into Reed's throat, and Reed staggered back. She saw the blood on his face. And on the front of his shirt.

Her heart dropped.

Livvy blinked back the dizziness and raced to get closer. They were there, right in front of her, less than a yard away, but she still didn't have a clean shot, and she didn't trust her aim anyway. The shooter would have to be out in the open before she could fire, and it didn't help that the man still had a weapon in his hand.

Reed's fist connected with the man's jaw, and that put a little distance between the two. Not enough for her to fire. But enough for her to catch a glimpse of the man's face.

It was Ben Tolbert.

God, had Ben knocked out his own son? And why was he doing this? Why was he trying to kill them?

"Stay back!" Reed shouted to her.

She didn't listen. Couldn't. Ben was armed and Reed wasn't. Plus, there was all that blood on Reed's shirt.

The milky-white moon cast an eerie light on Ben, and she saw him sneer at her. And lift his gun.

Ben aimed it right at her.

Her body didn't react as quickly as her mind did. Livvy recognized the danger. She realized she was about to be shot again, but she couldn't seem to get out of the way. Nor could she shoot. That was because her hand had gone numb. So had her legs, and she felt herself start to fall.

Reed shouted something. Something she couldn't understand. And she heard the shot the moment she hit the ground. The blast was thick and loud, and it echoed through her head.

"Reed," she managed to say. She prayed the bullet hadn't slammed into him.

Forcing herself to remain conscious, she turned her head and saw Reed lunge at Ben. This time, there was no real battle. A feral sound tore from Reed's throat, and he slammed his weight into Ben. In the same motion, Reed ripped the gun from Ben's hand. Both of them landed on the grass, not far from her. And she saw Reed put the gun to Ben's head.

"Move and you die," Reed warned. Every muscle in his face had corded and was strained with raw emotion.

Ben obviously believed him because he dropped his hands in surrender.

It was over. They were safe. Now, they just needed the medics.

Livvy tried to get up so she could go find them, but she only managed to lift her head a fraction before the darkness took over and closed in around her.

EIGHTEEN

REED paced, because he couldn't figure out what else to do with the powder keg of energy and emotion that was boiling inside him. Waiting had never been his strong suit, and it especially wasn't when he was waiting for the latest about Livvy's condition.

He heard the footsteps in the hall that led to the E.R. waiting room and whirled in that direction. It wasn't the doctor. It was Kirby, his deputy.

"Here are the things you asked me to get," Kirby said, handing Reed the plastic grocery bag. "I don't guess they've told you anything yet?"

"No. One of the nurses came out about ten minutes ago and said I'd know something soon." But *soon* needed to be *now* when it came to Livvy. "How's Shane?"

"He's got another bump on his head, but other than that, he's fine. The doc will be releasing him soon."

Good. That was one less thing to worry about, even though

this wouldn't be the end of Shane's worries. After all, his father had just tried to murder Livvy and Reed. Ben Tolbert would likely to go to jail for the rest of his life.

"I called the station on the way over here, and Ben's talking, by the way," Kirby continued. "Jerry's trying to make him hush, but Ben confessed to setting the cabin on fire and trying to scare Livvy into leaving town. He didn't want any evidence that could link Shane to Marcie's murder."

Reed felt every muscle in his body tighten. He wanted to pulverize Ben for what he'd done. "But Livvy's the one who cleared Shane's name."

Kirby shrugged. "Ben evidently thought Livvy wasn't done with Shane. He figured she'd keep looking for anything and everything to put Shane back in jail."

Great. Because of Ben's warped loyalty to his son, Livvy might have to pay a huge price.

"What about Charla?" Reed asked.

"The medics took her to Austin, to the psych ward. After they've evaluated her, they'll give you a call."

Kirby had barely finished his sentence, when Reed heard more footsteps. This time, it was Dr. Eric Callahan, the man who'd forced Reed out of the E.R. so he could get to work on Livvy's gunshot wound.

"How is she?" Reed demanded, holding his breath.

"She lost quite a bit of blood so we gave her a transfusion. She's B-negative, and thanks to you, we have a small stockpile."

"You gave her Reed's blood?" Kirby asked.

Dr. Callahan nodded, but Reed interrupted any verbal response he might have given Kirby. Yes, Reed was a regular blood donor, and he was damn thankful the supply had been there for Livvy, but a transfusion was the last thing he wanted to discuss right now.

"How's Livvy?" Reed snapped.

"She's okay. The bullet went through and doesn't appear to have damaged anything permanently—"

"I want to see her." Reed didn't wait for permission. He pushed his way past the doctor and went to the room where they'd taken Livvy nearly an hour earlier.

Reed stormed into the room but came to a dead stop. There Livvy was, lying on the bed. Awake. Her shoulder sporting a fresh bandage. Heck, she even gave him a thin smile, but she looked pale and weak. That smile, however, faded in a flash when Livvy's gaze dropped to the front of his shirt.

Reed glanced down at what had snagged her attention and immediately shook his head. "It's not mine." The blood on the front of his shirt had gotten there during his fight with Ben.

Livvy gave a sigh of relief and eased her head back onto the pillow.

"You shouldn't be in here," the nurse on the other side of the room insisted.

"I'm not leaving," Reed insisted right back. "Not until I find out how you really are," he said to Livvy.

"I'll speak to the doctor about that," the nurse warned and headed out of the room.

Livvy motioned for him to come closer. "I'm fine, *really*. The doctor gave me some good pain meds so I'm not feeling much." Her eyes met his. "Well, not much pain anyway. Please tell me Ben Tolbert is behind bars."

Reed walked closer, the plastic grocery bag swishing against the leg of his jeans. "He is. Or soon will be. I had Ben sent to the county jail. He's receiving medical treatment for the gunshot wound to his leg, but after that, he'll be going to the prison hospital."

"Good." And a moment later she repeated it.

Livvy might have been medicated, but the painkillers didn't remove the emotion from her voice or face. She'd been through hell tonight, and Reed had taken that trip right along with her.

He sat down on the right side of the bed so he wouldn't accidentally bump into her injury and, because he thought they both could use it, he leaned over and kissed Livvy. Reed intended to keep it short and sweet. Just a peck of reassurance. But Livvy slid her hand around the back of his neck and drew him closer. Even after she broke the kiss, she held him there with his forehead pressed against hers.

"I thought I'd lost you," she whispered, taking the words right out of his mouth.

Reed settled for a "Yeah," but it wasn't a casual response. His voice had as much emotion as hers, and he eased back just a little so he could meet her eye to eye. "I'm sorry I let this happen to you."

She pushed her fingers over his lips. "You didn't 'let' this happen. You did everything to save me."

He glanced down at the bandage and hated the thought that she was alive in part because they'd gotten lucky. Reed didn't want luck playing into this.

"You can't stay," someone said from the doorway. It was the doctor.

"Give me five minutes," Reed bargained. He didn't pull away from Livvy, and he didn't look back at the doctor.

"Five minutes," he finally said, and Reed heard the doctor walking away.

"Not much time," Livvy volunteered.

"Don't worry. I'll be back after you've gotten some rest." But first, he had something important to do.

He took out the candy bars from the bag and put them on the stand next to her bed.

Her face lit up. "You brought me Snickers?" She smiled and kissed him again. "You know, I could love a man who brings me chocolate."

The realization of what she'd said caused her smile to freeze, and she got that deer-caught-in-the-headlights look.

"Don't take it back," Reed blurted out.

She blinked. "Wh-what?"

"Don't take that *love a man* part back, because that's what I want you to do."

"You want me to love you?" She sounded as if he'd just requested that she hand him the moon.

And in a way, he had.

"Yeah. I do," he assured her.

But Reed lifted his hand in a wait-a-second gesture so he could lay the groundwork for this. He took out a map from the bag and fanned it open. It took him a moment to find what he was looking for.

"This is Comanche Creek," he said, pointing to the spot. "And this is Austin." He pointed to the space in between. "I want to find a house or build one halfway between. That'd give us both a thirty-minute commute to work."

And because he wanted her to think about that for several moments, and because he didn't want her to say no, he kissed her. He didn't keep it tame, either. But then, neither did Livvy. She might have been in the E.R., but it was crystal-clear that kissing was still on the agenda.

She pulled back, ran her tongue over his bottom lip and smiled. "You want us to live together. I'd like that."

"Like?" he questioned.

Her forehead bunched up. "All right, I'd *love* to do that. You really have love on the brain tonight." She winced. "Sorry, that didn't come out right. Blame it on the pain meds."

That had him hesitating. "How clearly are you thinking?"

"Why?" she asked.

"Because I'm about to tell you that I'm in love with you, and I want to make sure you understand."

Her mouth dropped open. "You're in love with me?"

"Yeah." And Reed held his breath again. He watched her face, staring at her and trying to interpret every little muscle flicker. Every blink. Every tremble of her mouth.

"You don't love me?" he finally said.

The breath swooshed out of her and she grabbed him again and planted a very hard kiss on his mouth. "I love you. I'm in love with you. And I want to live with you in a house with a thirty-minute commute."

She smiled. It was warm and gooey, and in all his life, Reed had never been happier to see warm and gooey.

"Good," he let her know. Another kiss. Before he moved on to the next part.

"Your five minutes are up," he heard the doctor say from the doorway.

"Then give me six," Reed snarled. He tried not to snarl though when he looked down at Livvy.

"Whatever you've got to say to her, it can wait," the doctor insisted.

"No. It can't." He looked into Livvy's eyes. "I don't want to just live with you."

She shook her head. "But you said—"

"I want to marry you, and then I want us to live together."

"You're proposing?" the doctor grumbled, and Reed heard the man walk away.

"Yes, I'm proposing," Reed verified to Livvy. "And now, I'm waiting for an answer."

An answer she didn't readily give. But she did make a show of tapping her chin as if in deep thought. "Let me see. I have a really hot sheriff that I love with all my heart. He buys me chocolate and jumps out in front of snakes and bullets for me. He's also great in bed. And he wants to marry me."

Reed smiled. "Does that mean you're saying yes?"

She pulled him closer. "Yes. With one condition."

Reed could have sworn his heart stopped. He didn't want conditions. He wanted Livvy, and he wanted all of her. "What condition?" he managed to asked.

There were tears in her eyes now, but she was also still smiling.

Reed thought those might be good signs. He was sure the lusty kiss she gave him was a good sign, too.

"The condition is—this has to be forever," Livvy whispered.

Well, that was a given. "It took me thirty-two years to find you, and I have no intentions of ever letting go."

And to prove that, Reed pulled Livvy closer and kissed her.

★ ★ ★ ★ ★

The Harlequin Intrigue® series brings you six new
passionate and suspenseful books a month
available wherever books are sold, including most bookstores,
supermarkets, drugstores and discount stores.

A BABY
BETWEEN THEM

Alice Sharpe

CAST OF CHARACTERS

Simon Task—This lawman has known and loved Ella Baxter for a long time, but he's recently had to admit love isn't always enough. Less than a week after leaving her, she disappears. Now he's either on a fool's errand or the rescue mission of his—and Ella's—life.

Eleanor (Ella) Baxter—She's always been secretive about her past. An auto accident leaves that past a secret from her. The trick becomes surviving events set in motion by an unseen hand. All she's sure of is her determination to reunite with her father and her growing feelings for the "stranger" who comes to her rescue.

Carl Baxter—Ella's husband or maybe her ex-husband. He seems to be caring for her after the accident, but there's no denying his very touch leaves Ella cold. What is he after and how far will he go to get it?

"Chopper"—This big, menacing man wields his knife with deadly accuracy. There is nothing he won't do to get what he wants.

Kyle Starling—Ella's father is a wanted murderer and thief who disappeared from her life many years before.

Jack—This larger-than-life man appears out of nowhere. He's a good man to have on your side in a fight. Just what—or who—is he fighting for?

ONE

A BLOB of color off to the left caught Simon Task's attention as he sped out of a town whose name he'd already forgotten.

He immediately pulled off the highway, the truck spraying gravel as he braked to a stop. Swiveling in his seat, he looked back. There it was, a pink-and-orange plastic ladybug, the kind that attached to the top of an automobile antenna. What was it doing buried in a wrecking yard?

His imagination got the worst of him as he waited for a break in the traffic before making a U-turn into the parking lot. He pulled up next to the shell of a rusty van with a shattered windshield.

It had to be a coincidence. There had to be more than one of those silly ladybugs in the world.

His mission, or quest or whatever you wanted to call it, had begun twelve hours earlier when he'd driven by Ella's house at three o'clock in the morning. Since their big fight and their subsequent breakup a few days before, he'd avoided her street, but last night had been a busy one. By the time his shift had ended, he'd been tired enough to take the old shortcut. It wasn't as though she'd be awake to see him drive past.

Much to his surprise, her house had been visible the moment he'd turned the corner, blazing with lights both inside and out. He'd pulled up to the curb in front and sat there until curiosity and uneasiness forced him out of the squad car and up the path to her door.

Wouldn't it be the ultimate irony if the instincts and skills honed on the police force, a job she'd begged him over and over again to quit, now provided the very abilities she depended on to rescue her?

Or was he reading this all wrong?

Wrenching his thoughts back to the present, he caught sight of the small snow globe on the passenger seat and picked it up, twisting his wrist, sending glittery "snow" falling over an otter "floating" on a sea of blue acrylic. On the night he'd found the lights on, he'd gone looking to see if her car was in the garage. No car. Instead, there was the snow globe, all alone where the car should have been, so out of place it caught his eye.

He was here because of this damn snow globe.

But was he in the right place?

He set it back down and got out of the truck, striding toward the fence with determination etched on the lean planes of his face. With his thirty-seventh birthday well behind him, he was a man accustomed to knowing what was going on or moving heaven and earth to find out. First things first.

Rounding a stack of tires, he could finally see through the chain-link fence and what he saw almost froze him in place. The antenna supporting the ladybug mascot was attached to a silver late-model sedan, or what was left of one, the same kind of car Ella drove. The hood was buckled inward and up, all but obscuring the windshield. The passenger compartment was partly crushed, shattered headlights and sprung doors attesting to the power of the impact that had put it here in the first place.

Had the driver walked away from this accident? More to the point—had Ella walked away or was she lying in a morgue somewhere? He swallowed hard.

Make sure it's her car. Bending at the knees, he perched on his heels as he tried to decipher the bent license plate three feet away. Every letter and number he could make out matched up to Ella's.

"You interested in that car?" a deep voice asked. Simon rose to a standing position as a man popped up from behind a dented SUV, a crowbar in one big hand, two hubcaps tucked under his opposite arm. With a shrill clang, he dropped everything on the rusty hood of yet another wreck and lumbered over to the fence, giving Simon the once-over.

He was fifty or so, pasty and short of breath, a layer of sweat glistening on his brow despite the cool May day. Simon started to reach for his badge but thought better of it. Finding Ella was personal, not official. He said, "It's in pretty bad shape," bracing himself to hear the worst.

"Ain't that the truth?" the man said, producing a can of chewing tobacco. He pinched off a few leaves, tucked the wad in his cheek and added, "Can you believe the driver walked away without a scratch?"

Simon let out a breath he hadn't realized he'd been holding. "Then she's okay?"

"*He's* okay, yeah."

Simon narrowed his eyes. "Wait a second. *He?*"

"The driver. Uninjured except for a scratch or two. Amazing thing. Course, his wife got bonked on the head pretty good. They had an ambulance take her to the hospital." With a wave of a thick arm, he added, "It happened just a mile or two down the road where the highway curves as it drops to the coast. Car went off an embankment and wrapped around a tree."

Okay, just a second. Since when did Ella allow someone to drive her car, and what was this talk of a husband? "Did you catch any names?"

"Sure. Carl and Eleanor Baxter."

It was on the tip of his tongue to protest that the Eleanor Baxter who owned this car wasn't married. This had to be a mistake. But he paused as he considered her nature. It wasn't inconceivable that she could keep an estranged husband a secret.

He'd actually liked that mysterious quality about her, at least at first. To Simon, coming from a large family with two sisters who never seemed to edit a word they said, Ella had seemed peaceful, composed. It was the churning oceans he'd since detected underneath her calm exterior that grew to worry him.

The wrecker's eyes narrowed. "The Baxters were tourists. How about you? You from around here?"

"No, I'm from Blue Mountain, high desert country. I'm a friend of theirs from back home. Can you tell me how to get to the hospital where Ella, Mrs. Baxter, was taken?"

"If you came from the east, you must have driven right by it. Won't do you no good to look for her there, though. She was released this morning. My wife, Terry, works over there in Housekeeping. She says everyone was surprised Mrs. Baxter left so soon."

Simon's mind was racing. "Was this woman tall with long wavy blond hair?"

"Tall, maybe. Truth is she was in the ambulance by the time I got to the scene. I got a glimpse of her, but her head was wrapped in bandages."

Simon hadn't slept in well over twenty-four hours and he'd been driving for eight. No wonder he couldn't make sense out of anything, no wonder his eyes burned in their sockets. Running a hand through his hair, he said, "Bear with me while I try to understand this. When exactly did the accident happen?"

"Three days ago," the older man said. "In the middle of the night. Every cop in the county showed up along with the fire trucks in case there was an explosion. It was a real circus."

"And the female passenger was released this morning?"

"That's right."

"Do you know if she's still in town? I mean she and her husband?"

The wrecker looked over his shoulder as though he'd suffered a sudden stab of conscience. His wife was no doubt cautioned not to gossip about the patients, but she obviously had and now the wrecker seemed to realize he was repeating her disclosures to a stranger. He spit tobacco with practiced ease, the brown glob landing a few feet away, and scratched his belly through a smudged shirt.

Simon casually took out the leather folder that held his badge. It didn't give him the right to go to the hospital and demand private information without a court order, but he flashed it just the same and the wrecker's face lit up.

"Oh, you're a cop. I get it now. What were they, bank robbers, drug dealers?"

"No, no," Simon said quickly. "I'm just a friend like I told you. I was supposed to meet up with them. I'm showing you the badge so you understand I know how to keep my mouth shut."

The wrecker appeared mildly disappointed. "Well, the answer is they ain't here anymore. Rented a car from Lester down at the Pacific 88 Station, and took off. The husband wanted to continue on their vacation over to Rocky Point."

Rocky Point—Simon had suspected as much. Actually, it had been a toss of the dice, either Otter Cove or Rocky Point, but he'd had a feeling it was the latter. He was itching now to get back in his truck and make it to the coast before dark. One way or another he'd find her. He still didn't know what was going on, just that he needed to see her with his own eyes. If she'd been playing him for a fool the last year or so, well, that was the past, they weren't together anymore anyway. But he had to know why she'd left the house all lit up and the snow globe in such an odd spot.

The wrecker, meanwhile, had continued rambling and Simon tuned back in to hear him say, "Doctors said as long as he didn't pressure his wife, it probably wouldn't hurt her, and might do her some good. They said it could go away overnight or take a few days or even weeks, just not to push her."

Once again, Simon found himself playing catch-up. "What could go away?" he asked.

"Like I said, her amnesia."

Amnesia? Ella had amnesia? Unsure how to respond to this, Simon worked at looking nonplussed as he racked his brain for a comment that made sense. The wrecker lowered his voice, leaned closer to the fence and added, "The wife heard he's not even supposed to tell her their baby lived through the crash unless she remembers and asks about it."

The shock these words engendered on Simon's face must have shown. The wrecker quickly added, "Her memory better come back pretty damn quick, you ask me."

Okay, this had to be another woman. It wasn't Ella, it couldn't be. Maybe she could have hidden a marriage, but a baby? The sudden image of her perfect nude body, of the taut skin covering her abdomen, flashed in his brain. He'd bet almost anything she'd never given birth.

Now all he had to do was figure out what had happened to Ella to separate her from her car so far from home.

The wrecker added, "My wife said the gal hasn't started showing yet, but nature will take care of that soon enough."

"She's pregnant," Simon blurted out, unable to hide the tremor in his voice.

The wrecker looked pleased with himself. "Yep."

That meant the woman in the car *could* be Ella.

And that meant the baby they were talking about could be *his*.

"IT'S GETTING COLD, Eleanor. Come inside," Carl Baxter called, his voice drifting out to the outdoor balcony through the partially open sliding glass door.

Glancing into the room, Eleanor saw that he'd stretched out atop the king-size bed and was watching the news on television.

"In a minute," she said, wrapping the thin blue sweater closer about her body.

Their room was on the tenth floor and overlooked the Pacific Ocean, the distant horizon flushed with color as the sun plunged toward the sea. The thin wind might be cold, but it was still preferable to being inside the small room with her husband.

Her husband! She absently twisted the gold band on her left hand as she tried yet again to conjure up a memory of Carl that preceded waking up in the hospital. Nothing. But the truth was, it felt funny to think of Carl as her husband. He was good-looking enough, with longish blond hair and an aristocratic face, but there was absolutely nothing about him that spoke to her on any level. He was older than she was, forty-one to her twenty-eight, or so their drivers' licenses revealed. His manner toward her was one of indulgent fondness, she guessed, though it seemed as though he might be a little on the controlling side.

For instance, on the drive from the hospital she'd begged him to drive her home—wherever that might be; no place sounded familiar to her. He'd told her they were going to continue their long-planned road trip, that the doctors had suggested traveling until she regained her memory. They would go back to Blue Mountain when she remembered who she was. It didn't matter that she wanted to go now; the doctors knew best.

Who was she to argue with the doctors? Except this plan seemed backward to her. Wouldn't her own space and belongings trigger a memory or two? And what about her parents or brothers or sisters?

All dead, Carl had told her, and then he'd folded her in his arms as though comforting her, but how was she supposed to mourn people she couldn't even remember?

Her sweater wasn't warm enough for the wind and she fought her reluctance to go inside. She needed better clothes if they were going to stay on the coast. A Windbreaker, for instance. She apparently wasn't much of a packer or maybe her suitcase had been lost in the accident.

She could remember absolutely nothing about the crash. It was as though her head was the inside of a pumpkin: mushy, stringy. The irony of being able to recall the look and smell and taste of a squash but not have a sense of self seemed absurd, and she thought more kindly of Carl. It couldn't be very pleasant to be saddled with a wife in such a befuddled state. She should be grateful to him for standing by her.

But why wouldn't he help her out a little? Why wouldn't he show her pictures or tell her stories about her past or explain what she did for a living, what she liked, what she didn't like?

The doctors. That's why. He was following their orders.

The door opened behind her. Carl stood half in, half out, the wind whipping his hair. Her own short brown locks barely stirred.

"Time to come inside," he said, standing aside to allow her to pass him.

He didn't try to touch her, and for this she was grateful. As she heard the door slide closed behind her, she paused in front of the TV. An announcer was offering details of a homicide, the cameras scanning a weeded lot as a gurney topped with a body bag was wheeled toward a waiting ambulance.

The picture disappeared as Carl clicked the remote. "I was watching that," she said as she turned to face him.

"It happened a long way from here, Eleanor."

"But—"

"I don't want you to watch upsetting, unpleasant things."

She took a deep breath. Was the man always this calculating or had her new vulnerable state aroused his protective instincts? "How long are we staying here?"

"Through Thursday," he said, moving toward her. He put a hand around her arm and, leaning forward, gently kissed her forehead. "You can rest tomorrow. Then the next morning we'll continue on our trip."

"Where exactly are we going?"

"Wherever we want," he said with a smile.

"I want to go home," she said.

"We've been through this a dozen times today," he said.

"Then let's get the map and choose somewhere else to go. I don't like the beach."

"We're staying through tomorrow," he snapped, his eyes flashing even as he resurrected a smile. "Why don't you let me do the planning? You just rest and get better. Are you hungry?"

"Not really. I think I'd like to take a bath."

"You got chilled staying outside so long, didn't you? Well, don't get the bandage on your forehead wet, okay? I'll order dinner from room service."

She resisted nodding, knowing from experience the motion would make her nauseated, then escaped into the bathroom, where she quickly flicked the lock.

TWO

SIMON knew he was looking for a blue car with chrome hubcaps, two years old. He knew the license plate number and the fact that it had a green rental sticker in the left corner of the rear window.

Thankfully, Rocky Point wasn't a big town, but it relied heavily on tourists, and as Simon drove into the city, he saw more motels and hotels than he could count. Before the light disappeared altogether, he wanted to cruise parking lots looking for the blue two-door coupe. If the car was parked underground or in a controlled parking lot, he'd be out of luck.

Not for the first time, he wondered if he shouldn't ask for police help. Or maybe he could march up to every front desk in town and demand to know if there was a Carl and Eleanor Baxter registered. But all of that came with official ramifications, and for now he didn't want anyone else involved. He knew if he started waving his badge around in a town this small, it wouldn't be long before the local cops came looking for him—no, thanks.

The beginning letters on the plate he sought were *YSL*. He

pulled into a motel on the beach and drove each row as though looking for a parking place, slowing down at every blue car. Who knew there were so damn many of them?

An hour passed, then two. He drove through a fast food restaurant and ordered a hamburger and black coffee, then went back to his task, gradually working his way north through town.

The task seemed impossible and more than once he was on the brink of taking a room, getting some sleep and heading home in the morning. But he kept at it, more out of perverse determination than because he thought his plan held merit.

A dozen lots later, his eyes burning like red-hot embers, his headlights picked up the letters *YSL* attached to a blue coupe. He pulled into a spot a few cars away and walked back. The rest of the plate checked out, too; the green sticker was right where it belonged. He used his pocket flashlight to briefly scan the interior. There was nothing in the car he could see except a road map.

He grabbed his overnight bag from his truck and walked into the hotel. It was eleven o'clock by now and the place was all but deserted. He toyed around with asking the clerk who gave him a room if they had a couple named Baxter registered, but held off—he didn't want Baxter alerted to his presence until he got a feeling for what was going on.

A few minutes later, he let himself into his room with the intent of taking a shower and then casing the hotel. He sat on the bed and pulled off his shoes.

If Ella was the woman in the car, then she was here, in the same building as he. Was her memory completely gone? Before that had happened to her, had she really left clues in the hope he would figure out she needed him, or had he jumped to a bunch of conclusions?

No. She might have lent her car to someone else, but she certainly hadn't willingly lent her identity. So who was the man acting as her husband and why had he brought an amnesic woman on a vacation instead of taking her home?

He took the snow globe out of his overnight bag and turned it in his hands, remembering the day a few months before when he and Ella had bought it at a gift store less than a mile from here.

Back when they'd been a couple.

Rubbing his eyes, he fell back on the bed and stared up at the ceiling. *She was here.* He could almost feel her presence. When he'd walked out on their argument just days before, he'd intended it to be permanent, but here he was and so was she.

Which added complicated dimensions to the question burning in the back of his brain: What in the hell was going on?

He woke up hours later, still lying on his back, gray morning light filtering through the sheer curtains. "Damn," he muttered as he tore off his clothes on the way to the bathroom. Five minutes later, he'd taken the fastest shower since his stint in the navy and caught an elevator to the lobby. He immediately crossed to the windows to see if the blue car was still in the parking lot. If he'd slept through their departure, what would he do next?

What could he do?

ELEANOR STARED AT THE PLATE of food Carl had ordered against her wishes and felt a wave of sickness rise up her throat. Thank goodness they were in their room and not the dining room.

"What's wrong?" Carl said.

She didn't have time to answer. Throwing her hand over her mouth, she ran to the bathroom and was sick. Sometime later, after she'd washed and brushed her teeth, she wandered back.

"I thought you could eat," he said.

"My stomach—"

"The doctor warned you'd be sick off and on again due to your head injury," he said.

"Well, the doctors were right." The smell of the congealing eggs was making her stomach tumble again. She grabbed her handbag off the chair. She'd searched her purse; she knew she had credit cards in the wallet. "Give me the car keys. I need different clothes and I need to get out of this room," she said, her hand on the knob.

He was grabbing his jacket. "I'll go with you."

It was on the tip of her tongue to add, *I need to get away from you most of all!* Instead she said, "I remember how to drive. The town didn't look that big yesterday—I can make my way."

She stopped talking because he'd put on his jacket and held the keys in his fist. "No, Eleanor, you will not drive yourself around with a head injury. I'll take you wherever you want to go. Besides, mine is the only name on the rental. You're not insured."

"Then I'll walk."

"Don't be absurd."

And because her head throbbed and her stomach roiled, she opened the door and left the room, Carl close on her heels.

It was a drizzly day outside. As Carl went to the front desk, she perused the lobby. Several people were standing or sitting in chairs in front of a big, hooded fireplace. She longed to be one of them, longed to go stand by the fire without Carl hovering nearby.

Her gaze met the gray eyes of a man in his thirties. He was tall and solid-looking, wearing boots, jeans and a black sweater. His hair was dark and thick, combed away from his face. His features were attractive, his mouth perfectly formed, but it was the intensity of his gaze that held her, that sent her left hand up to her cheek. His gaze grew even more piercing and a trill of excitement sputtered along her skin.

She looked away at once, but for some reason looked back. He had turned to stare at the fire.

"Ready?" Carl asked.

She startled.

"The clerk at the desk told me there's a nice clothing store less than a mile from here. Come on."

SIMON WAITED UNTIL HE SAW the taillights go on in their car before he left the building and ran to his truck. Within a few moments he'd caught up with them on the main drag.

A brisk, overcast Tuesday morning in April wasn't exactly high tourist time, he discovered, and wished there were a few more cars around. He'd already announced himself by allowing Ella to notice him staring at her. He couldn't afford another sighting.

But he hadn't been able to take his eyes off her. Her hair was short and dark, a fringe of bangs somewhat obscuring bruises and a bandage, framing her deep blue eyes. She'd looked wistful, vulnerable in a way he'd seen her look so few times. He'd wanted to walk up to her, talk with her, see if she knew who he was, ask her to explain what was happening.

Of course, he hadn't, and when she'd raised her hand to her face in an almost shy gesture, he finally noticed the sparkle of gold on her finger.

She wore a wedding ring. And the man who had come up to her wore one, too. A tall man with long fair hair, chiseled features and a hustler's tilt to his head.

Damn.

Simon hung back a block until he saw the turn signal on the rental. By the time he turned the same corner, the man was helping Ella out of the car. Simon pulled up to the curb half a block away and watched as they entered a building.

The man. Ella's husband. Carl Baxter. Call him what he was. But why had Ella dyed her hair? She had to have done it before the accident; surely she wouldn't use dye with scratches and wounds on her head, but again, why? Her hair was a source of pride for her, at least it had been, so why whack it off unless to disguise herself?

After getting rid of you, maybe she just wanted a change, an inner voice suggested.

Simon pulled his sweater over his head and put on the denim jacket he kept in the backseat, then snatched a green baseball cap out of a side pocket. As disguises went, it wasn't great, but it was as good as he could do without risking losing them, and he wasn't going to chance that. He darted across the street.

The inside of the store wasn't exactly booming with customers, but it was jammed with racks of clothes that seemed to go from floor to ceiling. The clutter made lurking a little safer. He'd just make sure they were in here to actually look at clothes, and then he'd leave and stake out the exterior.

Cap pulled low on his forehead, he caught sight of Ella fingering a rack of blue-green sweaters. It was his favorite color on her.

She took one of the sweaters off the rack and held it up against her supple body, the soft material at once clinging to her breasts and evoking a million erotic memories. It was a long garment and as she turned to look at herself in the mirror, he felt his breath catch in his throat. The night they first met came stampeding into his head and heart like a locomotive off its tracks.

Carl Baxter chose that moment to take the blue sweater from her hands and thrust a yellow one at her.

Simon immediately turned around and left the store, retracing his steps to the truck, where he took out his cell phone. He made two calls. One to work to request a few days' vacation and the other to an old friend. Then he hunkered down to wait.

"YOU LOOK BEAUTIFUL," Carl said, placing his hands on her shoulders and leaning down to kiss the nape of her neck. He was standing behind her as she faced the mirror, trying to arrange her hair to hide her abrasions and bandages.

She didn't really like the look of the yellow against her skin, and Carl's lips left her cold, which made her ashamed of herself. As he raised his head and their gazes locked in the reflection of the mirror, she said, "Do we have a good marriage, Carl?"

He smiled. "Of course we have a good marriage."

"Then why won't you tell me about it? You know, about one of our days, maybe. A Saturday, for instance. Tell me what we do on a Saturday when I don't have to go to work at the…"

He laughed. "Trying to trick me into telling you what you do for a living?"

"Can't you just throw me a bone? What do you do for a living?"

"Why this preoccupation with jobs?"

"I don't know, I just feel so lost waiting around, I want to do something. I want to know what I used to do, what we did as a couple."

He moved away toward the door. "Let's go."

"Carl—"

"You haven't eaten all day. You must be starving."

"But the reservation—"

"Is for an hour from now, I know, but they serve wine and cheese before dinner in the lobby. A little wine will do you good."

"With my head injury?" she said.

"One glass won't hurt."

There was just no point in arguing with him. The man never said or did one thing he didn't want to say or do, seldom let her out of his sight. *We better have a good marriage,* she thought as she walked past him into the hall, *because if we don't, I'm going to divorce him when I get my memory back.*

Though she would hardly admit it to herself, there was someone she was hoping to see again and that was the man from the morning. He wasn't in the lobby, however. She took a seat near the fire, the gray late-afternoon skies pressing against the tall windows at her back. Carl walked over to the informal buffet as she looked around the spacious room, glancing at the half dozen other guests sipping wine and laughing.

What would it be like to laugh? Did she laugh a lot? Was she morose or happy or contemplative?

One thing Carl was right about was the return of her appetite. It was back with a vengeance, and as she accepted a small plate covered with cheese and crackers and grapes, she noticed a tall man walk into the lobby from the outside and veer toward the front desk.

"Wine?" Carl said, and she accepted a glass of chilled white wine and set it on the table next to her plate. He stood by her seat, looking down at her as he sipped a dark red Cabernet and she tried a cracker slathered with creamy Brie. Why didn't he sit, why did he hover? She looked surreptitiously toward the desk, but the tall man was gone.

It had been the man from the morning, she was sure of it, the one with the gray eyes.

At that moment, a woman approached Carl. "Are you Mr. Baxter?" she asked.

He looked down his long nose at the woman who was wearing a hotel uniform identifying her as an employee. "Yes."

"Sir, we've been alerted your car has two very flat front tires. Would you come with me?"

Carl looked down at Eleanor and then back at the employee and said, "Just have it fixed. I'm not leaving my wife alone—"

"Oh, for heaven's sake, Carl," Eleanor snapped. "I'm not a child, I think I can sit here for ten minutes while you take care of an emergency."

He looked toward the parking lot, down at her and back again. The employee said, "It'll only take a few minutes, sir. We need insurance information."

"It's your damn parking lot," Carl fumed.

"Yes, sir, but it's well posted that your car is your responsibility. Not that we won't assist you, of course."

Carl set his glass down beside Eleanor's. "Stay here," he commanded, and marched off behind the woman and out the front door, glancing over his shoulder at Eleanor twice before he was out of sight.

Almost at once, a man sat on the chair beside her. His gray gaze delving right into hers, he said, "Your husband seems upset."

"It's you," she said, and realizing how lame that sounded, added, "I saw you this morning."

"I saw you, too," he said.

"You were staring at me."

"Yes. Well, I thought you might be someone I knew."

She leaned forward a little. "Really? Maybe I am."

"I don't quite get your meaning," he said with a smile, his voice playful.

She shrugged. "I had an accident a few days ago and my memory is a little blurred."

"A little?"

"A lot."

His voice dropped as he said, "Is that why your husband never leaves your side?"

She nodded very slowly and reached for her wineglass. The stranger's hand was suddenly there, as well. Somehow her glass sailed to the floor, spilling its contents. "I'm sorry," he said, producing a napkin or two and blotting her shoe. The rest of the liquid was quickly absorbed into the plush carpet. He set the unbroken glass back on the table and added, "Probably better not to drink when you've recently bashed your head, I suppose."

"I agree. I really didn't want it."

"Then why were you reaching for it?"

She met his eyes and smiled. "Because I didn't know how to respond to your observation about my husband. Have you ever noticed how you tend to do something with your hands when you don't know what to say?"

"I have noticed that," he said, his gaze once again penetrating. She should probably look away. She couldn't. Their conversation was harmless enough, but she found herself enjoying it in a way she hadn't enjoyed anything in days. She liked talking to this man. He made her feel something inside, made her feel less alone. "What's your name?" she asked.

"Simon."

"Just Simon?"

He brushed her gold wedding band with his fingertip. "Just Simon. What's yours?"

"Eleanor."

He withdrew his hand and she swallowed. Her reactions to this guy were giving her one of the few glimpses she'd had of her gut-level personality. She wore one man's ring and that man swore they had a good marriage. And yet she flirted with another man and wished she had no husband.

"Tell me about the woman you thought I resembled," she said.

Simon glanced toward the front door and then back at her. "I was in love with her once," he said.

"That sounds sad. Something happened between you?"

"Yes. Something happened."

"What was she like?"

"Well, let's see. She was very pretty, like you. She liked to garden, especially vegetables. Everything grew for her. And she liked to cook."

"She sounds like a homebody," Eleanor said.

"Kind of, yes."

"What did she do, you know, for a living?"

"She worked at a radio station, had her own show in the afternoons on Saturday. Gardening tips, food advice, stuff like that. She also had a slew of odd jobs because she said she didn't want to get stuck doing one thing forever."

"What kind of odd jobs?"

"Once she painted a mural on the side of an office building and once she walked dogs and house-sat. She also taught a few classes at the junior college and volunteered at an old folks' home. Stuff like that."

Eleanor smiled. "She sounds nice. What happened, you know, between you two?" As he looked away from her face, she chided herself and added, "I'm sorry. That was way too personal. I don't remember anything about myself, so maybe that's why I'm so caught up in hearing about this woman you're describing. Don't tell me any more, it's none of my business."

He opened his mouth, seemed to think better, and closed it. "How long are you staying here, Eleanor?"

"Until tomorrow," she said. "Carl insisted we stay through today."

"Then where are you headed? Home?"

"I wish," she said.

"You sound homesick. Been away long?"

"How do I know?" she said, turning beseeching eyes on him. "I don't know for sure when we left home or even exactly where home is except for the address on my driver's license."

"You don't remember anything about it?"

"No. The address on my husband's license is different from mine. When I asked him why, he told me we've moved recently. That's all he'll say."

"If you want to go home so badly, why don't you?"

"Because the doctor said we should stay away until my memory returns. Carl won't tell me anything about myself. He says it's supposed to come back naturally."

"Makes it kind of hard for you, doesn't it?" he said.

"I feel lost."

"I bet you do," he said, his gaze once again holding hers.

"How about you?" she said softly.

"I'm not sure about my plans, either." His gaze swiveled to the doors again, and he got to his feet quickly. "I see your husband stomping across the parking lot. He looks pretty angry."

"I'm beginning to think he's angry quite often," she said, instantly awash in guilt. She added, "He's taking very good care of me. It can't be much fun for him."

"You underestimate yourself," he said, and then as Carl pushed his way through the front doors, the man with the gray eyes disappeared toward the elevators.

Simon was right. Carl looked mad enough to kill someone.

THREE

"SO you agree she shouldn't be told she's pregnant?"

On the other end of the line, his cousin Virginia, a practicing psychologist in Chicago, paused for a second before saying, "Without knowing the specifics of her case, I don't know what to think. In associational therapy, the patient is exposed to familiar surroundings in hopes it stimulates the brain's neural synapses. Isolation from personal recollections seems counterintuitive, but if you know she's pregnant and sense trouble in her marriage—"

"If there is a marriage," Simon interjected.

"You said your partner on the force is checking into that, right?"

"Not my partner, no. I can't get Mike into a compromising position on the off chance Ella did something illegal before she left Blue Mountain." *Or since then, for that matter....*

"Then who did you call?"

"A private investigator I worked with a few years back."

"You're sure Ella isn't faking amnesia?"

"I'm positive. The only way the woman I know could react to things the way this woman does is if she wasn't aware of herself or her past. She's not faking."

"Okay. So, for now, all you know is she's with a man who was able to convince the police and the hospital he's her husband, which means he either planned her abduction very carefully or he is her husband—"

"In which case there is no mystery, just me jumping to conclusions," Simon finished for her. And yet her husband had told Ella they'd just moved to Blue Mountain, which was a lie. Ella had lived there for at least two or three years.

Virginia cleared her throat. "Didn't your mother tell me you and Ella were no longer a couple? In fact, you broke up with her just a week or so ago, didn't you?"

Simon stared out at the ocean and sighed. "Well, I guess you could say I broke up with her. She'd gotten even more secretive than usual and we had some words and I realized it was over."

"So maybe what you're feeling is guilt mixed with anger," she said softly.

"Huh?"

"Guilt for rejecting her. Then you find she has a husband all along and so really, she's the one who rejected you. That's why she wouldn't talk about her past and why you felt shut out of her life. Hence the anger."

"My mother has a big mouth."

"She talks to my mom, you know how it is."

He glowered at the moon sparkling over the sea and didn't respond. Spending the night staking out the parking lot wasn't his idea of a good time, but he figured it would serve a couple of purposes, and face it, he was anxious to get this settled in his mind and go home.

Home. "Ginny, do you think I should tell Ella who I am and ask her if she wants to come back with me? Give her a choice?"

"No. I can't advise distressing her when she's so lost already. Don't do anything to alarm her or frighten her. Listen, do you want me to call the admitting hospital and see if I can find out anything about her condition?"

"Will they talk to you?"

"I'll give it a try. I might know someone here who knows someone there. Call me back tomorrow night about this time, okay? Her name is Eleanor Baxter, right?"

"Yeah. Middle name Ann. Thanks, Ginny."

"Just be careful."

"Careful? Careful of what?"

"Think about it, coz," she said, and rang off.

He pocketed his cell phone and tried to get comfortable. He was parked across the row and three cars down from the Baxter rental so he could easily keep an eye on it.

And then he did his best not to think about Ella, but that was almost impossible.

She was different and it wasn't just the hair color. She was more open, as though not remembering her past had freed her from the burden of keeping it secret. She reminded him of the woman he'd fallen in love with, practically at first sight.

He got the feeling she wasn't too happy about her husband. For that matter, neither was Simon, who had seen the bastard hand Ella that glass of wine. Ella didn't know she was pregnant, but according to the wrecker's wife, Carl did, so what was he doing giving a pregnant woman alcohol?

That was Simon's baby she was carrying, and it pissed him off. At least he thought it was his baby.

But she'd been hiding something for the past couple of weeks, something that had her edgy, nervous...

He switched positions. He had a feeling he wasn't going to get Ella alone again. The tire trick had worked once; it wouldn't work again without arousing suspicion. The fact that Carl had insisted they continue this vacation and stay in Rocky Point made Simon curious. What if Carl had abducted Ella from her house in Blue Mountain? What if the accident had been just that—an accident? Had Carl pushed for her release from the hospital so they could make it to Rocky Point for some unknown reason? Or what if they were in something together but Ella couldn't remember they were partners? Would that explain her changed appearance?

It all came down to her houselights blazing, the abandoned snow globe in the garage and his gut feeling.

No answers right now, maybe tomorrow. He'd watch them come out to the car in the morning. See if Ella, once out of the hotel, appeared to be in distress. If she did, he would call in the cops.

"*Be careful,*" Ginny had said.

To hell with that. Carl Baxter was the one who better be careful.

Using his pocket flashlight, he opened the paperback he'd bought in the hotel gift shop and prepared for a long night.

"LET'S STOP HERE for breakfast," Carl said as he pulled into the deep unpaved parking lot belonging to a restaurant perched high above the ocean. A fog bank hovered out at sea, though the day had dawned clear but breezy. The few trees managing to cling to the bluff were shaped by the predominant winds.

"I'll stay here, you go eat," Eleanor said. "My stomach feels terrible. It must be that pill I take at night, the one for my head. I wake up every morning with a stomachache."

"Then skip the pill tonight," he said, reaching over to unbuckle her seat belt.

"Carl, I can't eat."

He looked at his watch, then at her. There was something different about him today, a tightening around his mouth and eyes. "How selfish can you get?" he snarled. "Do you think just because you can't eat, I should starve?"

Startled, she drew away from him. "You could have ordered from room service."

"I'm tired of room service. Come on, get out of the car, keep me company. We'll get you some toast."

She got out of the car, unsure why she allowed him to bully her. Was this what she was always like, or was this apathy because of her injuries? She hoped and prayed it was the latter, because the woman she was right now was a tiresome bore who had come to life only once since awakening and that was when she spoke with a stranger about his lost love.

How pathetic was that?

A bell tinkled as they opened the door. The restaurant was bigger inside than it had looked from the outside. Tables ringed the perimeter, which was fronted with glass and a panoramic view of the sea beyond.

Waitresses scurried with giant platters perched on their shoulders; others poured endless cups of coffee. A hostess led them to a table near the windows. Eleanor took a chair facing the door as the waitress handed them menus. "Coffee?" she asked.

"Just one cup," Carl said. "The lady wants tea."

As the waitress hurried off, Carl scooted his chair clear

around the table so that he was facing the door, too. He said, "Now, aren't you glad you came inside?"

She looked at the menu while taking shallow breaths. The place smelled like greasy seafood. Refusing to lie about her supposed joy at being talked into coming inside, she folded the menu. Carl looked up at the door, visibly tensing every time the bell announced a newcomer.

"Are you expecting someone?" she asked.

"Expecting? No. Why do you ask?"

"You keep staring at the door."

"So what?" he said.

His attitude toward her had taken a marked change from the preceding days. No longer overly solicitous, he was directing his general impatience at her. Truth was, she almost preferred it.

The waitress arrived with two coffees. As Eleanor had no plans to drink tea or anything else, she didn't comment on the mistake. Carl didn't seem to notice. "Crab omelet is our special today," the waitress chirped.

"That's fine," Carl said absently, twisting a little as a bell announced a family scurrying in out of the wind.

"Nothing for me," Eleanor said.

"Bring her unbuttered toast," Carl said.

The family was seated a table or two away while a man in a green baseball cap with his nose buried in a blue-and-white handkerchief took a seat at a table behind her. Carl finally noticed her beverage. "They brought you coffee? Why didn't you say something? Where is that stupid waitress?"

"It doesn't matter," she assured him. His nerves were beginning to get to her, too. Trying to soothe him, she looked around and added, "This is a nice restaurant. Maybe we could come back tonight and have dinner here."

"I suspect we'll be long gone before that," he said absently, tensing as the bell rang over the door again.

A different waitress appeared with a tray holding a tall stack of pancakes and a pitcher of syrup. As she started to lower the tray, Carl put up a hand. "I didn't order pancakes," he barked. "You've got the wrong table."

The tray tilted precariously as the waitress attempted to check the ticket buried in her apron pocket. Carl yelled at her, and she jerked. With a clatter, the plate slid right off the platter and landed in Carl's lap. The pitcher of syrup followed.

Carl stood abruptly, his face as red as a boiled Dungeness crab.

The waitress immediately began apologizing and dabbing at Carl with a napkin.

"You clumsy oaf," Carl sputtered, pushing her away.

"Sir, breakfast will be on us, of course."

"It's already on me!" he said, lifting his sticky hands. "Damn, I've got to go to the restroom and try to fix this." His gaze went from his watch to the door to Eleanor. "Stay here. I'll be back in two minutes." He stomped off without waiting for a reply.

SIMON, NURSING A CUP of coffee and hiding behind a menu, watched the incident at Ella's table with interest. He was willing to bet a week's pay the waitress purposely dumped the food on Carl Baxter.

Why?

That question was at least partially answered a moment later when an Albert Einstein look-alike slid into the chair across from Ella. As the waitress shuffled off with the spilt food and dishes, Simon carefully shifted position to sit directly behind Ella in order to eavesdrop.

"Good, you made it," the old guy said, his voice raspy. "Sorry about the mess with your friend, but I wanted to talk to you alone."

Eleanor said, "I'm sorry, but—"

"Do you know anything about Jerry? Last anyone heard from him was the day he came to see you."

"I don't—"

"Never mind, Jerry is clever, he can take care of himself. What's important is you. I'm real sorry about your brother. Oh, I know it's been months since his death, but I still remember him as a cute kid with a real gung ho attitude. Tragic thing to die so young."

Ella had a brother? This was news to Simon, who cursed his decision not to run a check on her background when he had had the chance.

"Okay, I'm stalling and we don't have much time," the old man continued. "Like Jerry told you, your dad set up this roundabout way of getting word to you to protect you and him. Jerry got you this far. My job is to tell you about the next stop. Go north to a suburb of Seattle named Tampoo. Be at the bus depot tomorrow right at noon. We all know what you look like. Come alone next time, okay?"

"I don't—"

"Listen, honey, there's a lot to explain, but don't ask me, I'm just a link in the chain. You need to ask your old man. You be careful now, it's likely to get dangerous before the end." The old guy looked up just then and after quietly patting the table three times with his fingertips, he got to his feet. "Don't let your father down," he said, and quickly faded into the shadows toward the kitchen.

Ella hadn't seen a man come out of the bathroom and pull

on his ear, but Simon had. That was a signal if he'd ever seen one, and it was followed within seconds by the appearance of Carl Baxter, a determined glint in his eyes and water spots on his clothes. Simon dived behind the menu again.

There was no time to trail the old man; he had to stay and hear what Ella said to Carl about this visit. His hope was she would say nothing.

"The strangest thing just happened," Ella said as another waitress arrived with a plate of eggs she set in front of Carl and toast she placed in front of Ella.

Worried Carl would start looking at the door again and notice Simon's interest in him, Simon turned his back completely, staring out at the sea and the encroaching fog. He heard Carl say, "What? What happened?"

"An old man sat down and spoke with me. He said something about my father."

"What did you say to him?" Carl asked, his voice fast and higher pitched than before.

"Nothing. I mean, what could I say?"

"The man must have mistaken you for someone else. Maybe he's a nutcase."

"Maybe," Ella said, "but he implied he had something to do with the food being spilled on you."

The bell on the door chimed and Simon glanced over his shoulder to get Carl's reaction. Carl didn't even look up. Instead he said, "Tell me what the old guy said."

Don't tell him anything, Simon chanted to himself.

"Well, he told me my father needed me. I thought you told me all my family was dead."

"He's a nutcase, just as I thought." A brief pause was followed by "So, did the old guy mention a city and a time?"

"Yes. Tampoo, Washington, tomorrow at noon. At a bus depot. He said someone would meet me. He said I should go alone. What does that mean?"

"How would I know?" Carl said with a clatter of silverware. "You're not eating, and I'm not hungry anymore. Let's get out of here."

Ella's voice was very calm as she said, "What's going on, Carl? How did you know he mentioned going to another city?"

"I didn't, you just told me."

"No, you asked. It's a strange question. I may not remember who I am, but I didn't suddenly get stupid."

"Just put your coat on. I'll explain in the car."

Simon heard chairs slide and watched as Ella stalked out of the restaurant. Carl stood by the cash register, glancing repeatedly outside as though afraid Ella would fly away. When no waitress appeared to take his money, he tossed a few bills on the counter and left. He'd apparently forgotten the waitress promised him a free meal.

Simon slapped a couple of dollars next to his empty coffee mug and followed, pulling on his cap, unsure how to proceed. If he'd been confused before, he was downright flummoxed now, but he also sensed Ella might be in danger from this man as she began to suspect his motives.

Ginny had said don't alarm Ella, don't frighten her. How was he supposed to get her away from Carl if he couldn't even talk to her?

He exited the restaurant with his head down so Ella wouldn't notice him. A quick glance; however, revealed that she'd made it to their car, which was parked close to the bluff. She stood with her back to the restaurant and to Carl's approach, arms linked across her chest, one hip thrust forward, her short, dark hair barely moving despite the strong wind. A lilac-colored coat flapped around her hips.

Her body language screamed *pissed off.* The bounce of Carl's steps and the faint whistling sound drifting back on the wind suggested Carl couldn't care less about his wife's frame of mind.

The weather had deteriorated, the thin fog blowing up the bluff, swirling overhead. Searching for an excuse to approach Carl before he talked Ella into getting into the car, Simon noticed movement in a dark sedan parked nearby. The door opened as Carl passed the front bumper. Carl didn't even turn to look as a big man with a very bushy gray-streaked beard got out of the car.

The huge man was dressed all in black and looked damn formidable as he peered around the parking lot, his gaze sliding right by Simon, whose instincts had warned him to step behind a pillar. Apparently making a decision, the giant fell into step behind Carl.

It didn't take Simon's twelve years in law enforcement to figure out something was going on.

Picking up his pace, the bearded man grabbed Carl from behind, twirling him around, throwing a punch that connected with Carl's nose. As he staggered backward, Carl pulled a gun from a hidden holster. The bearded man instantly kicked the gun from Carl's hand with an agility unexpected in a three-hundred-pound man. The gun flew over the bluff as the assailant produced a terrible, mean-looking knife with a curved blade.

Ella screamed. Simon started running toward her, taking his own gun from the waistband holster. Facing each other, jockeying for position, the two men backed Ella against the car. She pushed them away from her, lurching off to the side as blood from a knife slash blossomed on her palm. It ran down her arm as she continued stumbling backward.

Again and again, the bearded man swung his knife in wide arcs at Carl. Ella seemed oblivious of anything but the fight. The men kept at it, forcing her toward the edge of the bluff as the giant lashed out and Baxter recoiled.

Birds wheeling up the bluff caught Simon's attention. At once he realized the direction Ella's retreat was taking her. He yelled her name. The two men turned to look at him, but Ella kept moving as though oblivious of anything except escape. She stumbled backward against the knee-high rock and wood post wall, her hands flying, her purse launched into the air. She'd been moving so fast her momentum sent her sailing over the edge of the fog-shrouded cliff.

Both men lurched toward the bluff, became aware of each other again, and squared off. Carl peered at the empty spot where Ella had last appeared, obviously caught between his desire to find out what had happened to her and the one to save his own skin.

His skin won. He used the big man's momentary lapse of attention to get a head start back to his car.

Simon was only vaguely aware of the two men taking off in their respective vehicles as he reached the place where Ella had tumbled over the cliff.

FOUR

THE bluff was riddled with gullies and overgrown with Scotch broom, their brilliant yellow flowers dazzling despite the fog. More important than their color was the fact that they could cushion, maybe even stop, a fall.

"Ella!"

Twenty feet below him, he caught sight of movement, but it was impossible to tell if a person was responsible or if it was just the wind rattling the tortured boughs of a Sitka spruce.

Slapping his revolver back in the holster, Simon climbed over the fence and onto the narrow ledge, calling her name again. To his infinite relief, he heard her voice.

"Help! Someone help!"

As he took a cautious step, the sandy rocks beneath his feet shifted and he slipped. He grabbed one of the wood posts and caught himself but not before a shower of rocks skittered down the gully.

"Hold on!" he yelled.

Leaving her there was one of the hardest things he'd ever done, but he had to get a rope or risk stranding them both. He knew exactly where it was in his truck and dug his keys out as he ran. It was over twenty miles back to town. A call to the fire station would set a rescue in motion. Should he take the time to fiddle with his phone and instigate it?

No.

Grabbing the rope, he ran back across the lot. There was no one else around.

Fingers steady, he quickly rigged a bowline in the rope and hitched it over the wood post six feet north of where he figured Ella had landed or caught hold of a branch or root. The fate of the baby she carried flashed across his mind, but he let it go. There was nothing he could do except save Ella.

"Ella?" he yelled as he tore off the green baseball cap and pulled on the work gloves he'd grabbed along with the rope.

It took her forever to answer and when she did, her voice was faint. "Hurry. I can't hold on much longer."

"Keep talking. I'm rappelling down to your left, so no rocks will hit you, but I can't see in the fog. I don't know exactly where you are."

"I'm kind of in a tree," she called, her voice a little stronger.

The cliff below the post he'd chosen wasn't gullied like the other, but stuck out in weathered bare rock. Leaning backward and paying out the rope through his gloved hands, Simon backed down the face until his feet hit empty air. He swung back against the cliff, the impact briefly knocking the wind out of his lungs.

Below him and to his right, he heard Ella yell, "Are you okay?"

"Keep talking," he sputtered, and immediately pushed himself away. Now he could start veering toward the sound of

Ella's voice as she recited the alphabet, catching his feet in the gullies and fending off the brush as it became more dense. At last he spied a glimpse of lilac that almost but not quite blended in with the foliage.

Ella was wearing a jacket that color.

Another foot or two and he could see the gleaming cap of her brown hair and then two wide blue eyes.

She'd been stopped from the three-hundred-foot drop to the surf below by the branches of the spruce, themselves twisted by the wind. She clung to the end of a slender branch, one leg looped over the top, both hands clinging to the rough bark. The tree didn't look all that sturdy, but the thick foliage above her head explained why he hadn't been able to see her from above.

Pushing with his legs, he swung toward her, landing on the bluff right below her dangling foot.

"You have to let go," he said. The sound of the surf seemed twice as loud as it had from the top of the bluff and he raised his voice, reaching up to touch her denim-covered leg. "Trust me."

She looked down at him but hesitated. He wondered if she recognized him. Even if she did, why would she trust him? She didn't remember she knew him, and the basic Ella he'd come to understand was a woman who liked to control her own destiny and didn't trust easily.

"You sure that rope is strong enough for both of us?" she called.

He knew the rope was strong enough. They'd soon find out if the wood post at the top was. He said, "Would you rather hang around here all day?"

The tree creaked as she adjusted her weight. "Okay, point taken. Just be ready."

"I'll manage. Go slow. Keep a good grip on the tree as long as you can. Use me like a ladder. When you get down here where I can grab you around your waist, we'll figure out how to get back up the cliff, okay?"

"Okay," she said, and slowly began unhooking her death grip from the tree. He braced himself, tying off the rope around his waist so he could use both hands to grab her. Within a few moments, her foot hit his shoulder and his fingers wrapped around her calf. She all but slithered down his body until she paralleled him, one arm swung around his neck. The palm of her other hand was still bleeding and her clothes were splotched with blood.

She craned her neck and looked into his eyes. "What are *you* doing here?" Her voice was hushed and amazed.

"Saving you," he said. "Hold on," he added as he pushed them away from the bluff, shifting his weight to the left, landing a few feet back toward the direction he'd descended from. Ella caught on quickly and helped him by synchronizing her body movements to his, though he still wasn't sure how he was going to climb hand over hand up this rope with her in tow.

He heard voices from above.

"Who's up there?" she whispered, her breath warm against his neck. Hell of a time to feel a surge of sexual recognition.

"I have no idea," he muttered. There was suddenly new tension on the rope. Had some Good Samaritan figured out they needed help? "Other than your hand, are you hurt?"

"I don't think so." She glanced between their feet and added, "Just scared."

"Don't look," he cautioned, though he knew from his own brief glance all she could really see was thick fog creeping through the brush and trees. It was the faraway sound of the crashing surf that was alarming.

More voices drifted down the bluff, and the rope slowly started pulling them upward. "Hold on to the rope with your good hand and me with the other," he said. "Try to keep your feet against the cliff and walk with the rope." He didn't add that he hoped whoever was up there knew not to go too fast.

The most harrowing part was the last bump of rock that meant they hung suspended for what seemed an eternity, but after their feet hit the ground again it was simply a matter of taking the last few steps.

At the top, people reached for Ella and for him. Simon saw his rope had been tied to the towing wrench on a big four-by-four. The driver of the truck jumped out of the cab, clapping Simon on the shoulder, grinning ear to ear. Simon shook his hand and thanked him.

After a few moments, Simon sidled up to Ella, who stood shivering in the cold, a clean cloth someone had apparently given her wrapped around her left hand. "We need to get you to the hospital," he said.

"No. I don't have time for that," she said. "My husband. Where is he?"

"After he saw you fall, he drove off. The attacker went after him."

"Could you tell what direction they went?"

"North. Why?"

"Because we have to follow. The man with the beard was trying to kill Carl."

"I know. But you need attention. There's your head and the—"

He stopped a microsecond before saying the word *baby* and mumbled, "The cut on your hand to consider."

"No, please, you've helped me this much. Can't you help me just a little longer? Take me to the next town. I'll rent a car."

He wasn't sure it would be smart to admit he'd been spying on her, that he knew she had to get to Tampoo. Feeling his way, he said, "Is your memory back, Ella?"

She narrowed her eyes. "Why do you call me Ella? Carl calls me Eleanor."

"Well, I—"

She shook her head impatiently, wincing as her eyes refocused. "Never mind. It doesn't matter. No, my memory hasn't come back, but I now know I have a father who needs me. Something is happening that includes him, something Carl knows more about than he'll tell me. I have to find Carl. I have to get to Washington."

"The police," he said firmly. "They can put an APB out on your rental."

"No police!"

"But they can—"

"No," she insisted. "I don't want the police."

"Why?"

"I don't know," she said, biting her lip. "Just promise, no police."

"I don't—"

"Listen, whatever my father is involved in is dangerous for him and apparently for Carl, too. Carl has a cell phone. If he wants to call the cops, let him."

"Okay, okay, calm down."

"Can't we just drive north to the next town and see if Carl is there?"

Still he paused. Going about this on their own on the heels of that knife attack seemed foolhardy to him. But what about Ella? How deeply was she involved in all this? What had she done that she couldn't remember? He knew she didn't like police work, she'd complained about his job constantly, but without her memory, what was driving her to react to this extreme?

"Yes, okay, I'll help you," he said as though there'd ever been any real doubt he would.

She took a deep breath. Her hands shook as she ran them through her hair.

She began thanking their benefactors. Simon picked up his green cap from where he'd flung it. Nearby, a woman and her children seemed to be searching for the contents of Ella's spilled handbag and pressing it back into her uninjured hand.

As they left the parking lot, Simon heard sirens approaching from the other direction. It appeared someone had called the fire department to come to the rescue.

"SO, WHY DO YOU CALL me Ella?"

The road they traveled ran high above the ocean with hairpin curves and trees everywhere. Most of the scenery was obscured by the fog. She looked over at him and saw his brows knit.

"My mother's name is Eleanor. Everyone calls her Ella. I guess when I saw you fall I just switched back into an old habit."

"Oh." Well, that kind of made sense. She could see how that could happen. "I'm very lucky you saw me go over that cliff," she added.

"I'd just driven up to the restaurant," he said, "and noticed your husband and the big guy fighting. And then I saw you backing up to escape them."

"You yelled a warning. You yelled Ella."

"Yeah."

"And then you ran toward me."

"I didn't think you saw or heard me," he said, glancing at her and away as a big camper whizzed by going the other direction.

"I did but kind of in a hazy way. I was just so worried about that damn knife. And Carl had a gun. I didn't know before that he…" Her gaze swiveled to him. "You had a gun, too! I glimpsed it in your hand."

"Yes," he said.

"Why do you carry a gun?"

"I don't know if that's any of your business," he said, but his voice was gentle.

He had a point. Why was she grilling him? Why was she treating him as though she had the right to question anything he did?

He broke the awkward silence by adding, "Would you rather I call you Eleanor?"

"No," she said at once. "I prefer Ella."

"Then Ella it is."

"It was very brave of you to come after me like you did. You saved my life. Thank you."

"You're welcome."

"Are you a fireman?"

"Why would you—oh, because of the rescue?"

"Yes. You know all about ropes. It just seems like the kind of stuff a fireman knows. Don't they rescue people all the time?"

"Mainly we put out fires," he said.

"So you are a fireman," she said. "I was right." That explained the muscles she'd felt under his clothes as she slid down his body and the way he'd balanced her weight as they scaled the mountain.

"I'm used to helping people out of jams," he added.

"Let's get something straight," she said firmly. "I'm not expecting anything from you but a ride to a car rental place."

"I understand."

"I have to find Carl. He's been lying to me."

"Aren't you worried the guy with the knife will catch up with him first?"

It was her turn for evasion. Worried? Hell yes, if it meant he carved Carl into little pieces. She wanted to ask Carl about her father; she didn't want to find him dead.

Good heavens, was she really such a cold person that she could think like this about a man who claimed they had a good marriage? Yeah, well, he lied; he'd proven that this morning.

The silence was growing and, given the paucity of comforting thoughts in her brain, she blurted out, "You missed breakfast when you rescued me and then I dragged you away."

"I'll grab something later. Actually, I seldom eat before noon."

"My dad was like that. Just coffee with cream. I'd sit in his lap and he'd give me sips."

The words had left her mouth before she realized the significance of the thought behind them—or maybe a more accurate thing to say would be the lack of thought behind them.

Simon pulled the truck off the road into a lookout and set the warning lights. "You remember your father?" His voice sounded excited.

"Not really," she said slowly. "I just suddenly remembered sitting on his lap, drinking his coffee, liking the cream."

But there was more. The warmth of his arm around her waist as he held her, the faint odor of pipe tobacco, his deep voice booming above her head as she took tiny, sweet sips.

Already the memory, so tangible just a second before, began slipping away.

"That's great," Simon said. Hooking one strong arm over the steering wheel, he added, "We need to be honest with each other, not hold things back, don't you agree?"

"Yes," she said quietly, meeting his gaze. For a second, she was back in his arms, hanging from the rope. She'd been frightened, yes, but she'd also felt safe. She added, "I should tell you about the man in the restaurant. But couldn't you drive while I did?"

He blinked a couple of times. "The man in the restaurant?"

"This will all make more sense if you know about him." She motioned with her fingers. "Drive?"

He stared at her a second longer. "Okay," he finally said, and within a few moments, he had merged back into traffic.

She told him about the old guy and the way he'd contrived to meet with her alone and her conviction that Carl had known about the meeting days before. Simon asked if she was sure the old man didn't seem familiar in some way, and though she had to admit he'd appeared to be acquainted with her family, she had no idea who he was or who the man he'd called Jerry was, the man he'd said she was the last to see, presumably before she lost her memory.

They passed a sign announcing the next town a mile away. "So you can see why I need to get to Tampoo, Washington, can't you? I don't know what's going on, but it must be serious. My father needs me. And Carl—he knows something he's not telling."

Simon slowed down as they entered the city. To Ella's dismay it was bigger than Rocky Point. "I'll never find Carl here," she said.

"No, I don't think you will," Simon agreed.

"I thought I'd see our car, but there are hundreds of cars."

"If he has someone on his tail, he won't just pull over."

"And the last time he saw me I was flying off a cliff. He probably thinks I'm dead." She met Simon's gaze and swallowed. If not for him, she would have wound up on the beach a long, long ways down.

Finding Carl was impossible, that was clear to her now, whereas it hadn't been minutes earlier. What else was she missing? Was her light-headed wooziness her natural state of being or was it the result of the concussion?

As she stewed in her own inadequacies, Simon pulled into a grocery store parking lot.

"What are you doing?"

After he'd switched off the engine, he turned to face her again. "Do you agree it's pointless to try to find Carl in this city?"

"Yes. But Tampoo is in Washington and I need a rental."

"Okay, okay, just hear me out. Your eyes look spacey and you have a gash on your hand and Tampoo is easily reached in twenty-four hours. In fact, it will take a lot less than half of that, more like seven or eight. So I'm going to go into this store and buy what it takes to clean and dress your hand and you're going to go into the bathroom and strip off your clothes and wash up whatever got scraped and dirty and make sure you aren't cut and bleeding, um, anywhere important."

"Simon, really."

"It's this or the hospital."

"That's pretty heavy-handed," she said.

"I'm the cautious type. Does your stomach hurt?"

"No. Why would my stomach hurt?"

"You had a concussion," he said. "Nausea and, oh, cramps, maybe, can be a side effect." He looked decidedly uncomfortable as he added, "I just thought the fall might have exacerbated any…conditions."

"I feel queasy every morning. I think it's the medicine I take at night. Anyway, I'll do as you ask."

"You will?"

"It makes sense to me. You act surprised."

He shrugged. "The last woman I was close to wasn't quite as agreeable as you are."

"Is this the one you were telling me about last night?"

"Yes."

"I guess I'm just the easygoing type."

His smile seemed wistful to her and she wondered how long ago he'd broken up with this woman. Maybe the wound was still raw. That thought seemed to rekindle the throbbing in her left hand and she glanced down. What caught her eye was the slender band of gold on her ring finger, a band tying her to Carl.

Had he left her to die on the cliff or had his motive for leaving been to lead the man with the knife away from her? If so, that posed the question—what kind of loyalty did she owe Carl? Should she believe him when he claimed they had a good marriage? Were her current misgivings out of place? When she saw him again—and there wasn't a doubt in her mind he would show up in Tampoo unless the guy with the knife stopped him—should she give him the benefit of the doubt? He was her husband, after all....

She remembered the chill that raced through her blood when he touched her....

And the lies. He'd known about that meeting at the restaurant and now he knew about the one in Tampoo. What if Carl represented the threat to her father? She might not remember him to speak of, but she'd had one searing moment of clarity and this she knew—she loved her father. She would do anything for him.

"You okay?" Simon said.

"What? Oh, sure."

"You look upset."

"I guess I am."

"It'll all work out," he said softly, then shook his head and added, "I sound like a greeting card."

"You know, I still don't know your last name."

"Task."

"And I'm Ella Baxter. I can't remember if I told you my last name before."

"Pleased to formally meet you," he said, taking her right hand in his. The touch of his skin sent a million fireflies dancing up her arm.

"Let's get this over with," she said, withdrawing her hand and steeling herself for the moment Simon would drop her off at the car rental place and go his own way. The moment she would be alone except for the fleeting images of a faceless father who had given her sips of coffee some twenty-odd years before.

FIVE

SO, now he'd lied to her.

Repeatedly.

Simon put bandages, ointments and other supplies in a shopping basket before retracing his steps to the front of the store, where he waited near the alcove that led to the super-market restrooms. His concern was that besides scrapes and bruises and the gash in her hand, the fall had caused Ella to miscarry her baby.

Was her baby his baby? They'd been together at the time she must have gotten pregnant, but he couldn't swear that she hadn't been seeing Carl Baxter, too. He found it hard—and distress-ful—to think she would sleep with another man when he and she were lovers, but there was that secret side of Ella he had to consider, the side that led to her compartmentalizing her life so that he knew little about what she did when she wasn't with him.

And there was the recent withdrawn behavior, her unwill-ingness to share whatever was troubling her. It had begun a good month before and she'd countered his concerns by telling him being a cop didn't give him the right to butt into her business.

Hadn't loving her given him that right?

How in the world could he tell her she was pregnant and yet how could he keep it from her? And how would he convince her to allow him to come along on her trip to Tampoo and wherever it led next? He absolutely couldn't allow her to go on alone, not after that knife fight.

Did he have time to call home and see if the P.I. he'd called the day before had news or even to call Ginny and see if she'd found out anything from Ella's doctors?

He was about to reach for his cell when Ella appeared in the alcove, limping now, clutching her big handbag to her chest. For the first time he noticed the extent of the scratches on her skin and tears in her clothes. She looked pale and feverish at the same time, the bandage on her head sporting bright red stains as though bleeding anew. They were going to need some gauze.

"You're limping," he said as she drew near.

"I think I twisted an ankle or something. It's no big deal."

"How about other contusions and, er, bleeding?"

"Nothing serious. A few scratches. I think my clothes got the worst of it."

He motioned at her handbag. "I meant to ask if you've checked to see if all your belongings are in there."

"I haven't looked yet." She started to open her purse, then paused as her stomach made a gurgling noise. They both smiled. "Oops, pardon me, I think I'm hungry. It kicks in every day about this time, I guess when the medicine from the night before wears off."

"Let's see if we can find some sandwiches to eat on the run."

"Or maybe some good rolls and a few deli supplies," she said, and he smiled internally. His Ella had not been a fast food or ready-made type of girl. She'd been something of a closet gourmet, more likely to choose French Camembert than Wisconsin cheddar. "Whatever you like," he said.

His mind raced as they walked through the aisles collecting more first aid items and a supply of bottled water on their way to the in-store deli. Would she have told him if she was bleeding in a way that indicated problems with a pregnancy? Maybe not, maybe she'd be shy to mention it, but surely she would have bought herself something to help with bleeding and that would have meant she would have to open her purse and look in her wallet for change. She said she hadn't. No reason for her to lie about that, so he had to trust that, for now, the baby was safe. The thing to do was get Ella off her feet ASAP.

"Look at that," she said, stopping suddenly. She was staring at a display of sweatshirts and sweatpants, most of them dark-green-and-white and sporting a local high school logo. "I only have a credit card. Do you think the store would accept it?"

"Probably not," he said quickly as an idea flashed through his brain. "I'll get what you want."

"You wouldn't mind?"

"No."

She immediately began digging through the clothes for the right sizes. She'd set her purse in the top of the basket to have her uninjured hand free, and now with her back turned to him, he slid his hand inside the unzipped bag, groped around until his fingers touched what felt like her wallet and quickly extracted it. Bingo. It went in his pocket in a flash. Now she had no driver's license, and without a driver's license, she couldn't rent a car.

"What do you think?" she said. She'd managed to find a pale blue set of sweats and held them against her chest. A small painted dolphin leaped across her breasts.

"You look good in blue," he said softly. He'd always thought so.

There was a chair in the alcove. After they'd paid for everything, he slathered her up with antibiotics and wrapped gauze around her a couple of turns shy of a mummy. She went back into the bathroom and emerged a few minutes later wearing the blue sweats.

"I wonder if the real me would be as horrified by this getup as the current me is," she mused, putting her old clothes in an empty paper bag.

"I think you look kind of cute. Sporty."

"Let's go find a rental place, okay? I want to cross the state line into Washington tonight, and I'm sure you have a life to get back to."

"Absolutely," he said, "although the fact is, I'm on a few days' leave right now. That's how firemen in my area work. A day on, a day off, eventually four days off…it's called a tour and it leaves discretionary time." And that was true of the Blue Mountain Fire Department. It just wasn't true of him, though a call for time off had taken care of that problem with the Blue Mountain Police Department.

The next hour or so played out as he knew it would, although he felt crummy lying to her again. Once she found her wallet was missing, she insisted they call the credit card company until she realized she didn't know the name of the company or even remember what kind of card it was. As he knew it was safe in his pocket, he told her they'd worry about it when they stopped for the night. Between now and then, he'd have to figure out a way to get her wallet back to her.

Being without a valid driver's license had accomplished exactly what it was supposed to—it had kept her from renting a car. She'd accepted his continued help with a weariness suggesting she was just too frazzled to fight it. After she'd fixed them sandwiches from goodies she'd chosen at the deli counter, she'd fallen into a deep sleep, head against the door, cushioned on his jacket.

He glanced at her several times, wishing she'd wake up and be the old Ella, the one with answers instead of questions. True, he found this more open version of Ella very appealing in her way. She had all the wit and charm and beguiling oddities of the original woman without the wariness that had ultimately driven them apart.

What had she done that had put her in this position? He'd be willing to bet it had started when they were still together. The way she'd left her house, her odd haircut and color—and where in the hell had Carl Baxter come from? What did he have to do with Ella's father?

For that matter, how did they know this was really about Ella's father? The only time she'd mentioned family to him was to tell him they were all dead. Now, just because some old guy fed her a line, he was supposed to believe there was a whole secret plot going on? On the other hand, Carl Baxter and the big guy with a knife were absolutely real….

Bottom line: Was Ella in danger or was someone else in danger because of her?

He needed to get somewhere private and make a few phone calls.

ELLA WOKE UP as Simon pulled into another parking lot, this one belonging to a sprawling motel. The fact that it was already dark meant she'd slept for hours.

"Where are we?" she asked after a yawn that seemed to crack her face. She was stiff, sore, headachy and hurt just about everywhere.

"We're a hundred or so miles south of Tampoo. I'm too tired to drive any more. We can easily travel the rest of the way tomorrow morning."

She didn't argue. She wasn't the one putting in the hours behind the wheel.

"I chose a one-story motel," he explained as they got out of the truck, "just to be on the safe side."

"The safe side of what?"

"I just like having my feet close to the ground. You know, in case."

She let it drop. Maybe it was a fireman thing.

He checked them in as Mr. and Mrs. Simon Task, a fact she also didn't dispute. The man was paying for everything—she hoped she had enough money somewhere to reimburse him. If he wanted them both in one room, that was fine with her.

They immediately walked across the parking lot to the restaurant next door and ordered dinner.

"How do you do it?" Simon asked, sitting back in his chair and gazing at her across the table. His gray eyes were full of warmth and speculation and she found herself patting at her hair, wishing she'd thought to buy a comb.

"How do I do what?"

"Order food. How do you know you like morel risotto?"

"How do I know anything?" she mused. "It's a mystery to

me, too. I mean, if I can figure out what I like to eat, why can't I figure out who I am?"

"Today you remembered a detail about your father. Have you remembered anything else?"

"I had a dream about him this afternoon. I was riding in the back of a black pickup truck, sitting on a dragon. Well, not really a dragon, one of those floaty things that blow up, the kind kids play with."

"How old were you?"

"I don't know. Little, I think. There was a boy sitting next to me dressed like Tarzan. He had a toy gun."

Simon chuckled. "Where does your father come into this?"

"The boy turned into my father. One minute he was a kid with a red water pistol and the next he was my father and he was holding me in his lap and telling me it was dangerous to ride in the back of a truck but that he would protect me."

"Did you see his face? How did you know it was your dad?"

"No face. I just knew." Her eyes burned as she smiled at herself. "Crazy, huh?"

"It sounds as if you're close to your father."

"I know I am, I just know it. Oh, Simon, promise me you'll help me get to him. He needs help, I know he does. If I fail him I'll never forgive myself."

He narrowed his eyes.

"Promise," she said, uncertain why she was demanding this near stranger make such a pledge.

"I'll do what I can," he said.

"You must think I'm crazy."

"No," he said thoughtfully. "I think you're a woman with one person you can remember and I think he means the world to you."

"You do understand. I keep thinking about Carl. I'm sure he was using me to get to my father. What if Carl's goal is to hurt Dad? He had a gun, you know."

"The big guy with the knife kicked Carl's gun down into the ocean."

"But maybe Carl will buy another one. Why didn't I have the presence of mind to ask the old guy at the restaurant a few questions?"

"Probably because you didn't know what he was talking about. Go easy on yourself."

"Maybe we should have kept driving."

"Even if we drove all night, we can't do anything until tomorrow at noon, right?"

"Yes. Right."

They fell silent as salads were delivered. Ella noticed the waitress gave her a double take and wondered if additional bruises had blossomed on her face since the fall. Maybe it was better not to know.

Despite her nerves and the near silence they fell into as they ate, Ella enjoyed the meal more than any she could recall since waking with amnesia five days before. It wasn't just the food, either, it was the company, and perhaps it wasn't even the fact that Simon sat across from her as much as it was that Carl didn't.

He gives me the creeps, she thought.

"What?"

She'd spoken it aloud. She said, "Carl. I didn't like the look in his eyes."

"What do you mean?"

"He always looked as though he was laughing at me, inside, you know?"

"Very unpleasant."

"Creepy. Nice way for a wife to feel about her husband, isn't it?"

"You said you saw his driver's license."

"Yes."

"The same last name might mean he's your brother or an ex-husband, you know."

The thought Carl Baxter could be a blood relative made her queasy and she set aside her fork. "Not a brother," she said firmly. "The old man said my brother was dead."

"Then an ex-husband."

"Maybe. There's no denying the man knows things about me. I mean little things a man who didn't live with a woman wouldn't know."

"Such as?"

"Such as I have a mole on my, er, abdomen and another one on my breasts, neither in places people would normally see. And he knew about them."

"Intimate places," Simon said with a slow smile.

"Yes."

"How did he pay for your hospital stay?"

"I don't know. He told me not to worry about things like that. It makes me wonder if I'm always compliant."

He took a bite of his steak and shrugged.

"I keep wondering where I met Carl. I mean, I must know him in some capacity for our names to be the same. I just can't imagine myself being attracted to him. Maybe he's a long-lost third cousin once removed, but then why did he pretend to be my husband?"

Simon folded his napkin and sat back in his chair. "Good point."

"Tell me how you met her."

"How I met who?"

"The girl you broke up with. Tell me how you met."

His eyes took on a faraway look, though he didn't avert his gaze. "It was at a dance," he said slowly. "A masquerade dance I got talked into attending with a buddy of mine. I went as a pirate because I had an eye patch left over from something."

"And she was there?"

"She came as a mermaid. She had very long hair and it flowed all around her shoulders and down her back and she was wearing all this blue and green like the water. Every square inch of her seemed to shimmer when she moved."

"It sounds beautiful."

"It was. She was. She had on a mask so I couldn't see all of her face, just her eyes, but I knew she was it."

"She was the one."

"She was like a free spirit that night."

"You make it sound like she changed."

"She did, but that came later. I'll always have that night, I'll always remember the woman I met at the party."

She laid her napkin across the plate. "You loved her."

"I did."

"So how did it end?"

"I guess you could say I left her."

She tilted her head slightly as she looked at him. "But you still have feelings for her."

His gaze sharpened. "That's true, I do. She wasn't the kind of woman a man forgets overnight."

"Maybe there's hope you can get back together," she said. Had anyone ever loved her that way? Had Carl? Was he even capable of that kind of love? Was she?

"It's getting late," Simon finally said.

While he went back to his truck to get his luggage and the first-aid supplies in case anything needed redressing, Ella went into a small variety-type store with Simon's credit card in hand. There wasn't a lot to choose from, but she did find something to sleep in. They walked down the hall wrapped in their own thoughts.

Ella felt nervous about being alone in a room whose most obvious piece of furniture was a bed, but she told herself to grow up. If she could handle being close to Carl for several days, she could handle one night with Simon. At least she *liked* Simon.

"Why don't you use the bathroom first and then I'll take a shower?" he told her.

She pulled the knee-length sleeping shirt from the gift-shop bag and went into the bathroom, where a cursory look in the mirror revealed a total mess. Even her short hair looked defeated. When it grew out a little, she'd get herself to a decent beauty shop. This cut appeared to have been done by someone with their eyes shut.

A few minutes later, she walked into the bedroom to find Simon sitting in a chair next to a small round table. He looked up at her, his gaze flicking down her body as though he couldn't help himself. She saw all sorts of things flash in his eyes, things that made her insides sizzle. The T-shirt material suddenly seemed very, very thin.

"You're not limping anymore," he said.

"No, my ankle doesn't hurt."

"Are you finished in there?"

"It's all yours." He got to his feet in one fluid motion, re-minding her again of the way he'd clasped her to his side on the mountain, the strength in his arms. As six feet of potent mas-culinity walked toward her, she had to remind herself to breathe.

Simon paused a step away from her. "Do you need help re-bandaging anything?"

"No," she said, craning her neck back to look up at him. Their posture was perfect for embracing, for kissing; it was only the foot of space between them that sounded an off note. The hammering heartbeat, the flushed skin, the supersexual aware-ness—that was all there in spades, and unless she was even more clueless than she thought she was, it was there for him, too.

"I'll be a few minutes," he said as he went into the bathroom.

SIMON GAVE HIMSELF a stern lecture about poorly timed hormone attacks as he turned on the shower to cover the sound of his voice. He sat on the closed commode and punched in the number for the P.I. back in Blue Mountain.

"I thought you'd never call back," Devin Kittimer said as soon as he heard Simon's voice. Devin was a decade older than Simon, but a job at Devin's office one summer had been the deciding factor in Simon going to the police academy.

"It's been a little busy on my end. Did you find out anything about Carl Baxter?"

"He was born in Chicago forty-one years ago. Only child, parents alive but separated. Married Eleanor Thorton a few days after her eighteenth birthday when he was in his mid-thirties. The marriage lasted nine weeks before the split. There's some question about the legality of the divorce. Anyway, she apparently moved around quite a bit until ending up in Blue Mountain. She probably told you all this a year ago when you guys got together."

Simon was embarrassed to admit she'd never said one word about any of it. Not a single word. Why had she worked so hard to bury her past?

At any rate, it now appeared Carl Baxter was either her ex-husband or a husband she'd thought she'd left behind. It seemed unlikely Ella was carrying his baby.

Unless he'd come to town and won her back....

"What about Ella?" he said. "Did you call the radio station like I asked?"

"Yes. They have no idea where she is. Her boss was getting worried about her, in fact."

"So she left without telling them."

"I gave the guy some song and dance about a sick relative, and then I went by Ella's house and spoke to a few of her neighbors. Other than the fact that they noticed her house was lit up in the middle of the night, no one had wondered too much about not seeing her. I gather she often worked late hours and spent her free time in the backyard, gardening. No one saw anything suspicious around the time she apparently left."

"So, it wasn't a planned trip or she would have spoken to her boss."

"And stopped her newspaper, which she didn't. Other than that, the years before she got married are hard to figure. I have a few calls out, should know more tomorrow.

"Oh, one thing, Carl Baxter has a rap sheet a mile long. Mostly B and E when he was a kid, some con man stuff, bad checks, things like that. Got a little more inventive as he got older. Was part of a street gang running juice loans in Chicago. Car theft, et cetera. Did time in Tallahassee Road Prison down in Florida, been out a few months. He's also had a few aliases. Carl Stickler, Jay Mornajay, William Smith to name a few."

"Great," Simon said, running a hand through his hair. "You'll keep digging on Ella for me? Find out about her parents, if you can, especially her father."

"Sure."

"Thanks, Devin."

"No problem."

Simon's next call was to his cousin Virginia, who sounded as though he'd woken her up. She mumbled she hadn't been able to find anyone who knew anyone else at the hospital where Ella had been treated and a call to the attending physician had not yet been returned.

"I'm not sure how much he'll tell me even if he does call back," Ginny cautioned.

After hearing details of what had happened to Ella that day, she added, "This sounds increasingly dangerous, coz. I'm not sure you should allow her to continue this search."

Allow her? What a concept! Virginia obviously thought he had more control than he did. "She's determined to find her father. She had a spontaneous memory of him today and dreamed about him, too."

"Positive stuff?"

"Very. She obviously adores him. She's very anxious to find him."

"I wonder why she never told you about him."

"You and me both."

"But this is exactly why you should continue to protect her from too much truth. Her memory is coming back on its own."

"Following a knife fight and a long drop down a cliff," he reminded her.

"True. Still, play it close to the vest, give her another few days."

He'd known that was coming, but he'd hoped she'd tell him to spill his guts. "Okay."

"Call back tomorrow and stay away from steep cliffs and thugs with knives."

"That's my plan."

"You sound bushed. Go to bed."

He clicked off his phone, undressed and showered. He was too tired to shave and it wasn't as though he was going to kiss anyone anyway.

For a second, he was overcome with the not so distant memory of Ella running her fingers along his jaw while nibbling on his earlobe, whispering what they could do if he wanted to take a few minutes and shave—

He splashed cold water on his face. The Ella that memory belonged to was gone; those times were gone. If she was pregnant with his child, they'd have to figure out a way to parent together, but they couldn't be together; they'd tried and failed and he'd be wise to remember that. The excited gleam in her eye when she looked at him now made his groin ache with want, but he knew it would fizzle out and die the moment she remembered their shared past.

He let himself back into the room while holding a towel around his waist. He normally slept nude but not tonight. He'd just forgotten to take clean clothes into the bathroom with him.

He'd been away so long, he was pretty sure she'd be asleep. The lights were dimmed and he took a few steps toward his duffel before he realized she wasn't in the bed; she was sitting on a chair by the small table in the corner. Her face was deep in shadows, though he could see the glistening whites of her eyes as she stared at him.

And then he saw what lay on the table in front of her.

SIX

HOLDING the towel in place, Simon sat down on the edge of the bed, facing her. Gesturing at the table, he said, "You found my badge?"

"I saw the leather folder sitting in your open bag. I was curious so I looked."

"It's okay," he said.

"My snooping or your lying? Which do you mean? Which is okay?"

"Now, wait a second—"

"Are you going to try to explain why you told me you were a fireman?"

"I guess I'd better."

"Make it good," she said, and there was a deadly earnestness to her voice he'd heard before. This was the Ella from before the amnesia, the woman whose middle name was suspicion.

"Do you remember this morning when I suggested we call the police to help Carl and you wouldn't let me?"

"Yes."

"It wasn't ten minutes later that you assumed I was a fireman. It was obvious to me that you had a thing about cops."

"So you lied."

"You were shaken and upset and I didn't know how long we'd be in each other's company at that point, so I let you reach your own conclusions and went along with them. In other words, yes, I lied and for that I'm sorry."

She picked up the badge, ran her fingers over the surface and his heart sank. He'd completely zoned out on the fact that Blue Mountain was engraved on the badge.

"Now tell me why you never told me we come from the same town. It's quite a coincidence, isn't it?"

"What do you mean?" he said, taking the defensive. He didn't have time to review every last one of their conversations, but he was pretty sure he was on safe ground. "Are you from Blue Mountain, too?"

"You know I am," she said.

"How would I know that?"

"I'm sure I mentioned it."

"Nope."

"Are you trying to tell me it's just a coincidence we meet hundreds of miles from home and we come from the same place?"

"Why not?" he said. "Stranger things have happened."

She got up from the chair and walked over to him, the badge still in her hand. He prepared himself to have it lobbed at his chest, but she shocked the hell out of him by gently handing it over.

"I wish I didn't know you were a cop," she said.

Not what he expected. He said, "What does it matter?"

"I don't like cops. I don't trust them."

"Please believe me, I have nothing but your best interest at heart. Honest."

"Just tell me this. Are you the reason the thought of the police getting involved in my life makes me want to run for the hills?"

"No," he said, and that was the truth. Whatever had caused her to panic at the thought of police had started way before him. His job had been a bone of contention between them from the moment she found out about it.

Why was it such a big deal to her? It had never made sense to him and it didn't make sense now. Unless she had a record of some kind, unless she was on the run….

"Are you after Carl? Are you after my father? Are you using me to get to him the way Carl was?"

"Absolutely not."

"Are you here because you're a cop?"

"No. I'm here in this room at this moment helping you because of you. Period."

"Why?"

"Because you need help."

"And you spend your off time looking for damsels in distress?"

"Not usually, no. For you, I made an exception."

"Why?"

"You know why," he said.

"I don't know anything, remember?"

He took a step toward her and held on to her shoulders, resisting the habit of pulling her into a full embrace. She'd always fit against him perfectly. She was exactly the right height, exactly the right shape, her body a perfect match for his.

If it was just that easy.

"It started in the lobby when we exchanged our first words, when I touched your wedding band," he said softly. "I felt you tremble. The next day when I saw you disappear over a mountainside, what was I supposed to do, look the other way?"

She cocked her head. The bathroom light spilled across her cheekbones. Between the bandages and the short, dark hair, she almost looked like a stranger.

"Why do I want to trust you so much?" she said softly.

"Because somewhere in your heart you know you can."

"You could be part of this."

"But I'm not."

She blinked quickly. Her beautiful face was scratched and black-and-blue, bandaged, scraped, but there was nothing wrong with her lips. They were as luscious as ever. He knew she wouldn't stop him if he bent his head and...

And when her memory came back and she recalled the last night they had spent together, the things he'd said to her, the things she'd said to him, the past that lay between them? What then?

He dropped his hands from her shoulders, making sure the towel stayed in place around his waist. "Let's hit the sack," he said.

She mumbled, "I could use a stiff drink."

So could he. But if she couldn't drink, he wouldn't drink. There was a baby between them, too, and his gaze dipped to her midsection, where he thought he could detect a new curve against the cotton of her gown.

"Sleep will do us both more good," he said, dragging his gaze back to her face. "Maybe tomorrow this will all make sense."

Grabbing his duffel, he changed into clean boxers and a

T-shirt in the bathroom. When he returned to the room, he found she'd tucked herself under the sheets. It was obvious she needed sleep. He, on the other hand, had some serious thinking to do. Knowing he'd be out like a light if he darkened the room, he left the lamp burning and settled back against the headboard.

"Ella? Ella, wake up."

Though his voice was a whisper, the urgency in it cut through her sleep like a bullhorn, shattering a dream. Her eyes flew open.

Simon was sitting on the bed beside her, his body tense. As she met his gaze, his finger pressed against her lips and he motioned with his head toward the door.

She heard a very subtle rattle and then the knob slowly turned. She would have gasped but for the presence of Simon's warning finger.

She met his gaze and he lowered his head to whisper in her ear. "It may be nothing but some drunk trying to get in the wrong room. I'm going out the bathroom window. Lock it behind me."

"Why are you going to do that?" she whispered back.

"I want to know who it is," he said as though it was reasonable.

"We could just open the door—"

"Are you forgetting this morning?"

The gash in her hand seemed to spring into flames. No, she wasn't forgetting, but she wanted to beg Simon to stay. She didn't want to be alone and she was afraid for him. "Okay," she said, working to make sure her voice didn't betray her fears, though those fears were clawing their way up her throat.

Simon quietly slipped off the bed. He pulled on his jeans

and shoes, stuck his gun in his waist holster. She followed him into the bathroom, closing the door behind them so light from the bedroom wouldn't illuminate the window over the bathtub.

"Don't open the door for anyone," he cautioned as he stepped into the tub. "Make sure the chain is engaged."

"No kidding."

He slid the glass panel back and popped off the screen. All that was visible from Ella's point of view was a tall overhead mercury vapor lamp illuminating the side of a nearby building.

It took Simon a moment to twist his body through the narrow opening. When she heard his feet hit the pavement outside, she closed the window behind him and relocked it. Back in the bedroom, she double-checked the door before changing back into her blue sweat suit and shoes. When she heard another rattle at the door, she tiptoed across the room, waiting for a signal that it was Simon. Why hadn't they agreed on some kind of code knock? She stood so close to the wood panel the warmth of her breath bounced back on her face. If anything, her heart pounded harder than it had when she'd been caught on that tree, dangling above the ocean.

Who was out there?

The knob turned.

SIMON RAN AROUND THE PERIMETER of the motel, searching for a doorway back into the building. The only one he found was marked Hotel Personnel and was locked. He had to go all the way back to the lobby to reenter and then make his way cautiously back down the hallway.

The space in front of their door was empty, but he caught a glimpse of a man turning a corner into another corridor several yards beyond it. Staying close to the outside wall, he hurried along, peeking around the corner in time to see the same man push open the doors emptying out into the court-yard pool area.

He'd seen the man that very morning, wearing the same black clothes.

Obviously, the man with the knife had waited somewhere along the way and followed Simon and Ella to this motel. Had he dispatched Carl and was he now hunting Ella? Maybe he'd been trying to kill Carl to get to her that morning.

The questions were immaterial. Whatever this man knew, Simon needed to know. He had to get the jump on him; if Ella was in trouble with the law, so be it. He couldn't protect her forever if she'd done something terrible, and the sooner it was out in the open, the better. If Carl was dead, which seemed a likely scenario given the big man's presence at the motel, then it became even more important to make him talk.

Giving the guy a few seconds to get away from the doors, Simon practically slithered around the corner. He peered through the glass inset in the door and saw the big man standing with his back to the motel.

How to get out the door without drawing attention? When he heard raised voices, he realized there must be someone out there with him. The odds had just shifted. Nevertheless, the noise of the argument might cover the sound of him opening the door.

He took a deep breath and pushed on the glass, sliding out and into the shadows as fast as he could. The first place he found shelter was behind an electrical power unit that emitted a hum. As handy as it was for concealment, it was too noisy for eavesdropping.

Another peek revealed the men still talking, but they'd

lowered their voices even more as though aware a shouting match after midnight would draw attention. Simon kept low as he moved behind a handy clump of bushes and on to an equipment locker.

It was time to decide what to do. As a police officer in Oregon, he was on duty 24/7, but he wasn't acting much like a police officer right now. He could arrest the big guy for attacking Carl Baxter, and Ella could verify she'd seen the fight, but without Carl around to prosecute, how far would that go?

Of course, if Carl showed up dead, it would be a whole other matter.

Bottom line: if he used his official standing to try to get the big guy to open up, then he'd also have to be willing to hand Ella over to the authorities if that was appropriate. He needed a nonconfrontational way in which to get the man to talk.

He snuck another look, and this time the big man was pacing, obviously frustrated, grumbling as he walked, his voice spiking every few seconds. The other man suddenly stood up and moved into the light, grabbing the big guy's shoulder, spinning him around to face him, his back still to Simon. The two men jabbed at each other's chests, their voices still subdued, but loud enough for Simon to finally get the gist of the problem.

They were arguing about whether they should break down a door and take what they wanted. The big guy was in favor of waiting until morning. He'd tried the door; it was locked; a break-in would just create a scene. The other man said he could get in the room without detection, no problem, he'd done it before. He didn't want to wait until daylight; too much might go wrong.

There was little doubt in Simon's mind which door they were talking about and who they wanted to get their hands on.

The smaller man turned around.

Simon blinked a few times, his brain trying to assimilate what he saw and what it meant.

Carl Baxter.

The only reason he'd be here was if he'd joined forces with his adversary way back this morning. The two of them had to be working together, but why the fight, what was the purpose?

Wait, hold on, who cared? The reasons for everything could wait. What he needed right now were answers, and there were the two men who could fill in all the gaps, ripe for the plucking, only twenty feet away. Okay, they were both undoubtedly armed seeing as they were willing to enter a motel room where they must know Simon slept along with Ella. Surely they'd seen his gun that morning.

Could he take them both?

He felt a vibration in his pocket and ignored it for a minute. Voices lowered, the men started toward the far side of the motel where a parallel wing offered additional rooms. They were either refining their game plan or retreating until morning. How to tell?

He could follow them, maybe trap them in their room if indeed that's where they were headed.

The phone vibrated again. He grabbed it from his pocket and flipped it open to check caller ID. As he did, he heard the bigger man say, "Okay, you win."

That meant tonight....

He hit the button when he saw it was Virginia. Moving swiftly back toward his own door, he took care to stay covered in case the men turned around. "Ginny?" he whispered. "This isn't a good time...."

"I just got a call from that doctor I tried to get a hold of earlier today."

"It's the middle of the night," he said, incredulous.

"He called because when I left a message for him, I mentioned Ella's name. The police had just awoken him. Do you know your little Ella is wanted in connection with a murder back in Blue Mountain?"

"No," he said, his heart sinking. He looked over his shoulder to see both men entering through the far door. He ducked inside his own wing and walked quickly down the hall as he spoke. "Did you tell them I'm with her and where we are?"

"I don't know where you are, coz. You've been very careful to never tell me an exact location, and for that I thank you. But no, I didn't tell him about you, I made up something."

Why hadn't Devin said anything about this when they talked earlier? Murder? "Who's dead?" he asked.

"I don't know. Apparently the dead man was discovered in a vacant lot a couple of days ago, but now the police want to question Ella. I don't have details, I don't know how they knew she was in the accident or the hospital, but the other doctor is bound to tell them I was asking questions."

"Not necessarily, but if they do, tell them the truth, don't perjure yourself. I have to go."

"I want you to listen to reason. This is your career we're talking about—"

"Ginny? Not now. Thanks for the warning."

He snapped the cell closed and tapped on the room door. "Ella? It's me, Simon."

He heard the rattle of the chain and then the door flew

open. Ella took a few hasty steps back into the room. "Did you find out who was out there?"

He locked the door behind him, leaving the chain unhooked this time. If the thugs broke into the room, he didn't want management alerted. Better they should enter and see the room empty and go away.

"We have to leave," he said.

"Why? Who was it? That awful man with the knife?"

He started throwing his things into his bag. "Yeah, it was him, all right, but he's apparently in cahoots with someone else you know. Carl was out there and I think one or the other of them is on his way here."

Her face drained of color. "I thought the guy with the knife tried to kill Carl."

"I did, too."

She shook her head. "Even if they're cohorts now, why not just cut us off tomorrow? Carl knows where we're headed. Wait a second, how did either one of them know we were here in this motel?"

"They must have been trailing us all day," he said, his professional pride taking a hit. He hadn't detected a tail. He'd never even really thought to look for one. He stuffed Ella's few belongings into the gift shop bag. "Anything else?" he said, looking around.

"But that man tried to kill Carl."

"Unless it was staged."

"Why would they stage—"

"I don't know," he snapped, then took a deep breath. "I don't know," he said more calmly, meeting her gaze. "Maybe they had a falling-out, maybe the big guy caught up with Carl and they decided to go in together, I just don't know."

"They're coming after me," she said, her eyes growing hard. Every once in a while the old Ella showed up, and this time, he welcomed her arrival. "Just let them come," she said. "You have a gun, you're a damn policeman, right?"

"What about your father?"

Her lashes fluttered against her cheeks. "You're right, we can't risk my not getting to Tampoo, can we?"

"No. That's why we're going out the bathroom window."

Without another word, she turned on her heel and made for the bathroom. He unlocked the window again and slid it open, then threw their belongings outside. Since the drop to the ground was the more difficult part of the escape, Simon went first. Ella managed to get herself through the opening and more or less dropped into his arms, crying out softly when he grabbed her. No doubt he'd touched her hand or one of the other abrasions she'd suffered.

"Where's the truck?" she asked, looking around the parking area, trying to orientate herself.

"Out front." He'd been worrying about this since the moment he knew they had to leave. If he were trying to trap someone, he'd send one man to the room and the other to guard the getaway vehicle. Therefore, the best thing to do was abandon the truck.

But he'd signed into this motel using his real name and giving his license number, so it wouldn't be long before the motel would either tow the truck or have it impounded, and Ella's wallet was on the passenger-side floor under the seat where he'd put it a few hours before. If things ever got linked together, this would put her in his company.

All this meant it was time to take sides. He was either a lawman or a man dedicated to helping Eleanor Baxter figure things out. A man willing to risk everything for a woman who was probably carrying his baby or a man who threw her to the mercy of the court with the hope she actually wasn't involved in a murder.

No way. He did not want his baby born in prison and sometimes, as much as he hated to admit it, the law got things wrong.

Or had he got things wrong? Was it possible she carried another man's child? "We're walking," he grumbled.

"All the way to Tampoo?"

"It's coming up on closing time at the bars."

"*Now* you want a drink?" she said, her limp reappearing.

"Stay close to the side of the building," he cautioned as he pulled her onto the darker half of the sidewalk. "It won't take them long to figure out we're gone. I have a feeling the stakes are higher than either one of us can guess."

She fell silent beside him, her breathing growing strained as he hurried her along.

What had happened to make two men hell-bent on murdering each other this morning join forces now?

One thing was certain. Carl was no doubt at that moment storming their room, risking detection and possible arrest if hotel management got wind of things. That was the act of a reckless man.

And a reckless man was a deadly man.

SEVEN

ELLA soon discovered closing time at a bar was a great place to catch a taxi. Simon gave directions to head for the nearest town to the north with a bus station.

"There's a depot right here in Witchit, buddy," the driver announced.

"I don't want this one," Simon insisted.

"It's your dime," the driver said, "but just so you know, the next town is about twelve dark miles from here."

"That's fine."

Ella was seated very close to Simon, more or less in the same spot she'd landed upon getting into the cab, too tired and frightened to seek distance. "That's our plan? We're taking a bus to Tampoo?"

The light was spare inside the cab, reducing Simon to a shape darker than the shadows around him. He pulled her into his arms and spoke into her ear, his voice a whisper. "Not all the way to Tampoo. Too dangerous. We'll get off short of the place, rent a car and drive so we're not stuck when we get there."

"Good, because the last time we met with one of my father's contacts, I went off a cliff."

"Exactly."

They were silent for the rest of the ride. Simon paid the driver when he let them off, and though it occurred to Ella that he was going exceptionally far out of his way to help her, she let it go. Time would reveal his real motives; for now she had to trust what he'd told her—he was with her because she needed him. There was absolutely no denying that fact.

"Bus straight through to Seattle leaves at 6:00 a.m.," the depot manager announced.

"Too long a wait out in the open," Simon muttered, looking around the deserted building in such a way that Ella shuddered. She expected Carl and the man with the knife to burst through the doors at any moment.

"There's a puddle jumper comes through in about fifteen minutes, but it won't get you there any faster," the manager said, his gaze lingering on Ella's bandages.

"Did it stop in Witchit?"

"Yeah."

"Did it take on passengers?"

"How would I know?"

Simon bought the tickets and the two of them moved into the waiting room. Ella was too anxious to sit on the old chairs sprinkled about the area despite her weariness. She leaned against the wall instead.

The bus showed up on schedule. Simon shooed her into the restroom. "You're not getting on board until I make sure Carl or the big guy isn't on that bus."

"Why would they be on the bus?"

"If they figured out how we might leave town without our vehicle, one of them could be on board. I'll knock on the door, okay?"

She did as he asked. Every minute of the five-minute wait seemed to take an hour before she heard a couple of raps on the door and exited to find Simon standing there. "All clear," he said.

The bus was mostly empty. Simon guided her to the bench seat in the back. Ella sank onto the worn vinyl gratefully, scooting to the corner where she could rest her head. She closed her eyes, aware of Simon stowing his duffel and her bag in the overhead bin but too tired to care about anything.

Besides, maybe if she slept she would dream, maybe she would see her father again. The first time she'd thought of him, she'd been very small, sitting on his lap while he drank coffee. The second time she'd been a few years older and there had been a little boy there, too. The third time was just that night when Simon woke her up and she could remember none of the details, just that her father had been near her.

But sleep wouldn't come. The bus stopped too often, the secondary roads it traveled twisted and curved and she was very aware of Simon looking out the back window as though checking for someone following them.

She thought back the four, no, five days now since she'd woken up in the hospital, looked up at Carl and wondered who he was. In the next instant, it had come as a shock to realize she didn't know who *she* was.

It had been so frightening at first, so odd to hear people talk about her as though they knew her secrets and she did not. She'd been so frustrated at the curtain of silence that surrounded her, reinforced by Carl. She'd accepted his word that the doctors wanted her kept in the dark until her memories came back on their own, but now she realized she couldn't take anything about Carl for granted; everything he'd done or said since she'd met him in the hospital had to be reassessed.

She detected one bright light in the dark cavern of her mind; though her memory was still as full of holes as an old boat sitting on the bottom of a lake, she was beginning to gather a sense of self. Was that because she was recalling things on a subliminal level or was it because she'd just gotten used to living in a world less than a week old?

Was that why Simon seemed like a friend?

Was that what he seemed, or was it something a whole lot more and growing exponentially every moment?

"We're getting off here," he said suddenly, and she realized she'd been in a state so close to sleep his voice startled her. A glance out the window showed morning had come while she languished in a stupor. The narrow streets of the waterside town through which they traveled appeared all but abandoned.

"This isn't Seattle, is it?"

"No, but it's 6:00 a.m. and we just passed a car rental place. Let's go."

They walked the three blocks back to the rental agency, which was just opening for business. "Give me half an hour," the proprietor pleaded. "I gotta get things straightened away. We don't usually open until seven."

Simon looked down at her. "Are you hungry?"

"Sure," she said.

"There's a little diner right around the corner," the rental man offered.

At the door to the diner, Simon put some coins into a newspaper machine and extracted the *Portland Oregonian* newspaper. He scanned the front page, then tucked it beneath his arm and held the door for her.

The moment the warm, food-laden air hit her nose, Ella's stomach rolled over like a lazy giant getting out of bed. A giant in a foul mood.

"You okay?" Simon asked as they sat across from each other at a table near the back.

"I thought it was the medicine I take at night that made me nauseated in the morning," she said, "but I guess not. I didn't take it last night, so it can't be that."

"Maybe it's your head injury," he said quickly.

"And this nausea just comes around in the morning?"

"I don't know," he said, "except that this hasn't exactly been a normal morning, has it?"

"How do I know? Maybe I run away from thugs and husbands every day of my life."

A smile tugged his lips. "Do you want to leave?"

"I'm afraid so."

"I'll get a coffee to go."

"I'll visit the restroom and see if I can peel off a bandage or two. If my face is the key to people telling me what's going on with my father, I'd better try to make more of it visible."

As soon as Ella disappeared into the ladies' room, Simon opened the *Oregonian*. The front page offered nothing enlightening. He quickly scanned the A section, pausing only to order a large coffee to go.

The story was buried on page seven. The victim's name was Jerry Bucker, found murdered days earlier in a field Simon knew to be less than a half mile from Ella's house.

Jerry Bucker. Hadn't the old man in the restaurant said the contact Ella met before she lost her memory was a guy named Jerry? And hadn't he said no one had seen or heard from Jerry since that contact?

This revelation seemed to nail Ella against the wall.

His phone vibrated in his pocket. It was Devin on the other end and he led off with a question. "Did you hear the police want Ella as a person of interest in the death of a man dumped near her house the day you think she disappeared?"

Simon ran a hand over his face as though he could wipe away all the confusion and doubt. "Yeah, I heard. There's not much in the paper."

"It was big news a few days ago. I don't know why I didn't think to connect the murder to her right from the start, but the cops are bound to find out I've been asking questions."

"Tell them as little as you can without endangering your license," Simon said.

"It might help if you hired me."

"You're hired. First thing I'd appreciate you doing is contacting the Cozy Comfort Motel in Witchit and making arrangements for my truck to be stored there and not towed away."

"Sure."

"What do you know about the victim?"

"Probably not much more than you know. Former cop from Chicago, late sixties, retired up along the Columbia River. No one seems to know why he was in Blue Mountain."

"How was he killed?"

"The police aren't saying. I don't know why they're so close-mouthed on this. You could probably call your partner—"

"No. I won't get Mike into this. Do you know what connected Jerry Bucker to Ella?"

"They're not saying, but word on the street was his car was seen in front of her house and since she's gone, it looks suspicious."

"That's a very loose connection."

"Your girl still batting zero with the memory?"

"More or less. No way she can explain what a dead man was doing visiting her when she can't remember who she is."

"There's something else. Probably unrelated, but after missing the connection last time, I'm not taking any chances."

"What are you talking about?"

"There was an old guy found dead in his car at a parking lot in Rocky Point a few days ago. Isn't that where you said you were? Anyway, his last name was Connors, first name Robert. Ring any bells?"

"Where was the car?"

"North of town, out by a restaurant. Seemed emergency vehicles responded to a call about a woman going off the bluff and a guy going to her rescue. By the time they got there, the woman and her rescuer were gone. That's when someone noticed the old man in the car with a slit throat."

"Oh, God."

"I don't like the sound of that," Devin said.

"If it's the man I think it is, I know who killed him."

"Who?"

"I don't know a name, I just know a face."

"You have got to start thinking about yourself," Devin warned.

"Ditto. I'm going to get to the bottom of this in four or five hours and then I'll figure out the best way to go to the authorities. Don't call me anymore, I'll call you on a pay phone. From now on, the cell is out."

"Yeah, okay. I kept coming up against a wall while looking

into Ella's background," Devin said as the waitress delivered Simon's coffee and took his money. "It looks to me like she went to some trouble to distance herself from her past. I don't even think we got her maiden name right. Now that I know Jerry Bucker was a former cop in Chicago, I can do some digging back there and see what I come up with."

Handing over his debit card, Simon said, "Just be careful."

He snapped the phone shut and this time turned off the power. He was grabbing a couple of napkins when he saw Ella emerge from the ladies' room. She'd removed a couple of the bandages and combed her hair, and despite the fatigue and scratches, she positively glowed as the morning sun filtered through the window and bathed the delicate bone structure of her face.

God, how he'd once loved her. He'd looked past the things that drove him crazy and basked in the simple joy of being with her. The qualms he should have acknowledged right from the beginning he'd buried under blithe rationale. She would come around. She would open up. She would love him for who he was....

A knot formed in his throat as she approached.

She was depending on him to help her find the one person in the world she remembered.

Had Carl killed Jerry Bucker and forced Ella to come with him? Was that why she'd left the clues at her place, the lights on, the snow globe in the empty garage? Or were those inconsequential oversights in her rush to leave her house? Was she in this deeper than he could imagine? There were two murders now, two dead men, both of whom saw Ella right before their deaths. But at least he knew she couldn't have killed the second contact.

Did he? She'd disappeared outside for five minutes before Carl gave up paying the bill and went to find her....

No. This was impossible. That would mean she was faking the amnesia and he knew she wasn't; he'd bet his life on it.

His career…

"You look very worried," Ella said as she paused in front of him.

Resisting the urge to cup her face, to plead with her to remember something, anything, he reached for the door and held it open for her. "Just anxious," he said as they hurried back to the rental place.

THEY MADE IT TO TAMPOO with enough time to stop at a shopping mall. Ella loved the violet-blue tunic she found and wore it out of the store with her new jeans and a pair of sturdy walking shoes. She couldn't help but wonder if she always had such a hard time finding pants that fit in the waist.

They stopped at a men's store next. While Simon disappeared into the back, Ella looked through a rack of shirts. She found a dark gray one that would match Simon's eyes, just as her new tunic matched hers. When she looked around the store for him, she discovered he was already at the counter making a purchase.

Once outside, he stopped at a secluded bench, took a red-and-navy plaid flannel shirt from the bag and started pulling off tags.

"That's what you chose?" she asked, smiling. "Instead of the pretty gray shirt I found, you bought something my father would wear to chop wood?"

"Is that a specific memory or a generalization?" he asked.

She sagged onto the bench. "I remember my dad wearing a shirt like that one. I must have been ten or eleven and we were going to go cut a Christmas tree at a farm. There was a boy there, too, older than me, with dark hair, but he kind of ran ahead."

"I wonder if the boy is your brother."

"Maybe. I just remember staying with my father, holding his hand. I can hear a woman's voice say, 'Such a daddy's girl.' Being with my dad was all that mattered." She wiped a couple of warm tears from her eyes as the memory seemed to wrap its arms around her.

"You're getting older in each memory," Simon said softly.

"I noticed that. The way they just pop into my head as unrelated pieces of flotsam and then sucker punch me with the emotion that follows is unnerving. Wow, I really adore my dad. He must be a huge part of my life."

Buttoning the shirt over the T-shirt he'd started the day in, Simon grabbed a burgundy cap from the bag, as well. With the big flannel shirt and the cap pulled over his dark hair, he looked different.

"You bought yourself a disguise," she said. "The dark stubble on your jaw is a good touch."

"You think so?"

She looked down at her hands, suddenly swamped with a feeling of fear and despair. He sat down beside her. "What is it, Ella?"

"Why is my father going about reaching me in such a dangerous way? The guy back in Rocky Point said my father needed me. And what about my mother? Where is she?"

"Do you remember her?"

Ella clasped a hand to her chest as she nodded, more surprised by the realization she did remember her mother than by the significance of the actual memory. "It was her calling me a daddy's girl," she said, her voice hushed. "She had deep blue eyes and faint freckles. How can I remember nothing about her but her face and voice and so much about my father but not what he looked like?"

"It's curious, isn't it?"

She reached over and took Simon's hand, turning his wrist so she could see his watch, but enjoying the contact with his warm skin too much to let go. "We only have an hour before we meet the next contact. What about Carl and the other man? What could they possibly want with my dad?"

He shook his head as his fingers closed around hers. The motion sent heat waves up her arm and she looked at his face, at his mouth, and heaven help her, but she wished she could kiss him.

"I don't have answers for you," he said softly.

"Do you think the contact will be in danger?"

His look at her was sharp. "Why do you ask that?"

"Because the one back at the restaurant said no one had heard from the first man who came to see me. His name was Jerry."

Her stomach fluttered as something shifted in Simon's eyes. "What aren't you telling me?" She withdrew her hand and tucked it into a pocket.

"Nothing."

"You're lying."

"Okay," he said with a sigh, "I'm lying." He started stuffing tags and papers into the sack as he slid her a sidelong glance. "Listen, Ella, you've trusted me so far, trust me a little while longer."

"I'm trying," she said.

"I know." He looked in her eyes. His were the color of granite today. He added, "You don't have to go to this meeting.

We can get the police involved. They can meet your father's contact and capture Carl and the big guy. You don't have to do it."

"But my father—"

"Is not worth risking your life or safety."

"We've been through this. If you'll give me a ride to the depot, I'll take it from there. You can go on your way."

He cast her an impatient look. "Okay, we'll do it your way on one condition. I want to case the place before you enter. I'm sure Carl and what's his name will be there, but I think they'll think twice about trying anything in public."

"And Carl knows I have to speak to the contact alone, don't forget that."

"Right. They'll make their move afterward, out in the open. That's when they'll try to grab you."

"Have you figured out why Carl wanted to jump the gun last night?"

"My best guess is he wanted to control the situation going in."

"What does that mean, you know, in real person talk?"

"It means he's going to have to try to nab you today in broad daylight in a public place. If he'd gotten you last night, he might have been able to arrange the situation at the depot to his liking."

Her eyes grew wide. "I wonder if he's been giving me some kind of sedative or something, you know, to make me more submissive. Maybe that's why my stomach hurts half the day."

Simon's dark eyes flashed, and for a second, dressed as he was, his handsome face rough with beard, he looked more danger-ous than comforting. "The bastard better hope like hell he didn't," he said, standing abruptly as though a powder keg in his body suddenly exploded. He grabbed her hand. "Come on, babe, it's time to go. Let's get this over with."

The unexpected and casual endearment caught her off guard, but the surprise was short-lived, followed by a warm feeling of certainty.

She'd asked herself a question the night before, a question she hadn't been able to answer, but now she could.

Yes. Somewhere, someone either loved her now or had loved her in the past.

And that someone wasn't Carl Baxter.

EIGHT

THE Tampoo Bus Station occupied half a block of Second and Pearl in downtown Tampoo with large garages running at right angles to each other, surrounding what appeared from the outside to be the main lobby. An abandoned café took corner space with its own street entrance, boarded up now, windows blacked out.

There were three large buses occupying the garage area, including one with its engine compartment open. A truck with the logo Mobile Bus Mechanics was backed up to the bus. Three men in coveralls carried lunch boxes toward a cluster of trees in the far corner of the parking lot.

Simon had finally convinced Ella to lie down on the backseat so it would appear he was alone in the car in case Carl Baxter or the big guy with the knife happened to be watching and recognized him. The plaid shirt and hat weren't a very sophisticated disguise. He just hoped Ella was right about the dark stubble blurring the contours of his face. He drove slowly past the depot, pulling to the curb half a block farther on.

Turning in the seat, he peered into the back. Ella's huge blue eyes looked stark against her pale complexion. "Give me five minutes," he said, slipping his wallet into the glove box. He'd decided not to carry identification, though he wasn't clear why he'd made that decision. Was he still trying to protect his job? That seemed idiotic, but he locked his wallet in the glove box anyway and turned to hand Ella his watch.

She pulled it over her hand. "I'll just lie here and listen to my heart pound in my ears."

"Try not to look for me when you enter the depot. Judging from the original two contacts, this one will be another older man...."

The words were out of his mouth when he realized what he'd just done, that he'd told her he knew what her original contact, Jerry Bucker, now dead, had looked like.

"How do you know how old Jerry was?" she asked.

"I just know."

"Because you saw him at my house? Oh, God, Simon, were you there?"

"No, I wasn't there, I promise."

"Simon—"

And suddenly, Simon knew he couldn't send her into the bus depot and harm's way without being honest with her. She had a right to know what she was getting into. Maybe she'd change her mind if she realized how dangerous it was. "Because an older guy named Jerry Bucker is dead," he said simply. "It was in the morning paper."

Did he mention Robert Connors's stabbing death in Rocky Point? He wasn't positive it was the same man who had met with Ella though the law of coincidence leaned heavily in that direction. One glance at her face made the decision—that news could wait.

She closed her eyes and her words were blurred as she muttered, "When did he die? Where?"

"Days ago, back in Blue Mountain. His body was found in a vacant lot."

Her eyes fluttered open. "I think I saw it on television. Carl turned the TV off, but I think I saw the recovery of the man's body. Who killed him?"

"They don't know."

"How was he killed?"

"They're not saying."

"Oh, my God. Did I have something to do with his death? I can't remember—"

"I'm sure you didn't," Simon said.

"How can you be sure?"

How *could* he be sure? Truth: he couldn't. He said, "I just know it in my heart," and hoped she believed him. Before she could go further with this, he added, "Listen, it's getting late. Do you want to go through with this or do you want to drive away?"

"I can't drive away," she said, determination stealing back into her voice. "I have to find my father."

"Then give me five minutes," he said, "and when you meet this contact, warn him, okay?"

"Yes, of course."

Simon locked the doors as he exited the car. The first order of business was to walk around the building making notes of exits. He passed a room with lockers visible inside and several doors with chains and padlocks and no clue as to where they led. Once he had a feeling for the exterior, he entered the building.

The interior door to the abandoned café was right inside, occupying a front corner. Through the glass insert in the wood doors, Simon could make out stacks of dusty chairs. The doors were chained and locked.

The ticket counter, with a few people lined up in front of it, was to his left. He parked himself behind a young couple holding hands and proceeded to pat his pockets as though looking for his wallet or a misplaced ticket. While doing that, he surreptitiously looked around the place.

Five iron benches took up the center of the waiting area while a few plastic chairs and a couple of vending machines and arcade games were scattered against the walls. Five or six people sat in various states of boredom.

A minute later, the restroom door opened, disgorging a tall man with brownish skin wearing a tan raincoat. It took Simon a second to recognize him, and as soon as he did, he turned his face against the wall. It was the man with the knife. He'd shaven off his beard and looked younger, his face thinner, but Simon would know those intense black eyes anywhere. The man immediately made his way to a vending machine, where another peek revealed him making a show of studying snack choices. Simon saw how often his gaze went to the doors. There was no sign of Carl.

Okay, he hadn't expected them to come inside the depot. As far as he knew, Carl and the guy with the knife were just as anxious for Ella to get her next message as Ella was. He'd thought for sure they'd wait until she stepped outside. He guessed the man with the knife was there just to make sure Ella was covered when the meeting was over.

Simon scanned the gathering for a sign of an elderly man who might be the contact. Everyone was too young with the exception of one person, but that person was female and sat with her back against a wall with her eyes closed.

Simon moved up a step in line just as the door opened and Ella walked inside. Their formerly bearded adversary visibly stiffened at the sight of her and he looked away quickly. Ella chose a deserted bench in the middle of the room and sat down. She didn't look at anyone else, keeping her gaze directed at Simon's watch. She'd pushed it up her arm, where it was held in place by the bunched sleeve of her thick knit shirt. He could practically see her trembling.

The wall clock seemed to click the minutes off at glacial speed. Noon came and went. A bus emptied several people into the waiting area. Others left to get on a departing bus. An older man wearing a feather in his cap entered from the street and looked around carefully, and for a moment, Simon thought they had their contact, but a teenager by one of the arcade games yelled, "Grandpa!" The two hugged and left together.

If Jerry Bucker's death was well known, perhaps the contact had decided this was all too dangerous. A profound moment of relief quickly went up in smoke as an old guy with a newspaper rolled in one hand entered the depot through the same door Ella had used.

Simon knew the older man was ex-police by the way he carried himself. He might be retired but he was still wary, a man used to assessing everything and everyone around him. Simon would bet his life on the fact that the man was armed and ready to defend himself.

But he didn't expect what happened next. The old guy's gaze lingered on the bulky shape of the man with the knife so long, the other man sensed it and looked over his shoulder. Their gazes met and flashed away, but surprised recognition singed the air between them. The old guy immediately looked toward the door as though trying to decide what to do while the big man turned his back.

What was going on? They knew each other?

The older man apparently reached a decision. Walking quickly now, he approached Ella, sat down and started speaking. As she nodded and leaned closer to him, the man shook open his newspaper and the two of them disappeared behind it.

Once again Simon located the man he'd first seen on the bluff wielding a knife only a little over twenty-four hours before. He'd moved to a different vending machine and was dropping in coins, but by the way his gaze was glued to the glass panel of the machine, Simon was pretty sure he was really watching the reflection of the meeting going on across the room. There was still no sign of Carl, who was probably waiting outside to spring a trap once Ella left.

Simon had long since stepped out of the line and found an obscure corner. As he waited for the meeting to be over, he counted how many people were now in the depot. Including the woman selling tickets behind the counter, there were ten. At least four of them were here because of this meeting. That left six possibly unrelated individuals.

The newspaper moved as the old man rolled it once again and placed it on the seat next to him. Ella looked strained but resolved. The ex-cop patted her arm before getting to his feet. As he stood, his gaze darted to the big guy, who turned and took a step toward him.

The older woman who had seemed to be asleep also stood and joined the man, linking her arm with his. The big guy stopped abruptly. The older couple moved in unison toward the door. Apparently, news of Jerry Bucker's and maybe Robert Connors's deaths had reached Tampoo.

If so, what kind of loyalty propelled these old guys to risk themselves this way? And why were they being murdered *after* they spoke to Ella?

The big guy formed a fist and knocked it against his thigh. With hatred burning in his eyes, he turned his attention to Ella.

But Ella was looking at Simon, and though he tried to telegraph a warning, she looked away too quickly. He'd have to manually stop her from proceeding out the front doors, because that path would take her too close to the man in the raincoat, who appeared angry enough to throttle someone.

Simon heard passengers disembarking in the garage area behind him. Any second, they would barge through the doors. If he could waylay Ella, the two of them could get lost in the small crowd outside and circle the block back to their car. All he had to do was intercept her....

The metal door connecting garage and waiting area swung open. Several people flooded through, including a frail but spry white-haired woman using a four-wheeled walker who stopped right in front of Simon.

"What's the time?" she demanded.

He glanced at the clock. "Twelve-forty," he said, trying to get past the walker without bumping the woman.

"Where's my son? He's late. He's always late."

Over her head, Simon saw the tall man paralleling Ella's path. She appeared to be totally unaware of his presence.

"Excuse me," he added, sidling past the walker as he slid his hand under his jacket, unhooking the strap that held his revolver in the holster. There was no way he would pull a gun in a crowded building, but he suspected the big guy would usher Ella outside into Carl's waiting arms.

He'd see about that.

Instead, the man suddenly sped up and purposely rammed into Ella. She stumbled and turned to look up at him. Simon heard her intake of breath as the man placed huge hands on her arms. She seemed to sag against him.

Simon yelled, "Hey!" but it was drowned in the bellowing tones of the giant.

"Honey?" the big man said as he scooped Ella up like a rag doll. "Are you okay? You need fresh air." He knocked the door open with his broad back, supporting Ella's weight, his gaze briefly meeting Simon's. Simon looked at Ella's face. Her eyes were open, his lips moved, but the big man's continuing assurances covered whatever she was trying to say.

Simon had seen the man slip something into his pocket. He'd drugged her. He'd stuck the needle or whatever delivery system he'd chosen back in his pocket and covered her collapse with his booming voice and tan raincoat. That had to be what happened.

Simon quickened his pace. Damn. He'd screwed up; he hadn't expected they would make their move inside the building. A young boy ran into the station as Ella disappeared outside. The kid bumped against Simon's legs. Simon caught him and turned him away from the doors. "Slow down, buddy," he said.

The kid opened his mouth to speak, but the words never came. At that instant, an explosion rocked the building, blowing out the café doors. Simon, snatched from his feet, was hurtled against the ticket counter. Screams were followed by falling debris and frantic calls for help. The boy lay on the floor nearby. Simon crawled to him, clearing dust off his face and urging him to take slow, steady breaths. He couldn't see that any of the glass had hit the kid, who seemed more dazed than hurt.

A woman appeared through the gaping hole in the depot wall. "Peter!" she screamed, frantically looking every direction.

"Over here," Simon said hopefully.

She was there in a flash. "Peter, you ran ahead of me—oh, Peter!" She fell to her knees, taking the boy into her arms.

"Keep him still until help arrives," Simon urged.

She cast him an alarmed glance. "What happened?"

"A bomb, I think." He struggled to his feet, relieved to see the boy trying to sit up.

The woman caught Simon's wrist. "You're hurt," she said. "The back of your shirt is bloody. You'd better stay still."

"Can't," he said, peering through the gaping hole in the wall in time to see the tail end of a man shoving Ella's limp body into the backseat of a car.

"No," Simon yelled, but it was more of a croak. Behind him, pandemonium reigned; people sobbed and shrieked. As the car carrying Ella eased back into traffic, Simon staggered down the sidewalk toward his own vehicle, his head echoing with the concussion of the explosion, his movements unsteady and way too slow.

He heard approaching sirens. Pedestrians pushed past him on their way toward the depot. Fire and smoke filled the air. Traffic began plugging the street, but Simon could see the car Ella had been pushed into and it was still moving, ahead of most of the congestion.

A Harley pulled up alongside the curb in front of Simon. Throwing his feet to the ground and turning to look back, the driver tore off his helmet, revealing a head full of long dark hair. He was about Simon's age and very tan. He said, "Get on."

Simon wiped his face, barely noticing when his hand came away covered in blood. "What?"

"Get on," the man repeated with a slight accent.

"Who—"

"Your car is blocked in. If you want to save Ella, get on the bike. *Ahora.*" He pulled his helmet back on his head and revved the engine. Simon covered the remaining sidewalk as fast as his shocked and battered body could take him. He climbed on behind the stranger, who pulled back onto the street a second later, weaving the big bike through the stalled cars, moving quickly toward the corner.

ELLA SAGGED AGAINST THE MAN sitting next to her. Her brain was scrambled like morning eggs, but she did know a couple of things. She knew she wasn't supposed to be in this car and she knew the man holding her down on the seat was the same man who had bumped into her at the bus depot.

Another man turned around from the driver's seat and grinned at her. She recalled him at once, though it was hard to place him. Long blond hair gathered into a ponytail, long nose, thin lips. He looked at her for a heartbeat, then turned back to driving. Over his shoulder he said, "Did you give her the drug I bought on the street?"

"Half of it. She's not very big."

The driver grumbled. "It appears to be working. Slap her, don't let her fall asleep. Not yet."

A hand appeared out of nowhere. The slap came quick and strong, snapping her head back against the seat, bringing water to her eyes, but it couldn't dispel the bone-chilling lethargy that frosted her veins like an advancing glacier.

"Did she meet with an old man?" the voice from the front demanded.

"Yeah, and get this, it was Potter."

"I don't know anyone named Potter."

The big man grunted. "I keep forgetting you're in this for the money and nothing else."

"No shame in that," the driver said. Ella stared at the back of his head. A ponytail. She knew him. Carl. His name was Carl.

"The bastard got away," the big man grumbled.

"He's not important," the detached voice said.

He was her husband.

"He is to me. They all are. But I'll find him, you wait and see."

There was a pause as Ella touched her face, almost surprised when her fingers found skin instead of bones. What was wrong with her? Why couldn't she think?

"Where are you meeting the next contact, Eleanor?" the man in the front asked.

"Idaho," she mumbled, vaguely alarmed she'd responded and terribly sleepy.

"Where in Idaho?"

"Storm Creek." Her voice seemed to come from somewhere outside her body, like maybe from an overhead speaker.

The front-seat man snapped, "When?"

Before she could answer, her seat companion leaned forward. "The freeway ramp is up ahead."

"I see it. When, Eleanor?"

"Tomorrow," she whispered. She had a deep-down feeling she should refuse to answer any questions posed by these men, but she was unable to stop herself. All she really wanted was to lie down....

With a hard turn, the car, which had been veering right, suddenly swerved the other direction and she slid against the opposite door. A loud roar outside the window evolved into a motorcycle right beside the car. Carl swore as he steered the car under a bridge, missing the ramp completely.

"Damn it! He cut us off!"

There was a lot more swearing. Both men sounded furious. "What time is the meeting?" Carl demanded. "Eleanor, what time?"

She tried to close her eyes and ignore the raised voices and the demands, but the big man beside her grabbed her shoulders and shook her.

"Three o'clock," she muttered.

"What? What did she say?"

"Three," the big man yelled as he twisted to look out the rear window. "That bike is still back there."

"I know. And there's roadwork ahead. Look for someplace we can turn around."

"Up ahead, to the left, some old plant of some kind."

"Yeah, I see it. Hold on."

The car soon made another hard turn, the tires squealing. A loud metallic sound was followed by pieces of chain flying past the windows as the car broke through the rusted barrier and bounced on the uneven pavement of what had once been a parking lot.

"You got a gun?" the driver yelled.

"Just the knife. Gun in the trunk."

More squealing tires, more yelling, the big man twisting

again, hands bunched, knots in his massive jaw. "They're still back there."

"I know, I know. Get her head down, protect her face."

The car skidded as it turned again. The big man pushed Ella's head toward the seat. She felt an odd sense of detachment, a floating sensation as though only her body were in the car.

And yet at the same time a tiny fire flickered in her gut, a defiant flame braving the storm, beginning to spread warmth through her body again. In her mind, she walked toward the flame.

The dark figure of a man stood beside the rippling light, hand extended. She couldn't see his face, but his voice bathed her with comfort. He leaned down and said, *It's all right. Everything is better. I'm sorry, sweetheart. I won't leave again.*

Daddy?

The answer to her hushed question came in the form of a hand clamping down on her wrist, propelling her mind back to the inside of the car. The big man opened the door and jumped out, pulling Ella along after him. A scream died in her throat as she realized the vehicle was no longer moving. Her legs folded beneath her.

The big man bundled her against him like an armload of sticks and carried her around to the back of the car, where Carl was hiding. He held a big gun.

The next thing she knew, thunder roared from above as a huge black shape flew over her head and crashed somewhere in the distance. She covered her ears with her hands, melting into the gritty pavement, finally free to close her eyes where once again the flickering flame drew her to its warmth and the promise of her father's voice.

NINE

SIMON knew Carl was at the wheel; he'd seen the man when the bike prevented the car from taking the on-ramp. He hadn't been able to see in the backseat, but he knew Ella was back there.

Where would they take her? How could they go too far without finding out what she knew about the next meeting place?

His cell phone practically burned in his pocket. Things had gone too far. He'd let them go too far. Better Ella should be safe in a jail than in this situation. She couldn't have murdered Jerry Bucker, she couldn't be in cahoots with Carl Baxter…

But she could.

Carl wouldn't give her anything that would disable her too long until they knew what she'd learned from the contact and which direction to travel next. That meant just enough to control her for a while and hopefully, hopefully, that meant it wouldn't hurt her baby….

The road grew increasingly industrial and untraveled.

Orange signs announced roadwork ahead, and even over the noise of the Harley engine, Simon could make out the sound of earthmoving equipment. The car was going to have to turn around or risk being delayed, and Simon doubted very much they would take such a chance.

Up ahead of them, the car made a tight right turn into a vast parking lot, kicking up gravel and a dirt cloud as it bounced over torn patches of old asphalt, headed for the river where the hulking shape of a long sheet metal building abutted an aging wharf. Rotting piers jutted out of the gray waters of Puget Sound. It appeared to be an old fish packing plant.

The car went in a straight line toward the wharf. With the motorcycle, however, caution had to be used lest the bike spin out of control on buckled pavement and patches of loose gravel. Up ahead, Simon saw the car come to a screeching halt in front of the largest structure. Two men jumped out of the vehicle, the larger shape manhandling Ella to the protection of the far side. Simon saw the flash of a gun in Carl's hand. Shots whizzed past the cycle.

The Harley driver veered to the left, running the bike up a ramp that ran behind Carl and his buddy, bursting into the gutted shell of the structure behind them.

Simon was off the bike before it had completely stopped, stumbling once and catching himself on an overturned barrel. Revolver in hand, he knew he had to disable the car immediately. He darted to a glassless window and chanced a peek, but from this angle all he could see was the hood of the car.

The biker came up behind him, helmet removed. "What's the plan?" he asked, his voice deep and flavored slightly with a Spanish accent.

"Shoot a couple of tires out of the car, subdue the two men, rescue Ella."

"I'm not armed." He rubbed his jaw and added, "Be prepared, amigo." In the next instant, he'd sprung to his feet and disappeared into the deep shadows of the building, his footsteps all but inaudible, which was amazing considering the condition of the floor.

Simon didn't waste time shaking his head, but that's what he felt like doing. Be prepared? What, like a Boy Scout? Didn't look as though there was going to be a lot of help from that quarter after all. He shot a few rounds through the window opening just to announce his intentions, inserted a new clip and made for the door. If that car left again with Ella inside it, who knew what would happen? He had to disable the car.

From the door of the building, he moved to the shelter of a row of old steel drums. From there he could see the right side of the car. A bullet ricocheted off one drum. He shot out the rear tire, then aimed for the front.

Before he could pull the trigger, a man's voice announced, "One more shot and Eleanor dies."

Simon's trigger finger froze in place. He heard sounds of a struggle and then Carl appeared down below, in back of the car, a drooping Ella held in front of him as a shield. Her eyes fluttered open. Carl looped one of his arms around her neck while he pressed a gun barrel against her temple. Her expression immediately jumped from dazed to terrified.

"You won't kill her," Simon yelled. "You want to know what she knows. You need her face to open doors."

"You're right," Carl yelled, "I can't kill her. But I can wound her. What do you think? Leg? An arm?" Ella's gasps as Carl jabbed the muzzle harder into the side of her head skittered along Simon's nerve endings like firecrackers.

"Or maybe Chopper could use his knife on her, you know, someplace it won't show," Carl added.

Even from that distance, Simon could see the skin around Ella's lips grow white.

"Make up your mind!" Carl yelled, clasping her even closer to his body. "Drop your gun and stand up."

Decision time again.

Who was he trying to kid? Making a decision implied options, and he had none, but still, the first rule of police work was never to surrender a weapon.

"You win, Baxter," he shouted, bending slowly, putting the gun down carefully, sliding it into view. As he straightened up, he kept his eyes on Ella. Every bone in her face seemed to push against her ashen skin.

"Now you're being reasonable," Carl said, a smug smile playing over his lips. Raising his voice, he added, "Chopper, where are you?"

The big man who had abducted Ella from the bus depot sauntered out of the building behind Simon. The only thing more imposing than the size of Chopper was the curved cold steel knife he held in one hand.

"Where's the other guy?" Carl demanded.

"I found him hiding out by the old pier," Chopper yelled.

"Did you get rid of him?"

"I'm not a killer," the big man yelled. As his knife was one millimeter from severing Simon's future, Simon was happy to hear it.

Then he remembered Robert Connors found stabbed to death in his car.

"Since when?" Carl quipped as though the same thought had occurred to him.

"That's different and you know it. I'm not the one who set off a bomb at the depot."

"We all serve our own gods, Chopper. So, the bottom line is you left someone free to do what he wants."

Chopper pulled a roll of gray duct tape from his pocket. "No, I took care of him. He isn't going anywhere."

Simon hadn't held out a lot of hope for his Spanish-speaking friend with the light eyes, but now it looked as though there was no hope at all. He swallowed hard as Chopper grabbed him by the upper arm and marched him down the ramp. The tip of the knife blade was so close to his spine he could feel it all the way to his belly button and found himself arching his back as he walked.

Ella's eyes widened as she got a good look at him. "Are you all right?" she asked, her voice slurred.

"Couldn't be better. How about you?"

She managed a fleeting smile.

Carl yanked her closer again, strangling her for a second. "Chopper, check his wallet."

"He doesn't have one," Chopper grumbled after none too gently patting Simon down. The slaps jarred Simon's mincemeat back, causing shivers to shoot through his body. He was suddenly very glad he'd decided to leave his wallet in the car.

"So, just who in the devil are you?" Carl asked as Chopper once again loomed right behind Simon.

"A friend."

"Well, friend, you just bought yourself a load of trouble. If you'd left my wife at the motel last night, we could have wired her before she met the old guy today and none of this would have been necessary."

"Would that be before or after she fell to her death off the bluff?" Simon asked.

Carl shook his head. "It doesn't matter who you are. It's obvious you've turned into Eleanor's knight in shining armor. You're going to wish you'd kept your nose in your own business."

"You don't need to hurt her," Simon said, his fists clenched so hard his blunt nails bit into his palms. "She's not going anywhere, you know that. Loosen your grip. She's just as innocent—"

A bark of laughter escaped Carl. "My wife innocent. How quaint."

"I can't be your wife," Ella said, eyes gaining a little bit of the old flash. "I wouldn't marry someone like you."

"I have the papers to prove it, sweetheart."

"You left me on a cliff to die and now you have a gun pointed at my head. Some marriage."

He smiled again. Putting his lips close to Ella's ear, he added, "You've already told me everything I need to know about the next contact except where the meeting is to take place. Tell me that or I shoot your new friend."

"You'll kill me anyway," Simon said, still gazing at Ella.

Carl's voice dipped to a smooth, intimate tone, as he leaned in closer still. "Your friend is right, I probably will kill him anyway. But there are all sorts of ways to die, some a lot slower and more painful than others. How about it? Have you ever seen a kneecap explode?"

She shook her head.

"And whatever I do to him, I'll do to your father when I find him. With or without your help, I will find him. You can make it easier on me and you can make it easier on your father. Your choice."

"What do you want my father for? What did he do to you?"

"To me? Nothing. I just want to talk with him, that's all."

"Before or after you blow up his kneecap?"

Simon smiled internally. The old Ella was making a comeback.

"Maybe a little of the hero's blood will loosen her tongue," Carl said, leveling his gaze at Simon. "Go ahead, Chopper, use your knife."

Chopper raised the knife to Simon's throat, but he paused. "You want him dead, you kill him." He lowered the blade and pushed Simon ahead of him. The pressure of his hand hitting Simon's back felt like a million razor blades slicing through his skin.

They came to a stop a few feet short of Carl and Ella. "I'm in this for one reason, and you know it," Chopper growled. "I agreed to join up with you just to expedite my cause. That means I take care of the men who wronged me. They're mine. Someone like this man? He's yours."

"Why?" Simon asked. "And what is it you two want so much? I mean, besides spreading misery and mayhem, what is it you're both after?"

He was totally ignored as the two men glared at each other. Hoping to capitalize on their mutual animosity, he added, "You guys weren't buddies on the cliff. You were trying to kill each other. That's got to make trusting each other kind of tricky."

Carl cast him a withering look. Well, okay, it had been an amateurish attempt to play them against each other, but what other choice did he have? How could he possibly disarm both men? Carl might have relaxed his hold on Ella a little, but the gun was still positioned at her temple.

Carl finally spoke. "We're a team," he told Chopper. "I'll prove it. I'll kill the Good Samaritan." The clicking sound as he cocked the gun seemed to shoot through Simon.

"Wait! Okay, okay, I'll tell you," Ella gasped. "The meeting is at the last restaurant leaving Storm Creek going north."

"What's its name?"

"The Red Barron. No, the Red Barn. That's what it is, the Red Barn. Don't hurt him."

Carl rocked back on his feet, grinning. "That's my girl." Addressing Chopper, he added, "The leftovers from the bomb-making material and the receipts for all the equipment are in the trunk. Get them. We'll set the Samaritan up inside that building with all the evidence and stage a little suicide. That ought to take care of a couple of loose ends at once."

"But you said—" Ella began.

Carl kissed the back of her neck. "Since when did you get so gullible, sweetheart?" Once again addressing Chopper, he added, "Use that tape you have to gag and bind my wife first. We'll leave her in the car."

As Chopper once again began ranting about Baxter's tendency to issue orders, Simon glanced at Ella. There was a cold, detached look creeping into her eyes. If Simon was a betting man, he'd lay odds she was a breath away from trying to break free from Carl. It might work. The man was so disdainful of her strength of will, he might underestimate her, and from his position, he couldn't see the anger brewing in her face. He shouldn't have made fun of her, shouldn't have kissed her neck...

Simon had no idea how far she would get, but that wasn't the point. He was pretty sure Carl wouldn't risk shooting her.

Did she realize no one had picked his gun up from where he'd slid it? He didn't dare turn around and look, but he knew it was there. Chopper hadn't bent over to retrieve it. If she could make it to the ramp and remember the gun, she'd be armed.

A roaring noise seemed to come from nowhere. Simon looked up in time to see the motorcycle burst out of the dilapidated building behind the car and fly over them, missing Carl's head by less than a foot. The helmeted rider landed the bike with a jolt. Skidding, he turned the big machine and headed back, aimed at Carl.

As Simon looked around for Ella, he saw her fling her head back hard, hitting Carl in the nose. Between the advancing bike and the sudden impact on his face, Carl's grip loosened enough for Ella to break free. The two thugs dived for cover as Simon grabbed Ella's good hand and dragged her up the ramp, retrieving his revolver on the way. His aching body was forgotten in the need to find something better to hide behind than rusty metal and rotting wood.

Outside, he heard shouting and the sound of an engine. They had almost reached the far end of the building when the motorcycle appeared in the sunlit opening on the end they were nearest to, the sound deafening as it tore up to within a few feet of them.

Ella tensed as she stepped back against Simon. She was heaving. He knew exactly how she felt.

Without turning off the engine, the rider tore off the helmet and looked at each of them, his gaze lingering on Ella.

"Who *are* you?" Simon demanded.

"The name is Jack."

"Do I know you?" Ella said.

"No, *cariño,*" he answered after a brief pause. He handed the helmet to Ella and added, "Put this on." Pieces of gray tape hung from his wrists and circled the hem of his jeans.

"Get her out of here now," Simon said.

"I'm not going, you are," Jack said as he slid off the big bike. He touched Ella's arm and motioned her to climb aboard.

She paused. "But what about you?"

"I'm staying here." He looked at Simon and added, "The very large man found himself an automatic, I guess in the car, so now they're both armed."

"I can't leave you—"

"No time to argue," Jack said.

"Then take my gun."

Jack threw up his hands. "No, no gun. I don't need that kind of grief."

Simon stuck the weapon in his belt. "I'll call the police as soon as I get away from here," he said.

"No police." The response was quick and adamant.

What was it with everybody suddenly hating cops? "Listen," Simon said, "those men are murderers. Then there's the bomb—"

"No police," Jack repeated. "You heard Baxter, you heard him say Ella was involved in this. Until you find out how deeply, no cops."

"How do you know my name?" Ella asked. "Are you following me, too?"

"No, *mija,* I'm following him." He pointed at Simon; then his voice turned low and urgent. "Listen, both of you, there's no time to argue. I'm not suicidal. I'll keep them busy for a while, then escape via the water. Leave my bike on the same side of the street as your car, keys under the seat. Don't worry about me, think about her."

"But—"

"*Vaya rápidamente. Tenga cuidado,*" Jack said, and without a backward glance, ran toward the ramp where they could all hear the approaching footsteps of the enemy.

As ELLA HAD BEEN in a drugged stupor for the ride out of town, she had no clue how far they'd traveled. It came as a shock to discover they were only a few miles from downtown Tampoo.

She was very careful not to touch Simon's back as she sat behind him. The plaid shirt hid the torn flesh, but the dried blood and glittering glass shards embedded in the cloth suggested some slicing and dicing under the flannel. She'd seen the pain in his eyes as Chopper pushed him down the ramp.

The traffic was still snarled in front of the depot that was now surrounded with police tape and emergency vehicles. Simon stopped short of their destination, guiding the bike to a parking spot a couple of blocks away. She took off the helmet as he turned off the engine, running a shaky hand through her hair. Once she was on her feet again and Simon had deposited the keys, she propped the helmet on the bike seat.

She looked up at him, the world suddenly spinning. In a flash, he grabbed her arms and steadied her and she did what she'd been aching to do for hours. She leaned in against him, tucking her head under his chin, his strong heart thumping under her cheek, the warmth of his body stealing into hers, chasing away the chill. When she felt his lips against her forehead and the pressure of his arms around her, a sense of peace stole into her heart.

The sound of a siren snapped her out of the moment.

"Now what?" she said.

He took her arm and hustled her down the sidewalk toward

their car. "I don't suppose you lied to Carl about the contact information?"

"They gave me something. I told them everything." She ran a hand over her face, wincing as she rubbed scratches and abrasions raw again. "Except for the last thing. I lied about the Red Barn."

"Then the meeting isn't at a restaurant?"

"No. It's at a place called Thunder Lodge."

The corner of his lip lifted. "I could have sworn you were telling the truth."

"I hope my father doesn't have to pay for what I did. I can't believe I married Carl. Is it true he planted the bomb in the bus depot?"

"As a diversion to cover snatching you."

"Was anyone hurt?"

"Thankfully it was just me and a kid near the door, and he seemed okay. I'm not sure about anyone else. It must have been a pretty small bomb, but it did a hell of a lot of damage." He rubbed his jaw. "Listen, did you ask the contact any of the questions we talked about? You know, like what the hell is going on?"

"Of course I did. He wouldn't tell me a thing. He actually made the man in Rocky Point seem talkative."

Simon looked away at once.

"Just *who* is Jack?" she asked.

"I was hoping you could tell me. He seemed to know you."

"Everyone seems to know me," she said, and not without some exasperation. "But he said he was following you. Where did he come from?"

"Literally out of the blue. Let's hurry, I don't want to be caught standing on the street if..."

His voice trailed off, but she knew exactly where he was going with it. If Carl and Chopper defeated Jack. If they came looking…

The car was clear of most of the commotion. The knot in Simon's jaw as he looked back at the police directing traffic and the emergency crews investigating the scene tugged at her conscience. What had aligning himself with her cost him? Both personally and professionally, she was sure he was paying an awful price.

Why would a man give up so much of who and what he was for a complete stranger?

The answer seemed very clear—he wouldn't.

But he said he was.

She got into the passenger seat. Within minutes, Simon had circled the block, driving in such a way his back didn't touch the seat. He took the nearest on-ramp to the freeway, which happened to be one heading south, but at this point it didn't seem to matter that much where they went, just that they went. Maybe going the wrong direction for a while was a diversionary tactic.

With a million questions needing answers, they both fell silent, wrapped in their own thoughts.

Ella's eyelids kept closing, her head falling forward until she'd jerk awake. In those few seconds of stolen slumber, dreams pummeled her brain. In an effort to stave off sleep, she stared at Simon. For the first time since meeting him in the hotel lobby, he looked worse than she did. His face and hair were streaked with dried blood, his clothes covered with plaster and dust.

"We've been going southeast for almost an hour," he said. "It's time to loop back around and head north. We need a map.

I know where Idaho is, but I don't know where Storm Creek is."

"I don't, either," she said. Her voice sounded thick. For a second, she was back in the depot, heading for the door, anxious to talk to Simon, and then someone had collided with her and she'd turned, and just as she recognized Chopper without a beard, she'd felt a pinprick in her arm and her legs go limp….

She rubbed her arm now, realizing there was a small irritated patch of skin six inches above her elbow. Man, would she like the opportunity to give Chopper a little of his own medicine!

Simon eventually found a gas station, filled the tank and disappeared into the men's room. When he emerged again, his face and his hair were cleaner, several cuts now bright red against his face. He obviously hadn't tried to take off his shirt, and the spring in his step was subdued. Only the fire in his eyes revealed the anger she sensed inside him.

She'd bought a map and huge cups of coffee while he was gone. As he slid into the car beside her, she showed him the tiny speck in Idaho's panhandle that represented their next destination.

"It's practically in Canada," he said.

"Yes," she agreed, taking small sips of the hot, bitter brew.

They stared at the dot until Simon said, "First things first. The attendant in the station told me where we can trade in this car." He drained his cup as Ella refolded the map, then drove them a mile or two farther, pulling off at an exit promising an airport ahead. Before reaching the airport, he turned off at yet another car rental place. They traveled the rows of cars for a few moments until Simon hit the steering wheel and grinned. "Look," he said.

She looked. "You mean the dark blue truck with the tinted windshield?"

"Yes, but it's not the windshield I'm thinking about, it's the license plate. I was hoping this close to the Washington/Idaho border we might find a vehicle with Idaho plates, and there she is."

"So we won't stand out when we get to Storm Creek."

"Exactly."

"Good plan."

He was gone for almost an hour, but when he reemerged, it was with the keys for the truck. They moved their few careworn belongings, but before he inserted the key in the ignition, Simon paused. "The woman at the counter said Storm Creek is about six or seven driving hours from here," he said. "Before we go another mile, we need to consider the possibility that it may be time to stop this mad chase and turn things over to the police."

She'd known this was coming. Without her wallet and the ID it contained, she couldn't rent a car. She needed Simon's help and yet she was willing to admit it was asking too much. Gazing longingly across the way at a plane taking off from the airport, she said, "I can't buy an airline ticket but I can get on a train. Take me to a station. I understand how hard this all is for you as a policeman. I don't want to keep imposing—"

"Stop," he said, running a hand through his hair. "I don't care about me, this isn't about me."

"Then what's it about?"

"What it's always been about," he said, but then pressed his lips together. "I think we should stay off the main roads. They managed to follow us once before. We can't risk that again."

"Carl said I wasn't innocent in all this. What did he mean?"

"I'm not entirely sure."

"But you suspect something. Was he talking about the man who was murdered in Blue Mountain?"

"I think so," he said reluctantly.

"I wonder if I knew him. Did you?"

"No. And before you ask, I have no idea if you knew him or not. I have no idea if you know any of the older men you're meeting or why you're meeting them or what your father wants. I don't know if you're involved in a murder or if you're a hapless victim."

"I'm involved," she said softly. "I may not have actually killed anyone, but it's obvious I'm in the middle of it all."

"I guess it is," he admitted.

She pressed her fingers against her forehead.

"Carl Baxter and Chopper are dangerous men," Simon said. "They've set off a bomb that could have hurt who knows how many people. At least one man is dead. Not revealing their identities to the cops so they can be apprehended will put more people in harm's way. I can't justify that, even if it hurts you. Do you understand?"

"I think so," she said.

"I have to turn in their names and a description of their vehicle. I have to tell the cops where they're headed so they can be apprehended, which means I'll be leading the cops toward us, too. But thanks to you, they'll be in one part of town and we'll be in another. I'll do it anonymously, but it has to be done. I'll do my best to keep you out of it."

"It's not me I'm worried about. It's my father. He's going to such lengths to make this all a big secret and it seems everyone knows. Am I bringing disaster down upon his head?"

"Regardless of your father's situation—which we don't

really know—and your involvement, Carl and Chopper are both dangerous men who have proven they're willing to kill innocent people. We can't stand by and allow them to hurt anyone else."

"You're right, we can't. But you promise me you'll do what you can to keep my father out of harm's way."

"Frankly, it's not your father I'm worried about," he said.

"I know, but do you promise?"

"Yes," he said at last, but he didn't sound happy about it.

TEN

SIMON drove as Ella dozed fitfully beside him. Not familiar with the area, he ended up driving in circles and wasting most of an hour before getting back on the right track. The condition of his back made driving difficult. It would have been a lot easier to take primary instead of secondary highways, and for the entire time it took him to break free of the city, he seemed stalled in one road-construction project after another.

Plus, it was nearly impossible to get comfortable. He knew he needed his back attended to, but he couldn't bear the thought of stopping the truck. He might not see a tail back there, but he could feel one. He wanted the cover of darkness before they stopped.

He couldn't get Jack out of his head, either. Who was he? How did he know Ella, and more to the point, perhaps, how did he know Ella was in trouble? And why did he say he was following Simon? He flicked his gaze to the rearview mirror, expecting to see a parade back there, but the road was empty of everything except an old converted school bus. Hard to imagine Carl, Chopper or Jack driving that.

Beside him, Ella mumbled incoherently, her head rolling to the side toward the window. Her voice, thick with sleep, was soft but desperate when she mumbled, "No." Her hand fluttered on her lap and then rose to her face. "No!" she repeated.

Her eyes flicked opened and she caught a sob in her throat.

"You okay?" Simon asked, sparing her a long glance.

She swallowed. "Yeah."

He handed her a bottle of water he'd bought at the station when he'd found he couldn't quite get behind coffee. After she took a long drink, she straightened in her seat and looked out at the changing countryside. "Man, how long was I out?"

He glanced at his watch, back now on his own wrist. "Two hours and thirty-three minutes."

"I was dreaming," she said.

"I figured. Your father?"

"Hmm—we were dancing. I was wearing a pink dress and he was twirling me around and then he started to fade, like a ghost, just disappeared into thin air. I was frantic…."

He touched her uninjured hand. Between the two of them, it was getting hard to find an area of skin that wasn't bleeding or bruised. "It was a dream," he murmured.

"It was so real. Oh, Simon, I don't know what to do. What if the police want him? What if he, I don't know, robbed a bank for instance? Maybe that's why he fled the U.S.A. and moved to Canada."

"We have extradition agreements with Canada. He couldn't evade the U.S. law in Canada."

"Maybe he's hiding. Or maybe he did something else that wasn't illegal, just immoral."

"We'll find out tomorrow," he said firmly.

She stopped fussing, going as far as flashing him a smile. "I get tied up in knots."

"I don't blame you."

She narrowed her eyes as she studied him. Then he heard her sigh. "I'm also selfish. I forgot how hurt you are. Stop the truck."

"What—"

"Stop it. Right now." He pulled over to the side of the road as the old bus rumbled by them. "Change seats, I'm driving," she said. To punctuate her intent, she opened her door and came around to his side of the truck. Opening the door, she added, "Out."

Very gingerly, he got out of the truck, his back raging with fire. She took his place behind the wheel. "I'm driving to a motel and I'm taking care of your back."

"We should wait for dark—"

"We shouldn't have waited at all, I should have insisted earlier. Get in." Once he'd climbed into the passenger seat, she pulled onto the highway. He sat sideways, his left arm against the back of the seat. Without driving to concentrate on, he felt his back start to burn.

They passed a sign announcing a city up ahead. "We'll stop there," she said.

"Somewhere seedy and way off the beaten track," he told her.

"That goes without saying. I have a plan, trust me."

He smiled. The sleep had done her good. She glanced at him and grinned, laughing a little, shaking her head. It was a familiar gesture, and for some reason, it lodged in his heart. All that was missing was the mass of gold curls that used to dance as she moved.

Oh, God, he wasn't still harboring hope for her—for *them*—was he?

It was as though she read his mind. She said, "Tell me why you broke the mermaid's heart."

He shrugged and wished he hadn't, because it hurt like blazes. "We grew apart," he said.

"Explain that."

"Well, she wanted one thing and I wanted another."

"Do you always talk in circles like this?"

"She hated me being in law enforcement, for instance."

"Smart girl."

"Why do you say that?"

"It's dangerous work, right? Maybe she wanted to have babies, maybe she didn't want their father to be killed arresting some sleazeball."

Had her memory returned? Was she messing with him? He stared at her exquisite profile as he responded, "Or maybe she was running from something."

She smiled. "That's more exciting," she said. "I like that better."

He saw no subterfuge in the glance she cast his way.

"So you broke up with her."

"Well, maybe it was a little more mutual than that," he said. "She'd been keeping secrets and when I pressed her for details she blew up and called me a prying bastard."

"What did you call her?"

"Secretive. Controlling."

"Ouch. So now there's no more you and her. That's very sad, Simon."

"Yes, it is," he said.

They entered the town of Twilight around dinnertime. It

appeared to be a small town with lots of empty buildings, the kind of thing that tended to happen when a major highway bypassed a city. Simon spied a telephone booth in the overgrown parking lot of a long-closed miniature golf course. "Pull in there, park behind those trees. I've got to call a friend."

She did as he asked, getting out of the truck at the same time he did. When he reached the phone booth he looked back to see she'd wandered over to the fence surrounding the unkempt golf course, and was staring in at the old windmills and clowns that had once delighted children.

Though the booth didn't have a telephone directory any longer, the phone itself had a dial tone, and that brought a sigh of relief. Devin took the collect call. From the background clatter, he was either washing dishes or fixing dinner. "Glad you called," he said. "Guess what? Robert Connors was a retired policeman from guess where?"

"Chicago, like Jerry Bucker?"

"Exactly."

"Then Connors's murder is related to all this."

"It has to be. He has to be the old guy your girl met at the restaurant, which means other than the murderer, she's the last to see him alive, and there is a roomful of witnesses to identify her. The cops are going to want to question her."

Simon leaned his forehead against the glass panel of the booth. "I phoned in an anonymous tip to the police today about the identity of the men I think are responsible for the deaths of Bucker and Connors. When this is all over, hopefully tomorrow, I'll get back to Blue Mountain and go see the chief."

"He'll have your head. Withholding information, aiding and abetting—"

"Please, don't read me the list. I knew what I was doing when I took sides a couple of days ago. I just have to make sure Ella is innocent before those two spill their guts and try to blame everything on her. I can't take the chance she winds up in prison."

"Now, wait a second," Devin said with a rattle of pans that announced his inattention to what he was doing on the home front. "I thought you broke up with this girl. Why can't you let her go?"

Simon hadn't told Devin about Ella's pregnancy. He wasn't going to tell anyone other than his cousin until Ella remembered on her own or he broke down and told her himself.

Devin whistled. "You still have feelings for her."

Simon acknowledged as much. There was no denying—or quantifying—that fact. He had feelings for her, feelings that were beginning to make him doubt everything, but this wasn't the time to worry about it.

"Listen to me," Devin said. "I can't find her maiden name, but I know I've got to be getting close. Without a legal name change, however, her marriage to Carl Baxter might very well be invalid. But it might not."

"Let's take things one disaster at a time," Simon said.

"Speaking of disasters in the making, there was some guy asking around about you. Dark, speaks with a slight Spanish accent. Know him?"

"Kind of," Simon said.

After hearing that so far Devin hadn't been grilled by the cops, he hung up.

He wanted to call Virginia but didn't dare. He couldn't risk involving her and there really wasn't anything new she could offer. She'd told him to let Ella's memory come back on its own and it seemed to be happening. What they needed was time. What they didn't have was time.

Ella had memories of a mother and father now, and a brother, all two-dimensional figures moving through her dreams and sometimes stealing into her waking thoughts. He couldn't help but wonder who would be next. He could tell she suspected him of having prior knowledge of her—he thought it likely only the string of worsening circumstances kept her from really pressing the issue.

He walked back to the fence, his back in such pain it was hard to think straight. She was staring at a giant plaster bear balanced on top of a white flower. The bear wore lederhosen and held a giant beer stein in one hand. Its mouth was wide open as though it was yodeling.

"What are you looking at?" he asked as he put his fingers through the wire next to Ella's.

She leaned her head against the fence and gazed up at him. "A bird has built a nest in the bear's mouth. Listen."

He didn't hear anything until a small black-and-gray bird swooped over his head and landed on one of the bear's yellow teeth, setting off a cacophony of high-pitched cheeps from the hatchlings inside the nest.

"Starlings," he said softly. "The scourge of American songbirds."

"Starlings," she repeated slowly as though tasting the word. "Starlings. Why are they the scourge of American songbirds?"

"They're not a native bird. They drive out other birds, even destroy eggs."

"How do you know all this?"

"My mom and dad have several acres. They love their birds.

Want to hear about the innocent-looking but highly destructive house sparrow?"

She laughed, but then her eyes grew gentle. He loved it when she looked at him that way. In the past it had been an invitation for intimacy, not just sex, but a letting down of her formidable guard, a sign she was feeling safe and would allow him to get a little closer. His gaze dipped down to her waist and the small curve of her belly.

The thought her baby might not be his baby just about unhinged him. He wrapped his fingers around hers and looked deep into her eyes.

She didn't move, but her focus shifted to his mouth as their heads drifted together. A million remembered sensations coursed through his body as his lips touched hers.

In an instant, as her lips parted, he was whisked away to the night they first met. She, draped in a million shades of blue and green, skin sparkling with glitter, eyes so big and trusting he'd been mesmerized the moment he walked into the club and saw her standing alone. By the end of the night, they'd kissed a hundred times. By the end of the weekend, they'd been lovers.

He'd thought to build a future with her despite his mother's warnings about Ella's reserve. And now as her warm mouth and silken tongue merged with his, he thought that way again. He yearned to wrap her in his arms and back her against the fence, take what she was offering, make her his one more time.

He straightened up as, above them, the baby birds welcomed their mother or father back to the nest. He ran a finger over her lips. If she was willing, he was willing; why pretend he wasn't?

"For a moment there, I remembered what sex was like,"

she whispered, "and I wanted to have it again, right here, right now, with you."

"What a wonderful idea," he whispered against her cheek.

She looked down at her left hand. "I'm a married woman."

"Ella—"

"Even if the marriage is over, the fact is I was with him when we had the accident. He knew to expect the contact in the restaurant. In my mind, that means we were in 'it' together and a man is dead. I can still hear him saying I'm not innocent, and somehow, I think I believe him, I think he's right."

"You don't know any of this."

"And then there's Jack, showing up out of nowhere but knowing my name, and cautioning against calling the police…. Just how many men do I know? Are they all lovers or have they been in the past?"

Good questions. Simon stared into her eyes. "I don't know."

"I can see that. But you do know more about me than you're telling."

"Yes," he said. "Let me be honest. My cousin is a doctor. She said ideally, you should go home and come to your memories through familiar things. She called it associational therapy."

Ella took a deep breath. "I've always felt that's the way it should have happened. I've been wondering ever since I realized I can't trust Carl if he warped what the hospital doctors said, if he just told me what suited him. Maybe the doctors never intended me to have to go through this in this way."

"Maybe you're right. And maybe in a perfect world, you could go home. There're just a few little catches."

"My father needs me," she said firmly.

That hadn't been the catch he was thinking of. He'd been

thinking more along the lines of the dead men, a bomb and her possible involvement.

And yet she'd left her houselights burning and the snow globe—he was almost positive she'd been taken against her will. Did that mean she hadn't wanted to help her father or that she'd planned to help him all along and Carl Baxter showed up or she and Carl were in cahoots from the beginning but had a falling-out?

She'd been acting strange, she'd been keeping secrets. Was it Carl or her father or both?

"You look as confused as I feel," Ella said softly. As he'd been mulling things over, she'd slipped her wedding ring off her finger. "Well, I may be married to the jerk, but I don't have to wear his ring, do I?" And with that, she tossed the gold band through the fence, where it disappeared into the brush. She smiled fleetingly and added, "You're in such pain. Get in the truck."

"No sex right here on the ground?" he said only half jokingly.

"With your back full of glass?"

"You could be on the bottom."

She shook her head. "Get in the truck." She took one last look at the nest up inside the bear's mouth. "Bye, little starlings," she said, drawing out their name.

Back in take-charge mode, she dropped him off at a motel so disreputable they were both pretty sure the rooms rented by the hour. Then, against his protests, she drove off with assurances she would park the truck in the parking lot of a different motel she'd passed a few blocks away. He rented them a room and awaited her return with acid burning his throat.

But she did return, her step more full of vigor than he'd seen it so far, the very act of taking control seeming to empower her. Once again, he thought of the Ella he'd grown to know—the woman who could take care of just about everything.

She moved the two plug-in lamps in the dingy room near a chair she'd set up next to the bathroom door, angling their shades for light. He sat on a chair with his arms hooked over the rungs, his back exposed, as she peeled away his clothes. She was trying to be gentle, he knew that, but by now the blood had caked around the glass shards and the pain was excruciating.

"Oh, ack!" she said as she cut away the last piece of his clothing. Good thing he'd bought scissors when he'd bought antiseptic and bandages. "You're a mess."

"Less chatter, more work," he said, his breathing shallow. "There are tweezers in the bag, too."

"I have them. You want something to bite on?"

"No, thanks. Just get it over with."

The next few minutes passed in near silence as one by one, she located and extracted the splinters. When she muttered she'd gotten them all, she filled the sink with warm, sudsy water and carefully rinsed his skin. He almost jumped off the chair when the washcloth caught on a piece of glass she'd missed, but that was soon out, as well.

By the time she'd bathed his back and dried it, applied ointments and bandages and he'd found a clean shirt in his duffel, they were both frazzled but hungry for dinner and for information. But first Ella insisted on taking a shower, so while she lathered up behind a closed door, he lay on the bed on his stomach and prayed for the aspirin to kick in.

Thirty minutes later, they left the room carrying all their belongings, the key back on the dresser.

The truck was as Ella had left it, though they did hide out across the street in a Laundromat watching for signs of Carl or Chopper before approaching it. When it was obviously all clear, they drove to a fast food restaurant, where they both ordered chicken sandwiches and milkshakes. It was the first time he'd seen Ella eat fast food.

While dining in the truck, they studied the road map for the best route into Idaho. A long night of driving loomed ahead.

"There's a light on down the block, and from the size of the building, I'm betting it's city hall," he announced as he folded the map.

"What's at city hall?"

"Well, a newsstand probably, maybe someone who heard about the bombing. I can't go to the police department for information and I don't know where else to start to get answers, so let's try city hall."

He drove the few blocks down the road and parked on a side street. A sign directly in front of them announced the adjoining library, which turned out to be a small wing of the city building. It was open two nights a week and tonight was one of them. "We're in luck," he said.

"Closing time in twenty-five minutes," Ella noted as they approached the door.

The library might be compact, but it was connected to the Internet. After showing his driver's license, Simon was allotted time on the computer and immediately typed in *Tampoo, WA bomb.*

"Two Injured in Depot Bombing," announced the headline, and Simon sighed with relief. No deaths. One ten-year-old boy taken to emergency and released, one elderly woman held in the hospital for observation, no leads, which meant his anonymous phone call to the cops giving them Carl Baxter's name hadn't reached the press yet. Simon leaned back in the chair for an instant, then sat ramrod straight. Damn back.

He turned to tell Ella the good news, but she was standing several feet away staring at a poster of birds that was apparently part of the library décor.

As though she felt his gaze upon her, she turned to face him. Her expression caught his attention and he began to stand. Before he could get to his feet, she had crossed the small room and pulled a chair up next to his.

"His name is Starling," she said softly.

"What do you mean his name is Starling? Whose name is Starling?"

"My father."

"Are you sure?"

"The minute you told me what those birds were called, I felt something."

"Like what?"

"I don't know. A feeling of familiarity, maybe. And then when I looked at the poster and saw the word *Starling* in print, I knew. That's my father's name. Starling."

"Not Thorton. That name rings no familiar bells?"

"Thorton? No, why?"

"Because that's the name you used when you married Carl Baxter."

"How do you know this?"

"I have a friend who's a private investigator. He's trying to find out anything he can about you and Carl and Chopper and even your father. We need help if we're going to live through this and if we're going to help your dad."

She stared at him a second before slowly nodding. "Yes, of course."

"Starling, huh?" he repeated. He'd never heard her called that before. Of course, he'd never heard the name Thorton, either, or, for that matter, about a marriage, or a father. Her brother had apparently died tragically a year or so ago—she must have been dealing with his loss when they started dating and yet she'd never said a word.

"Why would I have a different name than my father before I was even married?" she asked.

Several possibilities occurred to him: she'd been married before; this father she remembered with such tenderness was a stepfather; her parents had never married; maybe even she'd gone to jail and had taken a new name upon release. All useless speculation.

Glancing at the computer screen, he said, "I could type Starling in, see what we get."

She stood abruptly. "I don't know."

"What are you afraid of?" he asked gently.

"Isn't it obvious?"

"No—"

"Are nice, normal people on the Internet? Isn't it mainly people who have made a name for themselves in some way? People who have, you know, done something hideous?"

"Or wonderful or notable or public—"

"I don't want to know," she insisted, and he could tell from the tilt of her chin that her mind was made up. "Please understand, I just can't." And with that she turned on her heel and hurried out of the library.

What now? He couldn't let her wander around town alone where she might be sighted. She was just anxious enough that she might not use her head. On the other hand, she had the keys to the truck and she knew the stakes and he was itching to type *Starling* into the computer....

"Ten minutes, sir," the librarian told him in a soft voice. He was the only patron left in the building. He nodded at her and typed in *Starling.*

Dozens of links to birds popped up on the screen. He scrolled through them quickly, moving on to lists of organizations and businesses, music groups and actors and finally *Starling, Tyler.*

He clicked on the link and went immediately to an archived article on a Chicago cop named Tyler Starling written over fifteen years before.

The librarian was quietly walking through the aisles, preparing for closing. He knew she wanted time to clear off the desk at which he sat, so he read as fast as he could, ignoring tempting links to other sites and possible further explanations.

And what he read started to explain a whole lot about Ella, about what was going on, and about the depth of the danger they faced.

But not everything.

He froze as another thought surfaced. He'd sent the police to Storm Creek to look for Carl Baxter and Chopper, and that's where Ella's father was planning a secret rendezvous with his daughter. What would happen if the police caught on to Ella's father's identity? It was true they would be in different parts of town, but Storm Creek was the smallest of dots on the map.

The whole thing was a giant recipe for disaster and he'd had more than a little bit to do with creating it.

Ella would hate him forever if he didn't figure out a way to make this all work out.

ELEVEN

THE sandwich that had tasted pretty good an hour before now was the eye of the hurricane brewing in Ella's stomach. She sat in the dark truck waiting for Simon's return, wishing he'd hurry and yet also wishing he'd never come back because she had a feeling she wasn't going to like what he found on the Internet.

She put a hand over her stomach and closed her eyes, willing the food to stay where it belonged. This was the first time she'd had nausea at night. Usually it was the morning—

Her eyes popped open.

Nausea in the morning.

No, it couldn't be, but her memory took her right back to the morning she'd tried on pants and found that although they fit her everywhere else, they were too tight in the waist. Both hands went to her breasts. Were they sensitive? Yes!

A knock on the window sent her scrambling to open the driver's door for Simon. He got into the truck slowly, carefully, sliding into the seat as though very mindful of his back.

"You want me to drive?" she asked.

"No. Give me a second to find a semi-comfortable position. I don't think we'd better risk an unlicensed driver at this point, do you?"

"Probably not," she said.

"Do you want to know what I found?" he asked as she handed him the keys. He inserted the right one in the ignition, but he didn't start the engine.

"Am I going to like it?"

"No."

The nausea rose up her throat. "Then let's wait. I need a bathroom. Now."

He started the truck and drove back to the fast food restaurant, where Ella bolted inside, making it just in time to lose her dinner in the privacy of a stall. She washed out her mouth, splashed water on her face and returned to the truck feeling slightly better.

Pregnant.

What if the nausea wasn't because of the concussion? What if it wasn't because of medication, which she hadn't taken in days anyway? What if it was because she was pregnant?

Which begged the question: Who was the father?

Jack? Was that how he knew her? Carl Baxter? Someone else?

And what about all the drugs she'd been given at the hospital and the truth serum or whatever it was Chopper stuck her with at the bus depot?

"Ella?"

She startled. Simon was staring at her, his gray eyes wide with concern. "Are you okay? What's wrong?"

"Dinner didn't sit so good. Guess it's been a rough day. Besides, I'm worried about my dad." She added that last part because it was the one overriding truth of her life right now. She loved her father. She needed her father.

Simon nodded once and started the truck again. A few minutes later they were rolling out of Twilight on their way to Idaho, the world reduced to the wedge of light illuminated by the headlamps.

She didn't want to talk to Simon and yet she did. Good heavens, she had to talk to someone, she couldn't carry news like this by herself.

If it was true.

Maybe it wasn't, but if it was, then there was one plea she would offer up to whatever stray gods might be looking out for her: *don't let Carl Baxter be the father....*

Her hands bunched into fists in her lap. She wanted to pound her head against the door until it spilled its secrets. All the reasons and the explanations and answers and knowledge were right there inside her and yet walled off. Her empty stomach gurgled and spat.

As much as she hated to admit it, she was worried what conclusions Simon might reach when he heard she might be pregnant. Would he assume Carl was the father?

She couldn't imagine rolling around naked with Carl. Couldn't imagine wanting him the way she'd wanted Simon all day. Stroking him. Loving him. Unbelievable.

"Ella," Simon said, and once again, she'd been so caught up in her tangled thoughts the sound of his voice caused her to jerk.

"What?"

He patted her hand. "I know how worried you are about your father."

"My father. Yes, I'm worried about my father."

"I think I found him on the Internet."

She nodded into the dark. "I had a feeling. Go ahead, it must be pretty bad if you're so worried about telling me it."

"It is pretty bad. He may not be the man you think he is."

"What do you mean?"

"He may not be the kind of man you'd want as a dad. It seems he—"

"Just a minute," she snapped. "I thought I was ready to hear it, but I'm not. My father is the only reality I have right now and what I can remember of him is wonderful. Don't take that away from me unless you are absolutely positive the Starling you read about is my father."

He was quiet for several minutes. "I'm not positive," he finally said. "It seems likely, but without knowing your past, it's hard for me to say."

"Then don't tell me."

"Okay."

She sat in silence as the miles droned on. Her hands clenched and unclenched, straying to her midsection whenever she wasn't thinking about them.

A baby.

She'd always wanted a baby.

How did she know that? Maybe she'd never wanted children. And with her father being so terribly important to her, how could she face bringing a child into the world without knowing who his or her father was? How did she deny her child a father?

She glanced over at Simon, who was making a big deal of not looking at her. If she was free to name a father for her baby, it would be him. He was big, but gentle. He was strong. He took care of people even if he was a policeman. He'd taken care of her from the moment he rescued her off the face of the bluff. He'd stood by her.

And he was the only man she really knew at the moment.

Besides, he was hot.

She smiled to herself, happy for the cover of darkness. He'd make a wonderful father for any baby, and a wonderful husband, too. She thought back to the moment when they'd stared at each other by the fence, to the feeling of his lips touching hers, his beard rough against her cheek, his intensity that had burned down to her shoes and filled her head with a kaleidoscope of images and impressions.

Then later, washing his back, her fingers brushing his hot skin, her eyes devouring the muscles in his shoulders and arms. She swallowed hard. If she was pregnant, then she'd already decided about a father for her child. There was no choice. The decision was already made and it wasn't Simon Task.

But maybe it was someone whom she admired and lusted after just as much. Surely her memory would return long before she gave birth and it needn't reveal Carl Baxter as her lover.

Maybe it was Jack. There was no doubt he was a very good-looking man with his tanned skin and long black hair, those light eyes and the velvet softness of his voice.

But he wasn't Simon....

Maybe she wasn't even pregnant. Maybe she was just spinning dreams.

Dreams. Maybe that's all she had. Maybe that's all she would ever have. She closed her eyes as she rested her head against the window. The miles sped beneath the tires. She tried to remember her last dream, or at least the beginning of it. The pink dress. The music. Her father. She could see herself looking up at him, way up, forever up, and there was never a face, no way of telling what he looked like, just his hands gripping hers and the music, and the spinning…

And then, again, he was gone, and she was still spinning, hands stretched out in front, but older now, no longer wearing pink, her hair long and floating, white, like clouds, like starlight. In her father's place was now a woman who reached out and caught Ella's hands and pulled her to a stop. A woman slapping her face, tears welling in her eyes, tears running down her cheeks…

Ella gasped and choked and sputtered, coming to her senses with ragged breaths and a hammering heart.

It was very dark and quiet. She sat there alone, catching her breath, not entirely sure she wasn't still dreaming.

Two lights appeared. It took Ella a moment to identify them as headlights on a big truck pulling into the same large area in which Simon had parked. In the instant the headlights illuminated the interior of the truck, her mind took a mental snapshot.

Simon sleeping, the dark stubble of his beard blending into the shadows, handsome beyond enduring. He was braced behind the steering wheel kind of funny so his back wouldn't touch the seat. She could hear the sound of his breathing, heavy and deep and regular as though he was so exhausted neither lights nor crying women could rouse him from slumber.

Here by herself in the very quiet dark, she could admit something very private: she was falling for him.

The truck pulled into a space a few cars over. It must be a rest stop they were in, or a park of some kind. But where? The only thing she was certain of was that she didn't want to wake

Simon. Not only did he need the sleep as he had to do all the driving, but she didn't want to talk to him right now, either.

However, sleeping was next to impossible. Not only had she already slept for hours, but her stomach was alternately empty and sick and her hand throbbed, probably because she'd had to tug to get the ring off. Every time she tried to get comfortable, something new hurt, and if she just sat still, her thoughts wandered back to dreams of her father and the crying woman.

Her mother, that's who that woman was. Crying. Slapping Ella. Ella crying.

Good heavens, what had happened in her past? Could Simon telling her about it be any worse than reliving it one miserable dream after the other?

SIMON AWOKE with the first morning light to find Ella staring at him.

He relaxed, wincing as his back touched the seat, but staying still until the worst of the pain subsided. It hurt less today although he felt lethargic, probably to be expected given the past few days.

"You been awake long?" he mumbled.

"Not long."

If he looked half as worn out and beat up as she did, they were in trouble. What they were going through was a more personal battle than anything he'd ever faced aboard ship in the navy, its outcome just as unpredictable as any war.

"Where are we?" she asked.

He rubbed his eyes and covered a yawn with a fist. "About ten miles past the place I should have stopped last night because my eyes kept drifting shut. It's a county park of some kind. There are no official rest stops off these little highways we're using. Let me walk around a bit and wash my face and we can get going."

"I'll join you," she said.

As she moved around the truck, he noticed the way her hand brushed her stomach and that made him notice the slight bump against her clothes. He looked away so she wouldn't see him staring.

They stretched their legs by walking down to a small river, used the minimal restrooms to freshen up, and met back at the truck a few minutes later, where they both stood for a moment, letting the sun bathe their faces.

"Are you hungry?" he said.

"Not really."

"I could use coffee."

"Simon, how far are we from Storm Creek?"

"A couple of hours. But I forgot to look up Thunder Lodge last night at the library, and that could be way outside of town. We need to hit another computer."

She nodded briefly. "If you look for additional references to the man you think is my father, are you likely to find them?"

"Absolutely."

"Could you find enough to know for sure this Starling you've found is really my dad?"

"I think so. If I can find an article that includes information about his family, it might mention you."

"What's this man's first name?"

"Tyler."

"And Susan," she said, tossing the word out as though it had been sitting on the edge of her tongue waiting to take flight. "Susan," she repeated.

"Your mother?"

"Yes."

"So the Tyler—"

"I don't know about Tyler, I just know Susan and I didn't even know I knew that until thirty seconds ago. But that could help, right?"

"Yes."

"Then we need to drive until we get to a city large enough to have a library."

"Okay," he said, and with this as their plan, they both got back into the truck.

"How's your back?" she asked him as he slid in behind the wheel.

"Not too bad. How are all your aches and wounds?"

"Not too bad," she said, and they smiled at each other.

The winding road out of the park was bordered by blossoming fruit trees. It was a windy day, so there were drifts of pale petals floating in the air, almost like snow. Simon darted glances Ella's way, but she seemed introverted this morning.

He'd seen her that way before, of course, and as they hit the highway again, he thought back to the times she'd grown distant and tried to relate them to a common thread. The last time had been at his parents' house where they'd gone for his father's sixtieth birthday party. His father had been delighted with Ella's gift of homemade cashew brittle and he'd spontaneously hugged her. Ella had withdrawn almost at once, pulling into herself, retreating.

That had been the moment Simon had begun to seriously contemplate the possibility that Ella didn't fit into his life very well, that for over a year, he'd been fitting himself into hers but there hadn't been much give-and-take.

And now he knew she had a thing about fathers, a difficult past with hers that had probably made the spontaneous show of affection from his dad unbearably uncomfortable.

Was that when she'd begun to get even more secretive? Had she made up her mind that night to drive him away or had Carl paid her a visit or had seeing his dad made her remember her own? Maybe she'd called him when she returned home, maybe that's what set all this in motion.

Face it. If Tyler Starling was her father, he was a crook and a murderer.

How did Simon tell Ella this and yet how did he let her keep risking her life for such a man? Undoubtedly, she had unresolved feelings about him and if her memories were progressing from the distant past to the present, sooner or later she would stumble across her true feelings. Was it better for her to discover that on her own?

How did he know?

And there was another thing that stung him more than he liked to admit and that was that she hadn't trusted him enough to talk about her past. It was pretty clear Carl Baxter knew about her dad—so why hadn't she told Simon? Was it an indication of how little she thought he could handle? Was it because he was a cop?

"Sure you don't want anything to eat?" he said. She glanced at him with a little of the old uneasiness flickering behind her blue irises. "Are you feeling okay?" he added.

"I feel fine," she said so quickly the words tumbled together.

"Your stomach isn't bothering you?"

"No," she said firmly, and looked out the window.

He turned his attention to the road.

Boy, the old Ella was coming back with a vengeance. He

smiled to himself, kind of glad. The sweeter version had been just that—more compliant, easier to talk to, sweeter. But this was his Ella. Kind of touchy.

Wait a second.

He glanced her way again. Her hand was hovering near her stomach area.

Suddenly he understood why she was acting different. *She knew.* She'd figured it out and she didn't want to tell him.

She knew or suspected she was pregnant, so she was going to pretend she felt no nausea and everything was fine so she didn't have to discuss it.

Yeah, well, he hadn't exactly been up front with her, had he? And did he want to talk about a baby with her, a baby he was hoping was his, when he'd sworn he'd never met her before a few days ago?

Uh, no.

"Aren't you going to stop for coffee?" she said as they rolled by signs announcing Coeur d'Alene.

"No. We'll bypass this city. Too big. Look at the map and see if there's a smaller town nearby. With Internet connection, it doesn't really matter how big a library is anymore."

She wrangled with the map for a few minutes. "Several miles ahead. Off to the left, a little place called Sellers. We ought to be there right around the time the library opens."

Eventually, they pulled off into Sellers, a town with a wholesome if isolated feel to it. While Simon filled the gas tank, Ella asked the attendant for directions to the library.

This time it was a new building, spacious with room to grow. Skylights overhead let in dappled sun; comfortable chairs held reading patrons. There was a whole bank of computers with several unused this time of day. The reference librarian studied Simon's driver's license for a few moments before allowing them both the use of a computer.

"You look up Thunder Lodge, I'll find out about Tyler Starling," Simon said. He noticed Ella took a machine angled so she couldn't see his screen. Her reluctance to know the truth about her father left him a little confused, but he let that go as he reconnected with the site he'd searched the night before.

It was a Chicago newspaper and the headlines were huge. Starling Steals Money and Runs. Simon quickly reread what he'd seen the night before, this time following links to other sites and articles detailing the depth of Starling's depravity, the manhunt, the condemnations from fellow officers right up to the commissioner, all repeating over and over again that Tyler Starling betrayed the public trust. He was a thief, a criminal, a murderer, and he would stand trial. Justice would be served.

He was never caught.

Looking for references to Tyler Starling's family, Simon kept searching. He about fell off his chair when he saw the man's wife's name: Susan. The children weren't named, but there were two of them, a boy of twenty and a girl of twelve at the time of the scandal.

He connected with another site that turned out to be an obituary for Susan Starling dated four years later. There was a graveside photo in a following article. It revealed a very pale young girl standing next to an ornate headstone.

The girl stood alone.

Short brown hair as she had now, blue eyes. Ella.

Younger, yes. But Ella.

He felt a hand on his shoulder and jumped, peering up to see Ella looking down at him. "I need some change to make copies of the directions to Thunder…"

Her voice trailed off as something of what he'd just seen must have registered on his face. Her gaze dipped down to the screen. Simon fought the urge to hit the keys that would send the photograph into cyberspace.

As he sat there pinned between the computer and Ella, she read the caption under the photo aloud.

"Eleanor Starling visits her mother's grave."

Sensing her shock, Simon turned the swivel chair in time to catch her, wincing when her arm fell against his back. She was chalky white as she sat on his lap, her eyes filling with tears.

"She used to hit me," Ella said, and Simon swore he heard a young girl speaking and not this beautiful, strong woman. He put his arms around her. "She was mean."

"I'm sorry," Simon said. He hit a key to send the photo away, unsure what to do next. They needed the printouts if they were to make the meeting in a timely manner, but maybe she'd give it up now. Maybe now that she remembered a mother who abused her, she would recall the crimes her father had run from and decide to hell with him.

"Do you still want to get directions?" he asked softly.

She stared into his eyes for a moment, then nodded.

"Can you stand?"

She stood quickly as if to prove her resiliency. He got to his feet, ready to grab her if she ran.

He had the feeling she'd been running for the better part of sixteen years.

TWELVE

"DO you want to talk about it?" Simon asked.

She shook her head. She didn't know what to say; she couldn't even dredge up an emotion past sadness. The beatings had happened, but it was as though they'd happened to someone else or to characters in a book.

"I'm sorry, Ella."

She nodded, still too shocked by the realization that her mother had abused her to process Simon's remarks. She knew she had to snap out of it, but while her brain had been blank to the point of distraction for days, it was now filled with fleeting images too hazy to decipher. And voices! Urgent whispers banged against each other. She put a hand on either side of her head and closed her eyes.

She knew she should be brave enough to ask Simon the rest of what he knew. About her father. About her mother's death. Instead she wanted to open the truck door and fling herself away from him, away from the voices, away from everything.

"Ella," Simon said. "Ella!"

She unclasped her head and opened her eyes.

"I'm taking you back to Blue Mountain," he said. "You're not going through this anymore."

"I have to," she whispered.

"No, you don't," he said. "Trust me, your father isn't worth it."

"That doesn't change anything," she said softly. Simon's voice seemed to have stilled the others in her head and she silently pleaded with him to keep talking.

He cast her an impatient glance. "How can you say that?"

"Because it doesn't. I have to see this through. For my mother. For my father. Hell, as far as I know, for my dead brother."

"What if I told you your father is wanted for murder?"

She swallowed hard and tried to think clearly. She finally said, "He's still my father. He helped me when I was little. I adored him and now he needs me."

"And you still want to help him even though he's wanted for murder?"

"Was he convicted?"

"He never stood trial. He ran away from the law and away from your family."

"It doesn't change anything. My father is the one real thing in my life. I'm here to save him, I know that in my heart. That's about all I know." She paused for a second before adding, "Why are you here, Simon?"

"Because of you," he said slowly. They were on a small road, the countryside around them growing increasingly wooded and remote.

"That's what you keep saying," she said. "But it doesn't really make much sense. You're risking everything for me. Why would you do that?"

He was silent for over a mile until he finally cleared his throat, looking at her briefly before he began speaking, then keeping his gaze on the road where it needed to be.

"Do you remember me telling you about the woman I loved?"

"Yes."

"Maybe I didn't mention how quickly it happened."

"What do you mean?"

"How quickly I fell for her. Almost immediately, in fact. I'm like that with women. No second-guessing, no *ifs* and *ands*, I just know."

"Wait a second," she said slowly. "Are you trying to tell me you've fallen in love with me?"

That earned her another quick glance. "That's what I'm trying to tell you, yes."

"And that's why you're risking life and limb and career."

"It makes me sound like an idiot when you put it that way," he said.

"How would you put it, then?"

He thought for a second before saying, "I guess I'm an idiot."

She smiled at his profile. She didn't believe him, not for a single moment. Her hands had settled on her abdomen as they were so likely to do lately, as though she knew without proof there was a life growing inside her. She couldn't tell Simon about the baby, especially when she wasn't positive there even was one, and yet the possibility of that child was the reason she had to see her father.

Anyway, Simon was keeping secrets of his own. There was

more going on here than he wanted to say, but he'd already told her about his cousin's warnings to let her come to these conclusions herself, so she decided to let him off the hook.

If nothing else, the exchange of words had cleared the voices and images out of her head, and she sat back now, taking a deep breath.

"What did you find out about Thunder Lodge?" Simon asked.

Happy to move along to a different subject, as well, she paraphrased the printout.

"Thunder Lodge was a privately owned campground back in the fifties. Some kind of legal hassle between warring heirs closed it down and it never truly recovered. Now only a few of the buildings are kept up and rented out during the summer for private functions. There's a river there and a waterfall called, guess what?"

"Thunder Falls?"

"Very good. 'Peaceful, remote, tranquil and serene' are a few of the adjectives they use." Peaceful and serene. The words sounded like impossible dreams.

"How far is it from the Canadian border?" Simon queried.

"It's actually right on it. There's a border crossing in a nearby town, but I gather Thunder Falls forms a natural barrier." She paused for a second before adding, "It sounds like an awfully remote place to meet, doesn't it?"

"Very. But your father is a man on the run."

"I get the feeling this is it, though, you know what I mean? I can't imagine we're coming all the way up here just to go farther."

"We can't go to Canada," he said as they entered the city limits of another small town. "We don't have passports." He stopped to pull on the knit hat. One glance in the mirror alarmed him—the beard was too long, too noticeable.

"We need to stop," he said. They had three hours to reach Thunder Lodge, which was only twenty miles away now. They hadn't eaten all day and both of them needed to be ready for whatever came next.

Once again they rented a cheap motel room, then walked half a block to a deli, where Simon bought and consumed a pastrami on rye and Ella picked at a grape and feta salad. Then they walked back to the motel, her stride finally strong again, keeping up with his. He wasn't sure how Ella was feeling about him right now, but he knew how he felt about her and it was disconcerting.

He didn't want to feel anything for her. He knew he cared about her welfare and that of the baby, but caring for her as a woman, as his woman, well, that was just plain nuts. The fact was, however, he was growing increasingly aware of her again, just as he had been the first time he fell in love with her.

He told himself to knock it off and keep his mind on the mess they were in. It would all be over in a couple of hours.

But once inside the room, she pulled her tunic over her head, revealing a skintight white T-shirt with a deep-scooped neck. The knit hugged her breasts and rose and fell as she breathed. Seemingly oblivious of what the sight of her half dressed did to him, she sat on the side of the bed and took off her shoes and socks, revealing trim ankles he knew all too well evolved into long, curved legs and from there to a body that was ripe and soft and lean at the same time.

He found himself itching to help her undress, curious what her naked belly looked like with a budding pregnancy cradled within. He wanted to lay his hand on her bare skin, over the developing child he hoped was his…

"I'll take the first shower," he said abruptly, and closed the door behind himself. Snap out of it! First he shaved off the beard, then climbed into the shower, cringing for a few seconds as the spray hit his back. Afterward, he emerged into the bedroom to find Ella ready with bandages and antibiotics.

She wore the T-shirt with her sweatpants, and though she was fully clothed, naked images of her ran rampant in his head.

"Sit down," she said, gesturing at the bed, and he did so. She climbed onto the mattress behind him, perched on her knees. Her touch started fires wherever her fingers lingered as she checked the wounds on his back. When she leaned forward, her hair brushed the side of his face, her breath warmed his skin, her breasts pressed against his bare arm.

"Most of your wounds were superficial," she said. "I'm just going to bandage two or three."

He turned his head a little to speak, but that brought their mouths within an inch of each other and he forgot what he'd been about to say.

She ran her fingers down his cheek. "Hmm, soft," she purred. "I like you all clean shaven."

That was it, that was enough. He moved the fraction of an inch it took to claim her lips, reaching around to clasp her shoulder and urge her around and into his lap.

She came with a sweet thud that made his nerve endings skitter like beads of cold water on a hot rock. His hands traveled up and down her supple body as his tongue teased apart her lips. Her warm weight melting into his lap drove him mad; the wet, hot touch of her tongue entwined with his sent flames shooting through his groin.

He inched his hands under her shirt, her skin so soft it rivaled satin. He kissed her with the longing of lost love and maybe something else, maybe with hope. He cupped her breasts and licked the lace cups of her bra, her moans echoing inside his head.

"Simon, Simon, time," she mumbled, and he reluctantly opened his eyes. Hers were open, too. They were deep, deep blue, her lips as she whispered reminding him of rose petals. "We don't have time," she whispered.

Time? What did time have to do with anything?

Everything....

He'd lost his head.

He swallowed the boulder in his throat and gripped her arms, leaning his forehead against her chest, the incredibly soft, rounded tips of her breasts cushioning his chin. They sat crumpled together for the minute or two it took for their heartbeats to slow, their hormones to recede. Every part of his body throbbed with either desire or pain. The truth was, there wasn't a heck of a lot of difference between the two.

She finally cupped his cheeks and raised his face to hers. He could tell she wanted to say something and was weighing if she should or not. Feeling he'd probably done enough to confuse her already, he was silent, but now that she'd mentioned time, it occurred to him they'd better get on the road again.

"A few hours ago you tried to convince me you'd fallen for me," she said at last.

He nodded but his mind was chasing its own tail in his head. He felt as though he'd been lying to her since the moment he found her in Rocky Point—would she ever forgive him and had the past few minutes just made things worse? He trailed a finger down her long throat. Knowing who and what she was when her memory was intact, he realized the answer was a resounding no. She would be furious he'd kept things from her.

And face it, she had one giant thing, or rather, one tiny being, she could keep from him if she chose. He glanced down at her stomach and then away. She could disappear as she apparently had in the past, and he would never know where she had gone.

"Well," he said, attempting to lighten things up, "I think I just proved it, don't you?"

"It seemed kind of mutual to me," she said, kissing his ear, her breath warm and sweet as it tickled his newly shaved skin. "After we meet with my father, after we find out what he wants, after we go back to Blue Mountain, do you think there's a chance for us?"

"There's always a chance," he said, alarmed at how her words touched his heart. Had he always hoped she would come around? He wasn't sure anymore. And what about her baby? How long could he keep a secret from her that involved her own body?

Unless she already knew and thought she was keeping it from him.

"Don't look so trapped," she whispered.

"I—"

"I know I'm not a mermaid," she said.

"No, you're not," he told her honestly. "No, you're real flesh and blood, all right."

"Damn straight." Their eyes met again. "It's getting late," she added. "Let me fix your bandages, and then we'd better get going."

With an assist from him, she got to her feet, gaze averted. She applied the ointments and gauze with haste, her touch almost impersonal. He finished dressing as she took a quick shower. When she came back into the room a few minutes later, she was dressed in her jeans and the blue sweatshirt. Her short dark hair curled enticingly around her face.

It struck him with a jolt she'd never been a natural blonde, that she'd been bleaching her hair. This new color wasn't a disguise; it was done to make her look more the way she used to when these old men apparently either knew her or had a photograph of her. The long blond hair had been the disguise. Judging from the hack job, he wondered if Carl had cut it himself.

He should tell her about Robert Connors knifed in the restaurant parking lot. He should tell her how Chopper had looked at the man in the bus depot with absolute loathing...

He should warn her.

If the police failed to act in time, they could meet up with Carl and Chopper again.

But she knew that. They both knew it. She had to go forward, and because she had to, he had to.

Their eyes met and they both looked away. Half-truths lay between them like buried embers, daring the wary to step carefully.

Five minutes later, they were back in the truck, headed for Thunder Lodge and the last contact before finally meeting Ella's father.

UNFORTUNATELY, THE ONLY WAY to get to Thunder Lodge was to travel through the very small town of Storm Creek. Simon drove as quickly as the law allowed while Ella kept her head down. Her heart hammered against her ribs as she considered the possibilities that lay ahead.

One, Chopper and Carl could be here; they could be

waiting to follow, madder than ever now because the Red Barn restaurant didn't exist.

Two, the police could have responded to Simon's anonymous call, arrested Chopper and Carl as early as last night if they drove straight through, and Carl could have told them exactly how much Ella was involved. There was the very real possibility that she could be arrested for murder.

Three, Chopper and Carl could have been waylaid by the law or by Jack and they could arrive at the lodge to find her father waiting with open arms. To hell with the open arms, she'd settle for an explanation. Was her father aware of how murderous his plan to reconnect with her was going to be or had it all snowballed at him the same way it had at everyone else?

Which would mean she would see her dad. She was alternately hopeful that seeing him would unleash all her memories and terrified it would open no doors whatsoever and he would be as big a stranger as everyone else.

She snuck an under-the-eyelash glance at Simon and amended that thought. Simon wasn't a stranger. Simon wasn't a dream or a threat or a snippet of memory. He was real and the thought of being in his arms, of feeling his lips on hers made her tremble inside.

She wanted more.

"Stop," she said suddenly.

Simon pulled the truck to the side of the road. "What is it? Did you see someone we know?"

She looked at him, careful to keep her face turned from the street. "No. I…I changed my mind. I don't want to go through with it. What do I need a father for?"

He stared into her eyes and nodded. "Okay."

She grabbed his arm as he lowered his hand to change gears. "No, wait."

He sat there and waited, didn't even check the dash clock or his watch to remind her they were running out of time. She finally said, "Didn't you expect I'd have my memory back by the time we got to this point in our journey?"

He thought for a second before slowly nodding. Wearing his black T-shirt with his dark hair combed away from his forehead, he looked like a man who could take care of anything. Even the scratches and cuts from the day before added a note of toughness to his face that she found reassuring. Simon Task wasn't an easy man to stop.

"Who is my father accused of killing?"

"A man in Chicago and his twenty-year-old son."

"Why would he have killed them?"

Simon looked as though he was going to avoid her question, but then to her surprise, he took her hand. "They got in his way. Listen, Ella, your dad was a cop, which might explain your aversion to law enforcement. He was involved in a huge loan-sharking deal with a street gang. He worked as a collection agent for them, him and another cop who was killed in the arrest. Your father made bail and skipped. He took over five million stolen dollars with him."

"And left me alone with my mother," she said softly.

He sat very still as though sensing she needed time to assimilate this discovery. Finally he sighed. "Okay, for the record, I think you're wise to pack in this thing. We can either surrender to the cops or to a lawyer—"

"No, that's okay," she said, resolve once again coursing through her veins. "Let's go."

"But I thought—"

"I just got cold feet, that's all. I want to know what happened. I *have* to know what happened."

She could tell he wanted to argue, but when he finally glanced at the clock and saw the time, he pulled back onto the street without further comment. She rested a hand on her abdomen and imagined a flutter beneath her fingers. It was almost over. She wanted—she needed—her life back.

They left town without seeing anyone they knew. There was no police presence, either, and Simon mused aloud that the small town might not even have its own department. But a bomb in a public building constituted an act of terrorism, he added, and that meant the feds would be looking for Carl Baxter, too. If they were undercover, they were doing a darn good job of it.

"Did I mention Thunder Lodge is closed until June?" Ella asked. "It's only May. How are we going to get into the lodge?"

"We'll cross that bridge in two miles," Simon said, nodding toward a road sign.

The trees crowded the road, shadowing it from the sun. Every once in a while there would be a spot where the trees thinned and they could see a river meandering through the forest. Ella's heart started pounding with nerves again, her stomach rolling.

"There's the turn," she said, pointing ahead, straining against the seat belt now, anxious to get this over with.

An iron gate stood ajar and they drove through. The road began a gradual incline, the pavement littered with pine needles and winter deadfall. Occasional shafts of sunlight revealed vague traces of tire imprints.

The truck rolled over a wooden bridge. The river running under it was dark blue and clear, dappled with sun that made its way through the lacy canopy of deciduous trees overhead. Birch, Ella decided, their white bark lovely against pale green leaves. As they rambled up the slope on the other side, the tree cover grew less rampant until they emerged into an open field.

The area seemed to be part of a natural meadow, surrounded by towering trees, but relatively flat. Several imposing log buildings ringed the area. There were no other vehicles and no sign of anyone else.

Simon stopped the truck in front of the largest structure and they both got out. As it was the only one without boards shuttering the windows, they gravitated to its wide stone stairs and wooden deck.

Ella gripped the metal handles on the big plank doors and tugged, but they were securely locked. "Are we that late?" she cried. To have come so far and be left with nothing was more than she could bear.

Simon checked his watch. "Five minutes is all. Remember, the gate was open. Let's look around the other buildings."

Before they could turn, Ella sensed a presence behind them. Something poked her in the back, something that felt an awful lot like a gun barrel.

A male voice demanded, "Let's get those hands up where I can see 'em, folks. Nice and easy, and no one gets hurt."

She looked at Simon.

They both raised their arms.

THIRTEEN

SIMON didn't recognize the voice, but that didn't come as much of a surprise. He was pretty sure neither Chopper nor Carl Baxter would have been so polite.

He knew what was coming next. Sure enough, whoever was back there slipped Simon's revolver from his waistband holster.

"You can turn around now," the man said.

They both turned.

The weapon turned out to be a Winchester repeating rifle in mint condition, the wooden stock gleaming with polish. The weathered man holding it appeared to be in his late sixties, of average height and weight, his skin deeply grooved. He wore scuffed boots, baggy jeans and a padded blue jacket with a patch or two. The threadbare edges of his quilted cap revealed wisps of longish gray hair.

He might look like a bum, but there was nothing remotely slack in the keen look of the old guy's eyes or in the way he shouldered the rifle. He looked from Simon to Ella, his gaze lingering on her face. Simon, who had assumed they'd run into a cagey caretaker, reassessed his conclusion.

"You haven't changed much since you were a girl," the man said, lowering his weapon.

"I'm sorry," Ella said. "If I ever knew you, I've forgotten."

His brow furrowed and his eyes narrowed. "Do I look that different?"

"I don't know. I was in a car accident a week ago. I've lost my memory. For a while, anyway."

Now his mouth seemed to drop open. "You have amnesia?"

She nodded.

"And yet you came all this way?"

"My father needs me, right?"

"He wants to see you, that's for sure." He glanced up at Simon and added in a censoring tone, "You her husband, what's his name, Carl Baxter?"

"Absolutely not," Simon said.

"My husband is one of the men after me. This man is named Simon Task. I wouldn't have made it this far without his help. It's been very—violent."

"I know about the violence," the old man said. "Jerry and Robert are both dead. I had to read it the newspaper. You know anything about that?"

"Those were the first two contacts," Simon said.

Ella sucked in a breath. "Both of them? The man from the restaurant, too?"

The old guy nodded. "I haven't heard from Potter, either."

"Potter the contact at the bus depot?" Simon said, remembering how Chopper all but spit out his name.

"Yeah. He was supposed to call. He didn't."

"I saw him leave the station," Simon said. "We both did.

But like Ella said, there are two armed and dangerous men following us. We've done our best to lose them, but—"

"Well, they aren't following you now. I've got someone on the gate." He reached in his pocket and withdrew a two-way radio. After fooling with the volume, he clicked a button that suspended the static and barked, "You there?"

The reply was equally terse. "Yeah, I'm here."

"You see anyone?"

"Nothing. Neither did Johnny. It's clear. I'm locking the gate. Good luck."

The older man pocketed the radio, then stuck out a hand toward Ella, who shook it. "My name is Reed. I'll take you to your father."

"But aren't you frightened?" Ella said. "The other men—"

"It's got to be done," he interrupted, "and trust me, if those fellows were still on your trail, Merle and Johnny would know about it." He looked down at her feet and added, "Good, you have decent shoes. Do you have a coat?"

"In the truck."

"Get it. My Jeep is around back. We'll drive a ways, but then we'll have to go the rest of the way on foot."

Simon stepped forward. "I'm coming with you."

"No, you're not."

Wondering if Ella would back him up, he said, "Then she doesn't go."

Reed glanced at Ella. "Is that your position?"

Much to Simon's relief, she nodded.

Reed narrowed his eyes as he studied Simon, finally saying, "You're a damn cop or military, something like that."

"Yes."

"You out to capture her father?"

"No. He's in no danger from me."

"Okay, you can come. Lock your truck. Come on, we've got a long way to go to reach camp."

As Ella and Simon gathered their coats and a few belongings from the truck, Reed disappeared around back, reappearing a few minutes later in a battered old Jeep. The rifle lay on the passenger floor, the passenger seat stacked with sleeping bags and backpacks.

Simon and Ella climbed into the back. Simon said, "How about returning my gun?"

"Later. Hold on now, it's a bit of a bumpy ride."

Simon exchanged a long glance with Ella. She'd pulled on the knit cap and looked like a kid on her first camping trip. Traces of her facial wounds were faint now, and in the afternoon light, her blue eyes sparkled more than the river. She was either excited to be out in nature or anxious to see her father, or maybe both.

They stopped after a couple of miles when the road came to an abrupt end. Climbing out of the old Jeep, they found themselves across a broad chasm from a waterfall that fell in a sheet of silver, pouring over the lip high above, falling into a pool before rushing down the river toward the lodge. The sides of the chasm were lush with vegetation, splashes of color thanks to wildflowers making it look like a secret garden. It was gorgeous and, at any other time, Simon would have itched to wander the isolated paths with Ella at his side.

Reed handed Simon his revolver. "Grab a pack," he added as Simon fit the gun back into its holster. "I only brought two but there's plenty of food."

"You're not leaving your truck here, are you?" Simon added.

"Where else would I leave it?"

"Someplace where it doesn't point a giant finger at us saying 'They went that away.'"

"I told you, no one came through the gate after you. Anyway, it's not my Jeep. Merle will get it later."

"Merle will just have to hunt for it, then. You don't know these two thugs who are following us." Simon stretched out his hand. "Give me the keys. I saw a big clump of trees and an old building half a mile back. I'll tuck it back in there. You two sweep the area, cover up the tracks in the clearing, I'll catch up."

Reed tossed Simon the Jeep key, shaking his head as he did so. Simon drove the truck back down the road and parked it out of sight. Dragging a branch behind him, he obscured the tracks on his way back to the clearing.

As soon as Reed saw Simon return, he shouldered his pack. Ella was leaning over a small white flower. "Trillium," she said as she stood. "I tried to grow some once."

Just like that, she'd gained another insight. She grinned. "I have a garden. I have a house. Gray with white shutters and a red front door. If only I could remember who used to walk through the door. Maybe my father."

"Maybe," Simon said. It wouldn't be long before she realized *he'd* walked through her front door a hundred times.

"Time's a-passing, folks," Reed said.

Despite Ella's insistence she be the one to carry the backpack, Simon got to it first. He took a deep breath as it settled against his back.

Reed took the lead and for an old guy he was no slouch. Simon brought up the rear. The path was easy going for a while, meandering its way up the mountain, away from the waterfall, and then back to it. But it was soon obvious the path was more or less abandoned. There were whole sections where the wooden supports for the stepped slope had rotted away, leaving it to each of them to find footing, holding on to branches and each other at times to keep from slipping.

Simon glanced behind them as much as he did forward. It was hard to picture Chopper or Carl climbing a mountain, but not impossible. He also did his best to put a lid on his growing annoyance with the whole situation. What in the hell was going on? Hiking? Her father couldn't just show up at the lodge like a regular guy? How many hoops were they going to have to jump through? He hurried past Ella, who had stopped to admire a patch of small purple flowers, catching up to Reed.

"I assume we're crossing into Canada," he said.

Reed spared him a quick glance. "We might."

"And judging from the sleeping bags and other equipment, we're out here for at least one night."

"Nothing gets past you," Reed growled. Simon was kind of glad to hear the strained quality of the older man's breathing. He'd hate to think a man pushing seventy had more stamina than he did.

"So what's in it for you?" Simon persisted.

Reed stopped walking and turned to face him. He took off his ratty hat, wiped his brow with his sleeve and gestured down the trail. "If your job is to watch out for her, maybe you ought to go tear her away from those flowers. We're losing daylight." And with that, he pulled on his hat and resumed climbing.

Simon swore under his breath as he watched Reed scramble uphill. He looked back for Ella, but she was already walking toward him.

Another hour put them near a small pool. Looking up the hillside, Simon could see the top of the falls disappearing into thickening cloud cover. The lush vegetation served as a reminder that spring was damp this far north. He found himself hoping Thunder Lodge got its name because of some old legend and not because of the weather.

The sound of the falls meant Reed had to raise his voice to be heard. "This is as far as we go tonight. Can't take a chance on falling. I remembered this spot being larger, but it's been years since I was here last and I didn't remember the trail being so bad, either. An old man's memory, you know."

Simon allowed the pack to drop to the ground, happy to stop. It had been torture having that heavy thing bounce against his back as he walked. He was either sweaty or bloody under his shirt and the truth was he didn't really want to know which.

As Ella unrolled their sleeping bag a few feet away, Reed started gathering fallen wood. Simon hitched his hands on his waist. "What are you doing?" he demanded. "You're not thinking of starting a fire, are you?"

"Sure, why not? It'll get cold soon."

"A fire will act as a beacon," Simon said.

Reed chuckled as he snapped a long branch in half across his knee. "Mr. Task, please. From Thunder Lodge, there's one way to go on this mountain and that's up. They don't need to see a fire to find us if they're back there, which I sincerely doubt. Besides, take a look around you. If we build it near the cliff wall, it'll be invisible from down below until you practically stumble into it."

Simon did just that—he looked around. Reed had a point, and one glance at Ella's wilted form and wan complexion sealed the deal. "Just make it a small one," he said.

"Sure."

Simon shook his head, but in the end, he took over fire duties while Reed produced a few freeze-dried foil-wrapped packets. As the last of the daylight fled, they sat around the small blaze eating reconstituted beef Stroganoff and drinking tea made from boiled water. Simon felt as though there were a target painted on his forehead and another on his back as he sat in the flickering light of the small blaze.

"How much farther do we hike tomorrow?" he asked Reed. Ella had moved close to the fire, her knees drawn up to her chest, her arms looped around her legs. She'd been gazing into the fire, but at the sound of Simon's voice, she looked up. Firelight played with her features as she stared at Reed, waiting for an answer.

"Less you know, the better," Reed said.

"I don't agree," Simon insisted. "How can I be prepared if I don't know what's going on?"

"That's what I'm here for."

"We don't even know who you are," Simon protested.

"I'm Reed. I'm the next link in her crazy father's crazy chain. That's all you need to know."

"Yeah, well, sorry for bringing this up, but our contacts don't seem to last long once they talk to us."

Reed dismissed this concern with a gesture of his hand. "I'm the most careful of the bunch." He produced a packet of cigarettes and shook one free. "Anyone mind if I smoke?"

"Yes," Ella and Simon said in unison.

He glowered at them. As he flicked the unlit cigarette into the fire, Simon pressed on. "Let's say you have a heart attack tonight," he said pleasantly. "Or maybe a bear eats you. How do we proceed?"

"Keep going up the trail to the top of the falls."

"And my father will be there?" Ella asked.

"Sooner or later. Stop worrying."

"Stop worrying?" Ella snapped. She sat up straighter. "Do you have any idea how many times I've almost died in the past week? And how about Simon? I believe we have more than a little right to be worried."

Reed studied her for a second before speaking, his expression difficult to read. "Okay, okay, all I meant is we'll keep the fire lit so the bears stay away." He smiled and added, "And there's nothing wrong with my damn heart."

"You smoke. That's hard on a heart," she grumbled.

"Just one after dinner," Reed said.

"Why this complicated and deadly system for a man to talk to his daughter?" she persisted.

"He's a wanted murderer. Some people want the cash he took, some want him held accountable for his actions."

"Did he really kill that man and his son?"

Reed stared at her a second before nodding.

"And now he's set in motion a plan that's getting more people killed."

"No one anticipated all the death."

"Do you know the two men who are after us?" Simon asked. "Carl Baxter and a guy called Chopper?"

Reed's bushy eyebrows knit together over his pale eyes. "I meant to ask about that, Ella. Your own husband is threatening you?"

"Ex-husband," she insisted, but ruined her authority by glancing at Simon and mumbling, "At least I hope so."

Things fell silent for a few moments as the fire crackled. All of a sudden, Ella said, "I remember a man saying he recognized someone named Potter. It's like it happened in a dream, though. Wait, it was in the car after they drugged me. That's where I heard it."

"It must have been Chopper," Simon said as he pictured the moment Potter and Chopper had locked gazes at the bus station. A sizzle of recognition had charged the air. He'd seen it. He'd *felt* it, he'd even mentioned it to Ella and then he'd forgotten all about it. "I saw them meet. They knew each other."

"Who are you talking about?" Reed demanded.

"The other man. We just know him as Chopper."

"Chopper," Reed mused. "I don't know—"

"Big guy," Simon added. "Dark clothes and complexion."

"Very fond of his knife," Ella added.

Reed looked at her quickly. "What kind of knife?"

"A long curved blade. Mean looking."

"A kukri?"

"I'm not familiar—"

Reed quickly grabbed a stick from the pile of collected firewood and sketched a knife in the loose dirt. "Like this?"

They both leaned forward to look. He'd drawn a knife about ten inches long with a curved blade. "Yes. Very much like that," Ella said.

"It's British army standard issue for the Gurkhas Unit."

"The what?"

Reed shook his head as he scuffed out the line drawing he'd made in the dirt with his boot and threw the stick in the fire.

"The Gurkhas are a military unit composed of men from northern India and Nepal," Simon said. Narrowing his eyes, he added, "So, Reed, why does the mention of the kukri make you look like you saw a ghost?"

Reed got to his feet so abruptly he stumbled and reached

out for a fallen log to brace himself. "I'll take first watch," he said. "Get some sleep."

"You're not going to explain, are you?" Simon persevered. "Why? You know, I looked up Ella's father on the Internet. I know what he did, I know why he ran."

"So many years ago," Reed mumbled. "Anyway, it's impossible."

"What's impossible? And sixteen years is not that long. I think you and the cops who have been acting as contacts must have all been still working together in Chicago—"

"I will not discuss this," Reed snapped, leveling a stare that announced question-and-answer period was over. "Flashlights in my pack, each of you take one." He shouldered his rifle and stalked out of their tiny camp, choosing a rock at the far end of the pool on which to perch, just out of the light cast by the fire.

Simon tore his attention from Reed's hasty exit to find that Ella had begun cleaning up the garbage from dinner. He joined her in sealing the used packets, cups and silverware in plastic so the refuse wouldn't attract wild animals, stowing it away to pack out with them the next morning. They went about their work silently, banking the fire, retrieving the flashlights from Reed's pack. There wasn't a whole lot to say, although Simon's mind raced. Who was Chopper? Potter had recognized him and so had Reed, or at least he'd recognized the knife.

"I have to visit the little girl's room out in the trees," Ella said, an urgent tone to her voice.

"I'll stand guard."

"No, that's okay, I'm fine," she said, and quickly grabbed her flashlight and disappeared into the trees, but he'd seen her hand fly up to cover her mouth. Morning sickness seemed to have been replaced by evening sickness.

Eventually, they both prepared for bed and lay down next to each other in the ample sleeping bag. There was only room to lay on their sides spoon fashion, and since his back was the one resembling hamburger, he took the outside position. This meant she was curled close to him, her back to his front.

"What are you thinking about?" he asked her when he found he couldn't get to sleep.

She turned her head to speak to him. Her breath smelled like peppermint. "I was thinking I wished Reed would go far away so you and I could finish what we started earlier."

He smiled into the dark. "Sounds nice."

"Nice? Is that all?"

"No, that's not all," he said, and inched closer. He licked her earlobe, something that had once driven her crazy, and by the way her hips moved, he was pretty sure it still did. In deference to their current situation, he limited himself to nuzzling her neck.

"Do you miss her?" Ella whispered.

"Miss who?"

"The mermaid. Do you wish she were here with you?"

"I don't want anyone here right now but you," he hedged, and once again chided himself. Something was going to trigger her memory. Something would bring it all back and he wanted her to understand where he'd been coming from, but that wasn't going to happen if he didn't find a way to level with her.

Keep telling yourself you don't care about her, his subconscious whispered.

"Me, either," she said.

"Good."

"Tell me what a Saturday is like for you," she said around a yawn.

"You mean when I'm not working?"

"Yeah. Just an ordinary Saturday. What do you eat for breakfast?"

As he described fresh bagels bought at a bakery in downtown Blue Mountain, she snuggled against his chest. The top of her head was cool against his arm, her hair redolent of campfire smoke.

"Then I work on an old BMW my dad and I are rebuilding together," he added. "I used to listen to the radio while I worked, to a gardening show my friend does. Sometimes her show is about cooking. She changes it up week to week. I just liked hearing her voice."

"That sounds nice," Ella whispered, her warm breath tickling the inside of his arm. "What next?"

"Let's see. Dinner, I guess. Sometimes I go out and sometimes my friend invites me over. Well, she used to. She's a wonderful cook. Her specialty is seafood. What she can do with scallops is enough to make a man cry."

Ella snuggled closer. Her bottom was against his groin and it was work not letting it get to him. "You're talking about the mermaid, aren't you?" she whispered.

"Yes."

"You're making me hungry."

She was making him hungry, too, but not for food. He stroked her hair, ran a hand down her arm.

As wonderful as it was to hold her, it was also deceitful. She had no idea of what she used to mean to him, what she still meant to him. Had he kind of hoped mentioning her voice on the radio and her scallops Provençal would tweak a memory? Yes, of course. After several minutes of arguing with himself over the right thing to do, he spoke.

"I have something to tell you," he whispered, stretching his fingers to brush the curve of her abdomen.

It seemed to him she stopped breathing. Before she could start asking questions, he continued. "I haven't been sure how much to tell you. Well, I admitted that once, didn't I? I told you my cousin, the doctor, suggested I play it safe and let you remember what you could when you could? And then so much has been going on, but the truth is I was also kind of afraid. I let you believe things—well, hell, okay, I lied. Anyway, here's the truth. Yes, you and I knew each other before you lost your memory. Back in Blue Mountain. We were lovers. Things started going wrong a couple of weeks ago. We had a fight. Oh, hell, the truth is I stormed out."

Her silence was deafening. On the other hand, she hadn't pulled away, so maybe there was hope. "Ella?" he whispered. "Say something. Ask anything you want."

Still no response. For several seconds he held his breath until it finally dawned on him she was asleep; his confession had gone unheard.

He considered shaking her awake, but in the end, gently kissed the top of her head instead. He'd try again tomorrow—before it was too late. Before he lost her completely.

FOURTEEN

HER father stood right in front of her, but when she reached for him, the movement of her hands dissipated his form into a mist that reshaped when she gave up trying to touch him. He had no face but it was him.

She closed her eyes. When she reopened them, she found Carl where her father had been. He was holding a plate and she screamed. The next thing she knew, they were flying. Carl held the plate in front of him, one hand on each rim. She grabbed for it and it shattered into a million pieces.

Tears rolled under her chin and down her blouse, between her breasts, down her belly, a virtual river of tears. She held her hands up and they turned into trees—

She awoke with a jolt.

The weather had changed. Her hair was damp, raindrops sliding down her forehead and cheeks. Simon knelt beside her, barely visible in the dim light of predawn.

"Are you okay?" he asked.

"I'm...I'm fine," she stammered, blinking rapidly.

"It just started raining," he said. "Let's get our stuff under the trees, okay?"

The trees. She looked over his head at the towering gray silhouettes of the trees, their boughs waving in the wind, their rustling vaguely evocative of the ocean.

"I dreamed about my father," she said.

Simon paused in his task of rolling his damp sleeping bag. "Anything we can use?"

"No, he disappeared as usual. Oh, get this, Carl made a cameo."

Simon's eyebrows raised. As anything to do with Carl was creepy, she quickly added, "Don't worry, he was just driving a plate."

Simon chuckled and kept working.

The rain increased and she pulled her hood up over her hair, hustling now to get her things under some kind of cover. Simon had earmarked a grove of evergreen trees. As they deposited everything in relative dryness, Ella looked around the campsite. It didn't take full daylight to see she and Simon were alone.

"Where is he?" she asked as she perched her rear on a fallen tree.

"Reed?" Simon sat down next to her. "I don't know. He woke me up a few hours ago to take over the watch, then disappeared again."

She hadn't heard Reed summon Simon, nor had she awoken when he extricated himself from the sleeping bag. She must have been out like a zombie. "He's a hard man to figure," she said.

"He turned white when he heard about Chopper's knife."

"True. Aren't you kind of wondering where Chopper and

Carl are? It seems too good to be true that Jack managed to stop them for good. For that matter, he said he wasn't even going to try to stop them, just delay them."

"Maybe the police apprehended them," Simon said. "Otherwise I think you could count on them being in this camp right now. Between the campfire and all our noise, this hasn't exactly been a stealth operation."

"If they're in custody, who knows what Carl is telling them? Probably blaming me for killing those two men."

He put an arm around her shoulders. "Let's take things one disaster at a time, okay?"

"I hope they didn't hurt Jack," she said.

"He seemed like the kind of man who can take care of himself," Simon said.

She could see the gray of his eyes now. His beard had started to grow again, defining the strong curve of his jaw. He added, "You're shaking. Are you nervous? Today's the big day."

"Hell yes, I'm nervous. It's not every day a person gets to meet her estranged father. But I'm shaking because I'm cold."

"I have a spare sweatshirt stuffed into my pack. Want it?"

"Absolutely."

While she took off her jacket, he dug in the pack, finally pulling out a university sweatshirt she hadn't seen him wear. At the same time, a sock came flying out of the pack and landed by her foot with a thud.

She instinctively reached for it, aware that Simon had, too. Her fingers closed on the soft cotton first, but it was obvious something roundish and heavy was stuffed into the toe of the sock. She lifted it and handed it to him, eyebrows raised.

He shrugged.

She pulled the sweatshirt over her head. What was he hiding?

By the time she popped her head out of the shirt and pushed her arms into the sleeves, he'd peeled away the sock. He held a small globe in his hand. Encased within the globe was an otter swimming on its back, a clamshell on its tummy. Silver glitter fell through the trapped glycerin like sparkling raindrops.

Zipping her jacket over the sweatshirt, she said, "What's that?"

"A memento," he said, and handed it to her.

She took it, her gaze fastened to his gray eyes. Looking down at the globe, she said, "It's cute."

"Would you like it?" he asked.

A smile tugged at her lips. "Yes."

"It's yours," he said, closing her fingers around the plastic dome.

A noise in the trees sent both of them to their feet. A moment later, Reed emerged from the underbrush. Ella slipped the globe into her pocket. She liked the way she could feel it resting against her leg.

"Where have you been?" Simon asked as his gun went back in the holster.

Reed held up a creel. In his other hand, he held a compact fishing rod. "Been catching breakfast. Anyone like trout?"

This time they found a rocky overhang under which to start a small fire. Reed produced a frying pan and with little fanfare fried three rainbow trout to perfection. They took turns eating the fish right from the pan. It took almost an hour to be ready to go again, but Ella had to admit the warm food sat better in her stomach than anything had in several days. Maybe she was getting over the incessant nausea. Happy thought.

But about the only one.

The nightly dreams featuring her father were growing increasingly bizarre and unfulfilling, and meeting Reed hadn't helped foster any warm, fuzzy scenarios. She fingered the globe in her pocket as she thought about the man she was soon to meet.

He'd taken huge amounts of money and apparently still wielded enough power to engage men like Reed and the others to do what he told them to do despite the danger. He had to be a cold, heartless man and Ella couldn't help wondering if she'd kept in close contact with him over the years or if she hadn't seen him since he ran away. She must have been twelve at the time. And he'd left her with an abusive mother, she was pretty sure about that.

This time, she got to the pack first and had it adjusted on her back before Simon could protest. They adopted the same formation as the day before, Reed in front, Simon bringing up the rear. This far up the mountain, the trail was more of a suggestion than an actual path. The waterfall was on their right as they ascended, though they lost sight of it on occasion. They climbed in silence, each caught up in the chore of just getting a little farther along.

An hour went by, then two. It wasn't until Ella stopped to take a deep breath and turned her face up to the sky in order to stretch her aching back that she realized the rain had stopped. The spring sunlight felt like a heat lamp.

Simon caught up with her. As he brushed a curl from her forehead he gazed at her with troubled gray eyes. "I want you to stay near me," he said as they resumed walking, this time more or less together. "Behind me, if you can. We don't know what to expect, so expect anything and everything."

He was talking about possible danger. He was talking about flying bullets and abductions and knives. The enormity of what she was possibly subjecting someone else to really hit home.

Her hand fluttered against her abdomen as she took a half-dozen steps and then she stopped and turned to look at him. "There's something you have to know."

"Okay. Go ahead. What?"

"I think I'm pregnant."

His gaze remained steady. The man was truly unflappable. She added, "I wanted you to know because it means there might be two of me to protect."

"How long have you suspected?" he asked.

"Since after the abduction, after the first time we went to the library. That's why I haven't had time or opportunity to buy a test."

She was sure she saw the gears spinning and turning in back of his eyes, but he didn't say anything.

"Okay," she finished lamely. "Well, now you know."

"Now I know. It explains a lot."

"I wish it explained who the father was." *Please, not Carl…*

"You'll know soon," Simon said. "We'd better catch up with Reed. We're almost at the top."

She nodded and turned, but he caught her arm and she looked back over her shoulder at him.

"You're going to make a great mother, Ella."

"Do you think so?"

"I really do. And I'll be there for you if you'll let me."

"Why wouldn't I let you?"

"Oh, you know, things happen and—"A sound up ahead cut off his words. "Falling rock," he murmured as he drew his weapon and stepped in front of her. "Reed?" he yelled.

The path twisted and turned as it climbed and though Ella peered ahead, she could see no sign of the older man. At last they heard his voice. "I'm okay, I'm okay. Just a little stumble."

Over his shoulder, Simon said, "Let me go ahead."

She nodded, falling into step a second behind him. Around the second bend, they came across Reed sitting on the ground, holding his ankle, swearing. From the look of things, he'd lost his footing on a patch of small rocks.

Simon reholstered his revolver as Ella knelt beside Reed. "Is anything broken?"

"No, just twisted or sprained. I'm okay," Reed said. He grabbed hold of a bigger rock and used it to push himself to his feet, glaring at Ella when she reached out to steady him.

"I'm fine," he insisted.

"Maybe we should take off your boot."

"No," Simon said. "Better keep it on in case his foot starts to swell. We can't have much farther to go."

"Not far," Reed agreed. He shrugged his arm away from Ella and started walking again. Ella and Simon exchanged glances when they saw his limp, but they fell dutifully in line behind him.

Eventually, Ella spied a red dot off to the west and pointed it out to the men. Shading her eyes and peering into the distant sky, she could barely discern the dragonfly shape of an approaching helicopter.

"My father?" Ella whispered, trembling inside. It was almost over. Her memory would come back—she would know who she was, she could go back to her life, she could nourish a new life—heck, she could know who to inform he was going to be a father. Her fingers danced over the globe in her pocket.

"He's early," Reed grumbled.

"Maybe he's just anxious to see his daughter," Simon said.

"Of course he is," Reed agreed, and once again continued walking, the limp growing more pronounced with each step.

"There's a gullylike thing we have to navigate up ahead, and then we're there," he added.

The gully turned out to be a narrow, rocky chute, deeply channeled and uneven. Reed stopped to lean against an exposed root of a towering pine. His foot obviously hurt him. The waterfall was very close at this point on the trail and it was too noisy to converse.

Simon tapped his chest and stepped ahead of Reed. He negotiated the tricky footing by climbing onto a boulder-size rock, then more or less sliding down the other side. Ella followed. As Simon gained ground, he reached out for Ella to help her. She, in turn, reached back for Reed, but he hadn't followed and gestured for her to go on.

At last Simon hauled her up the last precarious few feet, where they erupted onto the wide riverbed. The river itself was dark and swift, cascading over the lip, fed by the spring runoff from the Canadian Rockies. Huge flat rocks jutted up at random intervals. The forest crowded the edges of the bed. The ground beside the river was muddy, slippery.

Ella spared a quick look down the waterfall as Simon paused, she supposed to wait for Reed. It had to be a four-hundred-foot drop, a cascade of torrential water intent on fulfilling its destiny.

Simon tugged on her arm, pointed at himself and then back down the chute. She nodded her understanding and watched as he disappeared back the way they'd come. She shook her head—she knew Reed would hate taking help from Simon almost as much as he hated taking help from her. He wasn't the kind of guy who asked for or accepted a lending hand with grace.

She took a deep breath and perched atop a rock, searching

the sky for the helicopter, which she'd lost sight of during the past several minutes. It cleared the trees about a half mile away and began a descent toward her.

Though Ella was sweaty from the climb, she broke into chills as the pilot chose a solid-looking spot of smaller rocks set back from the water about a quarter of a mile away. The blades sent sand and grit into a swirling cloud as it hovered.

Merging worlds spun in her head. Her past and her future raced toward each other. Too late now to stop even if she wanted to. She got to her feet and began walking over the uneven rocks, breaking into a trot, her heart lodged in her throat as the copter touched down.

As the propellers spun to a halt, she shrugged the pack off her back and let it fall to the rocky ground. Bracing her hands on her knees, she took deep breaths.

This was it. The moment she'd been waiting for was upon her.

The pilot's door opened as she straightened up. An older man climbed out. He stood tall and straight, a leather bomber jacket worn with panache. The smile of greeting she'd felt flowering on her lips wilted and died as he pinned her in place with bright blue eyes.

She squinted against the glare off the helicopter, trying to see the man's features, trying to record them, recall them. He looked exactly as Ella had imagined he would, from the high forehead to the straight silver hair. Tyler Starling, her father, looked enough like her that she knew it would set every Starling bone in her body humming with recognition.

This was it.

Simon pulled Reed up the last few feet of the chute. The old man glowered at him. Well, what had he expected? They hadn't exactly been buddy-buddy during this trek; no reason for that to change now.

Once at the top, they both looked around at the impressive scenery, but Simon suspected Reed was also looking for Ella, just as he was.

They both spotted the bright red helicopter at the same time. It looked like a Bell JetRanger to Simon. Ella stood near it, facing a man wearing a brown jacket. The two of them reminded him of the acrylic snow globe Ella now carried in her pocket. Two figures facing each other, frozen in time instead of plastic.

"Damn," Simon muttered. "I shouldn't have left her up here alone."

"No one asked you to come back for me," Reed said as he dropped the pack from his back and leaned it against a rock. "I would have made it okay."

Simon ignored him and started walking. The old man limped but kept pace, navigating the uneven ground pretty well, all things considered. "Did her father come alone?" Simon asked.

"That was the plan."

"I can't see past the glare on the windshield. There could be someone else in the chopper. Let's go faster." Simon could think of nothing to do but get to Ella's side as soon as possible. There was no covert way to approach and rushing in like a storm trooper would be counterproductive at best. "If I'm right, that machine has about a three-hundred-mile range," he said as they walked. "Did her dad come from three hundred miles away or is he going to travel that far when he leaves here?"

"The airport isn't far. We're not as remote as it may seem. Things have become…uncomfortable…in Canada. He's leaving."

"Why a copter?"

Reed shrugged again. "Why not? The man is rich, he's on the run, not a bad way to get around, right?"

"I guess." He kept his opinion to himself, but a wanted murderer living the high life rubbed him the wrong way. He was surprised it didn't rub Reed the wrong way, too. His suspicions were right, Reed had once been a cop like the first two contacts. He'd known her father, or at least it sure sounded as though he had and maybe still did. According to the brief newspaper report he'd seen, Tyler Starling's actions had shamed the whole Chicago police department.

They were close enough now for Simon to see the face of the man by the helicopter. While he'd not really stopped to think about what Tyler Starling would look like, this guy was perfect. But no one seemed to be talking. As Simon crossed the last few feet to Ella's side, he tried to get a clear view inside, but the reflection on the bubble still obliterated everything.

Halting behind her, he touched her elbow. "Ella?" He met her father's impersonal gaze and tried a nod. "Ella, let's all walk away from the helicopter, okay?" With a glance, he included Ella's dad in the invitation.

Ella shook her head as she turned to look up at him. "I have a million images in my head," she said. "They're all disjointed. You, my house, thousands of trees for some dumb reason, my mother's face, my father disappearing into thin air—they're all inside my head but it doesn't make sense. Seeing my father has done nothing to jog my memory."

"Give it a bit."

Ella's dad remained statue still. Ella took a few steps toward him. "Dad?" she said.

Starling's expression didn't change. It was as though his emotions had been spent years before. Why didn't he speak? Why arrange such a meeting if—

No, wait a second. Starling didn't look indifferent, he looked terrified.

At the same moment Starling reached out to Ella as if to warn her away, Simon sensed movement in the helicopter interior. His hand went for his gun, but before he could draw, the crack of a bullet exploded and Tyler Starling sagged to the ground.

Ella ran to her father, catching his falling form in her arms as Carl Baxter jumped from the copter to the rocks. Simon had his gun out and he was pretty sure Reed had unshouldered the rifle, but Baxter already had his gun pointed at Ella.

Chopper rounded the front of the machine, his big curved knife held at his side, an assault rifle looped over his shoulder. He took one look at the fallen man and screamed. "You shot him, you bastard. He was mine to kill, not yours."

Baxter spared the big man an impatient sneer. "Will you please try to keep your eye on the big picture?"

Chopper sheathed the knife and slung the rifle around in front of him.

Reed whispered, "William Smith and Sanjay Chopra working together? God help us."

FIFTEEN

UNDER her father's sagging weight, Ella folded to the ground, cradling him in her lap. His blood seeped into her clothes, his breathing was irregular and rattled, blood bubbled on his lips. The pressure of a cold circle of steel against the back of her neck was the only sensation her brain registered.

"Once again, I seem to hold all the cards," Carl said, talking over her head. "You two put down your weapons or the little lady gets shot right where she sits."

Vaguely aware of the sound of weapons hitting the rocks, Ella leaned in close to her dad's face. "Can you hear me?" she whispered. "Please, answer me."

His eyes seemed to focus on hers and then he took a shuddering breath. In the next instant, his mouth went slack. With a growing sense of shock, Ella realized her father was dead.

Carl grabbed her arm, pulling so hard she had no choice but to stumble to her feet as her dad's body slipped to the riverbank. Tears of loss and fury burned behind her nose.

She turned on Carl and, heedless of the gun in his hand, beat on his chest with her fists. "You killed him," she screamed. "You bastard, you killed my father before he could say anything to me. How could you? How could you?" The tears rolled freely now, but she didn't care, she was too devastated to care.

Carl used his gun-free hand to slap her. Even as her neck jerked back, she saw Simon try to help her. For his efforts, Chopper swung the butt of his gun into Simon's mouth. Enraged even more, she went berserk, lashing out at Carl in any way she could until he caught both her shoulders and shook her.

"You silly bitch," he hissed. "You don't know, do you?"

Something in his voice and the smile twisting his lips froze the sobs in her throat.

He spun her around. Simon stood a few feet away, gray eyes blazing, blood dripping down his chin from the gash across his bottom lip. Reed stood next to him, pale to the point of bleached laundry.

"*That's* your father," Carl said, pointing, but not at the dead pilot.

Her gaze met Simon's for one heartbeat. In the next, they both looked at Reed.

"Is it true?" she finally whispered.

Reed stared at her, his lips drawn into a tight, straight line.

"Ah, come on, Tyler," Carl said. "Tell her all about it."

Ella glanced at the fallen man. "He looks just as I knew he would. Who was *he?*"

"Bob Rydell," Carl said. "Like the other contacts you met, he was a cop with your father back in Chicago when you were a kid. No relation, Eleanor, just a happy coincidence he seemed familiar."

Fixing her stare on Reed or Starling or whoever he was, Ella whispered, "Why?"

He rubbed his jaw. "Why did they risk their lives? Because they owed me. They were fulfilling a debt."

"Not that," Ella murmured. "Why didn't you tell me who you were yesterday?"

Her father studied the rocks, a knot in his jaw.

"Just give me a straight answer," she demanded.

"It wasn't supposed to be like this," he muttered, and for once he didn't sound so sure of himself. "I planned the hike up the mountain so we would have time to talk and get to know each other. I knew your brother had been captured and killed down in Tierra Montañosa. I knew you were alone.

"Anyway, I was leaving today to start over again somewhere new. This hike was my last chance to explain what happened all those years ago and to give you money, you know, to take care of you. When you got to the lodge and didn't know who I was, when you barely knew who you were, well, I wasn't sure what to do so I just let you assume I was the next contact. I just wanted to buy some time. I put off talking to you. I'm sorry."

"You're a stranger to me," she said.

"I can see that. Ultimate irony, isn't it? I risk all this, three men are dead—"

"Four," the man Reed had called Sanjay Chopra interjected as he stepped closer, the rifle clutched in his white-knuckled hands.

Starling groaned. "You got Cal Potter?"

"How else would we have known about the helicopter?" Chopra's dark eyes gleamed like shards of obsidian as he added, "You murdered my father and brother because they wouldn't go along with your schemes. They were good, decent men. My father was a former Gurkha, a man of strength and honor."

The big man's mouth twisted and his nostrils flared. In one fluid movement, he looped the assault rifle over his shoulder again and released the kukri knife from its scabbard. Holding it balanced on his fingers, he said, "When neither of them would be cowered by the murdering criminals you served, you killed them. Then you stole from the very thieving devils you worked for. You ran like the coward you were, like the coward you will always be."

"You've got this all wrong," Starling said carefully. "I'm not the one who killed your family. I'm the one who took the rap, I'm the one who got the others off free. I was the one who had the least to stick around for, the least to lose, so I'm the one they all paid off.

"So, yes, I'm guilty in some ways for your father's and brother's deaths. If I'd talked up when I first knew about the deep corruption on the force—and it went all the way up to the top—if I'd been as honorable as you say your family was, maybe it wouldn't have happened the way it did." He looked down at the man dead on the rocks and added, "This is the man who pulled the trigger. Him and the others, they're the ones who were involved."

"I will not listen to your lies," Chopra bellowed. "I've waited all these years, keeping track of each of the men who helped you escape, knowing sooner or later one of them would lead me to you. And now, thanks to your ego, they have. I've eliminated each of them with my father's knife." He glanced down at the dead pilot. "Except for him. Now it's your turn."

Starling lowered his arms. "I'm an old man, Chopra. Do what you have to do. But leave my daughter alone. She had nothing to do with any of this."

Carl Baxter cleared his throat. "Chopper? Hate to get in the middle of this, but there's the matter of the money. You go hacking Starling up into fish bait, how am I supposed to get what's left of his stash? We need him alive for a while yet. And my wife, too. She'll be his incentive to cooperate."

"Why did you marry my daughter, William?" Reed asked. "She was only twelve when you saw her in Chicago."

"I never even knew you had a daughter when I lived in Chicago," Carl said. "I first learned about her in the paper after you blew town, then later when your wife died. When I realized she must have turned eighteen, I tracked her down.

"And by the way, I'm not William Smith anymore. I don't work for a street gang, I don't associate with crooked cops. I have bigger fish to fry nowadays."

"You used Ella to get close to me."

"Fat lot of good it did. She hated you. Refused to talk about you. Blamed you for her mother killing herself, blamed you for everything and with good cause. We got divorced before two months went by, but I kept her in my sights and when I heard you were looking for her and your son, I got closer to her and you know what? She still hates you. When your first contact got to her house, she wouldn't even let him in the door, refused to listen to him, told him to tell you as far as she was concerned you were already dead. Good thing I came in the back way and…convinced her to be more agreeable."

Starling looked at Ella and said, "I wanted to explain all this so you'd understand. Nothing is really what it seems."

"You wanted to explain why you left me with a woman who beat me? Or did you want to explain how you were the cop who had the least to lose? Which?"

"You remember your mother's abuse?"

"It's about the only memory I have of her."

"She was sick—"

"And you left both of us. She was a bitter, unhappy drunk and you left."

"The others promised to take care of her, look after you, but they didn't. That's why they owed me. I kept my part of the bargain, I took the money and disappeared and let them all go on with their lives and act like heroes."

"And left your wife and children to carry the burden of your disgrace."

"She wouldn't take a dime of the money, wouldn't let me provide for you or your brother, wouldn't join me…all she wanted was to wallow in her misery."

"And who do you think wallowed with her?" Ella said. "At least I now understand why every dream I have of you ends up with you disappearing into a puff of smoke."

"I'm sorry," Reed said, and sounded genuinely contrite.

Ella said, "It doesn't matter. I have a feeling I gave up on you years and years ago." She turned her attention to Carl and added, "And *you* killed the first contact? *You* dumped that man in the vacant lot? I didn't have anything to do with it?"

"I didn't kill him. I just tied him up and left him at your place." He smiled to himself as he added, "Chopper found him before he could get free. They had a little chat and then Chopper carved him into pieces."

"You made me go with you. Why did you crash the car?"

"That wasn't my fault. You grabbed the wheel from me. You sent us off the road."

"No more talking!" Chopra spit, his voice deadly earnest. "The money isn't important. The past doesn't matter. Even if what you say is true, Starling, the men I killed were guilty and so are you." He looked at Baxter and added, "It's blood money. I will have this man's life in retribution for my father and—"

"Yeah, yeah, yeah," Carl interrupted. "Nice sentiment, good devotion, et cetera...but the fact is we have an agreement. You can do whatever you want with Starling as soon as he buys his daughter's life with what he's got left of the money. It better be a lot, too. She's been a ton of trouble. And let's not forget, he's the only one who can fly us out of here now that the pilot is dead."

For some time, as he'd tried to absorb everything that was going on around him and figure out a way to use the dynamics to his advantage, Simon had been aware of a noise coming from the forest to the west. Now it seemed they all became aware of it, because voices died down as everyone turned to look toward the bank of dense trees.

Chopper said, "What the hell?"

What the hell was right. Through a break in the trees something large and bright yellow came rumbling out.

"It's a school bus," Ella said.

Carl snarled. "Great, just what we need. Chopper, hold the knife lower before some busybody teacher with a cell phone sees it and calls the cops. Wait, prop the pilot up against the wheel, everyone look friendly or Eleanor isn't going to live long enough to have her baby."

Ella's gaze swerved from the bus to Carl so that the muzzle of Carl's gun now rested square on her forehead.

"You knew? You shot me with some drug, and you knew?"

"It's not my kid," Carl snarled.

"Well, thank goodness for that," she said.

"On the other hand, if *you* care about your baby's future, you'd better start playing the part of relaxed tourist." He waved the gun in a modest circle. "That goes for all of you. One false move and it's bye-bye, baby."

Ella, apparently taken aback by these words, looked down at her feet.

As they'd spoken, Chopra had pulled the dead pilot into a sitting position next to the helicopter wheel. Ella's father, who stood slightly tilted, due, no doubt, to his sprained ankle, watched the bus with a kind of fascinated horror. Simon knew how he felt.

"The damn thing is coming right toward us," Carl said. He lifted his free hand and waved at the bus, shouted for it to stop, but it kept coming, headed for the helicopter, sitting there with a full tank of gas.

The sun had moved around enough that the bus was now reflecting the light, but Simon began to get a funny feeling in the pit of his stomach.

"What's the matter with the damn driver?" Baxter sputtered. "He's going to run into the helicopter."

Hand held in front of him, Chopra took a few steps toward the bus. No doubt, with his size, he was used to imposing his will on anything and everyone, but even he was no match for a bus. When he saw it wasn't going to stop, he turned back to them. "We have to get out of the way!" he yelled as he grabbed Ella's father's arm.

"Let's get to that flat rock in the river. The damn bus can't roll over water," Carl said, yanking Ella along with him.

Simon realized that for a moment, he'd been pretty much forgotten. He dived for the abandoned revolver and rifle. By the time he was back on his feet, bullets pinged off the rocks around his feet. He quickly headed off in the other direction, running a zigzag pattern. It would do none of them any good to get back in the same kind of standoff again. He needed to find cover and plan a rescue.

The bus had left the relatively smooth ground of the riverbank and started across the larger rocks, which slowed it down, made it rock and lurch. As Simon ran past he saw there was no driver, no passengers he could see, but the side door was open. He turned to look back, knowing a collision was imminent. That's when he saw a man holding on to the spare tire mounted on the back bumper.

As Simon stopped to gape, the man let go of the tire and fell to the rocks. The bus kept going, but the way ahead was even rougher. It hit a rut that spun out the front tires. It recovered, but the course veered. Now it was aimed toward the falls instead of the helicopter.

Simon made a split-second decision to use the bus as a cover to approach the rocks where the others had fled. He changed his direction and took off after the bus. From the corner of his eye, he saw the newcomer jump to his feet, look around and make a decision to join Simon. They exchanged a brief glance. With a start, Simon recognized the man's wild black hair and lively eyes.

"Jack?"

"Miss me?" Jack said, drawing close.

Simon handed over the rifle and managed a laugh.

Meanwhile, the bus's movements grew increasingly erratic. It was only a matter of time before it got stuck in a new rut or broke an axle. Simon planned ahead how to stay clear when the damn thing fell over.

A moment later, the yellow vehicle seemed to rear up on its back tires. Both men slowed down, careful to stay out of sight behind it. It crashed down and rolled forward, but something had changed. The mystery was explained when the rear tires came up against what had caused the trouble—a downed tree lying across the bank. Somehow, the engine had become disengaged, and without sufficient power, the bus floundered against the tree, then flipped over on its side with a tremendous crash.

Simon dived for cover. As the clattering went on and on, he got back to his feet. Jack was right behind him.

"I had the pedal depressed with a branch," Jack said. "It must have snapped."

"You passed us outside a town called Twilight," Simon said.

"I did? You must have been the only vehicle I passed in a hundred miles. That bus was no Harley. The guy at the lot got the better deal."

"Listen," Simon said. "I don't think they know about you. If I give myself up, you might have a chance to take them out."

Jack regarded him with narrowed eyes. "That'll probably get you killed," he said at last.

Simon shrugged. "Do you have a better plan?"

"No. There's an emergency exit in the back of the bus. I could climb in with the rifle."

"Are you a good enough shot to take each out with one bullet?" Simon asked. "You'd have to damn near be a sniper."

Jack almost smiled. When he spoke again, his accent, which seemed to come and go like the wind, was back. "*Sí*, amigo. I think I can handle it. You just get Ella and her father out of the line of fire."

Simon paused in his efforts to help Jack open the emergency door. "You know about her dad?"

"Yeah. I followed your friends to Potter's place. I was too late to save the old guy. His wife was grateful I came along. She told me what I needed to know."

The door finally slid open, the noise it made covered by the crashing still going on inside the bus interior.

Jack immediately hoisted himself up into the opening. With the bus on its side, he'd have to step over the windows to get to the front and he'd have to do it without getting cut by broken glass or seen by Carl or Chopra.

Simon handed him the revolver, too. He didn't need it. He hoped Jack was half as good as he seemed to think he was. Then he put his hands high in the air and walked out of the shelter of the bus, knowing it was just as likely Baxter would shoot him dead on the spot as allow him to join them.

SIXTEEN

ELLA saw Simon first as all three men were staring at the bus wreck and she was staring behind it, searching for him. She saw him step out from behind the metal carcass, his hands up in the air. Her heart grew heavy in her chest. There was no hope now.

Carl saw Simon in the next instant. She knew when he raised his gun what he intended to do.

"If you shoot him, I will not cooperate in any way," she said. "Neither will my father. Kill Simon and you might as well kill both of us, too." And she meant it. The waterfall wasn't that far away, just a dozen leaps and she could throw herself into the maelstrom. Sure, she'd die, but Carl was going to kill her anyway, she knew that.

Carl's smile disappeared, a reward in its own right. She glanced quickly at her father to see how he'd taken her ultimatum. Hard to tell.

"Chopper, go take care of him," Carl said. "We'll follow."

As Ella furiously reiterated her threats, Chopra furrowed his brow. He glared at her dad and then, acting so fast it was little more than a blur, slammed the butt end of his rifle into her father's chest. Without another word, he left.

Ella's father doubled over, cradling his arm, which he'd apparently used to ward off the blow. As she reached out to help him, Carl grabbed a handful of her short hair and pulled her head back, forcing her to look up into his face.

"You've been nothing but a giant pain since the day I met you," he said. His eyes bored into her like drills. The skin on her exposed throat burned as he ran the muzzle of the gun down her windpipe. "How dare you think you can threaten me into doing what you want?" He cocked the gun, the click like thunder next to Ella's ear.

And then all of a sudden, he threw her down to the rock. She looked up in time to witness her father jump to the next rock and then the next, almost falling as his bad ankle took the landing, his injured arm supported by his uninjured one. Each faltering leap took him farther out into the river, toward the falls. Carl lifted the gun, seemed to think twice about shooting a man he planned to get rich off, especially as he might fall into the river and be lost. Instead of shooting, he took a leap and followed.

And for some reason Ella would never understand, she followed, too.

SIMON WASN'T THRILLED about Chopra's steady, deadly advance. Behind the man, he witnessed Ella's father making a break for it, leaving Ella stranded with Carl, who had her head bent over backward. A surge of anger flooded his central nervous system— Tyler Starling truly was despicable.

But then Carl threw Ella to the rock and took off after Starling and then Ella popped to her feet and followed Carl.

Chopper and his knife were getting damn close. Seeing as Chopper really didn't know if Simon had a gun tucked away, he was taking a big chance. Probably figured it would take more than a puny revolver to stop him.

Come on, Jack, Simon muttered to himself. *Any time now.* The fact was that Baxter was out of reach of the rifle. That meant Jack could stop Chopra but not Baxter. That meant he had to do it fast so Simon could stop Baxter.

The big man covered ground very fast. There was no way around him to help Ella; Simon had to go through him. He called out, "Sanjay? What do you suppose your father would think about his own son avenging his life by killing innocent people? You said he was a man of honor."

"The girl is a Starling," Chopra said calmly. "She is tied to her father's evil."

"You've killed three men," Simon said.

Chopra held up the knife. "I'll soon make it four and then five and then it will be over."

"Don't you see how Baxter's corruption is corrupting you? You wouldn't kill me yesterday, but today, here you are, lusting for my blood."

"Not lusting," Chopra said, close enough now to come to a stop. "Just taking care of business."

Simon lowered his head and charged Chopra. He hit him in the chest and almost bounced off. The sun glinted off the kukri's blade as Chopra shifted it into his right hand. Simon stumbled backward, tripping over a boulder, sprawling on the riverbank, faceup. Chopra was there in a flash. The curved blade of the knife started a downward plunge.

Simon took an instinctive breath to prepare himself for the worst. Instead, the knife fell from Chopra's grip as his hand flew backward. Jack had hit the guy's palm. Chopra advanced, another shot and his leg crumbled. He stumbled, giving Simon the opportunity to hit him hard and heavy. Wounded, the big man fell to the rocks. Simon scampered to his feet, heart pounding.

Jack showed up. Chopra lay writhing on the ground.

Without waiting to thank Jack, Simon took off toward the waterfall.

CARL WAS AT LEAST twenty-five years younger than her dad and uninjured. It wouldn't be long before he caught up with him. Ella doubled her efforts, practically flying between leaps. Looking ahead, she saw her father had almost gained the last negotiable rock. She made the first of her last two jumps and looked up in time to see Carl grab her father's coat by the back of the collar. The waterfall was so close the noise was deafening and river water washed over the rocks, making them slippery. She fell to her knees as she landed.

Carl shouted something, but there was no way to hear what he said. He pointed the gun at Ella, his meaning clear. All they'd accomplished was moving the hostage situation out onto the river.

She turned in time to see Simon upriver, jumping between rocks, and despite the knowledge his appearance out here was likely to get them all killed, felt a surge of love for him. He was such a controlled guy, such a cop, and look at him, behaving like a man willing to die for a woman.

It took her a second to realize there was another man behind him.

She looked back at her father, who had inched closer to the edge of the rock, and she knew, she knew, he was about to make a sacrifice to protect her. If he was gone, she would be safe; only it wouldn't work that way.

Meanwhile, Carl looked as though he was trying to decide who to shoot first. His arrogance changed her blood into lava. It pulsed through her veins, surged through her heart, burned in her throat. With a guttural scream, she rushed him, shoving him with her shoulder, emulating a linebacker.

Carl's eyes registered stunned surprise at her audacity. He stumbled backward, seemed to catch himself, then slipped again as his feet came down on a patch of moss. A triumphant smile disappeared as he lost his balance. As he went over the edge into the water, his flailing hand caught hold of her father's jacket. The older man went down on his belly and slid to the brim. Carl released the gun and grabbed the rock.

Ella immediately clutched her father's arm. She pounded on Carl's fingers with her fists. He lost his grip on the rock, but the death grip on the jacket remained.

Her father's lips moved as he stared into her eyes. She couldn't hear over the blood rushing in her head and the river and falls—it looked as though he said *pocket.* She stuck her hand in her pocket and felt the rounded dome of the snow globe. For a second, the river became the ocean; she was dizzy and disorientated.

Her father shook his head furiously. She took a deep breath as his lips moved once again and she finally understood he meant his own pocket. Of course. His jacket had deep pouches on the sides with fold-over flaps. She'd seen him stuff a half-dozen things in those pockets over the course of the past twenty hours. Reaching in, she gouged herself on a fishhook before claiming the prize: his pocketknife.

She flipped the blade from the cover and began sawing on the cloth. Carl had managed to swing his other arm into position and now gripped the coat with both hands. Raging water pummeled his face, blurred his features. He sputtered and gasped. She tried not to look at him.

The cloth was too strong, and wet, maybe even stronger. She made holes and slashes, but it wouldn't tear. Her father slipped farther forward and she held on to him with one arm.

Then it occurred to her to use the knife to stab Carl's hands. She raised it and steeled herself, but before she could plunge the knife into his flesh, the material finally started to give way. Her dad managed to twist his body and she saw that he'd somehow undone the buttons while she hacked at the cloth. The jacket slipped off his arms and immediately disappeared into the river. Carl was visible for just a second before the raging water sucked his body under and he was gone.

She and her father got to their feet. He was pale, wet; his arm hung uselessly at his side. His chest heaved with the effort of the past few moments.

She reached for him, half expecting him to dissolve into mist.

He clutched her extended hand.

AFTER WITNESSING THE DRAMA unfold as he jumped between the rocks, Simon landed on the rock a second later. Ella turned to face him, the smile on her face illuminating the air around her. She threw herself into his arms and he caught her. It was over, she was safe. He kissed her face a hundred times. It was a miracle.

He'd cupped her cheeks and was staring into her eyes when something caught her attention. Her eyes grew wide. He glanced over his shoulder and found Jack had arrived and was standing behind him.

Ella's hands flew to her face; tears sprang to her eyes. She moved away from Simon and toward Jack like a sleepwalker.

Simon had witnessed the expression she wore—the unabashed love, the depth of joy in her eyes. It had been directed at him a time or two—

He turned away from their embrace. Taking Starling's good arm, he helped the older man back across the rocks, vaguely aware that Jack and Ella followed close behind.

By unspoken and mutual consent, they kept going, past Chopra, whom Simon saw had been deftly wrapped in his own duct tape, past the overturned hulk of the bus, all the way to the helicopter and the pilot, whom Simon and Jack laid aside. Simon did everything mechanically. If he'd wondered before about the depth of his love for Ella, he needn't wonder again.

He loved her. Prickly, sweet, secretive, open, happy, sad…it didn't matter, he just plain loved her from the tips of her whacked-out brown hair to the depths of her guarded heart. He'd never stopped loving her and damn it, he had a horrible, horrible feeling he never would.

And that was a burden he was going to have to find a way to live with because Jack's identity was suddenly crystal clear. He had to be Ella's lover, the real reason she'd been distant before their breakup. Since finding out what had happened the night she was taken from her house, Simon had attributed her behavior to the mess with her ex-husband and her father; he'd not seriously considered the possibility of a wild-card lover.

Until now.

"Can you fly us out of here with a busted arm?" Simon asked Starling. All he wanted to do was get the hell off this riverbank. If Starling couldn't fly the chopper, then Simon intended on walking back the way they'd come. In fact, now that he thought about it, that was a better plan. He looked around for the backpack.

The old man shook his head. "'Fraid not. But my son can, can't you, Jack?"

Jack, his arm around Ella's shoulders, grinned.

"Your son?" Simon said.

"My brother," Ella added.

Simon looked from one of them to the next as it finally dawned on him she hadn't reacted to the news Jack was her supposedly dead brother, which meant she'd recognized him out on the rock. "You remember your family?" he said. Happiness for her and the fact that Jack wasn't her lover left him a little stunned. He abruptly sat down on a rock. "Your memory came back when you saw Jack."

She shook her head as she dug in her pocket and withdrew the snow globe.

"It started when I saw you racing out to save me—again— and then it just kept building until the moment I thought Carl was going to pull my father into the water. I touched the snow globe in my pocket and the day we bought it—you remember, it was raining that day and cold—came flooding back. Everything else followed. You, me, Jack, my father—everything."

"And your baby?"

"Our baby," she said with a dazzling smile.

He ran a hand over his face. "Thank heavens."

She caught his hand. "Of course it's your baby. Who else but you?"

"What's this about a baby?" Jack said.

Ella laughed. "Later, big brother."

Simon needed to get everything out in the open. He tugged on her hand, ran his fingers across hers, afraid to let go of her. "Can you forgive me?" he asked. Her features blurred and he blinked his eyes.

"Oh, Simon. Forgive you?"

"I've misled—"

"Shh," she said, leaning down to kiss him. "I've been running scared and hurt and angry for most of my life, my darling Simon."

"And that's my fault," Tyler Starling said. "I made a deal with a bunch of thieves mostly just to escape a bad marriage. I thought everything would be okay once I was gone. I thought Ella's mother would take the money I offered her and start over, but she got worse. And I couldn't come back, I couldn't help."

"And I was not only eight years older, I was already in the military," Jack added. "I was no help."

Ella shook her head. "It's too late now to change any of that." She turned back to Simon, meeting his gaze, lowering her voice. "You're the one good thing that's happened to me and I almost destroyed it. What do you want forgiveness for? For reading the clues at my house right? For coming after me even though we'd broken up and I'd been acting like an idiot? For risking your life, for saving mine, for giving up your career—what exactly do you want to be forgiven for? For loving me?"

He pulled her into his lap and buried his face against her sweet neck. He held her so tight she probably couldn't breathe, but he didn't care. She was his.

It didn't even matter that Jack and Starling were standing there, watching. Nothing mattered but Ella.

And the baby that bound them.

EPILOGUE

Seven months later

ELLA'S last memory of a holiday meal consisted of her mother passing out before the turkey was cooked. When she'd woken up and found it burned to a crisp, she'd slapped Ella so hard her cheek stung for hours.

But that memory was fifteen years old and it no longer held the power to hurt. There were two reasons for that, and both of them were within eyesight right that moment.

First and foremost, there was Simon, currently decanting a bottle of wine, tall and strong and so handsome in his red sweater it took her breath away. He was a detective on the police force now; being involved in helping solve multiple murders had actually brought him to the attention of his superiors and he'd been promoted.

Did she wish he wasn't a cop? Sometimes, but that was the weak her talking and Ella had learned not to kowtow to that weak self, to let her have her moment of gut-wrenching fear and then push on.

The second and no less dear reason lay asleep in her arms. Emily Rose, named after Simon's mother and grandmother, five weeks and one day old. Simon called her his miracle baby and who could argue that? Emily Rose had lived through more adventures while in utero than most people did in a lifetime.

Oh, there were other reasons, too. Jack alive—talk about a miracle. They'd invited him to join them for the holiday, and he'd said he would but expect a surprise. As everything about her brother was a surprise, she'd just smiled.

As for her father? Well, he sent cryptic postcards on occasion and was trying to convince her and Simon to bring Emily Rose to some undisclosed location to meet him. Maybe. She'd have to think about it.

They hadn't told anyone the truth about her father. They'd created an alternate story to explain Chopra and Carl. Considering Simon's bent toward the straight-arrow approach, she thought he'd been extremely generous to agree to let her father continue on his trek. There was no one to return the money to, no one left to prosecute. The only survivor from the old days who knew the truth about what had really happened all those years ago in Chicago was Cal Potter's widow, and she had no desire to see her husband's memory besmirched.

In the end, none of the men who murdered Sanjay Chopra's father and brother got away with it. The big man, along with Carl Baxter's help, had exacted retribution on every single one of them.

For now, the smell of roasting turkey filled the house, and Simon approached with a glass of wine. Later that night, they planned to put Emily Rose to bed and then retire to the big whirlpool bathtub he'd installed for her birthday, telling her it was only fitting a mermaid have a sanctuary.

They had a private holiday celebration to conduct.

"Trade?" he said.

She lifted the drowsy just-fed baby from her breast, kissed her downy forehead and handed her to her father. Simon passed her the wine goblet as he accepted the baby, and their fingers brushed. The brief contact set her hormones mad, screaming like crazy.

"The baby is sleepy and it's still a while before my brother and your family are due," she said softly, loving the way his eyes flooded with desire at the sound of her voice.

"You're on," he whispered, and cradling the baby with one arm, reached down to pull her to her feet.

★ ★ ★ ★ ★

The Harlequin Intrigue® series brings you six new passionate and suspenseful books a month available wherever books are sold, including most bookstores, supermarkets, drugstores and discount stores.

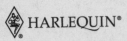

INTRIGUE®

IF YOU ENJOYED THESE 3 STORIES FROM THE HARLEQUIN INTRIGUE® SERIES BY BESTSELLING AUTHORS

DEBRA WEBB

DELORES FOSSEN

ALICE SHARPE

YOU WILL LOVE OTHER BOOKS FROM THE HARLEQUIN INTRIGUE® SERIES!

The Harlequin Intrigue® series brings you 6 new passionate and suspenseful books a month available wherever books are sold, including most bookstores, supermarkets, drugstores and discount stores.

www.eHarlequin.com   HI83756TR

 HARLEQUIN®

INTRIGUE®

**BESTSELLING
HARLEQUIN INTRIGUE® SERIES AUTHOR**

DELORES FOSSEN

**PRESENTS AN ALL-NEW
THRILLING TRILOGY**

TEXAS MATERNITY: HOSTAGES

When masked gunmen take over the maternity ward at a San Antonio hospital, local cops, FBI and the scared mothers can't figure out any possible motive. Before long, secrets are revealed, and a city that has been on edge since the siege began learns the truth behind the negotiations and must deal with the fallout.

**LOOK FOR ALL THREE TITLES AVAILABLE FROM
THE HARLEQUIN INTRIGUE® SERIES**

THE BABY'S GUARDIAN, *May 2010*

DEVASTATING DADDY, *June 2010*

THE MOMMY MYSTERY, *July 2010*

Available wherever books are sold.

www.eHarlequin.com   HI69472TR

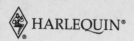 HARLEQUIN®

INTRIGUE®

WILL THIS REUNITED FAMILY BE STRONG
ENOUGH TO EXPOSE A LURKING KILLER?

FIND OUT IN THIS ALL-NEW
THRILLING TRILOGY FROM BESTSELLING
HARLEQUIN INTRIGUE SERIES AUTHOR

B.J. DANIELS

WHITEHORSE
MONTANA

Winchester Ranch

Nothing brings family together quite like a mystery, and the
Winchesters of Whitehorse, Montana, definitely have their
share. Pepper Winchester went into seclusion after the
disappearance of her son, Trace. When it is ruled a murder,
she demands that her far-flung family return to the ranch to
expose his killer. But the passionate Winchesters bring trouble,
and the town of Whitehorse may never be the same....

GUN-SHY BRIDE—*April 2010*
HITCHED—*May 2010*
TWELVE-GAUGE GUARDIAN—*June 2010*

Available wherever books are sold.

www.eHarlequin.com   HI69465TR